TO NOVA SCOTIA

BAHAMA ISLANDS

Mathewtown

INAGUA

CUBA

ATTACK!!!

COMANCHE

Puerto Plata

MIGs

WINDWARD PASSAGE

STORM CELL

HAITI

DOMINICAN REPUBLIC

Port-au-Prince

Great Inagua

AZTEC

CARIBBEAN SEA

DOMINICAN REPUBLIC

HAITI

15°N

'EC to Mexico

Salt Whistle Cay

10°

The 3 Megaton Gamble

All of the characters in this book (who are
not normally residents of the CCCP)
are fictitious and any resemblance to actual
persons living or dead is therefore
coincidental.

Copyright © 1978 by D. Terman
All rights reserved under International
and Pan-American Copyright Conventions.
Printed in the United States of America.
Cover and maps by Ted Montgomery /
Circus Studios / Waitsfield, Vermont.

First printing, September 1978.

Library of Congress Cataloging in Publication Data

Terman, D   1933-
   The three megaton gamble.

  I. Title.
PZ4.T2898Th [PS3570.E676] 813'.5'4   78-59875
ISBN 0-915248-21-2

Vermont Crossroads Press, Inc.
Box 30, Waitsfield, Vermont 05673

To R.E.L.

The 3 Megaton Gamble

D. Terman

Vermont Crossroads Press

Chapter 1

The device, measuring 0.88 meters in length and 0.63 meters in diameter, rested in its pneumatically cushioned transporter. The only protuberance to mar its cylindrical surface was a flexible woven-wire cable projecting from a quick-disconnect fitting. The cable led to monitoring instruments fitted in a panel on the side of the transporter that registered humidity, internal core temperature, and gamma-particle radiation.

The device, when mated with inertial guidance package, thermal battery pack, altitude-sensitive barometric switches, and housed in an ablative shield, would become a US Navy Mark 97 nuclear warhead; one of three multiple, independently targeted reentry vehicle warheads (MIRV) of a Trident I (C4) submarine-launched ballistic missile. The device was built by Weapons Project Group 17 in Zhignask, USSR.

The man largely responsible for the development of the weapon restrained his curiosity and stirred his lemon-flavored tea. His name was Yuri Striganov. Fifty-three years old, graying but with a thick, unruly crop of hair, he was marginally handsome. Fine gray eyes, caged behind yellow-tinted lenses, gave an impression of perpetual inner anger, when in fact, Striganov was a peaceful, untroubled man, content with his life and work.

He patiently waited for the balding colonel to complete his review of the test data and the device itself.

"What is the mention of this alloy?" the colonel said impatiently, stabbing the report on metallurgy with his blunt fingertip. The colonel could have been an actor, Yuri thought, noting the slightly shabby uniform, the cigarette ashes on the lapels, the abused and thinning hair raked carelessly across his forehead with a damp comb. Colonel Alexi Markoff looked the part of an incompetent. It was well known that he was not.

Yuri answered smoothly, without condescension. "That is a specific Alcoa alloy, Colonel. You will probably recall that it compares with our T-2887G except the Americans seem to use about 2 percent more copper for malleability. That is the only essential difference."

The colonel placed the report on the desk and stirred his Turkish coffee repeatedly with a tarnished spoon. The only sound was the soft hush of air conditioning and the muted vibrations of equipment in other rooms.

"It is not 'about 2 percent,' as you say, Doctor Striganov. It is 1.62 percent and I hope that you have spectrolysis data to confirm your 'about 2 percent.' I am responsible for the development of this device. I have been given very complete data to work with. I trust your attitude has been one of exactness."

Yuri said nothing and thoughtfully dipped the slice of lemon into the cooling tea. With exaggerated drama, he lifted his heavy brows, slowly raising his eyes from the cup to connect with the humorless, deep-set eyes of the colonel. He smiled slowly, as if his face revealed a slow motion shift in mood from apathy to comprehension to amusement.

Markoff's face remained turgid for a moment and then broke into laughter. And they both laughed together, Markoff slamming Striganov on the back, spilling his tea on the antiseptic tile floor.

They laughed for a long time, a laughter of relief and of jointly acknowledged success. And Striganov finally commented, pouring more coffee for the colonel, "And it is not 1.62 percent. It's 1.627 percent as we both well know."

Markoff lit a cigarette in complete disregard for the sterility of the clean room and squeezed the doctor's elbow for added emphasis. "It is an excellent job, Yuri. We test in two weeks. Inform AW-4 Special Situations that fabrication is complete."

Forty-three meters of reinforced concrete above their level in the nuclear weapons assembly facility, the arctic winds hurled across the steppes of Asia.

David Fox slumped moodily against the settee in the galley of the ketch *Hussar* watching the unrelenting fog roll in from the Strait of Juan de Fuca. *Hussar* surged uneasily at her docking lines, and David could hear the tiresome slat of a halyard aloft that had not been properly secured. He rose and limped over to the galley stove, poured a fresh cup of coffee, and paused to light his cigarette on the spluttering flame of the alcohol burner. "Christ," he thought, "will I never learn?" and stuffed the freshly lit cigarette out in the dampened bottom of the sink. He returned to the settee, dropping heavily against the cushions, and watched the gray fog smother the horizon.

Fox was 52 and looked 60. He smoked too much, ate too little, and drank an extraordinary amount of rum, a carry-over from Navy days. His tanned face retained the angular planes of light of his native Nebraska, but the leanness of a farm youth, Naval Academy graduate, and a ship's officer was now suffused with fat.

Mementoes were scattered throughout the big ketch; mementoes of moderate success. There was a somewhat faded photo of a young distance runner being handed a medal by an official. The photo was brown with age and without contrast but carefully preserved behind a gilt-framed glass. Another photo in a matching frame with a clipping from a newspaper showed the young ensign lounging easily over the rail of a ship, watching for an enemy in the empty western Pacific sky. There was a silver-plated lighter on the coffee table in the main salon, given by shipmates to a Lieutenant Commander Fox on his retirement. The plating had now worn thin and showed a trace of brass beneath.

He unthinkingly lit another cigarette and stared out of the galley windows at the fuzzy skyline of bollards, masts, yacht superstructure, and nothing.

Fox rumpled his thinning hair and then massaged the tendons in his neck, feeling the dull, pounding ache of a hangover. There had been friends over from the little Australian sloop anchored outboard of the *Hussar*. The invitation for a "sundowner" had lasted through five rounds of doubles, and Fox's evening had terminated on the settee in *Hussar's* salon, mouth agape and breathing heavily in the sleep of 86-proof Cockspur rum.

The pressure water pump cycled in the bilge and moments later, cycled again. Myra, his wife, was showering. The pump, running cycle after cycle, annoyed him. It mattered little that *Hussar* lay alongside a float where there was unlimited supply of fresh water from the high reaches of the Coastal Range of British Columbia. The very fact that Myra would use water so lavishly was annoying to a man who had spent the better part of his adult life showering under salt water, both in the Navy and even now, on the yacht.

The pump cycled for the sixth time. "Close to 12 gallons," he thought without specific bitterness. The lights dimmed noticeably during the last cycle, and he knew that he would have to start the generator soon to recharge the batteries.

He poured another cup of coffee, and this time laced it heavily with rum from the bottle that still rested on the galley counter. He hated the weakness of the act but knew that it would soften the edges of the nerves protruding from his fragile ego. Nothing more until sundown, he promised himself, and leaned against the teak paneling of the companionway to the galley and softly stroked the oiled finish as he sipped his coffee. The pump cycled again.

Hussar was a 64-foot, twin-screw motor sailer, built in Germany in 1951 by Abeking and Rasmussen to the designs of Van Statte. Her hull was 6-millimeter steel plating, and she had the water and fuel capacity to cross oceans. Like most of her breed, she was luxurious, overly complicated, and vaguely ugly. But she was designed to do one thing superbly. On inland seas in areas of indifferent winds, she could exercise her two huge Mercedes diesels for good speed with the sails dampening any motion. She had accommodations for the owners plus four other guests in three private staterooms. Her hull enclosed massive water tanks, a lavishly equipped galley, a 12-cubic foot freezer, a 20-foot refrigerator, air conditioning, which had ceased to function four months ago, and all the luxuries that sailors love and despise so well.

At first, Fox felt separation from the Navy had been a blessing. But the high-paying jobs were in defense-related industry, and the steady contraction of the defense budget became the kiss of death for this field. David made some tentative jabs in the direction of real estate, insurance, and mutual fund sales. All these attempts were prefaced with the explanation of "retiring young and enjoying a job for the job's sake." No one was impressed.

And so David and Myra Fox assessed their savings and their retirement income and bought *Hussar,* $42,000 down and the balance of $60,200 over eight years. The big ketch was to be their home, their kingdom, and their source of income.

David Fox had retained the memory of tropic seas on the western coast of Mexico from years past; a time when he served as third officer on an Attack Transport. There had been one stretch of six months, plying endlessly up and down the coast of Mexico and Central America in the fifties, a training cruise for a series of Reservists. Fox remembered little coves of powder sand, and langouste as long as your forearm, and people who did things as if there were no past or no tomorrow. And he still remembered the smell of driftwood fires on nameless beaches.

The Foxes commissioned a brochure, placed ads in *Yachting,* bought six months' supply of canned goods, and headed south for the Sea of Cortez. Off point Conception, the *Hussar* blew out a roller furling jib; that had cost $1600. And with their entry into Mexican waters, a customs official separated them from most of a rapidly diminishing stack of traveler's checks for lack of proper permits and inaccurate accounts of liquor stores. And then, off Mazatlán, they were flogged by winds that, dammed by the Sierra Madre, suddenly overflow from the central highlands toward the Pacific coast, creating storms of hurricane force within the span of a heartbeat. Retreating to what they knew, they turned the *Hussar* north for Seattle and with a pickup crew of four long-haired kids from San Diego, they sailed north and home. Fox was beaten. The *Hussar* stayed in the protected waters of Washington and British Columbia, chartering to weekend groups, the occasional summer cruise by a family, and on one occasion, two homosexuals whom they never saw except for meals during a two-week cruise.

Hussar's Bristol-fashion appearance had deteriorated markedly in the four years of David Fox's ownership. At first, the varnish was renewed every eight weeks, the decks scrubbed and bleached each Friday afternoon, and the area below decks kept ready for an inspection that never came.

But the owners' boredom and lassitude eventually overrode the daily, unrelenting demands that a yacht makes. Now, *Hussar* drew no admiring glances. Much of her varnish was painted out in neutral browns. Her topsides were marked by streaks of rust, and her once brilliant decks weathered black beneath multiple coats of linseed oil.

Hussar now lay alongside a floating dock in Sudder's Marina off Horseshoe

Bay, British Columbia. In these last days of March, the wind roared down out of Howe Sound, churning the bay with whitecaps approaching Force Seven. And when the wind didn't blow, the bay lay shrouded in fog, blanketing the horizon.

On this March morning, Clive Sudder, the owner of the marina, wiped a trickle of mucus from his ample nostrils, and leaned over the rail of the main pier, gazing down on the shabby decks of the *Hussar*.

"Shit," he muttered, as he critically eyed the slatting halyard and the loose ends of lines that had unlaid through lack of care. Clive had been a quartermaster aboard an old lend-lease four-stack destroyer during the Second World War, working on convoys between the Medway and Gibraltar. Four continuous months at sea in the paralyzing cold of the winter of 1940, and at the end of that hell-trip, his ship had sparkled with the care of men who loved their ship.

"Jesus, mistah," he mumbled and carefully threaded his way down the dockside ladder to the float that *Hussar* was secured to. Clive, out of courtesy, served as a mail drop for transient boats within his domain and although his position did not require personal delivery, he enjoyed this daily opportunity to make the rounds and yarn with each crew about the weather. And David Fox, he knew, was a good listener whose coffee would be laced with rum and whose galley was warm.

He paused near the boarding gate in *Hussar's* lifelines and bellowed, "Aboard the *Hussar*," even though he could see Fox plainly peering out through the misted port of the galley. He heard a muffled affirmative reply and boarded. Mud-covered boots lay on the deck at the companionway entrance. Clive winced, drew back the hatch and went below, leaving his sea boots placed neatly on the top step of the companionway steps.

"Letter for you, Davy," Sudder said, ignoring the traditional address of "Captain." Fox knew this was a slight and could not meet the older man's noncommittal look.

"Thanks, Clive. Sit down and have some coffee if you'd care to. The spice," indicating the bottle of golden Cockspur on the galley counter, "will give it some flavor."

Clive poured himself a heavily laced cup and settled his bulk in the dinette. He watched as David quickly scanned the letter and then reread the letter carefully. David quickly left the galley and Clive could hear him knocking on what he presumed was Myra's cabin door. There was a muffled but excited one-way conversation and he returned noisily from below, snapping the letter excitedly with his wrist and holding a small calculator in his other hand.

Fox kept muttering, "Christ . . . beautiful." Sudder waited patiently and with curiosity for the explanation.

Myra entered the galley from the below-deck companionway, flushed from her hot shower and with enough of her housecoat open to reveal the deep cleft between her breasts. Sudder made indefinite noises of greeting and pushed his spoon carefully to the exact center of the dinette. He raised his eyes and cautiously watched Myra bending here, reaching there as she prepared a light breakfast and waited as David punched hesitant fingers at the keys of the calculator.

Myra Fox was stunning in some haphazard way. She had reached that period in her late thirties when people either develop a mature grace and beauty or simply fade into some sad and slightly blurred image of their youth. In her twenties, she was slight of figure. But with the sun, alcohol, and less pressure to comply with the standards set down for a Navy wife, she had the aura of plump lustiness.

"So what it smounts to, My, is that Nichols Charters has a prospective charter for us from May first to September twentieth. We have to commit the boat for this period for a deposit of fourteen hundred bucks a month which works out to—," he paused to punch at the calculator again, "about sixty-five hundred. And that's without even leaving the dock! We get an additional one hundred bucks per day for any day we move plus actual expenses." David's smile broadened into an infectious grin and he downed the remainder of his rum-stiffened coffee.

Myra settled into the dinette alongside of Sudder. Their legs touched briefly and by accident. He quickly withdrew his leg, suddenly uncomfortable. She read the letter quickly and passed it back to David.

It's too good, she thought. Too perfect. But the money is there in the broker's account. Perhaps this time she could pull David out of his self-destructive spiral. Get away from this rain-lashed coast. Perhaps try for the Caribbean again. "Yes, let's take it," she finally said.

A gust, harder than the rest, heeled the *Hussar* slightly and her docking lines creaked heavily against the chocks. The flag aloft, edges frayed and red bars faded to pink, snapped a drum roll in the wind.

On that same March day, Plattsburgh, New York, was coated with a frosting of 2 inches of wet snow. The snow fell in the morning hours but by noon, the front which had brought the precipitation weakened under the influence of a strengthening high off the Carolinas, and by afternoon, the wind shifted from northwesterly to southerly. Temperatures rose, even in the lengthening afternoon sunshine, and by evening the underlying greens of spring were fed by patches of melting slush.

At 6:43 PM, the satellite swept through its trajectory, 93 miles above the city. The sodium-vapor lamps of the streets were switching on, section by section, giving the appearance of some gigantic electronic game in progress when viewed from altitude. The shape of the city was clearly defined, as well as the lake shore of Champlain, which was edged on both the Vermont and New York sides by lightly trafficked freeways. To the north, the mass of light from Montreal flickered and flowed in the refraction of the unstable atmosphere. And to the south, Albany, Syracuse, and a maze of lesser towns formed a loom of light that intensified as the Hudson flowed to the sea.

The satellite's infrared cameras swept the runway and hardstands of the Air Force Base to the east of Plattsburgh. The information was processed through a converter and fed to magnetic tape for storage. The satellite's electromagnetic sensors gathered information that was compared to patterns obtained in previous passes. Aberrations in the new sweep were updated and stored. Then the orbiting station's solar-paneled wings extended slowly and oriented toward the west, seeking new energy as it overtook the sunlight in its track toward the Pacific.

Far below, a man stood by the edge of the still-frozen lake and glanced at his watch as the satellite flamed into the sunlight in its westward path. He noted the time on a card and compared it to a handprinted schedule he had withdrawn from his topcoat. Satisfied, he carefully pocketed the papers and sighed. For more than an hour into the evening he trudged along the lake shore, picking stones at random from the semifrozen turf and flinging them out onto the frozen surface. The flattened shale rocks made brittle, ringing sounds as they skipped across the rotten ice.

The schedule had arrived in a plain envelope a week previous among his normal business mail. There was no return address, but the envelope was postmarked Orlando, Florida. Mark Sommers had examined the envelope, fingering its edges and feeling its surface, unbelieving. One of the technicians had come in from the shop and had handed him a list of TV components needed to repair a unit that had been partially destroyed by an internal short and realized that Sommers was just sitting there behind the desk, nodding and feeling the unopened envelope, not listening.

"Mr. Sommers. Anything wrong?" The technician shifted uneasily from one foot to the other.

Mark Sommers shook his head slowly. He took off the steel-framed glasses and laid them on his desk, next to the envelope. "No, Fred. Nothing. Just a sinus headache. Couldn't sleep very well last night." He yawned, trying to seem at ease. "Let's see your requisition."

When the technician returned to the shop area, Sommers opened the envelope, finding only the carefully handprinted schedule with the heading of "S-4" and a timetable for a date the following month. At the bottom of the page was a six-digit number. Before he finished reading the paper, a customer came in to inquire about installing a cable TV set that Sommers had sold him two weeks previously. The rest of the day was like that, but he found time to burn the envelope, after folding the schedule neatly and placing it in his wallet.

Mark Sommers was born in Kirovsk, USSR in 1922 of Estonian parents. His father worked for an Estonian paper mill and had been sent to Russia just across the Finnish border to manage tracts of forest under lease. Mark was given dual citizenship, a fact that seemed of small importance at the time. But in 1940, Mark was conscripted by the Russian Army and sent to Finland to work in a communications unit that attempted to jam Finnish field radio units. When the Russo-Finnish War ended and the partition of Karelian was completed, Sommers was withdrawn to Minsk for further training and commissioned a lieutenant in the MGB, later to become the KGB. In 1942, he was sent back into Finland as an agent, trained to work in the repair of electronic components. For a brief period of time, he sent out reports on German strength, troop movements, and the morale of Finns under the forced German alliance. He received no acknowledgement after the fourth report.

In 1944, he married a woman who lived in the same boarding house after sleeping with her once. All his papers now certified him as Finnish with no mention of the Russian birth. His wife, Stella, knew nothing of his background and they both faded into the lower-middle class grayness of wartime survival.

Sommers now began to erase his military background from memory, inventing stories of his childhood in the far north of Finland's lake country, where he said his father had been born. He came to believe these stories, elaborating on them and fleshing them out with local characters. He described in detail his home before the war and those classmates who would speak Swedish privately, because the Finnish language was beneath them and their wealthy parents.

Following the war, Stella urged him to apply for immigration to the United States, so that their son (she was sure that her swelling pregnancy would yield a son) would be born an American. A relative in Erie, Pennsylvania, sponsored them and in 1948, they received permission from the US Embassy in London to immigrate.

Four days before their departure, a man in a dull tweed overcoat stopped Sommers one block short of his apartment, asking for the correct time. The light was gone from the afternoon; everything was a washed-out, late-winter gray. The man reset his watch and then handed Sommers a small packet. "Your work is not finished, Sommers," he said softly in Russian and walked away.

The package contained a number of items: schedules of drops, recognition codes—the standard stuff. Instructions would come in letters unsigned bearing the postmark Orlando, Florida. As confirmation, the bottom right-hand corner of the postage stamp would be torn. There was a microfilm of a transposition code that Sommers remembered as being outdated, given frequently to agents of low worth. There was also a small enclosed note in Russian, wishing the best of health and prosperity for his wife and coming child. It did not mention Sommers' health.

At first, he felt compelled to tell his wife and the authorities. The war and his past were behind him now. He waited two days for the right time to broach the subject to Stella. But finally, he realized that if he did reveal his past, he would not only lose the right to immigrate but also his Finnish citizenship. And Estonia had been swallowed by Stalin. The night before they left, he memorized what he could from the package and fitted the microfilm behind the binding of his wife's bible. He had no occasion to use it for six years.

The Sommerses settled in Erie, Pennsylvania. He worked in a small radio repair shop, immediately useful to his employer, for the language of electronics is universal. And in the evenings, the Sommerses attended night school, learning their new government's history and functions. They studied English and would only speak English to each other, from the very beginning, though in the first few weeks it was more a communication of mime, interspersed with English verbs and laughter. Both of them successfully scrubbed all trace of accent from their speech.

During the early fifties, Sommers received an envelope from Florida with a torn postage stamp. After opening it he nearly discarded it from the day's mail before he realized its significance. The letter contained a small tourist brochure concerning the town of Plattsburgh, New York, and a section of classified ads showing houses for rent. One was circled in red ink. They moved within two weeks. Stella, who was usually placid, was furious with her husband for leaving Erie.

They settled 5 miles south of Plattsburgh, on the shores of Lake Champlain. The foothills of the Adirondacks rose to the west of them in spruce and maple, and there was an abandoned apple orchard for his son to play in. He opened a small TV shop and allowed it to grow slowly, doing only quality repairs at fair prices. By 1955, he had more work than he could accomplish and took on two assistants in the span of three months. He was beginning to prosper. Stella had a second son in 1957 and a daughter in 1958.

Twice in the early sixties, Sommers received envelopes from Florida. The demands were very detailed, wanting specific information on the Atlas ICBM sites under construction and the jet bomber wing assigned to Plattsburgh Air Force Base. He painfully collected the information, using as little as he felt would be acceptable. These bits of data were enclosed in a waterproof sack and left in the cistern of a toilet in a gasoline station on the New York State Thruway. During this time, Sommers began to develop high blood pressure.

He received nothing from Florida for another eight years and began to feel assured that his usefulness was now outdated by the multitude of spy satellites that the Russians were injecting into orbit. As a civilian, he could not gain access to the air base or missile sites. His reasons for travel were limited. It was finished, he thought.

One morning in April, 1976, he received a package with a small, high-frequency transceiver used in amateur radio communications. He looked for an accompanying note, thinking that it required repair. Checking the wrappings, he found only the Florida postmark and 3 dollars' worth of postage stamps, each one with a small tear. Depressed, he set the radio up in his basement and waited. At the age of 50, Sommers started to die of hypertension and regret.

Chapter 2

Fall in the Northern Hemisphere is measured by the retreat of the sun southward. September twenty-third is somewhat of a benchmark, for by this time the sun is over the equator and still southbound.

And with the southern migration of the sun, the instability of air masses in the Atlantic diminishes and is replaced by a massive high pressure area that forms an ellipse with foci over Bermuda and the Azores. This massive mound of high pressure air flows outward and because of the rotation of the earth, forms a clockwise flow in conformity with a law known as Coriolis Effect.

Thus, the air mass along the African coast flows south and then, responding to the clockwise demands of the system, travels 3000 miles across the Atlantic, gathering moisture and warming with the sun. On the western shores of the Atlantic, still moving clockwise, the air mass bends to the north and brushes the coasts of North America, bringing warmth to Mexico and the southern states, fog to the coast of the Carolinas, and moisture in the form of snow and sleet to a winter-weary New York.

The middle-aged man turned from his desk and watched the barren trees in his yard. What little remained of the morning snow had melted, but the ground was still matted with the brown grasses of last autumn. Nothing green. Just grays and browns and blacks. Depressed, he turned back to his desk.

Although Clifford Welsh was already in his late forties, he retained the body of a man ten years his junior. Just over 6 feet, he weighed 182 pounds and kept to within 3 pounds of that weight by habitually working through his normal lunch period, eating only a carton of yogurt. His straight brown hair was still full, and cut weekly by an Italian who would use nothing but a razor and patience. What little gray appeared was privately dyed into brown, except for gray around the temples, which was artificially encouraged with peroxide.

Welsh's face, framed by the artfully cut and dyed hair, complemented the image he affected. Plain enough, it was offset by a thin aquiline nose, sharpened and thinned to a fineness by generations of New England Welshes living through three centuries of bitter New England winters. His hazel eyes, widely spaced, had a softness and compassion that belied his true personality. And though his teeth were capped, Welsh rarely smiled, except in public and for the media.

Welsh picked up the brochure again and thumbed through it. It was one of those slick presentations that cost thousands of dollars and portray remote little resorts in the Caribbean with images that translate into privacy and prestige. And rather large amounts of money. Everyone was young and Caucasian and perfect. And there wasn't a cloud in the sky or a mar in the perfect blue-white beach. All accommodations were in private cottages without telephones. The staff was black and smiled continuously, at least while on duty. And the cost was high enough to maintain some degree of exclusion. Satisfied, Welsh scrawled a note across the face of the brochure and put it aside in a pile for his secretary to act on in the morning.

For some minutes, he toyed with his pen and yellow legal pad, doodling a sequence of sharp arrows and triangles, then overlaying them with graceful swirls and curlicues, hiding from himself his inner thoughts. Progressing to ovals, he elongated them, arming them with barbs. Welsh tore the paper from the legal pad, wadded it, and discarded it in a leather-sheathed wastebasket. In the morning, its contents would be committed to the shreader.

Unsettled, he swiveled in his chair with practiced ease to view the Hudson River and the New York skyline, thrusting into the March twilight over Manhattan.

"Poor bastards," he thought. The millions who treaded out their lives in the city, inhaling the unique combinations of oxygen, nitrogen, sulphur dioxide, carbon monoxide, and any other contaminants man could inject into the atmosphere.

And then he again thought of the fresh, clean tradewinds that swept the Atlantic; the outpouring of the mid-Atlantic high. His father had told him that, sometimes, one could smell the cooking fires of Africa on the eastern shores of Barbados. And the sun would feel good on his back and shoulders. But it would have to wait, and he reluctantly turned back to the reality of his life and ambitions and the millions who faced him from across the river.

The study was growing dark in the diminishing twilight. Clifford Tannis Welsh II, Junior Senator from New York, switched on the antique brass lamp over his desk and drew the curtains behind him. For the next hour, he carefully reviewed a list of political achievements he had attained, both for New York State and in terms of his voting record in the Senate on national matters.

There was no fault. His record for New York State and specifically for the city across the Hudson was one of a series of bills that Welsh had introduced and fought through the Senate to make New York City literally a ward of the federal government. Indirect loan guarantees had not been enough to salvage the city from its creditors and even direct federal grants for redevelopment, job training and make-work projects had done little to stem the outflow of the affluent, the corporate giants, and the disillusioned. But the city still functioned and payrolls were met, credit largely due to Welsh. And the voters knew it. His reelection for a third term was guaranteed by the polls.

Nationally, his record was undistinguished but marketable to a liberal audience. No on the B-1, Yes on the Canal Treaties, although that was now a disaster, but with two-thirds of the Senate voting as he did, who was to be singled out? Yes again on withdrawal of aid from Taiwan. No on gas rationing. No again and again on the Personal Credit Reduction Act and its thirteen amendments. Bankruptcy was now a national epidemic, but Welsh had argued with a straight face that bankruptcy was a way for the disadvantaged to close the gap with the middle class.

And he had the background. Moderate wealth, raised in this same stone mansion on the bluffs of the Hudson and schooled in law at Columbia. His father, also a Congressman, had groomed him for his first political campaign as Attorney General with the single guideline of "be visible and vote straight blue-collar issues." The formula, however trite, worked. Welsh kept in touch with the people, spent time in the ghettos, the garment district, and in the factories.

With his elbows on the desk, he created a steeple with his hands, resting his chin on the apex. Everything there, he thought. Liberal voting, visibility, and background. Everything that Kennedy had, except that one missing ingredient. A neck-snapping national issue to lean on. One that he must create, and one that would have to be so controversial that it would split the nation. If he lost, it would be political immolation, but if he won, Pennsylvania Avenue and the real estate thereon would be his for four years. Longer if he had his way.

He leaned back, eyes closed, testing the edges of his teeth with his tongue. The speech in Utica, he thought, would be the litmus paper.

The study door opened without a knock and his wife, Judith, entered, peeping hesitantly around the age-darkened oak.

"It's 5:00 PM," she said. "How goes the platform?" She set a moisture-hazed glass of Irish whiskey squarely on the legal pad. It glowed with refracted warmth and light beneath the solitary lamp.

"Thanks." His eyes rose only enough to take in her form but not her face. He slid the castored chair back over the rug, arching his back and stretching his legs far out beneath the desk. He threw the pen like a projectile toward the pad. It clinked against the glass and lay glowing with 18-karat gold in dull imitation of the whiskey.

He raised the glass toward her and said, "Cheers."

"Cheers," she whispered, her lips forming the word as they both drank.

Random noises filtered down from the floors above as the children and the servants made the transition from day to evening. A train whistled in the distance. Welsh removed his wire-framed aviator's glasses and laid them carefully over the pad of legal paper, as if in slow motion. He applied his long fingers to his temples and absently worried the wrinkles which radiated upward from the corners of his eyes.

"It's still garbage," he said dully.

"John Humberstall called and said that he would call you back about seven and," she paused to take a deeper sip of her wine, "State called about the Senate Committee meeting on Intelligence activities in Iraq. You're supposed to call them back tomorrow. It's some kind of a flap from what Charlie Hayle says. But not immediate."

He rose from the desk and walked stiffly over to the fireplace, fiddled with the gas valve, and then applied a match. The maple logs slowly took hold and burned in subdued yellows and oranges. He returned to the desk and sat next to his wife, putting his arm around her waist.

"Gets old, doesn't it?"

She rested her head against his shoulder and groped carefully for an answer. "Sometimes. But I probably see more of you than if you were selling steel or bonds or whatever." She drained the little remaining wine in her glass.

They sat together in silence for a time, both watching the growing flames consuming the wood, listing to the hiss and crackle of the damp wood.

"Seriously," she said, "how is the platform coming? I thought you weren't worried about the election."

Welsh got up and went to the concealed cabinet, drawing out a bottle of Bushmills. He poured himself another glass and then refilled hers with wine. "The platform?" He shrugged and sipped the whiskey, slowly this time. "Don't know. The same thing, I guess. DeSilva thinks I should push for making city employees federally funded. Maybe a federal pension fund for teachers. I haven't been doing much work on the state election stuff."

She craned her neck, looking down at the legal pad. "What's this then?"

"I'm thinking about not running." The words seemed to echo in the long silence that followed. Her eyes were avoiding his, watching the flames.

"What, then?" she said evenly.

"Health, Education and Welfare. Maybe an ambassadorship to a politically hot country. Something with national visibility."

She turned on him, her face flushed. "*Why*, for God's sake?"

"Two years of time is *why*. Two years to build an image, a platform, a national identy. For a crack at the presidency."

She carefully set her glass down, watching the moisture spread across the desk blotter. "You're sure of this?" she said finally.

Welsh made an exasperated sound in his throat. "Sure? Christ, no, I'm not sure!" He paced across the rug to the fireplace, jabbing a poker into the flames. "DeSilva won't stand for it. I lose my power base here. And it means going against my own party and an incumbent president. In a nutshell, I'm unsure as hell."

"Then, why do it?"

He dropped the poker back into the rack, turning to face her with his hands thrust deeply into his pockets. "Like DeSilva once said, it's the reaction of a man who finds a fire on the first floor of the building and runs to the roof for safety. New York—for that matter, most of the big cities—is living on borrowed time. We have the aid now, enough to sustain us from month to month. But the tax base is going. Going to the sun belt or the smaller cities. Each tax dollar lost from a fleeing corporation needs five dollars in aid to replace it, because with the corporations go the jobs. New York will last another four, six, eight years. But comes the first major economic crunch and the federal aid will vanish, and with it, any politician in office. I don't want to be holding the bag when it happens. But while it lasts, I can capitalize on it, add a vital issue, and work from a safe base. HEW sounds like a first choice."

She stood up, smoothing her dress. Judith Welsh was a graduate of Radcliffe cum laude. Dark brown hair, falling in a full mass framed gray eyes and a small, evenly proportioned face. She bore children without trace, attended teas, and had an IQ of 140, which she hid well, even from her husband. She loved him, but she knew he hadn't the strength, the conviction, the stamina, and the sheer guts for survival that would win him the presidency.

"You need an issue. What is it?"

He picked up a sheaf of notes and laid them beside her. "I want you to read through this. I need your opinions. It's the foundation of my campaign for the presidency."

Judith Welsh unsnapped her two strands of pearls and laid them on the desk. She picked up the notes and glanced through them. "I'll read them later. What's it about?"

"It's the outline of a speech which I'm going to make up in Utica this weekend. I've called it 'The Science of Peace.' Basically, I'm going to test public reaction to unilateral disarmament. The game plan is to convince the people that we can safely disarm the nation and then use those funds to finance a whole spectrum of social programs."

She tapped the notes with slim fingers. "Would the voters buy it? More important, would the country be safe?"

He shrugged and turned to the window, pushing back the drapes. "Who knows. The Pentagon would have collective apoplexy. But I think we're better off completely disarmed than being a poor second best to the Russians. They don't want war any more than we do. And with the military budget diverted to social programs, we'd free up twenty, maybe thirty billion a year. That's over one hundred bucks for every man, woman, and child in this country."

"Fewer administrative costs," she said. "With the bulk of the money earmarked for the big cities?" She tried to keep the irony out of her voice but he hadn't noticed it.

"Of course," he answered, drawing her against his chest.

The satellite swept west across the plains states, chasing the sun. Fed by sunlight and drawing heavily on the copper-selenide thermoelectric generator, three cameras, the infrared scanner, and magnetometers were running at full output, constantly feeding the data storage bank. From the near-space of 93 miles, the continent was dead of color, showing only contrast of earth and snow. The Rockies were still capped in white as were the Sierras, the deserts between a contrast in umber.

Over the Mojave, a light winked on the desert floor, flickering as it tracked the satellite. Forty-two solar cells of the left wing panel burned out in the intense, blazing heat of the laser, reducing the total solar input by 6 percent. Output wattage monitors reported this to the memory banks as the Russian orbital laboratory slipped past the California coast and sped toward its apogee south of Guam.

In 43 minutes, with the batteries fully recharged, the satellite extended microwave antennas, locked onto a ground antenna located in Dobrekinov in the southern Urals, and disgorged 89 minutes worth of reconnaissance data in a 30-second, high-speed transmission. Data banks empty, *Salyut III* swept on toward Europe.

The facility at Dobrekinov was still a partial unknown to Western intelligence planners. In the conflict that the Soviets still call the War for the Fatherland, thousands of German prisoners were shipped by open coal cars beyond the Volga and the Kirgiz Steppe into the southern range of the Urals. Over two-thirds survived the seven-day journey without food or shelter.

Dobrekinov was originally intended to be a complete underground facility for the production of ball bearings and some aircraft parts. The facility was constructed in a deep valley and blasted out of solid rock to a depth of 123 meters, then built in eight levels with reinforced concrete. Access to the facility was through an S-shaped blast tunnel, protected by eight steel doors sequenced in such a way that only three could be opened at the same time. A compound was built on the surface to house the German prisoners and administrative staff. The winters were so cold that the Germans were forced to stack their dead like cordwood to await burial in the spring thaw.

Following the Soviet victory in 1945, Dobrekinov's future was assessed by many of the same advisors to Stalin who had advocated its use as a ball-bearing production plant. Because of its southern location and remoteness from Moscow, it had little use as a center of Soviet communications, air defense, or even of munitions storage. But in 1951, a committee under the Ministry of Defense decided that its very remoteness and lack of vulnerability to all but a direct hit by a multimegaton warhead would allow Dobrekinov to become a secure record-keeping facility and ultimately, a center for planning and assessment of strategic intelligence data. A bureaucrat examined a list of available designations and assigned the concrete pit the title AW-4.

The facility at first was staffed by a cadre of eighty members of the Red Army. Records, dating as far back as the beginning of the century, were stored in random stacks among the disused machine tools of the obsolete ball-bearing production plant. Later, a primitive microfilming facility was set up at Level Two. Slowly, improvements were made and the illiterate soldiers were supplanted by members of the GRU and by members of the Soviet Academy of Sciences. Four microwave links were established in the mid-fifties, tying AW-4 directly into the Kremlin. Additional hardening was ordered in 1961 so that the facility could take an all but direct hit from an American Mark Five nuclear warhead. Twenty-two hundred political prisoners were shipped down from the Gulag and bodies were again stacked like cordwood through the winter of 1962.

Today, the village of Dobrekinov is listed infrequently and casually on the Ministry of Sports List of Athletic Facilities as a winter training spa. The only aboveground structures are a speed skating rink, two wooden barracks, and an unmarked cemetery containing the bodies of over forty-five hundred Germans, Poles, Czechs, and Russians. This was paved over in 1965 and is now used as a helio-pad.

But despite this preparation, it was not until a Marshall of the Red Army, Gorki Penkovsky, took command and integrated AW-4 into the mainstream of Soviet planning and strategic analysis that the unit became an essential part of Soviet planning.

Marshall Penkovsky, as a lieutenant of the Czar, had been assigned to attend Sandhurst in England in 1910. During this period, he learned English, German, and polished his French. He blotted up the training, jumping one class, and in the process made the friendship of a military scholar, James Duncan. Duncan was one of the first to evolve the strategic military game. Initial efforts were merely moving lead soldiers in sandboxes. But the concept rapidly expanded to battlefields and then continents.

Penkovsky maintained close touch with political events in Russia, bending when necessary, but never becoming involved. What he planned was for Russia, not for the transient ruling clique. He was granted Order of the Soviet Hero by three separate administrations. His photograph appeared only once in the Western press, poised in the background as an Aide to Marshall of the Armies Zukov, who, with his hand flung westward, directed the fire of Soviet artillery along a 2000-kilometer front against the forces of the Third Reich. Penkovsky was a colonel then.

Before his death in 1969, Marshall Penkovsky had assembled a nucleus of staff planners, implemented the Division of Strategic Planning, and filled

Dobrekinov with the equipment necessary to accomplish his aims. He died peacefully in his sleep at the age of 77, an ancient terrier the only one to mourn him. But his ideas survived.

Penkovsky had argued repeatedly in the sixties that the age of planning by generals and admirals was over. Nuclear wars of the future would be fought, as he drolly commented, "during the span of a bowel movement." And the factors necessary for successfully waging war were temperatures over the poles, the depth of the isotherm in the Pacific, the morale of a fighter squadron in Minnesota, and ten thousand other unrelated factors, updated daily and preferably hourly. Computers would compute; men would program. Definite goals would be stated and all effort would be for their attainment.

Penkovsky had one precept for the conduct of both peace and war. "If you are not winning, you are losing. The situation is never static." The cadre of officers beneath him had understood. The most terrifying period was 1958 to 1963 when the American military was at its strongest, with its Atlas and Titan ICBMs, thousands of jet bombers, and nearly forty nuclear submarines. Penkovsky and his cadre cautiously predicted, with the aid of their first vacuum-tube computer, that the US would not strike unless the Americans believed the level of their casualties could be held under 500,000 with no major damage to industry. The period passed, not without tension, but Penkovsky's theory was vindicated. As Soviet strength grew and American strength waned, Penkovsky turned his efforts to appraisal of Soviet chances for winning a war of initiative. He argued that if Russia lost no more than 18 percent of its industry, 12 percent of its population, and could regain its present level of gross national product within five years, a war would be a success, providing of course, that the US was brought under Soviet control without major loss of industry or agricultural output. This objective would be attained by a one-time, all-out strike on US military installations with a planned overkill factor of 5.

From this evolved a multi-layer cake of intelligence gathering; each factor was weighed according to its worth. To bring the percentage chance of winning a preemptive war to 100 percent was wasteful, Penkovsky argued. Some risk must be accepted. And it was decided by the Presidium that 89 percent probability of "winning" was acceptable. Penkovsky didn't care. He would have accepted 60 percent with relish. For in the end, he believed determination and initiative, not sheer force, would win. But there could be no vacillation. The first strike must be made based solely on computer projections and not by political consideration. No withdrawal of diplomats, no breaking of ties. Just a clean, surgical strike, based on the printout of a machine.

On this day in March, four men and a woman were seated around a situation display table on Level Six discussing factors that would be programmed for the Eighty-nine Percent Level (ENPL), as it was now known. The ENPL situation display was a miniaturization of a much larger display that dominated the walls of a mammoth chamber, which their glassed-in balcony overlooked. By verbal request to attending technicians or by keyboarding the *Zudypo IV* computer directly, raw data could be retrieved, new data inserted, or projections drawn.

The meeting comprised five of the six working members of the Committee for Data Gathering, a rather innocuous title for a group of technocrats that held the power to decide the conditions favorable for war. The chairman was Marshall Georgi Zhivotovskiy, Assistant Deputy to the Premier, KGB. He stuffed out another cigarette and turned to the woman addressing the group. His voice was cracked and hoarse and he habitually whispered. "Conclusions, Alexandra. Conclusions. The data you have there can be read by the Committee at leisure. Get on with it."

She flushed slightly, leafing through the report to the final pages. She was a woman of 50, features slightly mongol. Her coarse black hair, drawn back severely and tied in a bun, gleamed under the lights as if it were oiled. Pushing her glasses back on the bridge of her nose, she continued. "The findings of my section indicate that last year the Gross National Product of the United States has risen only 2.43 percent, adjusted annually for inflation, which is presently in excess of 11 percent. Specifically, we do not feel that the US military can sustain its present growth. In the sector of my group's concern, we are projecting a slippage of eight months in the start-up of the production of the Boeing 86 Model C cruise missile. We also think that this, in turn, will result in immediate pressure on spares procurement for the Model B. Overall, we estimate a reduction in mission capability of 4 percent beginning in April as funds are diverted from operational expenses to research and testing. Any questions?"

A tall, bony man raised one finger. He wore a white lab coat and puffed methodically on a dead pipe.

"Comrade Korkin?" she said, inclining her head toward him.

He rose slowly, unfolding his frame. "Just one question, Alexandra." He hesitated, looking down at his notes. "Why the direct link between spares procurement for the Mod B and the development of the Mod C, which your circulated memorandum indicates is a longer range version of the B?"

She smiled condescendingly. "They are both part of the same program, thus the same funding. If the prime contractor and the Air Force feel that development of the longer range version will be hindered by lack of funds, they will probably divert money from operational necessities to research and development. Satisfactory?"

He nodded, tapping his pipe into an ashtray. "What is the overall effect on the ENPL?"

She looked into her file again, knowing the percentage to three places, but delaying the answer for greater impact. "Ah, 1.38 percent by April. Perhaps over 2 percent by July if we get verification of our projections through our US sources."

"Agreed?" The Marshall looked at the members of the Committee. There was no dissension. He then keyboarded the classification code, subroutine, and percentage points. All eyes of the Committee rose to the ENPL display, which flickered briefly and rose from the morning's projected level to a figure of 71.88.

"Bit by bit," he muttered, hardly audible. Lighting another cigarette, he checked his notes and then turned to the short Ukranian opposite him. "Developments, Doctor Lostnev?"

Lostnev remained seated. He scanned his report and keyboarded data into the *Zudypo IV*. "No relevant data at this time, Comrade Marshall. In terms of Air Defense, we have added eighteen of the MIG-23 interceptors to the bases in the Kola Peninsula. I will suggest a shift of some of these aircraft to the Warsaw Pact areas. We need some additional strength on the Polish border. My report will be complete for tomorrow's meeting." He paused, scratching his chin. "There is one thing. *Salyut III* reports loss of 6 percent of her solar panels. The loss was occasioned by a tracking laser device in the western United States. We have been anticipating this."

The Marshall raised his dense eyebrows. "In what way?"

Lostnev smiled thinly. "Because we are doing the same. The remedy lies in a selective wavelength transmission coating for the solar panels. We feel that this will allow incident sunlight to penetrate the cells and yet retain a 95 percent rejection factor of the laser frequency the Americans are presently using. *Salyut IV*, which is scheduled to be launched on the twenty-first from the Tyuratam Cosmodrome, will have this coating. I will report further at that time. Otherwise, I have no input for the ENPL."

Marshall Zhivotovskiy nodded slowly, his shaggy gray head hardly moving. "Agreed." His voice was a bare whisper. His eyes swept around the seated members of the Committee. He never smiled, only indicating pleasure with the intensity of his look and a slight crinkle around his eyes. He lit another cigarette from the tip of the last one. He spoke carefully, referring to a teleprinter message before him. "Good. All your inputs are acceptable. But the fact of the matter is that the ENPL has risen less than five percentage points in the last year. We are reaching a point of diminishing returns, where major technological advances matter less. We must maintain our lead in weapons and extend it when possible. But as long as the United States has a nuclear strike capability, we will be on a very thin edge." He paused for effect, looking at the faces before him. There was a careful raising of eyebrows.

Zhivotovskiy continued. "You are all aware that," he chose the words carefully, conscious of the tape recorders, "there is some political relaxation by the US with the Chinese, who are growing stronger. Should we wait until we have the military supremacy to accomplish the ENPL, we might well find ourselves vulnerable to an effective Chinese strike force." He paused for effect.

"I have before me a message from the First Secretary and the Premier. It has been decided that our attentions must be turned toward developing special situations in which it might be possible to effect US disarmament. These are political considerations and quite justly fall under the Department of Political Affairs for this Committee. Doctor Vassell Rametka, whom you all know—," the Committee turned toward the scientist who had now entered the room and stood before the Committee Table, "was responsible for our successes in Angola. His most notable achievements to date have been political factors underlying the withdrawal of Italy from NATO. Doctor Rametka has developed a two-pronged scenario for the disarmament of the United States within a period of nine months. I think it bears our consideration." He turned toward Rametka. "Doctor?"

Chapter 3

The dawn of April 11th brushed the west ridge of the Sugarbush Valley with grays and reds, which slowly turned to pinks. The first sunlight refracted through the crystals of the last spring snow and illuminated the crest in brilliant white. Rock outcroppings on the ridge were a contrast in gray, their contours softened by the blur of a new snowfall.

Spruces on the valley's walls were overloaded with mounded snow and branches drooped to the point of fracture. With each fresh breath of wind, the snow fell from the branches in muffled thumps.

Lower in the valley, the freshly fallen snow melted, forming rivulets to feed the roaring waters of the Mad River on the valley floor. Meadows and corn fields showed the first green and cows moved from their barns toward the rocky fields. A tractor fired irregularly and then settled into a steady beat, exhaust rising in the morning light. It would be a day of not-still-winter, not-yet-spring.

On the eastern side of the valley, north of the Common Road and beyond Applewood Farm, a single dirt lane led up into the tree line. Despite the night's snowfall, the road was a mush of rich brown mud. Just at the tree line, an ancient Jaguar XK-120M with mud-spattered sides was parked beneath a grove of young maples. Beyond this, set back into the spruce, was a partially completed A-Frame of indifferent design, still in the shade of the east wall of the valley. The roof was covered only with black tar paper and the spruce siding was unpainted except for dapples of different shades of brown stain, which represented the builder's half-hearted attempts to decide on the shade of finish.

A tan Land Rover with dented fenders was parked close under the overhang of the projecting balcony. Packages of shingles were stacked haphazardly in the vehicle along with partially opened kegs of rusting nails.

A silver-gray Siberian husky loped from around the back of the house, slowed beside a pile of firewood, and sniffed. Rejecting it, he selected a stack of fresh building lumber to urinate on. The husky stood there in the morning shadows, leg lifted, breath steaming and tongue lolling in obvious satisfaction. Finished, he scrambled up the rock stairs to the front door and nudged against the sill with his nose. No one was there to open it for him and he lay down, whining softly.

The interior of the house was silent, except for the occasional hissing of embers in the carefully banked wood stove. The bedroom still lay in the subdued grays of early morning. Clothes ranging from a blue blazer to muddy Levis lay about the shag-carpeted floor. A smaller pair of jeans, a T-shirt embossed with a faded profile of Daffy Duck, and a down-filled parka lay folded on the dresser. A leaking faucet from the adjoining bathroom tapped its steady, muffled beat.

The bed was a shapeless lump of twisted comforters and indistinct forms. A swatch of long blonde hair flowed across a pillow, face hidden beneath the covers.

"Uhmmmmm," sighed the woman as she stretched her full length. Her hand appeared above the blanket, testing the temperature and withdrew.

The bed underwent a rearrangement of shapes and was still for many minutes. Then another arm, scarred from the elbow to the wrist with burn tissue, projected up from beneath the covers, flexed at the elbow, rotated at the wrist and exposed the dial of a Rolex. The owner's eyes peered out between the comforter and pillow that covered his head.

"Crap," he muttered and withdrew the arm back to warmth.

"Uhmmmmm," she sighed.

The husky waited by the door for another hour, breath rising in small clouds, the morning sun melting snow from his silver fur.

Brian Loss had started the chalet two years ago. The land had been a gift from an aunt, now dead. Starting with no plan, he used only hand tools. He recognized that the slow, clumsy work was a form of therapy but tried not to analyze it too closely. It took three weeks to dig the foundation and another four to pour the concrete, which he mixed by hand. At the end of each day, he would take the four-wheel drive down to the river and bathe, sometimes lying in the shallows, barely covered by the tepid water, and watch the clouds form and dissipate above him. He kept to himself, cooking his meals on a propane stove and reading until the light was gone.

She drifted back from Alaska with the dog and helped him frame the house. Twice she left on backpacking trips, but both times she came back. Neither of them spoke about it but it was a form of union, delicately balanced between dependence and independence.

Sometimes while paneling the roof, Loss would stare at the sailplanes that thermaled beneath building cumulus clouds, playing in the sun like hawks. He tried to forget about the black gunship and the skies of Southeast Asia.

After the gunship crash, Loss had been sent back to California to recover from the burns and, ultimately, to shuffle papers. A flying evaluation board was convened to rehash the accident. A brisk young major who had never flown combat chaired the board and the findings were that Loss might have saved the plane and the other four crew members had he landed with the gear up on a foamed runway. They reinstated his flying status but denied his request to return to combat. Disgusted, Loss didn't appeal the verdict.

Two months later and by a chance occurrence of scheduling, he flew with the young major and told him, as they parted in the debriefing room after the flight, that the major made a better asshole than a pilot. Loss found out later that the major's father was a lieutenant general in Washington.

Loss resigned his commission and three months later met Kitzner in a bar in Denver. Kitzner was the vice-president of a small airframe subcontractor which was making stressed-skin aluminum bodies for recreational vehicles. Kitzner hired Loss based on the friendship that had started that evening, but now Loss tried to forget about him ever since he had learned that Kitzner had blown his brains out. He tried to forget about Kitzner's pathetic little firm, Amtechnik, which had expired one dull Friday morning in the fall of 1975.

Actually, the pink slip had informed him that he was "furloughed." An accompanying letter (xeroxed) informed him that a reorganization of the firm was under way with some interested backers, and he would be notified as soon as his services were required. The letter concluded:

> We here at Amtechnik are proud to have been associated with a person of your high ability, energy and faith in our collective future. Thanks for your loyalty during these difficult times. In the near future, Amtechnik will be rolling again and we hope that you will be part of the team.

Collecting his check from the personnel section, he cleaned out his desk and exchanged the usual platitudes with fellow employees. The one that counted was Kitzner.

But Kitzner's secretary said that he was unavailable. Beyond her, Loss could see Kitzner, alone at his desk, a half-empty bottle of Wild Turkey set squarely on his blotter. Kitzner finally glanced up. His shoulders contracted in a shrug and he turned away, looking far beyond the blank wall.

With his last paycheck Loss had paid off the balance of his lease on the apartment and had closed his utility accounts; he then had packed the Rover and headed north toward Canada. Screw unemployment handouts, he thought, wanting to see only bare, silent snowfields. There was enough money to ski for a while, and he didn't want to think too much about the past or future.

For the first two days, he drove recklessly. He cursed Amtechnik and Kitzner. And he cursed himself for being stupid. The Rover bit into the mountain roads, tires squealing through the turns.

By the third day, he was in northern Montana. The isolation and stark beauty of the country began to bring him composure. Toward sundown, he picked up a girl with long, straight hair carrying a rucksack. There was a dog with her. She said her name was Holly from New Mexico. Just like that.

"Where are you going?" Loss asked as she and the dog climbed in. The rucksack and dog had divided the back seat into two fuzzy spots of darkness.

"Alaska, I think." She pulled back the tasseled ski cap and turned toward him and smiled. Her complexion was tanned and flawless. "It's a beautiful four-wheel drive," she said, brushing her hand along the top of the dash with awe, as if it had been hand-tooled leather instead of roughly finished aluminum.

They floated along in the gathering darkness, the road a dark track of asphalt walled on either side by aspens and deep snow. She sat there in the glow of the dash lights, humming softly. The dog moved forward and rested his muzzle on the back edge of her seat and laughed, his tongue lolling. He was a Siberian husky. She said his name was Total.

He smiled at this and realized that this was the first time he had smiled in three days. Total. It seemed like a name for breakfast food or gasoline or something you rolled into your armpits. "How come the name?" he asked.

"He was hit by a car when he was just a few weeks old," she said, reaching back and gently scruffing at the dog's ear, "and they thought he was totaled. He was all broken bones and blood. A real mess. His owner was going to shoot him, and I just took him away and saw a friend who was a vet student. He made it OK."

"Ya still limp a little, don't cha?" She buried her face in the dog's fur.

They stopped south of Missoula for dinner. Both of them had tacos and split the bill. Finished, he leaned back in the booth and drank the stale coffee, watching her chew each bit endlessly.

"Sixteen times," she said without looking up, poking a piece of lettuce back into the taco shell. "It's good for your digestion. But they taste like plastic, don't they?"

He smiled and felt fine.

After dinner, they pushed north again. She asked him why he found it so difficult to laugh, and he told her about the minor disasters of the last few years, and it sounded ridiculous, even trivial. She sat in silence for long minutes after he finished the explanation, and they listened to the whine of the snow tires on the bare road beneath them.

"It really sounds like you hated the whole thing, anyway." She turned to him and smiled again, just as she had when he had first picked her up on the highway south of Anaconda.

They drove on into the night, talking about little things. She said that she had worked in Vail Pass as a night clerk in one of the inns, and she skied during the day and that the phony architecture and the beautiful people and the rich freaks had messed it all up. She wanted to see Alaska in the spring. Someone by the name of Donny worked on the crab boats up in Anchorage, and she would be with him for a while.

The three of them drifted up into the mountains of British Columbia for three days and then turned west toward the coast.

The nights were spent in motel rooms. She would unpack a few things from her rucksack, unself-consciously strip off her clothes and slide into her side of the bed. Brian did the same, and on both nights she would simply take his hand

and hold it tightly, then reach over to brush his lips and say goodnight. He awoke in the early morning of the second night toward the first grays of dawn, with her hand holding his over her breast. He lay still in feigned sleep, feeling the steady beat of her heart.

On the morning of the third day, the sky was clear with the startling blue of high altitude. Range after range of the Canadian Rockies and the Monashee Mountains unfolded to the west, peaks covered in white. High on the summits, snow streamed off in dazzling banners blown in the wind.

She said her name was Holly Stowe and that she was 28 or 29, and that she always forgot her birthday. She laughed a lot and hummed and was delighted with the beauty. He asked her how long she had been skiing.

"Oh, about three years like this." She vaguely waved her hand across the horizon. "I was an architect and I just got tired of drawing straight lines." Pausing for a few minutes, she looked toward the side of the road, watching fenceposts step across the fields. "There was a marriage that didn't work out. And then Vail. I just had to get away and think about it. It's better now."

The Rover wound down through the coastal ranges and down the Fraser Canyon, skirting the eastern fringes of Vancouver. He turned north along Howe Sound for Garibaldi Provincial Park.

They rented a single bedroom house behind the grocery store at the base of Whistler Mountain, and she said that she would stay as long as she shared in the rent and the food. That night, she made spaghetti and they drank two bottles of Mateus Rosé. The dog finished the remains, coughing happily and rattling the scorched pan against the flagstone floor.

They sat in front of the fire and drank the last of the wine. She watched him in the firelight and traced the broken ridge of his nose with her fingertips. "How did that happen?" she asked.

"An airplane stopped moving and I didn't." He opened his eyes and looked at her and grinned. "I lost a tooth, too. They put another one back in. It was a fair trade. I didn't even have to pay for the plane."

"When was that?" she asked. The dog was making clanking sounds with the spaghetti pot, shoving it across the kitchen floor.

He ran his fingers down the asymmetrical ridge of his nose. "Two years ago. Three, actually. I was flying an airplane and one of the main landing gears wouldn't come down." He could still remember the final approach in the disabled C-47 gunship with three of them in the back, dead or dying. The right engine was feathered and partially hanging on its fire-blackened mounts. Lt. Vaughn Harris, whom he barely knew, sat in the copilot's seat with both hands clasped over a reddish-black thing that had been his stomach, his face white and eyes staring blankly at the aluminum cabin top.

The left main gear was down and locked. The right gear hung askew, partially torn away by the 50-millimeter cannon fire they had caught near a hilltop south of Quang Tri. He touched down at 90 knots with the controls held progressively more to the left, balancing on the one good gear. The gooney bird wobbled awkwardly and despite full deflection of the yoke, settled onto the right gear, cartwheeling into noise and blackness.

"Did you ever fly again?"

"Once or twice after I got out of the hospital. They sent me back to shuffle papers, mainly. I irritated a few people and someone suggested that I might make a good civilian. I haven't flown since."

She pushed the hair back out of her eyes. "And now?"

Loss shrugged and looked into the fire, watching the flames lick around the bark of the aspen. "Now—" he paused, thinking. "Now, I think I'll go to Vermont after I've skied myself out. I've got 5 acres there. I'll sell it or build a home. Maybe try flying again, but nothing very serious. I think it'll work out." He thought about it and somehow it made sense.

She turned to him, studying his face in the firelight. She reached down and held his hand. "I think, Brian, that you're already there. It's just that you have yet to realize it."

She pulled a cushion from the sofa and lay down in front of the hearth. Holding her arms up to him, she said, "Can you help me get this sweater over my head, Loss?"

For three days they skied the face of Whistler Mountain, dropping down through the powder-snow-filled bowls, falling and laughing and breathless. And each night they went home to the little cottage to eat and fondle the laughing husky and to make love before the bed of dying embers. Once he started to tell her that he loved her and she turned away from him, crying.

In the early afternoon of the fourth day, they sat beneath an outcropping of rocks in the Western Bowl, eating a lunch of cheese and Canadian wine and sourdough bread and looking out along the curvature of the earth. The visibility was clear and the sky cloudless. Out beyond the Coastal Mountains he thought he could see the Strait of Georgia and a blue haze beyond that—the Pacific.

She cut a slice of cheddar for him. "It's clean up here, isn't it?" she said.

Loss just continued to stare out at the west and slid his arm around her waist. "Clean isn't the word for it. Maybe one of the last great places God made. I hope that the Canadians will learn from our mistakes. I think of Denver now, sitting on the edge of those beautiful mountains, and yet all the people are swimming around in a sea of smog." He turned and grinned at her, his sun-blackened face contrasting with the white band from the sunglasses.

"You look like a raccoon," she said.

He kissed her nose and cheeks. She kissed him back and then rested her face against his.

She drew back from him and took off her sunglasses. She had the small beginning of tears. "You're OK, Loss," she said, standing up and brushing the snow from her jeans. "Be careful."

She kicked into her bindings, shuffled off the ledge, and fell away in long sweeping turns through the fresh powder.

He watched her until she disappeared into the tree line, and then he could see her again along the brow of the East Ridge, skiing very fast but carving out turns of perfect symmetry. Her blue parka finally disappeared in the distance.

I'll have to get used to that, he thought, but her changeable moods and independence were part of her whole personality, and it seemed to fit together. He gathered the wine bottle and the bits of lunch, loaded them into his knapsack, and sat back again to light a cigarette.

Looking south toward Vancouver, he caught a long thin contrail of a jet climbing toward the sun. And he thought again of the beauty of high altitude flight and realized that he had missed it. He laughed out loud, remembering how it was at first, when he was first learning to fly. There was no beauty to it then, just the unrelenting terror of failure to pass his flight checks, of the first solo, of the ancient captain who sat in the back seat of the two-place trainer, shouting into the intercom. "More right rudder, mister," or "Get your airspeed up, stupid." The first fourteen hours of instruction had been a bath in hell and Loss's performance had been totally mechanical and unfeeling.

On a July steamer of a morning, Captain Slokum and Loss had done three circuits of the pattern and landed. Slokum was grumbling into the intercom about keeping proper airspeed control on final. He directed Loss to taxi off the active runway. Slokum got out of his cockpit and came forward on the wing. The big Lycoming ticked over, and Loss could barely hear his instructions.

Slokum blew his nose and then leaned down on the canopy sill and shouted into Loss's ear, "You're so bad I doubt that you will ever make it through this program. Your only hope is to get this *thing* safely into the air and go find some uncluttered sky. Maybe this thing can teach you something about aviating that I surely can't." He thumped Loss on the shoulder, briefly grinned, reminding Loss of a horse baring its teeth. Slokum jumped off the wing and walked away without looking back.

Teeth gritting, Loss spun the T-34 through a 180-degree turn, savagely braking short of the active. He asked for and received takeoff clearance.

The cleaning up of flaps, retraction of gear, the adjustment of power settings and rpm were automatic blurs. Although he knew that Slokum expected him to shoot touch-and-go landings, Loss cleared the control area of the field and headed east. He climbed for the base of the growing cumulus clouds, which grazed like obedient sheep along the edge of the Texas Gulf Coast. Passing through 8000 feet, he felt the cockpit cooling to a clean crispness. Leveling off at 9000 feet, he headed for a towering cumulus that bulged with turrets and ramparts and convoluted towers. He eased in power and banked sharply, scraping the cloud-fabric with his wing; then he reversed direction in a chandelle and tore down in a dive with the engine screaming at redline, smoking through the canyons of the clouds. His mind merely said, "Go there," and the plane obeyed. For two hours, he played with the aircraft, alternately bathed in sweat or chilled. He and the T-34 explored the corners of the envelope of flight, from stalls at low power settings to cheek-sagging, high-speed turns. He snap-rolled the trainer, working from his memory and ended up inverted. Shouting at the top of his lungs with the mike button unconsciously depressed, he rolled the aircraft upright. He knew that the sky was his, at least on loan.

Back in the tower, Slokum heard the joyful laughter on the receiver and knew it for what it was.

Loss looked again at the contrail, now dissipating to a blurred chalk mark in the blue horizon. I guess it's time to climb back into a cockpit, he thought.

He reached the cabin by sundown. The fire was lit and a pie sat cooling on the top of the oven. Her things were gone, of course. He read the note she had left on the pine table. It simply said, "We'll come back. Love from Total and me." There was no signature. He smiled and wished her well.

Chapter 4

The device rested on its pneumatically cushioned transporter in the cool, dehumidified darkness of its bunker. An identical twin to this device was stored in a duplicate vault one-half kilometer away. The third device of this design had that morning been detonated 2880 meters below the Dzhelinde Steppe of Central Siberia. Test data on the shot were still flowing into the evaluation center at Zhigansk by teleprinter, fax transmission, and by computer link.

Professor of Soviet Nuclear Science, Yuri Striganov, munched on jam-covered toast and examined the teleprinter message, which lay before him. He occasionally underscored passages of the text with a silver-plated pen, grunted, reread passages, and finally pushed the message aside.

"I think, Colonel Petrov, that our test data conform exactly with our expectations." Striganov looked up at the blonde man with the brittle blue eyes and nordic features.

The man in the uniform of the Soviet Long Range Rocket Force sat slouched in a chair, facing Striganov's desk. He made no effort to look up and sat expressionless, brushing a particle of nonexistent lint from his dun-colored trousers. He then opened his mouth as if to speak, hesitated, and then spoke in flat tones with almost German accent.

"Yes, Professor. I have seen the test data. I question the yield, as it seems to be nearly three megatons whereas we had expected the device to be in the range of 2.0 to 2.3. Other than that, the signatures match exactly, the generation of manganese 56 seems to be within limits, and I conclude that you and Marshall Markoff are satisfied. By the way, could I have some more coffee? Cuban, not Turkish, please." He then smiled and said mechanically, "I know that this has been a great effort on the part of your group here at Zhigansk. I have been instructed to inform you and Marshall Markoff of the personal expression of thanks by our leaders."

The standard statement of praise by the young colonel brought a polite smile to the face of Striganov, but he wondered at the importance of the device. He paused and pressed the bar on his intercom. "We wish another cup of the Cuban coffee. A glass of tea for myself and, yes, bring more toast. With currant jam." A hollow voice distorted by the speaker repeated his order and he released the bar. "I am surprised, Colonel, that the construction data were so complete, but you in the, ah, Rocket Forces must know of these things." Yuri paused and decided to probe for some reason why a nuclear device designed to be used in the Poseidon SLBM would be copied in the USSR down to the exact shape, metallurgical composition, and even umbilical plug connector. How the exact design was obtained was beyond comprehension. "We have found the design of the device to be quite sound," he continued, "but the miniaturization was rather difficult to duplicate in the arming circuits. The design of the radar altimeter is, as the Americans say, 'state of the art.' I presume that you will be using the device for—"

The young colonel injected, "For evaluation, Professor. We will be using these devices to evaluate the feasibility of certain special situations."

They sat in silence for a moment. The explanation had been made complete in its absence. Yuri Striganov rejected further probing as both unwise and unsettling to the stomach. A light blinked on above the shielded door and an older matron pushed it open as Yuri depressed the magnetic release. The young colonel rose from his seat and walked to the far end of the office to inspect the model of the new high speed cyclotron being constructed by the Academy of Sciences. Petrov's casual withdrawal gave Striganov the impression of suppressed impatience.

The matron served the coffee and tea, deposited a dish of toast, and wheeled her trolley back out through the double set of doors. The colonel returned to his chair.

He started without preface, ignoring the coffee. "I will not fence with you, Professor. I am an officer of *Glavnoye Razvedyvatelnoye Uparvleniye,* seconded to the KGB, Section V. I am doing so under the direction of Comrade Yuri Andropov, Director of the KGB. I hold these orders." He withdrew a thin leather case from the inside coat pocket of his jacket and laid it carefully before Striganov. "Here also is my identity card. My fingerprints have been scanned by your security people. I believe it is all in order." Striganov opened and read the orders.

```
GOSPLAN TO GROPSYNC SECURITY LEVEL NINE STOP
BEARER OF ORDERS COMMA IDENTIFIED COLONEL
ANATOLI ANTONOVICH PETROV COMMA TO CONTROL
MOVEMENTS OF UNITS TWO AND THREE BUILT ZHIGANSK
STOP UNQUALIFIED COOPERATION REQUIRED BY
EVERY AGENCY PRESENTED THESE ORDERS STOP
```

```
TELEPRINT KGB/5 IN TACTICAL CODE DELTA COMMA

QUOTE SALMACIS UNQUOTE STOP  AUTHENTICATION

REPLY IS QUOTE PORT ARTHUR UNQUOTE STOP

SIGNATURE FIRST SECRETARY STOP  END MESSAGE
```

Yuri studied the documents carefully, folded them, and returned them to the far side of the desk facing Petrov. "I begin to understand the importance of this, Colonel Petrov. Excuse me." Yuri took a deep swallow of the Georgian tea and set the cup to one side. He withdrew a directory from his desk safe and thumbed through the pages, finally noting the teleprinter index number of the KGB, Section V. The room, which was regulated at 20 degrees Celsius, seemed very warm. He walked to the teleprinter and awkwardly punched the coded address and waited. In twenty-two seconds, the answer-back code appeared. He then coded the word *SALMACIS* through the automatic enciphering unit and pressed the TRANSMIT GROUP key. The machine chattered softly and then was quiet. He could hear the colonel stirring the cooling coffee. Approximately one minute elapsed and then the machine came to life, indexing the roll of paper through two lines and then printing in clear black print the words *PORT ARTHUR.*

"You're out of your fuckin' mind, Clifford." The speaker was a little cock of a man, dark complexioned with a beak nose. Scuffing back and forth across the parquet floor, he left small streaks on the waxed finish. He paused by the bay window and brushed the curtains aside with the vexation of a thief who hasn't cracked the safe yet and has heard the police pulling up outside. His name was Harry DeSilva and he saw nothing except the gray of New York's distant skyline.

Clifford Welsh said nothing, smiled by remote control, and waited for the rest of it.

"No way, Cliff, are you going to get reelected on this sort of a platform. Why blow it? You just keep your mouth shut, attend luncheons, pose with some hard hats, visit the hospitals and you're in. You're *in* right now." DeSilva rubbed his forehead, his cheeks, his nose, and his jowls as if trying to separate the skin from his skull. His eyes had the desperate look of a cornered animal.

Harry DeSilva had managed the campaign of Clifford Welsh for two terms of office. For despite the workingman exterior of appearance and speech, DeSilva was a Wharton School of Finance graduate with heavy experience in mass marketing. He felt the pulse of public opinion by computer surveys. And he believed that political superstars were made by research and not election-year trivia.

DeSilva composed himself and continued. "Cliff, in no way am I saying these ideas aren't workable, but it just doesn't mesh with your position over the last five years. This speech here," he slapped the document down on the desk for emphasis, "is for the birds as far as vote getting. Look, you got elected on the basis of campaigning for a federal bailout for New York. And a lot of people in that city know just one thing—they've got federal funds paying for their jobs and their retirement funds. You beat the governor and even the mayor in pushing the bailout through Washington, despite Ford and Carter and the fuckin' Congress. So why this other stuff?" DeSilva sat down heavily on the leather divan, scowling.

Senator Clifford Welsh looked down at his manila pad for some minutes, not wanting to speak so that DeSilva would digest what had been said. Welsh also wanted to project an attitude of calm and decision. In reality, he had known that DeSilva would resist a radical swing in the platform, and Welsh had rehearsed for just this moment.

He had met DeSilva in 1972. Welsh had a good campaign going, but it lacked punch. His platform had had a very broad scope, covering crime in the streets, nuclear power stations, and the environment. But it needed something else.

DeSilva had come to his campaign headquarters in lower Manhattan in July, 1972. In the space of three hours, DeSilva convinced him that the Welsh platform was cold turkey. People voted for one thing: jobs and security. The rest of it you can stuff, he had said.

DeSilva drew up a simple three-point campaign, a schedule of events, and probable result in voter impact. And the incredible thing was that DeSilva had personally conducted and financed his own poll of 2200 New Yorkers and had the results to prove it. And with DeSilva running the organization, Welsh moved from fifth place to win the race going away.

But DeSilva was getting sloppy now. Good salary, top staff, and firmly entrenched in his position. The talent was still there, but the security of knowing that his candidate would win had taken the edge off.

Welsh knew that there were other men he could hire to replace DeSilva, but they wouldn't be as good or tough or canny. It would be a waste of energy to try. He looked down at his pad for the first item in his attempt to drag the little man into a new political challenge. Opposite the figure 1, he had written in a neat scrawl, "Establish Authority."

Clifford pushed back his chair, stood up, and walked over to stand before DeSilva, who still sat drooping on the couch. Welsh stood over six feet. He looked down at DeSilva and said, "You can't support me in this position, Harry? You think it's a stupid thing to do?"

DeSilva, finding Welsh standing directly in front of him, had to arch his head up to reply. He felt small and awkward. "No, Cliff, I didn't say that exactly. That speech you made in Utica. That was a potential disaster. I mean, like this thing on disarmament. Everybody agrees that disarmament is a good deal, but there are a lot of defense contractors in New York who won't like that kind of comment and you have the Street to contend with. Merely say "unilateral disarmament" and the Dow Jones will fall on its ass. And, Cliff, you just can't ignore the money that comes from those guys in election years. And then think—"

Clifford cut him off brusquely. "Harry, you're not really thinking. You were really good once. You understood what people thought. We anticipated public feeling, and we shaped the platform to accommodate these shifts in mood. But are you telling me now that people want to continue paying for massive defense budgets at the expense of social programs? Do you honestly feel that the Russians pose any real threat? We're Number Two now in the arms race and if we continue like this or try to become Number One again, we're going to get beat up on. No, damn it! It's better that we don't present any threat and keep our nose out of both Europe and Asia. We have an inflationary economy to contend with, and we can't have guns and butter at the same time."

DeSilva was on the defensive now. "Cliff, these are national problems. The people that elect you are concerned with state and city problems. That's OK for a speech to farmers in Iowa or liberals in Chicago, but it's stupid and unrealistic to think you can make points with the whole spectrum of voters in New York on an issue like that. Talk about better garbage disposal or teacher's retirement funds, but leave the heavy stuff to presidential candidates who . . . ," DeSilva's voice trailed off, and he sat in silence for several minutes, thinking.

The second point on the tablet read "Define Goal." The tall Senator turned from his aide and walked over to the mantle and silently examined the portrait of his father. It glared down from the canvas to the viewer, expression forever set in distaste. The brass ship's clock on the desk chimed two bells.

Clifford spoke. "Yes, Harry. I think you see the point. The platform *is* designed for farmers in Iowa and liberals in Chicago. I don't want to be Senator from New York forever. I don't have national support, but somehow I have to get out of the state into some position where I can build a political base for the presidency. I'm young but so was Kennedy. I'm willing to take stupid posts in the UN, ambassadorships to unheard of countries, anything. But I have to establish a national profile with national identification. If anything, I have to overcome voter rejection in the farm states due to my stance on New York. But I need you, Harry."

"Jesus." DeSilva sat with his head in his hands. "Jesus. You're committing political suicide, Cliff. You've got the election sewn up right now, and we could go for governor in 1984 and then we could begin to think about it, but you're talking about withdrawing from the Senatorial race *now,* and what in hell are you going to do for the next four years? If the Republicans win this election, you could be sitting out in the boondocks for the next eight years. Did you ever hear of Adlai Stevenson?" DeSilva went through his face-scrubbing routine again, kneading and massaging the skin. Welsh decided it was a sign of frustration and made a mental note. He had never seen DeSilva so unsure before, but, he reasoned, that up until now, the coarse intellectual with the dockside mannerisms had been in absolute control. He now showed a new facet of indecision and the knowledge undermined the confidence of the young Senator. "Look, Harry. Either you have confidence in me or not. It might mean that I *do* spend four years in the boondocks. But during that time I can build nonpartisan support. I can write a book to state these positions. I'll be disaffiliated with New York. But I need you or someone like you. I need the organization down deep to direct my efforts. Judith and I have gone over the whole thing, and I think that I can make it if we build a good organization starting right now." It sounds like I'm pleading, he thought. DeSilva just sat there on the sofa, staring into the fire, expressionless.

Finally DeSilva spoke. His voice was flat and expressionless. "I have faith in you, Cliff. You know that. I wouldn't have come to you in the first place. But it's not time yet. Let's win this election and then begin to build up something. Just don't make waves now. You'll be in a much stronger position in four years' time." He turned and smiled weakly. "Look, you're going down to that place in the Caribbean for two weeks. Take some time and think this over and I will too. We'll discuss it when you come back, and I promise that I'll do some research in the meanwhile. I may be wrong, but I have to run a poll to see whether it works."

"You may be right, Harry. Let's both think about it. Don't discuss this with Judith. She thinks I'm set on it, and I don't want to get involved in rethinking my position with her on a vacation. She's always had faith in your computer survey predictions, and if the decision is negative for breaking away, it will be easier for all of us to accept."

The Senator turned his back on DeSilva and stood at the window, parted the curtains, and watched the progress of a small freighter stemming the muddy Hudson. It was snowing lightly. The overcast was under 800 feet.

Clifford could hear DeSilva getting up and walking toward him. He felt anger and yet relief at the decision that was probably now made, tacitly agreed upon by each of them. The time was too early in his career.

DeSilva stood beside him and shared the view of the Hudson and the rust-streaked freighter. "I know how you feel, Cliff. Just get some sun and forget about people like me and those fourteen million turds across the river. How are you going down, Pan Am?"

The freighter was nearly out of sight beyond the bend in the river. The snow was getting heavier.

"No, Harry. I'm taking my Aztec down. Incidentally, call up my pilot. His name is Brian Loss. His number is in my appointment book. Tell him to bring charts for everything from the States south to Grenada and meet me at Albany International on Friday morning at 11:00 AM."

"OK, Cliff. I'll take care of it. Ciao." DeSilva turned and left the room without another word.

The Junior Senator from New York watched DeSilva walk to his Mercedes, get in, and slowly disappear down the snow-covered driveway to return to his apartment on East 58th Street.

"Fourteen million and one turds," he thought and turned away from the window.

They lay together in the darkness of predawn, each retreating from sleep, aware of each other but not moving or waking. Finally, he murmured and turned toward her, fitting his body to hers, his chin resting lightly on the back of her neck, his knees fitting against her calves. She made a small sound and he felt her pushing back, her buttocks to his groin. Her body was warmer and the cadence of her breathing mismatched his.

He tried to edge back into sleep, wanting those few more minutes. But he was awake now. The window framed grays, growing lighter, and he heard the husky whine.

"Awake?" she said, voice muffled in the pillow.

The nape of her neck smelled of fresh bread, intermingled with the scent of soap. He pulled her more closely to him. "No," he answered.

The clock chimed seven and Loss came to the edge of wakefulness again. He lay on his back with the down-filled sleeping bag, which had been opened to its full width, lapping his nose. He reached to his left to touch Holly but her side of the bed was now cool and empty. The bedroom door was closed, but he could hear the Siberian husky prancing excitedly over the bare maple floors of the living room, down the passage to the bedroom, sniffing and then trotting back to the slate kitchen floor. And he could smell the perking coffee.

The temperature in the room was 43 degrees. Consolidating his nerves and muscles, he counted to ten reluctantly, leaped from the bed, and raced for the bathroom. He flicked on the steam timer and raced back to bed, shivering uncontrollably before his body heat regenerated some warmth beneath the down-filled cover. Holly's side of the bed was covered with her down-filled bag as well, opened to its full width and zip-mated to his own. The cold seam of the brass zipper had been covered with tape, which seemed to be the maximum effort that either of them had made toward any permanence in their relationship. Loss sighed and looked at his Rolex, adding ten minutes for the steam to fill the bathroom with heat.

DeSilva's call had arrived at five last evening, ordering the Aztec to pick up the Senator at 11:00 AM. Brian and the mechanic crew from the valley's small airport had worked late into the evening, completing the 100-hour inspection and cleaning the aircraft. There were bound to be photographers in Albany, and Welsh would want the aircraft flawless. Brian checked his watch, decided to give the steam five more minutes, and drifted back into the semianimation of dozing and waking.

He could barely hear her in the kitchen, singing something about a cowboy down in Colorado that rides the ro-de-o. He checked his watch again and found that he had three more minutes. Fully awake now, his mind began to synchronize in real time. He would have to be up at the airport by 8:30, preflight the Aztec, file a flight plan, and get the Lycomings run-up by 9:30. Assuming about an hour between Vermont and Albany, New York, he would touch down in time to refile and get the aircraft wiped down before Welsh's arrival with the press.

Loss didn't like or dislike Welsh. It was a paycheck without too much of a commitment. When Welsh wanted him to go somewhere, Loss made the trip regardless of time or day. But when the aircraft wasn't in use, Loss flew back to the valley to work on the house and be with Holly. In Loss's mind, it was a good arrangement.

But this was a little different. Welsh wanted to take a trip to some resort in the Caribbean. With the fuel shortage, it would be better to go commercial airlines. But Welsh was like that—the fearless politician image. And this time Loss would be gone for more than two weeks. He wondered whether Holly would be here when he got back. The thought bothered him, but he knew that he would not press her for an answer.

She had come back from Alaska in the spring, six months after they had met in Montana. She helped him finish the framing, and they accomplished more in two days than he normally could have in a week. During that spring, he answered Welsh's ad for a pilot position and was hired, leaving her to do much of the work. Holly was delighted, explaining that although she had worked as an architect, she never had the experience of actually building.

She had done most of the construction herself but in rushes of enthusiasm interspersed with backpacking trips. She characteristically would announce one morning that she would be gone for a while, kissed him, and left with the dog bounding ahead into the countryside. Once, she had gone to hike along the Maine coast, and he didn't see her for two months, receiving only mildly pornographic postcards from Italy to mark her existence. Where she got money to travel on was an unknown.

He glanced at his watch, sighed, and jumped from beneath the covers. Running to the steaming bathroom, he stubbed his toe and slipped on the bathroom tile. Hopping and holding his toe, he swore loudly. She appeared some minutes later in front of the glassed-in steam bath, holding a large mug of coffee.

"It looks like the Tropic of Cancer in here," waving the steam from her eyes and handing him the mug. He stuck out his tongue, and she retaliated with a rude finger gesture.

She closed the door to the bath and called out behind her that there were some eggs awaiting his pleasure when he was ready.

In ten minutes, he sat down opposite her. She rose, took the eggs from the oven, and set the plate down before him on the rough pine table. She poured another cup of coffee for him and made herself a cup of tea.

He pointed at the eggs encased in a shell of sausage with his fork and prodded them gingerly. "What do you call these?"

"Scotch eggs or scrofulous eggs, depending on what state you vote in." She smiled. The husky sat behind her on the slate tiles, laughing. The sunlight spilled through the window and highlighted her hair. I'd miss her if she goes, he thought.

"Where is it that you're flying to?" she asked.

"Place called Salt Whistle Cay. Umm. Eggs are great. It's a little 100-acre rock in the Grenadines, which isn't too far from Barbados. Any more eggs? Seriously, they're tremendous."

She dished out two more eggs and spooned some sour cream on them and then sprinkled freeze-dried chives over the sour cream.

"This is my own added thing. I didn't think you would go for it on the first course. What do you think?"

He nodded his head enthusiastically, his mouth too full to answer. Actually, he liked them better without the sour cream. He sat back after finishing the eggs and lit a cigarette.

"How soon do you have to leave?" she said, looking up at the wall clock over the refrigerator.

"By 8:15 I guess. Can you take me up in that antique of yours?" referring to the elderly Jaguar, which she had driven back following her last unannounced absence.

"Yes. I already put all your stuff in it. Your flight case is in the mud room. I stuck in the new Jeppesen approach plates that came last Monday. There were two new ones for Fort Lauderdale."

He raised his eyebrows. By some genetic trick, his eyebrows seemed to be linked to his ears, and they flattened back, just as his father's had always done. The serious effect was ruined. "I didn't know that you knew about filing approach plates. You're hired. I hate doing that. It's like taking the same pill every day and not getting better."

"It's easy," she said. "I just read the instructions and put them in and removed the old ones and signed it off the little list that they have in the front. You have to explain approach plates to me sometime. It's not that easy, is it? I mean, you're surrounded by pea soup and trying to find the airport and getting into line with all the other airplanes that are doing the same thing. It sounds busy." Her blue eyes looked into his without wavering. "That was a nice approach you made earlier this morning," she laughed and leaned forward to touch his nose with her lips. Her shirt was unbuttoned at the top and his eyes fell to the cleft between her breasts. I've known her for three years now, he thought, and she can excite me still just by a word or a touch.

"Oh," she said, pushing the newspaper toward him. "Did you see what your boss said, supposedly off the record?"

The local paper carried a small clipping about a speech Senator Clifford Welsh had made at Utica College in March. The article reported that he had been there to dedicate a new wing of the Science Building and had made an oblique reference in his dedication speech to diverting more funds from the military into the quest for what he termed "The Science of Peace." The reporter in an interview after the ceremony had asked the Senator to elaborate and he had hedged, saying that US withdrawal from the scenes of potential world conflict would be an inducement for other nations to do so. The reporter had asked whether the Senator was really advocating unilateral disarmament. The Senator would only further comment that such proposals were always under study and terminated the interview. Response to the speech had been mixed.

Brian pushed the paper away in disgust without finishing it. "Sometimes I think that man has rocks for brains. He's all right personally, but the country would be a lot safer if he was running a stock brokerage house or playing at city councilman. But why is it that some speech he made in early March comes up in an April newspaper?"

"You should read the rest of it, but—well, it goes on to say that the *Manchester Guardian* picked it up and when the reporter was questioned about it, he admitted that the interview was correct but that Welsh's political manager had personally called that evening and asked him to keep it off the record. I guess someone overheard the conversation between Welsh and the reporter, or maybe the reporter actually leaked it. But save it and show it to him. He'll love you for it."

He stubbed out the cigarette and folded the newspaper. "Yes, but I can imagine he will love that reporter in Utica all the more. Let's get up to the field."

Brian pulled on his long sheepskin jacket and stood impatiently by the desk in the living room, waiting for Holly to get ready. He absently thumbed through yesterday's mail, which he had not had time to read because of the late evening work on the Aztec. He noticed on the back of one advertising circular addressed to Occupant, Box 318, Warren, Vermont, the green felt-tipped writing that Holly invariably used. The words were only, "$3800 for Rover, will call back or see you at airport."

"Hey, Holly. What's this note?" he called toward the bedroom. She came to the doorway, flouncing her long hair from beneath the collar of her down jacket.

"Oh, Brian. I forgot to tell you. This guy called from Plattsburgh last night and said that he wanted a Land Rover and that he had heard that you had one. He's offering thirty-eight hundred subject to inspection. He was supposed to call you this morning although he said that he had to come over to the valley anyway and might stop up at the airport this morning. That's all."

Total pranced around the door, alternately looking out at the yard and then looking back at his mistress.

"He's out of his mind," Loss said. "My Rover isn't worth more than twenty-nine hundred and probably not that much with the wear it's got on it." He quickly calculated that with thirty-eight hundred he could make a substantial down payment on the new diesel van that GM was marketing. Ideal for camping, hauling stuff for the house, and decent mileage.

He opened the door and the three of them walked to her car in the crispness of the early April morning. Suits me, he thought, as he glanced toward the Rover.

Ten minutes later, they arrived at Sugarbush Airport and drove directly to the plane to transfer his baggage. The manager of the airport, John Malcomb, wiped his hands of grease and walked toward them as they transferred luggage to the aircraft's baggage compartment.

"Birds fly south earlier in the year, Brian," John laughed.

"Wish I could take you along, John. How's the port engine running up now?" He referred to the slight rpm loss on the left engine they had noted during engine checks last night.

"I replaced the harness and it checks out fine. The insulation was just getting old on the ignition leads around number three and four cylinders." Malcomb stood back and looked at the gold and white Piper Aztec, absent-mindedly wiping his hands. He started for the office then stopped and turned to face Loss. "There's some guy from Plattsburgh who says he wants to buy your Rover. He's waiting in the operations office. I'll tell him that you'll be in when you're finished preflighting." Brian nodded his thanks and turned to help Holly with loading the luggage. Her blue nylon seabag lay among his luggage.

Holly, what's your bag doing here?" He smiled, puzzled.

"I'm going on a vacation too. I need a ride as far as Albany. Should I get out on the runway and stick out my thumb?" That damn smile again.

"Yes, no, I mean sure you can come down to Albany with me. How about Total?" he asked, turning toward the dog who was sniffing the aircraft's wheels.

"No, he gets to stay with John. It's all taken care of, Captain." She saluted. "Go ahead to the office. I'll get the stuff stowed."

He walked to the operations building through the remains of corn snow, avoiding the muddy areas where possible. He was pleased that she would be with him for the short flight, and with the arrangements for Total, he knew that she would be back. The day seemed to be sunnier, despite the low stratus that hung in scattered patches over the valley.

A tall thin man in his late fifties smiled at Brian as he pushed open the office door. He wore a long wool lumberman's jacket and his hair was speckled with gray.

"Good morning, Captain Loss. I am Mark Sommers of Sommers Electronics over in Plattsburgh." The man extended his thin hand.

Brian shook the hand with his own left, because of the flight bag he carried in his right. "Yes, good morning, Mr. Sommers. Listen, I'm sorry but I really am in a rush. I have to leave for Albany ten minutes ago."

Malcomb peered out from his office and waved a paper. "I'll have your bill in just a minute. I called Flight Service for you and they say three thousand scattered all the way to Albany. Winds 290 at 15 knots. Be with you in a sec."

"Yes, Captain Loss," Sommers injected. "I'm sorry that I couldn't meet you before now. But it's not very easy to get over here with the roads and my business. It's about your Land Rover."

Loss cringed at the title "Captain." It was like calling a guy who drives a 16-foot powerboat "Captain." He felt uneasy with the man.

"Look, Mr. Sommers. I would sell it for thirty-eight hundred but it's not worth that much. It's a '75 and it's the short-bed version. You're welcome to take a look at it. Here are the keys. You can drive it around locally. Just leave the keys back here with John," he said, pointing to the office where the sounds of an old electric calculator chattered.

"That sounds fine, Captain. No, I've seen it and it looks fine to me. It's just that I have always wanted a Land Rover and used ones are so hard to find. I only have a few days off because of the business. If there is anything wrong with yours, then I will probably go up to Montreal to see one advertised there. Can I reach you somehow this afternoon and give you my decision?"

Loss was puzzled because his Rover had not been used for two weeks due to a dead battery, which he had only replaced yesterday. Sommers must have seen it near the house, but it seemed unimportant.

Loss shook his head. "I'm afraid that I will be boring holes in the sky over the mid-Atlantic states by this afternoon, and I don't know where we'll be stopping. But I would like to know what you decide and if it would be possible for you to place, let's say 500 dollars on deposit with John here; that will hold it until I get back from my trip in two weeks."

Sommers zeroed in on his prime question. "Yes, Captain Loss, that will be fine. But how am I to reach you over the next two weeks?" Sommers stepped back and removed a notebook from beneath his jacket and took a ballpoint from his shirt pocket.

Loss thought briefly of the admonition that Welsh had given him five days ago. He had not wanted their destination known to anyone because this was to be a complete vacation without even local reporters requesting interviews. But thirty-eight hundred was a gift for the Rover. Brian took the notebook and wrote "Salt Whistle Cay, The Grenadines, St. Vincent, West Indies."

"Just cable that address care of me, Mr. Sommers. I'll be there tomorrow night. I'll send a reply to John as your authorization to buy it. But please don't mention this as my destination. My boss wants this to be a quiet holiday. He's bothered by reporters sometimes. All right?"

The man nodded his agreement and extended his hand. "It's a pleasure, Captain Loss."

The twin-engined turbosupercharged Aztec F fired on the left engine, missed and caught again, throwing blue exhaust as it picked up revs, and then settled down into the smooth, assured idle of a well-maintained engine. Sparrows pecking at the newly seeded grass beside the hangar took to startled flight. Patches of corn snow exposed to the prop blast scattered at buckshot velocity downwind of the aircraft. The right engine turned stubbornly at first, then caught and held evenly. Loss taxied from the parking spot on the ramp toward the taxiway. The pucks on the disc brakes squealed lightly as the aircraft turned downwind on the runway and taxied to the takeoff position.

The first traces of April buds hazed the maples near the end of the runway in a suggestion of green. Where there wasn't snow, there was new grass. And the birds were returning.

The Aztec pivoted on the end of the runway and turned through 180 degrees in the narrow space of the runup pad and aligned on the centerline. The flaps were lowered to their limits and returned to the trailing position. The props were cycled between the fine pitch of takeoff and the coarse pitch they would assume for efficient cruising speeds. There was a small frame of time when the aircraft sat, seeming reluctant to commit itself to the air. The wind was quiet; the shadows of clouds moved across the fields.

Then both engines rose in pitch and the aircraft, piniioned by the brakes, crouched down on its nose gear, waiting to leap. The turbos spooled up, and with brakes released, the Aztec rolled. From the cockpit, the movement of the centerline stripes progressed from individual movement of each stripe to a blur, to a solid line, and then with lift-off, the line fell away.

The landing gear hesitated and then tucked up into the aircraft belly, and the Aztec climbed through the thin stratus and into the raw spring sun of early-morning New England.

Loss settled the airspeed into best rate of climb, trimmed out the control pressures, and slowly eased back the rpm. The not-white, not-green valley fell away to the ragged ridge of the Green Mountains. And then the ridges melted into the snowscape and the horizon spanned the White Mountains to the east and the Adirondacks to the west; the blur of Montreal to the north and the haze of the Hudson Valley to the south.

He leveled the aircraft at 10,500 feet, slowly eased back the power and rpms, retrimmed and cut in the autopilot.

"Now I understand why you do this." She sat relaxed in the right seat, scanning out over the nose and alternately pressing her nose against the right seat window, looking down.

The pentagonal starform of Fort Ticonderoga lay in the neck of Lake Champlain to her right, 2 miles below. And to the immediate south, the valleys of Vermont and New York spilled out onto the plains of Schenectady.

Holly reached into the aft seat and retrieved a thermos of coffee. From her purse, she withdrew a plastic glass and filled it. "Why don't you ever talk about this? It's beautiful." She looked down suddenly, stretching over the instrument panel to watch a flight of Canadian geese vectoring north less than a thousand feet below them.

"It's not always like this," he replied. "Sometimes it's boring and sometimes it's just hard work. But you're right. It's times like this that make it worthwhile." He turned and smiled at her and raised the coffee cup in salute.

"Will you teach me then, Brian?" She hesitated. "I mean, in a little airplane. Not this. It's too big." She stumbled for words and smiled helplessly.

"Yes. OK. I will but you have to start in sailplanes. That's where it all started and probably that's where it will probably come back to. That's difficult to explain so we'll save it for when we get back. But it's a promise. For when we both return."

She digested his words in silence, sipping coffee and pouring him more from the flask.

"Where do you go from Albany?" he asked, keeping his voice level and disinterested. He pulled back the power slightly and retrimmed.

He thought that he had spoken too softly or that she hadn't heard but eventually she answered. "It's a place called Carriacou. It's not too developed, but it's nice."

To Brian, the name sounded almost familiar. Venezuela or maybe in Scotland. He thought and couldn't place it.

She slid her left hand up behind his neck and rubbed his muscles. "I have a friend who is staying near there and I want to see him."

Loss called Albany Approach Control and was fitted into the sequence of aircraft approaching from the north. The farmlands slipped beneath the wings, much greener and more cultivated than those to the north. They flashed over a river and both could see the smudged outlines of Albany.

"Brian, you're a stubborn bastard. Damned if you're going to ask me where Carriacou is." She looked straight ahead and leaned over the instrument panel, watching the countryside roll beneath the Aztec, her face set, cheek muscles hard.

He sighed. "Look, Holly. We don't have much time left. Things are going to get busy in about two minutes and when we land, I've got to let you off and get the aircraft ready for Welsh. But, yes, if it pleases you, I *am* interested in where this place is. You live your life the way you want to and I have to accept that as part of being with you." He paused and pulled back the power, adjusted the revs, and spoke to Albany Approach Control. Then, he turned briefly toward her and then looked forward against the glare of the sun.

"Look," he said. "I asked Welsh if I could take you along and he flatly said no. I wish I could have, but I can't. All I can say is that I wish you could be with me. OK, so where is this Carriacou?"

He eased down flaps and switched to tower frequency. She turned in her seat and watched him manipulate the controls, delicately feeding in power, adjusting pitch, willing the aircraft to follow some perfect path.

"Carriacou," she said, "is just as far as you want to make it," and faced forward to watch the runway grow larger in the windshield.

Chapter 5

Mark Sommers stood in the cloud-dappled sunshine, watching the Aztec evaporate into the distance. Without knowing why, he felt disturbed that he had been able to capture the information from Loss so easily. By itself it had no meaning, but he knew that correlated with other innocuous scraps of intelligence, some larger picture would emerge, and with this, a decision. Because the emphasis had been on Loss's employer and his destination, it must concern some attempt by the KGB to use Welsh or possibly to–. But Sommers turned his mind off to further speculation and set about the last stages of his involvement.

The plane had been gone for long minutes and he could only hear the wind moving through the barren branches. Sommers looked out over the airfield, noting the symmetrical rows of sailplanes parked in neat rows of tie-downs. Soaring. Riding on the wind. Quiet freedom. It would be something that he would want his children to experience. He himself felt very old and somehow fragile.

Malcomb came out of the office, banging the door, whistling something from a pop opera, hands thrust deep into a denim jacket. "It sounds like you have yourself a Rover, Mr. Summers." Malcomb passed him and walked over to the aviation gas pump, noted the gallonage, and printed a figure on the palm of his hand with a ballpoint pen.

"Sommers, not Summers. I know it sounds the same." Mark Sommers stamped absently at the granular snow beneath his boot.

"Sorry, Sommers," repeated Malcomb displaying a smile that showed even white teeth. He looked again at the gas pump and booted it gently. "We can hardly get fuel anymore. The Aztec has a ration allowance and some of these other owners do," he said, waving his hand out toward the fleet of small aircraft, "because they have some authorization for the use of an aircraft for business reasons. But the rest of these poor bastards get enough to fly about five hours per month. Great for business."

Sommers nodded sympathetically. "Tell me, Mr. Malcomb, you know Captain Loss. Is this Land Rover of his a good machine?"

Malcomb shrugged. "Yes. It's a good bus, Mr. Sommers. Brian has had it for the three years that I have known him, and he seems to take reasonable care of it.

It's not new, mind you, but I see him do most of the maintenance. Harry, our other mechanic, helps him on stuff like setting tappets. I think they ground the valves this winter, and I know it has a new battery." Malcomb pulled at his nose as if it irritated him. "Yeah. It's good as far as I know."

"Well, I think I'll go look at it now. Captain Loss told you of our arrangements, did he not?" Sommers said, gesturing vaguely toward the direction of the departed Aztec.

Malcomb shook Sommers' extended gloved hand.

"Yes, he said it was fine. Just drop back and tell me what you've decided and then wire him or telephone him, whatever. I know that he's anxious to buy some sort of RV. Drop back and let me know." And Malcomb walked off through the soggy grass and snow toward the hangar.

Sommers was finished inspecting the Land Rover in twenty minutes. He had no reason to buy the Rover once discovering Loss's destination, which would be, of course, Welsh's destination. But he meticulously went through the motions of an interested buyer, tracking up the snow around the vehicle, driving it out to the road and back several times, and playing with the four-wheel drive. He was careful to avoid going near the chalet. His final act was to slam the door in simulated disgust as if he had found some fatal flaw, and then he trudged back to his VW.

He dropped the keys by the airport office. Malcomb wasn't there, which Sommers was grateful for. He left a note with the secretary indicating that the transmission had a whine that probably indicated major power-train problems, left the keys, and departed for Plattsburgh. The secretary stared after him, blankly.

The trip to Plattsburgh took three hours. There were still tourists driving into Vermont for spring skiing, clogging the two-lane highway that ran down through Sugarbush Valley. Once on the Interstate, he made good time to the ferry landing on the Vermont side of the lake, taking care to keep under 50, the national speed limit, but fast enough to stay with most traffic. Two state police cars passed him slowly, and his heart beat with labored agony for the few minutes of each occurrence. The ferry was late, and he had to sit in his car on the Grand Island Ferry Terminal for twenty minutes, rasping at the delay.

Since receipt of the instructions, Sommers had lost 7 pounds from his already slight 160-pound frame. The instructions he had received had been written with invisible borate ink on the inside of the envelope. He was instructed to slowly accumulate as much information as possible on Senator Clifford Welsh; his speeches, personal and financial background with particular emphasis on political leanings, feelings toward disarmament, socialism, and détente. Of particular interest was a speech Welsh had given in Utica, New York, earlier in the year.

Sommers had gone about collecting the information carefully, building up Welsh's case file starting with Welsh's college records and progressing on through his terms as Senator. He was able to obtain all Welsh's voting record and speeches on the floor of the Senate through microfilms of the Congressional Record. Of financial records, Sommers could obtain nothing, with the exception of a credit rating. In all, the material was voluminous but lacked any real depth of information. Sommers bundled the material into a box and left it in the waste bin of an Italian Restaurant in Syracuse, New York, as instructed.

Two days after he had dropped the file on Welsh in Syracuse, he had heard a car driving along the gravel road that bordered his home's property to the west. It was late evening and only his youngest daughter was home, talking on the telephone in the upstairs hallway. He waited for the car to turn around or back up. The lane was a dead end. For minutes, he heard nothing and decided that it was only kids necking. He smiled, thinking of how it would be and turned the TV up again.

He heard a light knock about ten minutes later. Stella has forgotten her key, he thought with irritation, and then realized that the bowling league would not be over until after eleven. He turned on the front porch light and peered out between the curtains. A woman, no taller than 5 feet and wearing a pink cloth coat, stood stamping her feet on the concrete steps. He opened the door immediately.

She looked up thankfully at Sommers, her breath visible in the chill evening air. Smiling apologetically she said, "I'm very sorry to disturb you but my stupid car is stuck in your lane. I think I've flooded it or whatever it does when it won't start."

Sommers smiled hesitantly and looked out beyond her into the darkness. He could see nothing except the wan light of the porch lamp washing over the dark lawn of last autumn's leaves. He was reluctant to commit himself to anything. He hesitated and said with a forced smile, "I can call the tow truck, but I can't do much else. My wife has the car and my heart isn't too good. Will you come in, please?"

She smiled and shook her head. She gestured toward her car and said, "Oh, I was hoping that you could just start it for me. I'm just not used to the car. I'm so sorry, it's rude of me not to introduce myself. I'm Mrs. Stratton from Orlando, Florida. I'm just up here visiting old friends." She beckoned to him with her gloved hand.

Sommers looked at her stupidly, his mouth slightly agape. The silver bristles of his day-old beard shone plainly in the porch light. He stared at her uncomprehendingly.

She returned his stare, the muscles under her cheekbones flexing, and she handed him a calling card. It contained only the firm's name, Star Enterprises. There was no address. Sommers recognized the identification and followed her out into the night. His heart hammered as he followed her across the lawn. She walked swiftly over the partially frozen ground, not looking back, until she reached the fence bordering the western lane.

She stood in the darkness with him, unmoving, listening for several minutes. Satisfied, she turned to him and said, "Sommers, your information has been useless. You made no real attempt to obtain the information that we needed. You now have another chore. Are you listening?"

Sommers stood hugging himself, the sweat beneath his armpits soaking through his thin shirt. He shook uncontrollably.

She continued in a sharp, thin voice, "Here is an envelope containing a one-time cipher and the newest *Salyut* schedule. Use it once and burn it. We have to find out where Welsh is going this coming Friday. You will use the method outlined in your instructions to obtain this information. This is essential." She turned and left him standing in the night. Moments later, her car started and she drove up the lane toward the highway with her lights extinguished.

By 14:04 the car ferry docked. Sommers calculated that he would be back home in time to make the scheduled transmission at 17:53. He didn't feel very well, the strain of the past few weeks and the work today bearing heavily on his nerves. His face was flushed with perspiration and tingled. There was a vague pain in his side.

The cars were offloading now and he reached to switch on the electric engine. A knuckle rapped against the glass window. He turned and saw a gray uniform and a holstered revolver at eye level. A pain spread through his chest and his heart hammered erratically. He felt jagged slivers of glass probing at his heart.

The face came level with the window and waved canceled ferry passes. Sommers rolled down the window weakly and handed his ticket to the security guard. The guard tore off the ticket, returned a stub, and waved him on without any comment, aggravated with the delay and wanting only to finish passing the cars through. He absently thought that the gray-haired man in the VW looked very ill. Screw it, he muttered to himself, and walked back to the warmth of the shelter.

By 17:41 Eastern Daylight Time, Mark Sommers had tuned up the UHF transmitter in the basement of his Plattsburgh home. The location of Salt Whistle Cay had been translated into latitude and longitude with the aid of an Atlas and then enciphered into five-digit groups. Rechecking his chronometer and the schedule, he waited patiently, listening to the receiver.

At 17:44 *Salyut IV* crossed from darkness to sunlight over the Canadian Maritime Provinces, streaking west-southwest. Within the 8-ton satellite, sensors and cameras were already probing the North American defenses, translating images and infrared data through analog computers, storing the information on magnetic drums for later transmission.

At 17:47 incoming telemetry data were received from a fleet of twenty-eight Soviet block fishing vessels in the Atlantic, giving temperatures at many depth levels over the Continental Shelf, surface wind direction and velocity, locations and levels of temperature thermoclines beyond the 100-fathom line, and placement of US naval units along the Atlantic seaboard.

During all these simultaneous operations, the satellite's position was computed 408 times a second by inertial navigational computers that directed the frequency schedules for transmission, reception, and data correlation.

At 17:49 the satellite transmitted coded messages on 17.155 kilohertz directing Soviet Fleet Submarine Z-689 to return from its patrol two days earlier than schedule and to Soviet Attack Submarine RZ-122, congratulating the Navigation Officer on the birth of a 3.9 kilo son.

At 17:53:30, *Salyut IV* extended a parabolic antenna toward northern New York State and transmitted a seven-dot grouping on 144.217 megahertz.

Sommers heard the identifier and quickly transmitted his code groups three separate times within the span of forty seconds and then listened carefully. The transmission was repeated back at a slightly less rapid rate, frequency shifting slightly as the Doppler effect altered the satellite's transmission. Satisfied that the message had been received and recorded, Sommers continued transmitting in normal Morse code, tapping out, "This is a test . . . this is a test . . . this is a test . . . test out." He shut down the transmitter, disconnected it and replaced it on the top shelf above the workbench.

His heartbeat was shallow and rapid but the pain in his chest had subsided. Above him, he could hear his wife's footsteps in the kitchen, moving about, preparing dinner.

I will do no more for them, he thought, and slowly burned the schedules and enciphering sheets, spreading the ashes beneath the workbench. Turning off the desk lamp, he sat in the cellar's darkness for another half hour, listening to his weakened heart pulse against the cage of his chest cavity.

While Mark Sommers sat in his basement, *Salyut IV* passed across North America, dipped into the Pacific, and recurved north over Southeast Asia. By 18:38 a multichannel microwave link was established between AW-4 and the satellite. Eight minutes later, the processed and decoded message from Sommers was torn from the teleprinter in the Directorate of Special Situations, Western World.

"I read this to be 12 degrees 34.2 minutes North, 61 degrees 19.7 minutes West." The older man pushed his trifocals up over his forehead and looked down upon the young colonel of the Soviet Long Range Rocket Forces. Petrov was stretched out on the wine-red leather couch, his tie loosened and blue eyes fixed on the ceiling. He lifted one boot and used the heel to scratch absently along his other shin. Speaking in a low voice, the words hardly audible, he said, "Look it up. Central Data will have something on it. I would guess that it's located somewhere near the north coast of South America; probably in the lower Caribbean." He withdrew a cigarette from his shirt pocket and lit it, propping his head up on the armrest of the couch.

Vassell Rametka, Chief of Special Situations, lowered his eyeglasses again and reread the coordinates. He depressed a bar on the intercom and spoke softly to someone in Central Data Section whom he called "Iosif." Satisfied, Rametka released the bar and sat back in his chair and thoughtfully chewed on the end of his pen. "You consider the devices produced by Striganov and his group to be adequate, Colonel?"

Petrov nodded. "You have the reports. When it detonates, the radioactive signature will be undetectable from that of an American weapon. I have submitted a recommendation to the First Secretary that Striganov be awarded the Order of Lenin. The job was creditable."

Rametka gritted his teeth and slammed the pen to the desk. "Petrov, I want you to understand one thing. My directorate has conceived this operation. The KGB has been assigned to carry out the operational phases of this work, but I am directing it. I have personally asked for you to head up the teams based on the merit of your work in Ethiopia and Mozambique. You come well recommended, Colonel. I would like to work in harmony, but let us have no doubts about chain of command."

Petrov shrugged and tapped an ash from the cigarette. "Let us say it in this way, Doctor. You and your people here are in charge of planning and evaluation. I am in charge of operations. Once I am in the field, you will have only supportive function. I think we can work only on that basis." Petrov sat up on the couch, snuffing the cigarette out in an ashtray. "Let us not have to resort to solving this question by taking it to our superiors." He smiled thinly, watching Rametka's face.

Rametka was about to reply, looking for a face-saving gesture. The teleprinter bell chimed and started printing. Line after line of material fed out of the machine on a tongue of yellow pulp paper. Finished printing, the unit indexed through three more lines and fell silent. Both men rose to read the information. Petrov noted Rametka's breath was sour and his armpits smelled. There would be no future conflicts of power, he thought absently.

The file was sparse. It read:

```
12/580   CENFIL TO SIRSPCSIT AW-4 STOP   LOCATION

SALT WHISTLE CAY CARIBBEAN SEA WINDWARD ISLANDS

GROUP STOP   RESORT ISLAND APPROXIMATELY ONE

KILOMETER SQUARE VOLCANIC AND CORAL GEOLOGICAL
```

```
STOP  FORMERLY BRITISH COLONIAL TERRITORY NOW
ALLIGNED BARBADOS/TRINIDAD BLOCK COMMA PRO
WESTERN DASH NEUTRAL STOP  ISLAND USED SOLELY
AS LUXURY RESORT COMMA SEE FILE TAPE 2958889ARG
STOP  TOPOGRAPHICAL PROFILE AND SALYUT 4 SCANS
FOLLOW SOONEST BY FACSIMILE TRANSMISSION STOP
COMMUNICATIONS TELEPHONE AND MARINE RADIO
TELEPHONE STOP  TRANSPORTATION TO ISLAND ONLY
BY SEA WITH LIGHT AIRCRAFT LANDING STRIP ON
NEIGHBORING UNION ISLAND STOP  STAFF POPULATION
APPROXIMATELY FORTY STOP GUEST ACCOMODATIONS
FOR FIFTY STOP  ADDITIONAL DATA BEING FORWARDED
BY RESIDENZ COMMA BARBADOS COMMA ON REQUEST FOR
SPECIFIC INFORMATION STOP  SECURITY CLASSIFICATION
NONE CENTRAL TAPE 2203795ARG  STOP END MESSAGE
```

Petrov smiled. "A Caribbean resort island vacation for Senator Welsh. Perfect, I would think."

Vassell Rametka ran his hand over his balding head and reread the message. Pulling three folders from his safe, he seated himself at his desk and leafed through the separate binders. Finally, he pushed them aside. "Welsh is not ideal, Colonel. Of the three politicians under consideration, he would be my second choice. The most promising subject is still our Indiana Congressman. Welsh shows strong psychological profile identity. He might be very difficult to deal with."

Petrov glared at him from across the room. "We've been through that, Rametka. In order to contact and work with any of these three men, we must approach them during their vacation period. I think that it will take a minimum of five intensive days of work with any of them, plus drugs, to achieve reasonable control. The man in Indiana spends his holiday in a religious retreat. It would be an impossible situation. Can you see me as a priest?" Petrov paced across the room and back, rapping his knuckles against the wall as he turned. "No, Rametka. Welsh will do. The area is isolated and it will be simple for me to meet him. From there on in, it will be a question of subduing him with drugs and feeding him with sugarplum visions of power and wealth. There is no man alive who will not respond to this treatment. And Welsh, as we can see from his dossier, is hungry for power."

Rametka nodded. "True. The situation does seem favorable. But I caution you now that you must proceed slowly. If Welsh seems in the least hostile, it will be necessary for you to withdraw. He must feel that he is making his own decisions." Rametka reamed out the bowl of a clay pipe and loaded it with coarse tobacco. Lighting it, he leaned back and rested his head against the wall behind him. Both men said nothing for many minutes, thinking, blue smoke from the pipe rising in a stream to be suddenly fragmented as it was drawn into the air conditioning ducts. Finally, Rametka leaned forward and handed the Welsh dossier to Petrov. "Welsh it will be, Colonel Petrov. How do you intend to handle it?"

Anatoli Petrov smiled slowly, lips barely parted. He inserted the Welsh folder in his leather case, snapping the lock closed and spinning the combination. "Handle it? Quickly, I should think. Welsh is already en route to the resort. I will fly to Zurich tonight and then onward tomorrow. As usual, I will be using a 'wife'; probably the German woman whom I used in Amsterdam last fall. She is excellent with drugs. For the rest of it, I will use Heiss for documentation and camera work. We will probably dispose of him after the meeting with Welsh. There are great many details to be worked out. Incidentally, I want the psychological profile and background on Welsh's wife. Also his pilot, Loss."

Rametka nodded and spoke into the intercom. There was a short delay and then a muffled reply. "They will have the information in half an hour. Let's go up on the surface. I haven't been out of this place in five days. I've forgotten what the sky looks like."

Both men donned coats, Rametka pulling on the Bond Street tweed with the enameled pin of the Order of Lenin in its lapel. Petrov shrugged into the dark sage military coat and they left, walking along the carpeted corridors of Level Seven. Signing out through the security station, they rose by private elevator to Level Four. Petrov excused himself for a minute and entered the office of KGB Liaison, firmly shutting the door behind him, leaving Rametka in the corridor. Irritated, the Soviet planner waited.

In twenty minutes, Petrov reemerged and warmly took Rametka's elbow, guiding him down to the main bank of elevators. Petrov seemed animated now, relaxed. He spoke to Rametka about small things, the record of the Dynamo Soccer team. They rose to Level Two and passed through the final security station. Petrov called the man by his first name, commenting on his promotion to sergeant. Smiling, the guard snapped to attention as they left.

The two men passed through the sequence of blast doors, slowly climbing the shallow concrete ramp, finally seeing blue sky beyond the last door. Both of them surrendered the interior identification passes to the control desk at the entrance to AW-4, substituting green outside-area passes. They walked into sunlight.

The Urals rose on each side of the valley. There was still snow in the higher elevations. Rametka put on his fur-trimmed hat, the black mink contrasting with his pallid face. He guided Petrov along a wooden walkway to the edge of the ice rink. Three off-duty technicians were skating. One of them, a red-cheeked woman with Kazakhstanian features was very good, gracefully pivoting in mid-air and then landing on one skate, back arched, arms spread in icy flight.

"I have always wanted to do that, Anatoli," Rametka said, watching the skaters. "I have two children, both young. It will be good to retire and spend my time with them. It seems an insane thing, but I sit at my desk often, imagining the three of us skating together in Gorky Park, hands together, listening to the music. We have chocolate later and then go to the theater."

Petrov watched the face of the older man, the tributaries of wrinkles forming in the corners of his eyes, running to the rivers of his sagging cheeks. The skin was white and unhealthy. Only the eyes were strong. "I understand, Vassell. There must be a time in all our lives when we get tired of this. Perhaps in a few years we will have won. Then we will all rest. It's a tiring struggle." He stooped and picked up a handful of snow, compressing it tightly in his bare hand, squeezing the moisture from the white granules.

Rametka removed his hat and turned to face the sun, closing his eyes. "It feels good, doesn't it?" he said unnecessarily. "The device. How soon will you ship it?"

"I already have. It's being positioned in Vladivostok in Weapons Depot Number Three, awaiting *my* further orders." Petrov accentuated the word. He dropped the wasted ball of snow to the ground and kicked it with his boot.

Rametka nodded, accepting without protest the implication of command. "And after Welsh? I want final confirmation with our group of psychologists as to their analysis of the recordings between you and Welsh before we finally commit ourselves."

Petrov barely raised the corners of his mouth in a smile. "Yes, I have thought of that too. I will not have enough time to bring the material back here. I will probably fly from the resort to Mexico and then on to Cuba. I will meet you there with your team. If our timing is satisfactory, I will have time to return to the resort while Welsh is still there, should it be necessary." He patted Rametka carefully on the back as you would do with a fragile grandfather. "It will work out well, Vassell. Your retirement pension and Order of the Soviet Hero are well assured."

The two men looked south from the valley toward the plains of the Kirgiz Steppe where they would be planting wheat now. Petrov was smiling.

Chapter 6

There is some question as to the creation of the Blue Antilles. Geologists have assumed that the chain of islands, arranged like a handful of emeralds strewn on blue velvet, are merely the tips of extinct volcanos thrusting up from the sea bed.

But Carib Indian legend relates that God placed his hands side by side on the ocean floor and, thrusting down, formed ridges between his fingers. The eternal sea and timeless trade winds eroded these ridges, leaving gaps as wide as the land remaining.

The Blue Antilles range from Hispaniola and Cuba in the north of the Caribbean Sea to Trinidad in the south and are divided by size into the Greater and Lesser Antilles. Cuba, sweating in the sunlight, Puerto Rico, cowering beneath eternal clouds, and Hispaniola just wishing to be left alone, are the Greater Antilles.

The Lesser Antilles really start with the Virgins, leap the Anegada Passage to Saint Maarten, and arch south and east to Trinidad. The southern half of this chain is called The Windwards and the seven islands that grace it are named for saints and sinners, navigators and thieves, all long dead.

At the very bottom of this chain are the two islands of Grenada and St. Vincent and between them, an archipelago of tiny islands, thundering reefs, and still lagoons called the Grenadines. One such island, for a reason long forgotten, is named Salt Whistle Cay.

The Aztec eased over into level flight from its climb, leaving St. John's International, Antigua, 41 miles behind and 12,000 feet below. Loss adjusted manifold pressure, rpms and mixture, settling the aircraft down into cruise power. Number one VOR receiver was indicating solidly on Guadeloupe and number two was just coming to life on Lamentin in Martinique, 170 miles to the southeast.

Welsh sat beside him in the copilot's position, playing with the time and distance computer. He fidgeted with the ADF radio, trying to pick up a local station and finally snapped off the switch with impatience. Clifford Welsh was never at ease in an aircraft. Loss hated to fly with him, for his presence was one long succession of tapping instument dials, questions about fuel remaining, times of arrival, and imagined engine noises. And yet, in the media, Clifford Welsh was known as the Flying Senator. He knew the terms, had taken a few lessons, and affected the manner and dress of a pilot. The deep gray sunglasses, languorous movements, clipped sentences. Someone had forgotten to tell him that that stuff went out at the end of World War II with the fifty-mission crush. But the press gobbled it up.

"How long now?" Welsh asked, adjusting his sunglasses. He looked at the wine-dark sea below.

Loss retrimmed the aircraft slightly and punched numbers into the computer. "I make it to be about forty-eight minutes to Martinique and one hour forty-six to Union Island. I called Salt Whistle Cay from Antigua with our estimated time of arrival. They should be able to meet us there on time. We're running about five minutes ahead of schedule."

Welsh visibly relaxed. He looked out ahead toward the string of islands lying before them. "What do you think of this, Brian?" he said, waving his hand across the front of the canopy.

Loss leaned against the plexiglass and looked down at the sea before him. The ocean out to the east was the indigo of deep water, burnished to brass by the western sun and flecked with white by the wind. Before him spread a chain of islands, perpendicular to the steady flow of the tradewinds and sea, each island ringed with white surf and mounding up in humps and folds of olive green. From the summit of each mountainous island, a stream of cumulus clouds trailed downwind to the west. It was spectacular. "It's very nice, Senator," Loss said, wishing he was over this quiet sea alone, with only the sound of the engines and the rush of wind past the cockpit.

Welsh settled back in his seat, adjusting the sunglasses. "You can forget the 'Senator,' Brian. I appreciate it but we've got two weeks of unwinding. Just make it 'Cliff'." He adjusted the ribbed polo shirt beneath the camel's hair jacket. "I'd just as soon not have the hotel guests know that I'm a senator. We just want to relax."

Loss nodded, knowing that Welsh would smoothly let the senator-thing drop within the first two hours; probably first to the manager. "Fine, Cliff." Loss turned on the boost pumps and switched from the mains to the auxiliary tanks, watching the fuel pressure gauges for fluctuation.

Welsh had turned in his seat and was looking aft. His wife lay curled sideways across the aft seats, a blanket pulled over her body. Her mouth was slightly agape and she was asleep. Welsh adjusted her blanket and turned back. "Judith's really tuckered out," Welsh said. "Actually, so am I. The reelection thing is coming up in a few more months. Between that and the normal workload, I'll be ready for the zoo by November." He laughed, more of a grunt.

Loss eased in an increment more cabin heat and glanced sideways at his employer. "It looks like you've got the election sewn up. Will you have to do all that much campaigning?" In his peripheral vision, Brian saw Welsh make a small shrugging movement.

"It depends, I guess," Welsh said quietly.

Guadeloupe was passing below the left wing tip. They both watched the verdant, convoluted coastline unfold beneath them into shallow bays and bold peninsulas, spotted with small fishing villages. A large schooner was running free, with sheets eased, down the coast, white wake contrasting with the blue coastal waters.

"Picture-book stuff," Welsh remarked, pointing downward toward the city of Basse-Terre. Then, he pointed off to the left, toward the mountains on the southern part of the island.

"LaSoufrière. The volcano that erupted in seventy-six." The crater was plainly visible, the center filled with a small yellow lake. Mud-colored mist trailed off downwind from the crater.

Loss nodded and eased the aircraft into a shallow bank to the left, leveling on a more southeasterly heading. Before them now was a broad channel spotted with islands and beyond that, Dominica shrouded in cloud. And beyond that, Martinique and St. Lucia and St. Vincent. Loss was happy that Welsh was relatively relaxed and quiet. The islands were unbelievably beautiful; one long chain of poetry flowing south. He whistled softly between his teeth.

"You like flying, don't you, Brian?" Welsh said.

"It gets me there. The pay's good. No complaints," Loss said, irritated with Welsh. It was like asking a kid with a sweet tooth whether he liked candy.

Welsh nodded wisely, settling back into the seat. "It must be nice to have a profession where you don't have to deal with a bunch of idiots. Between the party bosses, political managers, the goddamn voters—it begins to get to you." Welsh was quiet for several minutes, thinking. "You know, Brian, I checked you out pretty carefully. That is, when you first applied for the job of flying me around."

Loss raised his eyebrows in surprise. "How so?"

"Well, beside the flying part of it, the licenses and flying hours, I had the FBI check your security clearance, political affiliations, Air Force records. That sort of thing. Everything checked out fine except one thing that was never explained. How is it that you resigned? You were a regular officer, not reserve. Why did you quit?"

The aircraft droned on, Loss sliding back in time. The little major. A real prick, that one. Loss realized that Welsh was still talking to him and he snapped back into the present.

"...and at first glance the crash you had in Viet Nam seemed to rule you out." Welsh laughed, embarrassed. "Of course, you realize, I didn't want someone flying me around who was pranging airplanes into the ground. But I read the accident report and realized that you were pretty well shot up." Welsh smoothed his hair back into place, lifting a few stray strands carefully over his ears. "But then the reports go on to say that, even though you were reinstated in flying status, they assigned you to staff work. Six months later, you resigned. What was the story?"

Loss told him briefly, omitting the details. It sounded almost trivial to him now.

The Aztec droned over the open sea. The mountains of Dominica were cast in shadows under the building afternoon cumulus. Loss finished the story. "And it was just a combination of the crash, the flying evaluation board, and then me finally mouthing off to a major who had connections in the Pentagon. Nothing would ever appear in my file, but, I'd be lucky to make Lieutenant Colonel in twenty-five years. That and the fact that the military services are dwindling in terms of quality and funding. Viet Nam was just the final straw. It was a dead-end career."

Welsh rubbed his finger over an imaginary blemish on the cowling, his eyes averted. "I see your point. Undoubtedly, you made the right decision. And philosophically there shouldn't have to be a military in the first place, should there?"

Loss made no answer. This wasn't a discussion he wanted to get into with Welsh.

"I mean what do you think would happen if there was no US military?" Welsh said, watching Loss's face carefully from the corner of his eye.

"You're talking about what would happen if the US was disarmed, but the Russians retained their present military?"

"Exactly."

"I think they'd run over us with a steamroller, as quickly as possible. We'd be flattened."

Welsh snorted. "That's a standard answer, Brian. But there's no valid reason to assume that they would take advantage of us. I think the opposite would happen. The Kremlin would probably sigh with relief and let their own military dwindle to forces adequate to cope with the Chinese.

"There's just two problems with that logic, Clifford. It assumes that the Russian military is willing to be dwindled, as you put it. The other one is that, economically, they don't want to have to compete with us."

Welsh leaned back and sighed, removing his glasses and rubbing the bridge of his nose. He placed them back on his face and scowled against the molten afternoon sun. "I don't know, Loss. We can't go on with this arms race forever. An accident, some trigger-happy bomber pilot, some psychotic ICBM commander and the whole thing goes up in smoke. Someone has to take the first initiative in disarmament and it should be us."

Loss leaned down and retrieved the newspaper from his flight bag and handed it to Welsh. "You're going to do the initiating? I saw this in the local paper."

Welsh read the article and handed it back. "Just feelers. My political manager, DeSilva, tried to retract it. Thinks I should stick to improving garbage collection schedules in The Big Apple." Welsh paused and tapped one of the fuel gauges, frowning. "If we could disarm, Brian, it would free up 200 billion a year for social programs. Think about the changes that could bring about."

Loss thought about New York and make-work programs and federally guaranteed life-styles. "That would be something, Mr. Senator," he said, looking at the far horizon. "That really would be something."

Welsh laughed, the nervous laugh of a man who has just learned that the pain in his throat isn't cancer. He sat in silence for many minutes and the conversation was at an end. Except that finally he said, "Well we'll see, Brian. I think it could work. The people want it."

Which people, Loss wondered.

Seventy minutes later, the Aztec squeaked down on the asphalt airstrip at Union Island and in ninety-five minutes, the Welsh party was on board the twin-diesel yacht sent to collect them. They pounded up through a light chop, a small island growing larger in the windshield.

Carl Heiss thoughtfully read the coded letter from Rotterdam for a third time, and then shreaded the paper into vertical strips and flushed them down the toilet in two separate flushes. One small strip remained in the bowl, and he disdainfully flushed the bowl for the third time.

He reentered the living room of his small flat and spread the gray lace curtains, looking out over the Straits of Dover at the white-capped sea. He sighed, thrusting his hands deeply in the pockets of his terrycloth bathrobe and then smiled. Some days bring unexpected pleasure, he mused.

Scratching absently at a pimple over his right cheek, he dialed a Surrey number.

A female answered. "Mulgraves Film Processing."

"Yes, love, this is Carl Heiss. Is Martin there?"

She answered in a slur of words and the receiver was mute except for a distant conversation. Heiss could hear the background noise of BBC-1 rock music. He waited, without impatience, picking at the pimple and rubbing the back of an ancient cat, which brushed ingratiatingly against his bare leg.

"Martin here," the receiver said, the "A" squashed and the "R" strung out. Heiss kicked the cat absently, its tail and genitals presenting an end view in retreat.

"Martin? Carl speaking." The breath at the other end sucked gently for air. Heiss continued. "Look, Martin, old bag. I've been called away on assignment, some damned travel thing. You know, a layout thing on Caribbean travel. Can you take care of my work while I'm gone?" Heiss paused and listened to the breathing. He thought that some day soon, Martin would have a heart attack.

The receiver made protesting noises although no coherent sentence emerged.

Heiss overrode the conversation. "Look, Martin, it can't be helped. This is a good assignment and I'm afraid that you'll just have to bear up. I'll be back in about three weeks." He hung up.

Carl Heiss walked to the full-length mirror inset on the wardrobe door and looked at the lean figure standing in a slouch before him. The blonde hair was straight and overly long, even for an Englishman, which he was not. Tufts curled forward over his ears, and he thoughtfully twisted at each in turn, curling them with his fingers. The long, narrow face was bland and without bone structure to diminish the monotony of shallow planes. He pursed his lips and parted them, revealing synthetically perfect teeth, straight and even like rows of dice. His pale blue eyes were pieces of stained glass.

The cat watched his master from the bedroom doorway sill, swishing his tail in agitated strokes.

Heiss opened his robe to reveal his body to the mirror. The face, which was ordinary, seemed at odds with the strong, graceful frame. A thin hairline scar traversed the right hip to the groin. Heiss was almost hairless. His legs were stark white in contrast to the rest of his tanned body and well roped with muscle.

Above in the upstairs apartment, he could hear the muffled laughter of canned TV audiences. You could almost pick out the words of the announcer.

With annoyance, Heiss pondered the cat, which now stood rubbing his face and whiskers against the divan leg. He had no time to arrange for its care, and he couldn't leave it to fend for itself in the alleys of Ramsgate. And inevitably, it would return to his doorstep.

He reached down with affection and grasped the cat by the scruff of the neck.

"I'm afraid that you will have to go, Peter," he said to the cat, brushing the moist pink tissue of the tom's nose with his lips. Peter responded by splaying his feet, frightened. Heiss adjusted his grip on the cat's fur to encompass the neck and squeezed abruptly. The cat's eyes widened to an impossible angle and it convulsed in spasms. Heiss made a snapping motion with his wrist, and the cat hung limp in his hand. He placed it in a paper sack, dropped it in the plastic garbage pail, and washed his hands.

Forty-three hours later, Carl Heiss finished the last of a Beefeater's and tonic and placed his forehead against the cool pane of the double-layered perspex window to watch the sea below. Through a scattered cloud deck more than

30,000 feet below, he saw areas of empty indigo sea and nothing more. The low-humidity, high-altitude flight made the aftertaste of the gin and tonic slightly metallic.

"Boring trips, these." The statement, without the inflection of a question, came from the passenger to his left. Since they had left Heathrow, England, the elderly man next to him had dozed, eaten only a small portion of the in-flight dinner, and consumed two copies of the *Economist*. His accent was public school.

"I suppose," Heiss replied, discouraging a conversation. He made an attempt at a smile and turned toward the window again, touching his forehead to the cool pane.

"Camera boffin, eh?" The voice of the pudgy man inquired, pointing down at the aluminum case between them on the middle seat. "Good hobby. Remember years ago my wife used to play with these things. Had quite a mess of lenses. You know, the usual thing. Cost a fortune. Dead now." The speaker waved his clutched *Economist* for emphasis. He was short, florid with a hawkish face. The thin gray hair was swept straight back covering a bald spot and continued over the back of his head to curl along the nape of his neck. His tie was Royal Thames Y.C. and slightly askew.

Heiss sighed inwardly, wanting to be alone with his thoughts, and he replied unenthusiastically, "Yes. I do enjoy cameras. I sometimes do photojournalism assignments. Nothing much. Just for my enjoyment. Tax thing, you understand."

A stewardess came down the central aisle toward them, giving passengers a cool, synthetic "We're nearly there now" smile. She picked up the plastic glasses with accustomed grace and continued aft toward the economy class section.

The pudgy man lit a Dunhill, sucking the smoke down and then hacking lightly. "Cigarette?" he inquired, thrusting the pack toward Heiss. "Damned habit. But I can't quit now. About the only thing I enjoy." Heiss lifted his hand in a negative gesture and sat back into the seat, irritated but his face an expressionless mask. The pudgy man leaned back in imitation.

Sunlight and shadows wheeled slowly across the cabin of the Boeing 747, picking up motes of dust, pinpointed in suspension. The engines, barely noticeable in their constant tone, dropped an octave.

The background tinkle of music stopped and a confident voice said, "Good afternoon, ladies and gentlemen. This is Captain Goodwin speaking. We are presently descending from 34,000 feet and expect to be in Barbados in twenty-three minutes. Surface temperature is 22 degrees Celsius under mostly sunny skies."

The smooth baritone continued, "Please fasten your seat belts and observe the *No Smoking* signs. We hope that you have enjoyed your flight with Euro-Caribbean Airways as much as we have enjoyed having you with us." The Musak resumed and the seat belt sign winked on.

"Good weather, eh?" the pudgy man intoned. Heiss nodded, uncaring whether the passenger to his right understood or saw his acknowledgment.

They touched down on runway 08 at Grantley Adams International Airport, Barbados, twenty-six minutes later.

Heiss was one of the first of the passengers to Immigration. He passed through without question, giving Barbados as only his overnight stop before traveling onward. The customs officer displayed no interest in his two-suiter but pondered the aluminum case. The dark face searched Heiss's, looking for telltale unease or too cool an expression. He found only flatness and impatience in Heiss's eyes.

"Open this case, please."

Heiss rammed his hand in his pants pocket, searching for the key, his face expressionless. The locks were opened and the lid lifted. The interior was lined with sponge rubber and fitted depressions. A Hasselblad camera with three lenses, a Minox, and a pocket tape recorder were nested in the recessions.

"These are expensive cameras, suh." The black customs official lowered his hand to a lens but watched Heiss's hands which held the case on either side. He saw no contraction of the muscles in the white tourist's hands.

"These are all personal possessions, Officer. I don't intend to sell them." Heiss paused, looking directly into the dark pupils of the customs officer's eyes. "And be careful with that lens. It cost 300 quid."

Their eyes met for a second. The dislike was mutual. The sergeant turned from him and beckoned the next in line. Heiss found his armpits wet beneath the cord jacket. He brushed aside a baggage porter and walked out into the incandescent sunlight of Barbados.

The pudgy Englishman turned from the second floor of Barbados Airport Security window and smiled at the black lieutenant of the Barbados Home Defense Force who sat behind the desk. The lieutenant adjusted his Sam Browne belt first and then eased back into the chair.

"What do you think?" queried the Englishman, stabbing his cigarette at the set of photographic prints. To no one, he muttered, "Damn bastard, filthy bugger," and paced the office puffing jerkily at the cigarette, finishing it and lighting another from the tip.

The black lieutenant calmly ignored his visitor and listed each item shown in the photograph, cross-indexing to a manual for the weight of each specific object. He applied the results to a pocket calculator. "Well, I make 9.22 kilos. That's according to the manual. And yet our Mister Heiss has a case that weighs 2.3 kilos more. Our telephoto shows only the Hasselblad, three lenses, and the recorder. The case is a common one. It is conceivable that he could have filters under some section of the foam rubber, but not over 100 grams worth. However, Mr. Campbell, it is not the policy of our government to, ah, insert ourselves in your Foreign Office affairs. We are anxious to cooperate if there is an infringement of our laws. Otherwise, it is your affair."

The Englishman thrust a packet of cigarettes at the black lieutenant. The lieutenant declined. "No, I sometimes think that I'm the only one left in the world foolish enough to smoke these filthy things," he commented, and stood before a portrait of the Queen, looking at the familiar face as if to draw some guidance from it. "No, lieutenant. It is strictly our affair. You're right, of course. I don't think Heiss is up to anything here. We shall find out who he contacts, if anyone. But Heiss showed onward reservations to Miami. We'll check his flight, you can be sure. But for your own knowledge, there goes," he pointed toward the draped window with his cigarette, "a Section V KGB German who is absolutely top drawer in surveillance, photography, and on two known occasions, political assassination."

The lieutenant looked again at the photographs, two taken from directly overhead the customs counter by a camera with a 600-mm lens. The others were full face and profile, again, taken by telephoto lens. The surface was still damp from processing. He looked up at Campbell, tapping the photos with polished fingernails.

"I suppose that you are something less of a menace to our security, Mr. Campbell?" The question could be taken as a statement. They looked at each other and Campbell shrugged.

The telephone rang once and the lieutenant answered. Campbell paced to the window again and looked out over the flat plains hatched by canebrakes and palm-lined highways. The horizon shimmered in the heat.

The lieutenant hung up and spoke hesitantly. "Heiss left our first cab, took another going in the opposite direction, and left that one on a corner in Bridgetown. We've lost him."

Campbell felt his eyes aching in the glare of sunlight, and the portrait of the Queen offered no inspiration.

Heiss pushed his way past a lottery-ticket seller on Church Street and went down the stone-paved alley. He glanced back fleetingly and could see no one following. The smells of cooking and urine smothered him. He looked up between buildings and saw the face of a black woman office worker raised toward the open sky. She didn't look down. He pressed into a brick-arched doorway and tried the handle of the door. It was locked and possibly barred. Deeper into the alley, Heiss could see an open garage door. Waiting for several minutes, he stood in the arched doorway, watching the mouth of the alley. No one entered. His watch read 4:23.

Finally, he slowly walked down the alley to the garage and glanced in. It was empty. There were the remains of a washing machine in one corner with the motor assembly exposed and wires splayed from a terminal box. It was rusting badly. The rest of the garage was barren. The rafters overhead were partially covered with plywood and a small stack of scrap lumber.

He looked out of the garage again. There was a small boy at the head of the alley, walking toward the garage, perhaps 300 feet away. Heiss quickly made a decision. He tossed the bags up onto the rafters and, scrambling on the washing machine, drew himself up in a swinging backhanded vault with the ease of a gymnast. He quickly walked across the rafters to the floored portion and drew his bags onto the platform. He had over forty seconds to spare before the boy scuffed by, kicking a stone.

It was unbelievably hot in the attic of the garage. The platform was partially occupied by three bald tires, thick with dust. The near corner of the door to the garage contained stacks of the *Barbados Advocate, Town and Country,* and journals on rock collecting.

Heiss opened his photographic case and extracted the Hasselblad and a telephoto lens. He disassembled both with a small screwdriver he carried in the case. The Hasselblad yielded the aluminum frame and cartridge clip of a Polish Laskoy 7-millimeter automatic. The telephoto lens offered two choices of slides and barrels. He selected the longer 9-centimeter barrel and fitted it to the frame. From a close-up lens, which he disassembled, he withdrew a baffled silencer. He assembled the weapon in less than ten seconds. Working the action, he chambered one cartridge and eased on the safety. He would wait now.

Heiss was agitated. In fourteen years now, he was reasonably sure that British Intelligence had no knowledge of his existence. On only two occasions in those fourteen years had he made contact with his control and the result was the simple act of waiting in the parking lot until his designated target had approached a car. Heiss had called to the person in each occasion, asking change for fifty pence and then had fired two hollowpoint bullets at close range with his silenced Laskoy automatic. Always the same. Always effective.

During his residence in England, he worked as a free-lance photojournalist for trade magazines and in particular for labor unions. A lot of the material on union leaders, their weaknesses and indiscretions, found its way to the diplomatic pouches of foreign embassies representing countries east of the Po River. But it was all very discreet.

No, he thought, it had to be pure chance or perhaps imagination or mistaken identity. He reasoned that had there been doubt of his identity or the contents of his camera case, he would have been stopped at customs at Adams International. From a matter of routine, he had switched cabs and only at the last moment had the Austin Princess behind him tried to execute a U-turn. He caught the faces of three men, one Asian and two blacks, in the Austin staring at him. One was pounding the back of the seat with his fist in frustration. He had lost them. But the doubt remained.

Heiss dozed most of the afternoon, lying in the stupefying heat, his clothes saturated with grime and sweat. At 6:42, a small truck or car entered the garage and moments later, the overhead door was drawn down and locked from the outside. Heiss listened to the footsteps receding up the alley.

He decided that it would not be safe to move around in the garage until 11:00 PM. The meeting with Control was not until 9:00 AM tomorrow. The wait would be a pain in the ass.

Heiss removed his shirt and suit coat and used them to wipe the dust and grime from the platform beneath him. He stifled sneezing repeatedly until finally he fashioned his undershirt into a crude mask against the dust. With this done, he discarded the remaining clothes he had on and lay back to rest and let the sweat on his body evaporate.

The evening had lowered the outside temperature, and the roof overhead was growing cool to the touch. Heiss lay there, feeling his body with strong fingers, relaxing and slowly regaining confidence. Turning aside, he opened the two-suiter and withdrew a flask of vodka, which he used to cleanse his body, using the undershirt as a washcloth. Cooler now, he lay back and waited until his body dried.

He heard a truck or auto drive slowly down the alley and he tensed, but it drove by without apparent decrease in speed and did not return. His watch read 7:55. Three hours to wait.

The one small windowpane in the peak of the garage, long ago broken, admitted only the dankness of the tropic night and distant street noises. Heiss sighed, and groped for the thin plastic tube that rested in the false telephoto lens. Carefully, he unscrewed the cap in the dark and tapped the tube gently into his cupped palm, using his lighter to determine the amount. He recapped the tube and replaced it in the lens and extinguished the lighter. Raising his palm to his nostrils, he inhaled sharply and felt the warm rush of cocaine. Lying back, he waited for the world to turn.

Chapter 7

Carl Heiss awoke, chilled and stiff. His watch read 4:18. Hunger gnawed at the edges of his stomach and he was reluctant to begin. But for 10,000 quid one could endure all kinds of things, he thought.

He crawled to the edge of the platform and looked down into the darkness. He could sense, rather than see, the vehicle parked below. Flicking his lighter, Heiss saw the outlines of a small blue van 1 meter directly beneath him. He dropped lightly down to the roof of the van and then vaulted to the floor. Listening now, he could hear no sound, even from the distant street. The front seats of the van were empty except for the sports section of the *Barbados Advocate* and an empty cigarette pack. With the weak interior light on, he found an assortment of tools, cannisters of freon, and an elaborate set of pressure gauges in the rear of the van. The owner was obviously in refrigeration repair. His eye caught the glint of a bottle, partially wrapped in an oil-stained towel, and he withdrew it to find the remains of a fifth of white rum. Smelling it carefully first, he took a swallow. The raw liquor blossomed in his throat and hit his stomach with the impact of raw acid. He gagged and spit out the remainder, but he was fully awake now. Laughing to himself, he returned to the rear of the van. He could imagine the headlines. *Master Spy Caught Nude in Barbados Garage...* then in smaller print... *Denies Spying Whilst Intoxicated.* Heiss felt good now, vital.

Leaving the dim interior light on, he retrieved his two-suiter and camera case from the loft and returned to the interior of the van. Using shaving cream and cologne to lubricate his skin, he shaved carefully, nicking his chin lightly. Then using cotton, he packed his lower jaw gum line, giving his bland face the appearance of fullness and age. From a plastic container, he removed tinted contact lenses and slipped them in changing the cold blue to hazel. The hair would have to wait.

He dressed in a fresh pair of hopsack trousers and a lightweight blue blazer, leaving the nylon shirt open at the neck. From the camera case, he removed the bottom padding of foam and peeled it open along an almost invisible seam. He withdrew a Dutch passport, identity cards, credit cards, and odd bills, which he exchanged for the contents of his wallet. On the most recent entry in the counterfeit passport was stamped an entry for Barbados. With careful practice, he entered a date of two weeks ago and the signature of the immigration officer, which he copied from his Carl Heiss passport.

He appraised his mirror's image with the passport photo of one Pieter Bolken. Except for his real blonde hair not matching the gray of the Bolken identity, he was ready to face any casual inspection. The image was one of a middle-aged Dutch businessman, not wealthy, not poor. For the time being, he would wear a faded tan cap to cover his hair. It didn't match the tone of his outfit, but it might be the exact thing a man, unaccustomed to a tropic sun, would wear to protect a balding head.

At first, Heiss was reluctant to leave the luggage behind in the loft, but he reasoned that carrying luggage would make him too identifiable. With reluctance, he returned the cases to the loft but retained the weapon, which he stuffed in his inside blazer pocket. It created no more bulge than a heavy wallet.

By now, it was almost six and the owner of the van would soon pick up the truck for his day's work. Heiss carefully examined the floor around him and the truck for any trace of his night's presence. Satisfied, he returned to the loft.

At 6:48, the owner opened the garage door, started the van, and left. And at 8:00 AM, Heiss, now Pieter Bolken, dropped gracefully to the floor of the garage and strode with complete assurance out into the deserted alley and headed for the central taxi stand on Bridge Street.

One hour and ten minutes later, Heiss slowly walked along a palm-shaded avenue, holding a large bag of groceries, for all appearances a white resident of Barbados on his way home after a morning's shopping. The luxurious apartment building across the street had only four units set back discreetly from the street. The upper unit displayed a Red Cross sticker in the left-hand window; the meeting was now confirmed. Heiss looked both ways down the residential lane and crossed over, then walked down the hibiscus-edged path and climbed the stairs to Apartment 2. He pressed the bell for seven seconds by his sweep second hand, waited three seconds, and repeated the seven-second ring.

The door opened inward almost immediately, held from behind. Heiss entered. He made no sudden movements but placed the groceries on a low, ceramic-topped table to his right. Carefully removing his jacket but without turning to view his host he said, "I am Carl Heiss."

The Laskoy was gently removed from behind his waistband where he had transferred it prior to obtaining the groceries. A woman's voice behind him said, "Yes, we have been expecting you. Please take a seat. I will serve you coffee. The bathroom is directly back at the end of the hallway to the right."

Heiss walked to the sofa and sat down and looked back at the woman. She was a medium-tall blonde in her early thirties, thin and with fine bone structure. Her long straight nose spoiled prettiness but added character and complemented the high cheekbones.

"You may call me Lousje. Pronounce it Loo-sha. I am an East German national," she added, unnecessarily.

Heiss sat for a few moments, absorbing the atmosphere of the room. It was furnished in cane, brightly upholstered in pink and yellow batik prints. The terrazzo floor was covered by a beautifully woven grass mat, perhaps 4 meters in diameter. The drapes, drawn against the heat of the morning, were of richly textured, coarse woven linen. The apartment was obviously expensive.

The woman returned with a small tray containing a cup and saucer of coffee, a creamer of warm milk, and a small silver dish of coarse brown sugar. She set it down before him, and he could smell the freshness of her hair and body. She indicated the sugar.

"Try it. It's the local variety. Quite better than Fidel sends us, I think." She smiled for the first time and Heiss found a form of sexual arousal in watching her deft fingers arrange the tray before him. The pressure of the last twenty hours had produced a high state of hormone activity, which was unrelieved. He felt tense, excited, wanting something. He touched her wrist, watching for her reaction. She withdrew from him abruptly without comment and returned to the kitchen. Heiss smiled, wanting her positively now. The bitchy ones were always the best.

"Remain seated. I am your control. Call me Robert Klist. Tell me in detail about your trip from England."

Heiss looked up at the lean, sensitive looking man who stood in the hallway. Heiss moved to rise and the young man dismissed the effort with a curt flick of his hand, and said, "We need no formalities. We have relatively little time to discuss the complete operation. Lousje and I must leave by cab for the airport in three hours. Go ahead with your report." Petrov-now-Klist seated himself with easy grace on a wicker lounge chair and leaned back to stare at the ceiling.

Heiss started, unsurely, picking up the threads of the assignment from the first in Ramsgate to the landing in Barbados. He described the pudgy Englishman and their minor conversation. Klist had listened without comment but now he held up his hand. He called to Lousje, "Describe the MI-5 man that the Residenz briefed you on." She came from the kitchen, drying a wine glass, a small apron tucked around her dress.

"Short, long gray hair curling in the back, alcoholic's face, beak nose, gray eyes, about 85 kilos, English public-school accent, smokes excessively. No distinguishing marks on face or hands." Klist dismissed her with a nod. "That is the one, correct?"

Heiss nodded and continued to relate the immigration and customs inspection, the change in cabs, and the Austin Princess that tried to follow him as he changed cabs.

Klist interrupted him to ask if Heiss touched anything that would leave a fingerprint.

"No, I touched nothing unless I rotated my fingers to smear the print, just as always."

Klist sat up in the lounge chair and patted his shirt pockets for a cigarette. He found one and lit it. Heiss thought that Klist had been picked well for the role. His features were nordic. The English was almost accentless with just a touch of German or Dutch. The mannerisms were that of a man who commands.

"The man who sat next to you on the flight is a second-rate MI-5. They probably have a file on you because of the labor union connections you have, Heiss. I would not be too worried about this. I think that had you been important to them, they would have searched your luggage thoroughly. Bringing in the weapon was sheer stupidity. You were not instructed to do so. The photographic equipment was far more important. Now, tell me the rest."

He continued, telling Klist of the garage, the switch in identity and passport, and the baggage that still remained in the garage.

Klist got quickly to his feet and left the room without explanation. He returned in less than five minutes.

"Heiss, I have a very strong desire to send you back. Every move you have made has been amateurish. I have called the Residenz through an outside number. A telephone company van will pick you up here at 8:00 PM and you will retrieve the bags. The lock should offer no difficulty. You will depart tomorrow afternoon for Guadeloupe, stay overnight there in the La Belle Creole Hotel, and fly by charter flight to Union Island the following afternoon. Reservations will be made in your present passport identity. Take care of your hair to see that it matches your passport. The Residenz can offer all the necessary materials should you require anything. I will dispose of the weapon. You won't need it. We'll eat now."

The three of them ate a late breakfast in strained silence. On two different occasions, Heiss started to ask questions relative to the assignment and was left unanswered. He was starting to feel both hatred for Klist and a sadistic lust for Lousje. Watching the open throat of her shirt, Heiss made repeated attempts to catch a glimpse of her breasts. She turned at last to face him directly, catching his glance toward her opened shirt. Without changing expression or raising her voice, she simply said, "Heiss, you are a pig." She excused herself and cleared the dishes, returning with a flask of coffee.

"Carl," the Russian said, pushing back his chair and crossing his legs, "I am hardly pleased with anything you have thus far done. On the surface, your dossier seems perfect for the assignment. I think that you will understand the importance of the assignment when I tell you that I am directly responsible to the First Secretary for the proper execution of this job. Yours will be a small but significant part. You should have no difficulty in doing it well. The choice will be very simple. A very fat carrot or a very dirty stick. In more direct terms, if you do your part well and as I direct, you will have 10,000 pounds sterling deposited to your usual account in Luxembourg. If you fail in any part—," Klist left the sentence unfinished.

Klist continued. "I want you to take notes, memorize them, and, of course, destroy them. I will have very little chance to talk to you after today. Have a beer or whiskey now if you wish, but just one. What you drink after we leave is left to your discretion."

For the next hour, Klist briefed both Lousje and Heiss on the assignment. They discussed a map of the island, the number of staff, both local and foreign, communications, and finally the part Heiss would play.

"You are to simply play one role, Heiss," Klist said, walking slowly back and forth across the lounge area. "You will play yourself, a professional photojournalist. You are staying at Salt Whistle Cay mostly for relaxation but with the concept of producing a few articles for the British trade press. You will meet us," Klist indicated himself and the woman, "just through normal social contact. Remember that this is a very expensive and select resort. Lousje and I are there as man and wife. I will simply be known as a European industrialist. Here is a prepared text of my background, which you are to memorize. Do not give it freely or all at one time. Only if the opportunity presents itself. I merely want you to reinforce my image as a successful industrialist.

"My purpose in being there is to meet and talk to an American by the name of Clifford Welsh. He may be a key element in the future of certain special situations that have been devised. I hope to talk to him a great deal, and I want each and every conversation carefully recorded. I want every syllable, every nuance, every inflection. I also want excellent quality photos of him and his wife, and of Welsh and me together. If it is possible, I will want infrared photos of Welsh with his wife having sex. It may also be that Lousje and Welsh may be photographed together. And when I feel that we have enough material, you will be the delivery boy. We have made extensive arrangements to get this material back to—," he hesitated, feeling for a word, "to where it can be properly analyzed."

Heiss finished writing and ran over his notes. Klist left the room and returned, a glass of iced coffee in his hand. He seated himself in the wicker lounge. He leaned back, eyes closed, his face composed in rest.

Heiss went over the details carefully, making notations in the margin. He transcribed these into a list. Klist appeared to be asleep, his eyes closed and his respiration slow and even.

Heiss was about to speak, but Klist interrupted. "You have three questions, I believe. First, I have the miniaturized recorders, three of them. They are the standard RGK-21 type. They each have a capacity of over 4 hours. Second, your cottage will be near the Welsh cottage. It is a remote part of the island, and you should have no difficulty with placement or retrieval of the units.

"Thirdly, the Residenz will supply any additional equipment or film that you may need. You will have complete equipment to do your work properly. Lousje will see you from time to time on the island to get your reports. Is there anything else?"

Looking down at his list, he saw that Klist had answered all but one question. Heiss rapped the pen against his list for emphasis, and asked, "Who is the Residenz?"

Klist yawned and pointed vaguely down the corridor to the bedrooms. "The Polish consulate. His driver is waiting in the back bedroom. He will give you further briefings on your equipment and travel. You will not move until 8:00 PM." Heiss knew that he was dismissed.

He stood in the earliest dawn, when the flat black of the sea is crazed by the first streaks of light. Then, the sun came up as a distended bubble, erupting from beneath the eastern sea's horizon. In a few short moments the illusion was gone; men had started their clocks for the day.

Clifford Welsh watched the sun with the intensity of a man who has forgotten what the sun looks like, just as he had done for the last three mornings. The particular quality of early morning light tinted the small world of the island in cotton-candy pinks. He breathed a deep sigh of contentment and sipped the pungent coffee.

He wondered whether he should wake Judith and looked automatically at his wrist for the watch that still rested in the drawer of his dressing table. The white left by the band had disappeared into the tan of his skin. He looked at his arms and body, pleased that his skin was browning.

The Welshes' cottage was poised on the edge of a high bluff, overlooking the eastern beach of the small island. Century plants, reputed to bloom only once in a hundred years, dotted the area in front of the veranda. The bluff fell away to a sugar-sand beach 200 feet below. Beyond that, the sea was contained by reefs that encircled the eastern approaches to the island and beyond that stretched the Atlantic.

Welsh looked down the beach to the south and saw a solitary man running the hard, surf-packed sand. The man neither avoided the waves nor the softer berm, but ran in a straight line, his legs lifting high, directly toward some imaginary goal. One moment, Welsh could see the showers of soft sand spraying from beneath his feet and the next, splashes his legs made in the foaming surf. The man neither asked for nor accepted favor from his environment. Welsh speculated that the man would live his life like that, directly, avoiding no obstacle. Perhaps a difficult man to deal with.

Her arms enclosed him from behind. He turned to his wife and they watched the solitary man driving down the beach until he was lost from sight. The gulls and frigate birds were climbing in the wind that swelled upwards and over the bluffs. Soaring on the rising current of wind, one frigate hung stationary before them, his eyes fixated on the sea below, motionless in flight.

"It's really a marvelous place." She hugged him enthusiastically.

He brushed her hair with his hand. "I thought you might like it." He sipped at the coffee and offered her the remains. "I'm sorry that it's cold. But there's more in the thermos. They make up a batch for me every night."

She smiled and accepted the cup, drinking the remainder. Setting the cup down, she sat on the stone wall that edged the veranda, overlooking the sea. Her white terrycloth robe fluttered in the wind like something alive. But she remained motionless, a statue cast in bronze, forever looking out over a copper sea. They remained on the terrace for many minutes, not speaking, watching the sun grow.

Far out beyond the reef, a native sloop beat its way up to windward, only the sail visible. Up to the east, a pinnacle of rock stood out from the blank horizon, its top white with bird guano. Sail Rock Welsh had heard it called. And he understood how a man aloft in a sailing vessel could mistake it for a man-of-war, hull down on the horizon.

Judith Welsh unfolded her legs and stood up. She turned to her husband, brushing her long hair from around her eyes. She walked into his arms, drawing the knot that held her robe. He bent down to kiss her, noting that her face was warm with the heat of the sun.

Much later, they sat together on the terrace, eating breakfast. Welsh had finished off two halves of papaya, a rasher of bacon and was still eating a two-egg omelet. While he finished, she sat there watching him, amused.

"Not your usual boiled egg and tea," she laughed.

He nodded several times, his mouth full. "Getting old," he said and forked in another bite of omelet. "Need the protein."

She stretched and leaned back, sun hot on her face. "Never know it, Mr. Welsh. Never know it. You get a B for technique and an A for effort." She punctuated it with a laugh.

"You sound like my secretary," he said straight-faced, and she kicked him hard in the shin. "Uncooth sod," she said, and the frigate birds squawked at his shout of surprise and dove toward the lagoon.

He finally finished and wiped his mouth, smiling. "I've put on 2 pounds already. Got to stop eating or get out and do some exercise."

"Swim?" She poured both of them another cup of coffee.

"We could go snorkeling if you'd like." He pointed to a section of the reef to the southeast near a small rock just awash in the seas. "That's where the manager's wife says to go. Take a dinghy and anchor it over the coral. Work from there into the current."

She thought for a moment. "Is it difficult? And what about big fish and things that go bump in the night?" Taking a strand of hair, she drew it across her upper lip.

He took one step and stood behind her chair, massaging her neck, finally kissing the golden down of her neck. "Only *we* go bump in the night," he whispered, and as he said it, he felt young and foolish and alive. Like it had been when they both were 15 years younger. He straightened, trying to be serious. "No, Mrs. W. It's a piece of cake. Easier than swimming. The mask over your face is full of air and that gives you buoyancy. You just breathe in slowly and snort out. It clears the tube of water. And kick your flippers slowly to keep moving." He stepped into the cottage and rummaged for the hotel literature.

"All explained here in fine print," he said, laying the folder down before her. He stood back, legs spread and hands deeply thrust into his bathrobe. She thought he looked younger. Much.

"You like it here, don't you?" she said, looking up at him, shading her eyes. "How's the sunburn?"

He rubbed the tops of his shoulders and swore. "God, that was stupid lying in the sun yesterday. But I'll use some blocking cream today. If it doesn't peel, I'll be beautiful. The darling of the working class."

He had tainted their private amusement, and they thought in silence for some minutes and then she reached up to hold his arm. "It's a long way from New York, isn't it, Cliff? You know, I listened to some of your conversation with Brian when we were coming down—I mean about disarmament. You sounded less sure of it. Have you changed your mind?"

He rubbed his unshaven face, enjoying the day, not wanting to be dragged back into the reality of his political life. "Changed my mind? No, not really. DeSilva's dead against it. But I think mainly because it means that he loses the security of running a two-time winner into a third term. He's pushing me to run for Senator again and then for the Governor's slot in four years. Like he wants to keep me locked into New York. But he did say that he'd run some polls on voter reaction to unilateral disarmament. He should have it finished by the time we get back."

She sighed, leaning back in her chair and fluffing her hair from around the collar of her bathrobe. "But you're still having second thoughts, aren't you? And Loss seemed to be against it, didn't he?"

Welsh snorted derisively. "Loss is an arch conservative. Born and bred in an era when the Russian tanks were just waiting to roll over Berlin. Tunnel vision. Can't reframe his thinking. What he and everyone else like him don't understand is that we *have* to rethink our military commitments, both in terms of what our economy can support and what the Russians are going to do if we don't back off on this damned rearmament thing."

He paused, looking out over the sea, aggravated. "Judy, you know that I'm on the President's Intelligence Watchdog Committee. What goes on in there can be hair-raising. But basically it boils down to what most intelligent people already know. That we're behind the Russians in just about every category. The B-52 bomber force is just about junk and the cruise missile program won't be up to full strength for six more years; longer if Congress can have its say. The

Trident sub program is just starting to replace the old Polaris class and some of the Minutemen ICBMs are over 12 years old. People keep talking about us as a first-class power. Goddamnit, we're not! Every freeborn son of a bitch in this country thinks that it's our collective God-given right to be Number One in the world. If the Administration goes along with this rearmament thing, it's going to shove up the inflation rate even higher and ruin the economy. And more important, it's going to destroy every program that we have now or in the future for rebuilding the cities and for all the social programs that we need."

She got to her feet and held his arm. "Calm down, Clifford," she said, smiling. "I've read your platform. You can convince the voters. It's just going to take time."

"And lots of money," he added. "But more important than that, Judy, it's going to take something special to get me nationally known."

She lead him toward the bathroom by the hand. "Maybe you could help me take a shower and explain your position a bit better. Any position will do," she said laughingly. "Come on, big shot."

He followed her, swatting at her rump with his free hand. "You're on, he said."

Chapter 8

Brian Loss pulled the light coverlette over his head and pushed deeper into the pillows. He lay like this for some minutes, slowly coming awake, picking up sounds of the new day. A diesel engine barked into life and settled down to a steady throb, followed by a second diesel, more hesitant to start than its mate.

Loss looked at his watch. Ten straight up. Pushing back the covers, he sat up, yawned, and scratched his scalp with his nails. His mouth tasted of stale cognac and too many cigarettes. Ambling over to the balcony, he looked out over the anchorage. Two more sailing yachts were in, one just dropping its mainsail and shooting up into the wind, gradually losing steerage way and letting go the anchor with a flash of white water.

The sport fisherman *Striker* lay stern-to at the dock, warming up for the run over to Union Island; Hendrick, the skipper, was on the foredeck, washing down its aluminum surface.

Gulls wheeled in the anchorage. The day was brochure-perfect. Small cumulus, already formed, were sailing in formation down to the west. The wind was probably east-southeast and from the few white-flecked waves in the channel, the wind would be about 12 knots. God had cranked this day out of the machine, letter perfect. What was it that the manager had used to describe the endless, perfect summer?—"another shitty day in paradise."

He missed Holly and imagined her sitting on the end of the bed, brushing her hair, unaware of the beauty of her nakedness. He thought of how they could pass the days together: swimming out beyond the reef, sailing the small sloop out to the smaller islands to the north, and picnicking on cheese and wine and love.

So much for that, he thought, depressed and filled with a doggy inertia. Pushing his feet into leather sandals, he showered and shaved, beginning to feel good in spite of himself. There were always beautiful women around such a hotel, and the stunning girls who came ashore from the charter yachts looked friendly enough. God, he thought, in just the last evening there had been a Rhodesian, an Australian, and two English girls, all from the same yacht crew. The skipper never showed up—probably resting. He laughed now at the thought of a man of thirty, burned out by birds in paradise.

Humming now, he put on white cotton slacks, a striped crew neck shirt, and sunglasses. Breakfast sounded like getting stuffed with food that would be barely digested in time for lunch. Tennis maybe in the cool of evening. And then he decided that he would ride over to Union on the launch, just to check the tie-downs of the Aztec, and see a bit of the island while the crew of *Striker* picked up supplies and met the next contingent of guests.

He started down the shallow lawn toward the dock. Two departing guests were being helped aboard and the twin diesel was making ready to cast off. Loss gave a piercing whistle, waved, and ran the length of the dock as the crew kept one remaining docking line on. He leaped aboard, out of breath, and they cast off, and with engines in low revs, threaded out through the anchorage.

The departing guests, an older couple, had settled down in deck chairs in the aft cockpit well. They looked up and gave him a polite smile. They were both deeply tanned and in their late fifties. He exchanged greetings with them and went forward to the bridge deck where Hendrick was at the controls.

"Morning, Hendrick," Loss said, settling down into the upholstered chair on the port steering station.

"Good morning, sir." The youth flashed back a smile, teeth white against the dark skin, hair in unruly tight curls beneath the skipper's cap. "What brings you out this morning? The last I saw you were still playing backgammon. You win?"

"No, dammit. You know bloody well I got squashed by the manager as well. But you realize that backgammon is a game where you can lose a string and win a string with equally good players. It's how you use the doubling cube. So tonight, my friend, we are going to play for green bills and not drinks."

Hendrick shook his head, his eyes half closed, and silently laughed. "You don't learn easily. OK, Mr. Loss, we do it your way." He laughed again and slowly eased in more throttle as they came abeam of the south end of Salt Whistle Cay and skirted through a break in the reef. The *Striker* slowly came up in the bow and settled onto the plane, rolling slightly as they ran across the channel to Union Island, which lay 4 miles to the northwest.

Loss went aft a few feet to the tuna tower and climbed to the first level, 12 feet above the deck. There the smell of diesel fumes had vanished in the fresh trades. The roll was more accentuated, but he felt free up here and alive. Union was now dead on the bow, about 3 miles distant, rising up out of the sea, looking like a small edition of Morea: volcanic peaks and upland forests. To the north lay numerous small islands with the outline of the main island, St. Vincent, barely distinguishable in the haze. And to the south was a larger island, only 4 or 5 miles distant, with the outline of Grenada much further in the distance. Every island he could see within 5 miles was ringed by a reef to windward and marked by long lines of breaking seas advancing to crash against the coral, leaving rainbowed mist along the summit of each shattered crest. Christ, he thought, you could understand why these people lived out their lives in contentment; bartering, boatbuilding, fishing, and living a completely fundamental life.

He climbed back down the tower and settled in the seat once more, offering a cigarette to Hendrick and lighting one for himself.

"It's a beautiful part of the world, Hendrick. I've got to get a chart of the area. Better yet, I'd like to sail through it."

"We got some charts of the area, Mr. Loss. Admiralty charts, but plenty better than the US charts. All of them are screwed up. Think the last survey through here was 1855, HMS *Scorpion.*" Loss looked incredulous.

"No joke, man," Hendrick continued. "But it doesn't change that much."

The *Striker* slowed as it passed through the reef surrounding Clifton Harbor on Union Island, and the deck boys started to lay out fenders along the port side and prepare docking lines.

"How long will you be over here, Hendrick?" Loss asked, trying to estimate the time it would take to walk to the small airstrip and back.

Hendrick shook his head. "No sweat, Mr. Loss. We pick up vegetables, drop mail, and some other things. These guests are staying one night here at Union and going out on the LIAT flight in the morning for St. Vincent. But we have to wait for some guest coming in by charter flight from Guadeloupe. I guess all the space was booked up on LIAT. You ought to bring that plane of yours down here for charter. Good money in it." He laughed again. "Then you can play me in backgammon."

"Get stuffed, Hendrick," Loss said, smiling. "Just bring some money with you tonight."

After they docked, Brian went ashore, passing the children and older men lining the dock. A small black boy approached Brian and held up a small snapper, offering it for "a shilling" although English currency had disappeared from the islands over thirty years ago, replaced now by Eastern Caribbean Currency. The boy followed him, not nagging but curious, singing to himself and running ahead sometimes, only to sit in the shade while Brian caught up.

By eleven, he had checked the tie-downs, aired out the cockpit, and hired the boy to wash the undercarriage of the Aztec with soap and water. Loss cleaned the leather interior with a chamois and emptied the ash trays. After the boy was finished, he ran up the engines for a period of five minutes. Satisfied, he locked the aircraft and wandered over to the small restaurant, situated on a knoll overlooking the airfield. He had an excellent lunch of quiche Lorraine and a light Chablis, musing at the great diversity of foods which the Islanders had integrated into their culture. The West Indies had seen the French, the English, the Spanish, the Dutch flags. Added to that, the influence of North and South America and the basic underlying culture of Africa produced both remarkable language and food.

Loss had a flan for dessert and ordered another carafe of wine. It's not so different from Vermont, he thought, sipping the wine. The people down here and those in Vermont were both relatively removed from government. When you wanted to launch a boat or rebuild your fences, you asked a neighbor, not the bureaucracy, for help. Isolation breeds independence. Loss's Law Number One.

He thought of Welsh's plan to help the cities. The solution for any problem would always be the same: more money, more officialdom. But in the end, money rarely solves human problems. The cities would have to partially die and then regenerate themselves. Their problem, not mine, he mused.

He picked up the faint drone of aircraft engines, aware of the sound like any pilot, long before those that bind their lives to the earth. The blue and white Cessna 310G came down the valley between the mountains doing better than 180 knots. It pulled up into a sloppy chandelle, dropping gear and partial flap. Loss grimaced as the twin-engined aircraft turned on short final, pitching up as it lowered full flap. It touched down, well over one-third down the runway, slamming the gear onto the asphalt. The pilot stood on the brakes and the aircraft hunched forward over smoking tires. The Cessna stopped 5 feet short of the seawall, swung through 180 degrees and taxied clear of the runway.

"Our new guest might need a rum punch." Loss turned to find Hendrick standing against a wooden roofing support, relaxed and smiling.

"I believe that the aircraft is French," Loss said, punching his thumb over his shoulder toward the aircraft. Hendrick nodded.

Loss got up, leaving a few bills for the waitress. "I have been told that the French consider sailing, flying, and sex a big hairy adventure. Personally, I would yank that idiot's ticket if I were in the French government, but then again, he would probably kill himself before the paperwork got through." He wiped his lips with the napkin and tossed it onto the table. "Let's go down and meet your new guest."

They walked down the flagstone steps and across the tarmac to the aircraft. The pilot was heaving the luggage out of the cargo compartment, chatting with the black customs officer who had met the plane. The lone passenger turned to meet Loss. He was in his early forties and graying around the temples. His face was bland and noncommittal, but his eyes were expressionless.

He extended his hand, with only a trace of a smile. "I am Pieter Bolken."

The three of them had dinner on the veranda, beyond the dining room of the pavillion. The wind had dropped and the stars were out. They spoke little during the meal, requiring nothing more than gestures. The dinner was elegantly simple: green turtle soup followed by tanya cakes, glazed carrots, and fresh dolphin.

There was no flamboyance, flaming sauces, or obsequiousness. Just quiet, discreet service. They finished the dinner with cognac and Martinique coffee.

"I wonder why there are so few places like this in the world," Judith Welsh said. She leaned back in the canvas officer's chair, more handsome than Loss had ever remembered her. The three-day tan on her face and arms was a deep cocoa and she wore no other makeup.

"Do we have a moon tonight, Brian?" Welsh asked, swishing his cognac around in the snifter.

Loss nodded. "Later on. It's a gibbous moon. Nearly full." He paused and smiled. "That was an excellent meal. Many thanks."

Clifford Welsh showed his excellent teeth in a quick flash. "It's our pleasure, Brian. We're enjoying ourselves." Loss wondered whether Welsh's cordiality was an invitation to leave. Welsh had mentioned that they were meeting another couple for after-dinner drinks.

Neither of the Welshes offered any more conversation and Loss felt awkward. He raised his glass to both of them and finished the cognac. "A wonderful evening. Again, thanks," and he rose from the table. "I'll have to leave you both to hold up the stars. I've got a tennis date at six in the AM," he lied.

"Good night then, Brian," Welsh said, making no effort to rise, but toasting Loss with his near-empty snifter.

Brian left them, sitting in the dark shadows, holding hands beneath the table, touching each other like young people in love, or whatever it was that young people felt. He passed through the bar, pausing to watch Richards, the manager, and Hendrick working out the end phase of a backgammon match. The man named Bolken sat on a barstool alone, watching, saying nothing. They exchanged glances without greeting.

He stopped briefly to say good evening to a Canadian couple who lived in the cottage fifty yards down the leeward beach. They were from the Maritime Provinces and retained the languid ease of colonial English inflection; they drank tea in the afternoon. In their vocabulary, whiskey meant scotch, and not blended, please. And he liked them for saying what they felt, perhaps their only Canadian characteristic.

She tossed her short-cropped, curled gray hair and said, "Do sit down, Mr. Loss. I have been watching all evening and the young crew of ladies from that lovely yacht has not yet come ashore." She inflected each adjective with an upward lilt. But her fixed smile was more conspiratorial than admonishing.

"Thank you, Mrs. Kent," he replied, easing down into the camp chair. "I'm just on my way down the path. May I offer you something?" Brian motioned for the waiter.

"No thanks, Brian," Edwin Kent replied, "but take care of yourself. Sam," he motioned to the waiter, "please place this on my account. A whiskey for Mr. Loss." He turned to Brian, immediately at ease and old school. "Damned fine aircraft you have there, Brian. Margaret and I had a look at it yesterday over at Union. Beautiful thing." He was graying and touching on sixty, but Loss saw the fine muscle structure, good reflexes, and most of all, the decisive use of his hands in everything Kent did.

Loss answered, pausing to raise his newly arrived glass. "Thank you. The Aztec's not mine. I am what you would call a company pilot. Mr. Welsh, who I think you have met, is the owner. But yes, the Aztec is great for what it is."

She touched his arm lightly, which he thought was a singularly English thing to do.

"Edwin flew for the RCAF. He always drools over airplanes. Scruffy little things, big aluminum things; if it flies, he drools. Like some old dog, without teeth, over a bone." She had no malice to her voice, and Loss knew she loved her husband.

"I still shamble around," Kent said. "I've got an old Piper Super Cruiser. Had it since '51. I put floats on it in the summer and skis on it in the winter, just to get away from the old girl." Edwin Kent chuckled gently. "No, Margaret is right. I flew first in the RAF, no Battle of Britain thing. Just Lancasters. Then later I came back to Canada and we did air defense for a while. CF-100s and the usual lot."

Loss suddenly remembered who Edwin Kent was. Kent, a Vice Air Marshal of Canadian Forces in NATO, had pulled two flaming, fuel-saturated men from the fuselage of a burning Canberra bomber that had crashed on a fog-shrouded runway in France. Because of that, Kent had left his left leg buried in a field of France. But he had demanded and received permission to still fly first-line interceptors. Kent was still legend in Canada.

Loss looked again at Edwin Kent. "I think I've heard of you."

Kent laughed. "Shouldn't believe it all, Brian. They're likely to say some good things about me when I kick off. Damn liars all." He raised his glass.

"Good evening." The voice passed behind Brian's head and he turned to watch the attractive couple take a table near the Welshes on the patio.

"Nice couple," Margaret Kent said without conviction. She lifted her hand in recognition, but they had not looked back.

"Klist, I believe their name is," remarked Kent, watching them settle at their table. "I believe the journalist chap over there," indicating Bolken, "says he's some sort of industrialist in Holland. Transistors and things."

"It's a fairly international group," Loss commented. "I like to see people other than Americans abroad. This couple, Klist I think you said their name was? They seem young. He's the one who pounds up and down the beach every morning, isn't he?"

"So Margaret tells me," said Kent. "I'm still tucked in at that hour. But I'll vouch that he's not originally Dutch. I spent three years in Germany during the last go-around. I'd swear he's not Dutch." He paused and smiled. "Margaret is telling me with her foot that I should be more discreet, but then again, here we are, good Canadians with a closet queen. Keep a Union Jack hidden under the mattress. That sort of thing," and he snorted with laughter at the illusion.

"What nationality do you think he is?" Loss questioned.

Kent rattled the cubes of ice in his drink in a circular motion, thinking.

"I can't say exactly, Brian. German or Polish, perhaps. European traits have tended to merge over the last thirty years. But it's partly the bearing, the assurance, the devotion to a strong body. Just strikes me that way. Can't exactly pinpoint it. But he's not Dutch." Kent looked toward the couple and noted that they had joined the Welshes. Kent nodded discreetly in their direction.

"Looks like they have joined your employer and his wife. Incidentally, it's Senator Clifford Welsh, not just Mister, isn't it?"

Loss hesitated just long enough to confirm the statement. He shrugged, answering, "I guess that he wanted to keep it quiet. Something of a vacation. But I would ask that you not make that information public."

"Edwin's such a snoop," Kent's wife remarked to Brian. "No, of course we won't say anything. But you know, Canada is not such a long way from New York. Senator Welsh has gotten wide coverage in some of our newspapers. He seems to be trying to pull New York up by its scruffy bootstraps, and that's just the same thing that is going to have to happen in Montreal." She paused and put her hand beside her mouth and said in a stage whisper to Loss, "Don't talk to Edwin about French Canadians. He goes livid."

Kent laughed and pushed back his chair. "Pay no attention to her. Just as long as I don't have to learn to speak French in my lifetime, I can put up with them. Incidentally, why don't you take a sail with us tomorrow? Margaret and I have chartered the hotel's sloop. Plenty of room for you as well."

Brian thought briefly, knowing that there was no likelihood of the Aztec's being used. "It sounds like a great idea," he answered. "Where are you going?"

Kent dug around in his jacket pockets and came up with a small printed brochure. He read through it, holding it almost at arm's length. "Eye's don't accommodate well anymore. Ah, yes. It says that we go down to Tyrell Bay on Carriacou."

"I beg your pardon," Loss said.

"Tyrell Bay," repeated Kent, drawing a pair of glasses from his jacket breast pocket and putting them on. "It's about 12 miles from here down the west coast of Carriacou. Nice hotel there, I take it that it's the only one. We have lunch there, drive around a bit, and sail back in the late afternoon."

And Loss, warming with a rush of blood to his head, remembered that Holly had said "Carriacou was as far as you wanted to make it."

"Yes," replied Loss, smiling broadly, "I think that I'd very much like to go."

Chapter 9

Carl Heiss sat uncomfortably on the barstool, bored and restless. The backgammon game continued at the far end of the bar, now drawing a group of dining room staff who had finished up for the evening.

The Canadian couple sitting with Welsh's pilot had left, and the pilot himself left moments later after signing for his bar bill. Two other couples, whom Heiss didn't recognize, still were in the game room annex, playing darts. He finally realized that they were off one of the yachts. The younger woman in their group obviously wore nothing beneath the thin shift. She looked Scandinavian.

The bartender broke off from watching the backgammon game and started to mix another round of drinks. One of the drinks was a Campari and soda, the drink that Klist would normally order. Heiss waited patiently and watched the waiter carry the tray to the patio. One round of drinks would give Heiss a clear twenty minutes. He left a 5 dollar bill on the bar top and left through the now darkened dining room. Four figures sat at the Welsh table, their faces indistinct in the single candle flame. They were raising glasses to each other.

Heiss stood beyond the stone wall of the dining room patio, waiting for his eyes to adjust to the darkness. Except for pathway lights leading to the pavillion and muted stateroom lights in the yachts riding at anchor, the island was dark. He picked out the sound of an outboard motor running in the anchorage and strained to watch if someone were coming ashore. Spreader lights on the schooner anchored furthest out in the bay flooded the deck briefly and went off. Just crew from one yacht visiting their friends.

As his eyes accommodated, the forms of trees emerged from the blackness, and then he could see the outlines of the dirt path the staff used to walk to their quarters. Heiss followed the path, pausing every fifty steps to listen. The path steepened as he climbed the hillside and became coarser with spalls of chipped rock. Unexpectedly, he stumbled and fell heavily, pain from his hands forcing a rush of breath from his lips. Lying for a minute in the pathway, Heiss drew the injured hand to his lips and licked at the wound. The blood was warm and salty, like melted butter. He got slowly to his feet and could feel the pain throb steadily with each pulse of his heart. A cool draft blew through a vent in the knee of his pants. Heiss cursed inwardly. The pants had cost 20 pounds on Bond Street, and they were new. "Fucking sod," he muttered.

In ten minutes the path leveled again and over the rise of the hill he saw the indefinite shapes of the two large staff buildings. The area before him was open, and he altered his course to the left, avoiding the buildings and moving down through the high lemon grass toward the road that led to the four cottages on the eastern bluff.

A spent cigarette arched into the blackness and died in a shower of sparks not more than 20 feet to his right. Heiss froze and slowly lowered to the ground. The grass pressed up into his face, and he thought that he could hear the sound of insects scattering beneath his body's weight.

The West Indian accents were indistinct, thick monosyllables. One of the two voices was a woman's. She giggled and then very distinctly said, "Keep you hand still." But she laughed again. The man's voice was blurred by his deeper tone: short, insistent words. Heiss looked at his watch, alarmed by the high luminosity of the dial. He had consumed twelve minutes already, and he painfully began to inch his way down to the left, relying on the sounds of the wind in the grass to mask his movements. In four minutes, he gained the protection of a clump of scrubby trees and rose to a crouch, pausing to listen. The voices were nothing now, and he could hear more distinctly the numbed roar of seas breaking on the windward reef.

The Welsh cottage, Number 4, stood alone on its individual bluff. The access road was dark, but a few lights illuminated the path leading to the front doorway.

Heiss listened for two minutes more, straining to hear or see anyone approaching on the path. Satisfied, he calmly walked across the road and strode up the bluff, keeping clear of any illumination from the lighted path. He listened at the door and scanned the road again before entering the cottage.

The three rooms were vacant. Switching on a penlight, Heiss examined his wounded hand and torn pants. He gritted his teeth in anger, cursing his stupidity. Obviously, he should have walked from the pavillion to his own cottage and then simply approached the Welsh cottage from the beach side of the bluff. "Twenty fucking quid," he mumbled again, squeezing the open wound in his hand and watching the dark blood flow thickly. He licked it again, holding the taste in his mouth like a bubble of sour wine.

He removed his shoes, noting carefully that no dust or mud had been tracked upon the tiled floor, and then stood on the backboard of the bed and scanned the ledge of the stone wall with the flashlight. The recorder was undisturbed. He carefully changed the tape, substituting a fresh reel from his inside coat pocket. The battery indicator showed that the cells were still fresh.

Tapping the contact microphone with his thumbnail, he watched as the reels moved a fraction of a revolution and stopped again. The recorder had a voice-operated mike, recording only when a sufficient level of noise was present. It was unavoidable that the sounds of the shower, toilet, and human movement sometimes actuated the mechanism, but the tape had a capacity of 4 hours, easily spanning a normal day of conversation.

Heiss serviced two more recorders, one on a beam in the patio and one hidden under dirt in the frangipani bushes bordering the patio. It was a chance that Welsh would look for surveillance devices, but unlikely. A microphone had also been attached to an FM transmitter under Welsh's dining table but the range to Heiss's receiver-tape recorder in his cottage had been too great for actual use. There was a great deal of fading so that only one-third of the recorded conversation was usable. Heiss had considered moving the unit closer to the pavillion but thought that Lousje would have a recorder in her purse, for any important meetings.

A sound startled Heiss as he finished changing the tape in the third recorder. Flattening himself behind a lounge chair on the patio, he heard the voice of Judith Welsh. The bedroom was suddenly bathed in light and shadows from forms passing in front of the bedroom lamps spanned the patio in rapidly shifting shapes: oblique characterizations.

Knowing that any movement would probably be seen, Heiss lay still, heart pounding. Raising his head minutely to clear the cushions, he saw Welsh and his wife changing to bathrobes. He noticed that her stomach had traces of flab but the rest of her body was firm and tanned; her breasts were small but satisfactory. They both moved into the bathroom, and Heiss counted to 10 slowly, planning to vault over the stone retaining wall. He tensed, carefully planning his movements, and then Judith Welsh walked back into the bedroom and spent several minutes stirring around the contents of her cosmetic case. Clifford Welsh re-entered the room and sat down on the bed, examining his sunburnt shoulders before the mirror as his wife walked back into the bathroom area, pausing long enough to pass her hand across her husband's neck.

It seemed too risky to move, thought Heiss. It would be better to wait for an hour or so and then move off after they were asleep.

A toilet flushed and Heiss imagined three tape recorders faithfully committing to permanent magnetic memory the sound of waste being passed down a pipe.

His wound was oozing again and Heiss sucked on it.

The lights were extinguished first in the bedroom, and then as Judith Welsh reentered the bedroom, the last bathroom light flicked out. He could hear them talking in low tones at first and then silence and then the sounds of love making. He timed them, counting off thirty-one minutes. "Fucking sod," thought Heiss, growing stiff in the night wind.

The two men jogged along the beach in the early morning sunlight. They passed the southern tip of the island breathing heavily in the loose dry sand, then gained the broad sweep of tide-washed flats that ran north beneath the windward bluff. Browsing land crabs scuttled to their holes, sensing the vibrations of the running men.

The younger of the two forced his breath to a faster rate, and faltered in his pace. He would seek not to embarrass.

Welsh looked over at the young European and staggered to a halt. The Dutchman was breathing heavily as well, but there was no visible triphammer pounding beneath his rib cage. Welsh felt his own heart thudding, the sound reverberating in his mind. They both sank to the still-cool sand and silently watched the lagoon rising to feathered whitecaps in the fresh wind.

Welsh spoke, surprised at the harshness in this throat. "I should be doing that every morning, Robert." He exhaled heavily, thinking that at least he had matched the younger man.

"I find it difficult to do every morning," replied the Soviet colonel, pouring sand through his hand, allowing it to engulf two ants struggling with some particle of food. The ants reappeared from the sand in seconds and Klist showered them again with a fresh avalanche. They did not reappear.

They had talked briefly last night of their backgrounds. Klist asked him directly, within the first five minutes of conversation, whether he was not the Senator from New York. Welsh acknowledged this, pleased that a European would know his name and recognize him.

Klist spoke, so softly that Welsh had to lean toward him to hear. "I follow American politics closely, Clifford. It seems much more of an honest–," he groped for the word, "game than in Europe. What are your aspirations?"

The question was so direct and blunt that Welsh answered without much consideration.

"Robert, I really don't know. I guess that every politician wants a shot at the Presidency. I've thought about it, but I'm young. Perhaps in several years, perhaps sooner, I'll make a try at it."

"So was Kennedy young," replied Klist with a shrug, as if it were nothing. He turned and looked at Welsh directly, again speaking softly. "Many people in Europe are worried about the drift of American political thought. Others, including myself, find some hope."

Welsh tensed slightly. The subject seemed directed, but he discounted this after thinking for a minute. Klist was obviously no reporter. He remembered that the opinions of others concerning politics were difficult, no, impossible to obtain, just because of his political position. He decided to milk this Dutchman of as much European bias as possible and resolved to give nothing in return.

Klist sensed the change in the man's mood and discussed his admiration for Welsh's handling of the New York City financial crisis. They talked for another twenty minutes, the sun warming them now, the heat easing cramped muscles.

They drifted in discussion of European money matters and the return to gold as a monetary standard among the fractured IMF countries.

"Yes, I grant you that it was a major mistake for Burns to continue the policy of demonetization of gold," Welsh said. "We forced France into this corner repeatedly." He made a throwaway gesture with his hand. "I'm glad that it's changed."

"It's not really over, Clifford," replied Klist. "The gold boom in Europe is stabilized, but those who hold South African gold shares are worth great fortunes." Klist said this evenly, with no inflection in his voice.

Welsh erupted in laughter. He started to speak and then stopped again to laugh. "I wish to God that I had a few shares of Vall Reefs tucked away, Robert, but the closest relationship that I have to gold is a batch of fillings in my teeth."

Klist turned toward Clifford Welsh, shading his eyes with a hand. He looked awkward, about to salute.

"Didn't your father, a Senator himself, I believe, favor the policy of backing currency with gold reserves?"

Welsh didn't stop to analyze the depth of this question. "Of course," he replied. "My father fought Roosevelt tooth and nail on the subject. Thought it was irresponsible to allow the amount of paper currency in circulation to be tied to the whims of politicians. I personally think he was right. But I don't recall that my father ever personally invested in gold."

Klist stood up abruptly and brushed the sand from his warmup suit.

"We must talk some more, Clifford. I think that Lousje will be ready for breakfast soon. Will you join us for cocktails this evening at our cottage?"

Welsh staggered to his feet, one leg numb from restricted circulation. "Yes, of course, we'll join you. What about five?"

And the Russian nodded without looking back, striding easily north along the tide line.

They met again as agreed, on the patio of the Klist cottage, high on the road edging Telescope Hill. Klist was wearing perfectly tailored slacks and a shirt of raw silk. The shoes were probably Pucci and by comparison, Welsh felt shabby. Klist's wife, Lousje, served catered canapes, swimming around the room like a graceful, exotic fish, her full-length dress strangely not out of place. Welsh and his wife both sensed that the meeting had been carefully planned, in the manner that good hosts plan perfect things.

"Your hospitality is a little less than overwhelming," Welsh commented, raising his glass in salute to the women. Neither Klist nor his wife commented but merely returned the toast, smiling evenly.

They all sat for some minutes, watching the anchorage. *Mintar,* the hotel's chartered sloop, could be seen, hard on the port tack, close-reaching up the bay. The shadows had lengthened with the last of the sun pinking the mountain tops of the islands to the south and west. And as always, the wind seemed to abate as nightfall approached.

There were seven yachts in the anchorage now, ranging from a traditional staysail schooner far out in the roadstead to a small fiberglass cruising ketch, moored stern-to to coconut trees lining the beach. An hibachi flared at the stern of an English-rigged cutter further down the bay. Welsh swallowed appreciatively at the vodka and tonic, letting his mind slide.

The sun was just touching the western horizon, a globule of orange fire, flattened by refraction.

"We will have a green flash, yes?" Lousje said, more statement than question. "There are no clouds on the horizon." She stood behind her husband, an obedient servant waiting his command.

Judith Welsh felt ill at ease. The Klist woman was too perfect a sort of showpiece. She doubted secretly that Klist and this woman were married. She never saw the small touches of either dislike or love that pass between all married people. The Dutch couple were more like actors, playing some role, unrelated and only artificially adept at small gestures. She was about to say something, vaguely supportive, when the Dutch woman turned to her and said, "Judith, I wish to go down to the boutique to pick up a shift. You know these prices, I think. Can you come with me?" It was a line from a script.

Klist nodded as if he had excused her, and Welsh, caught unexpectedly in a situation he did not understand, nodded as well, not quite knowing what was agreed to. The men rose, and as the women departed, Lousje said something in Dutch, repeating in English for Welsh that they would meet them in the pavillion for dinner in one hour's time. She blew a kiss and they were gone.

Klist first spoke, indicating the sun as it was swallowed by the western sea.

"If you look carefully, there will be the lightest blink of green. It is rare to see it, only when the horizon is free of clouds." And as if on cue, the sun poised on the horizon, the top arch flattened by distortion, and disappeared, leaving behind a divided second's flick of emerald. The sun was gone now, but radiating from its invisible point below the horizon were graduated blues and tones of gold across the sky, like sun rays on Sunday School posters.

Klist got to his feet and took the partially empty glass from the table in front of Welsh. He refilled the glass and his as well, and eased back down into his chair. He looked intently at Welsh for a long period of time, his face open and relaxed. Finally, with a measure of reluctance, he said, "You know, Clifford, I have not been honest with you. But I think you know that."

Welsh looked at him, with a gaze as steady as he could manage. Klist's eyes, blue by daylight, were points of black in the gathering darkness of the tropical evening.

"Yes, I sensed that, Robert," Welsh replied, waiting for an explanation, slightly afraid. His palms felt moist, despite the coolness of the evening.

Klist picked up a cigarette from a flat gold case and lighted it, relaxing with his exhalation as if the alchemy of the nicotine brought some inner peace and decision. He started, slowly building the explanation.

"First of all, Clifford, I am not Dutch. Let us say that I am European. Perhaps all of us there may someday feel that way. Also, I am not what I appear to be. I am wealthy, yes." Klist paused to inhale the cigarette and then continued, exhaling as he lay the words down in neat, precise bundles.

"I represent, along with myself, a select number of European industrialists who are, surprisingly enough, not specifically interested in profit. But," he continued, "we are interested in stability."

Welsh held up his hand in a gesture of denial, starting to speak, but Klist interrupted. "No, let me finish, Clifford. It is not what you think. I am approaching you for my group *because*," he paused for emphasis, "because we think we can support you in an early bid for your Presidency without attempting to dictate to you any terms. Simply put, we want to help you."

Welsh was staggered. He sat in silence, his mind trying to reach ahead, probing through his experience with Klist for some recognizible point of contact.

"Continue," Welsh said flatly, letting no emotion alter his voice.

As if the roles were reversed now, Klist became sincere, open, sometimes faltering for words.

"To allay your obvious opinion of me, Clifford, I must say that had we been seeking a candidate who would grant trade concessions or other sorts of favoritism, you know as well as I that there are men who stand much closer to the Presidency whom we could buy. Politicians the world over are open to bribes. No, that is exactly what we do not seek.

"We do seek a man who can take command of your country with the full will of the people and bring a halt to a new race for armaments. This is what we fear in Europe."

They sat together in the darkness, the sea wind bringing coolness. Welsh slowly digested the words, repeating in his mind their implication, feeling already caught up in something. "Put it straight to me, Klist," Welsh said, pleased with the note of firmness in his voice. "You are saying that you and other people in Europe will support me financially in a campaign for the Presidency without attempting to dictate policy. Is that it?"

"Yes," the Russian answered, "within the limitations of what we know you stand for. The major position that we are concerned with is disarmament. We are not concerned with your internal policies. We feel that we have no legitimate say in such things."

"Keep talking," Welsh said, feeling detached.

Klist finished the cigarette, the ash glowing, subtly lighting his high cheekbones. "NATO, as you know, Clifford, is a hollow shell. As long as America retained the balance of power, the weaker nations felt obliged to contribute to the common European defense. We wish it were otherwise, but your country has greatly reduced her commitment both in Asia and in Europe. The Eastern Bloc, conversely, has made sizable gains in power. Although your intelligence organizations may feel otherwise, we feel in Europe that there is no danger of war, *as long as you do not challenge the Russians.*"

There. It was out, thought Welsh. How did they know his feelings on this? Perhaps it was just self-evident that some US politician would make this opinion felt. They had done their homework. "Where did you pick up any indication that I was inclined toward unilateral disarmament?" he asked, trying to seek out some truth in the face opposite him, now cast in shadows.

"It may surprise you, Clifford, but we know of eight such men who we feel are within range of the Presidency. It is not an uncommon thought now, but as you would say in America, the idea has not been market-tested. No, we follow the lives of men we feel are important on a global basis. Your speech in Utica . . . " Klist trailed off in his explanation.

Welsh sat in the darkness, carefully rethreading the words, testing them against his own beliefs. It would be unthinkable to allow Europeans to interfere with American policy or, for that matter, politics. But if the goal were common— "Peace in our time" crossed his mind, and he angrily rejected the quotation. But he could listen to their proposal. He already thought in terms of "their" rather than "his," Klist was nothing more than a messenger. "If I were to agree in principal with your concept of disarmament, what would your friends be able to do in assisting my campaign?" Welsh asked, relaxed now. Smooth.

Klist replied, almost eager. "A great deal, but all of it indirect. For example, you know that Europe has expanded its trade boundaries to include much of the Middle East, the Far East, and South America. Consequently, we can bring economic pressure to bear that will be beneficial. For example, if you were to propose a bill in the Senate, ceding *all* US rights to bases in the Canal, plus the US's right of intervention in the Republic of Panama's territory, that new leftist government would respond by ceasing all hostilities, allow presently positioned US troops to withdraw, and would make every attempt to praise your initiative. You would be invited to Panama on a 'fact finding commission.' You would return home with a draft for a treaty of peace and friendship and for passage without charge for all US ships in perpetuity. Thus, such a move on your part toward conciliation would gain you national prominence. I don't think that I have to mention that a similar proposal by any other member of your government would be met with indifference. Similar situations could arise by your introduction of a bill to allow Cuba to take back ownership of Guantánamo Bay over a three-year transition period. I think that you would find Cuba would take immediate and effective steps to remove her military force from Africa. There would be extensive praise in the foreign press citing your vision of a new détente."

Klist seemed confident, and the two scenarios had been carefully presented, as if there were no doubt as to the outcome. "Who do you represent, Klist?" Welsh said. "This is unbelievable. What you're saying is that your group controls the top echelons of major governments. Is that correct?"

Welsh has bitten, thought Klist, and he smiled in the darkness. It will work now, if I feed him bit by bit. "No, Clifford. Don't forget that the US has always been dictatorial in its demands. Concessions are rarely made by your country unless under duress. There is strong sentiment for governments to respond to an open-ended gesture. We merely supply enough influential opinion in the halls of power to effect the results desired. And in regard to your question concerning our members, you could probably name ten of the top industrialists or second-level leaders of government in Europe and have a fair idea of our membership. But it was decided that your knowledge of those names might influence you unduly in future years. We want no favoritism, nor any possibility that you might feel obligated to us. Our influence will only be beneficial to your rise to higher office. You will have no past to shed."

"Then all this, ah, assistance hinges on my stand on disarmament," Welsh said.

Klist stood up and walked slowly back and forth across the patio, his head bent, his hands clasped behind his back. He made several attempts to start speaking and each time stopped, reforming his words. Finally, he said, "It is difficult for you, as an American, to appreciate the European mind. No, I know. You have spent many months in Europe and speak two languages. But you must remember that Europe has been a battleground too often for there to be any firm national commitments, even from the West Germans, to fight in a nuclear war that will basically be between the US and Russia. And it is a commitment that your country can ill afford to bear alone.

"On the other hand, we have the Russian leadership, still stupified by losses of twenty million people during the Second World War. It is a reflexive action on their part to overarm. If they see one of your tanks in Europe, they will build three to counter it with. But they cannot maintain this insane pace of weapons manufacture. There is too much demand from beneath for housing, consumer goods, food, and better transportation to sustain this effort.

"The crucial point has arrived. The world now views yours as a second-rate power, but there is much discussion now within the United States for massive and rapid upgrading of weapons within the limitations of the SALT II agreement. If this were to happen, we greatly fear that the Russians would launch a preemptive strike before you could accomplish your goals."

Klist paused. "I'm sorry, Clifford," he said. "You know these things as well as I. I don't mean to sound so academic." He picked up the glasses and started to refill them.

"I don't care for another," said Welsh.

"I think you will," Klist said, placing a filled glass before his guest. "There is yet more to what I have to say. It is the most important part."

Klist settled in his chair, pausing to drink from his glass. He lit a cigarette and paused, trying to compose the words. The effort was discernible, even in the darkness. "Clifford. What I am about to tell you now cannot be proved. I have no, . . . as you would call it, documentation. Let me tell you in the way this came about.

"One of our members was in Prague last spring to discuss building a rolling mill for high-tensile steel. While he was there, he was invited to the estate of one of the party members whom he had been dealing with. After the dinner was over, the host detained our associate until the guests had left, asking that he remain behind for a meeting. At eleven or shortly thereafter, a man entered the study of the host. This man was, and still is, third-ranking man in the Soviet Presidium. He discussed with our associate just what we have been speaking about. This Russian claimed that it is impossible for them to initiate major concessions in disarmament due to their somewhat dogmatic approach as leader of world communism. Any relaxation at present, if initiated by the Soviets, would destabilize control of their satellites.

"On the other hand, they view rearmament by the US as a warlike act and militant members of the Presidium would demand what he termed, 'surgical removal of US military capacity.'

"However, he feels that if the US were to make moves toward unilateral disarmament, the Soviet Union could respond in kind on a gradual basis, finally falling to a level sufficient only to achieve a balance of power with the Chinese."

"I find this difficult to believe," said Welsh, wanting to believe.

"No," replied Klist. "I assure you that it is true. I would not have come to meet with you if we thought otherwise. The obvious question is why this Russian should approach us rather than meeting with US policy makers directly. The answer is simple. The Russian claimed that such an approach has been made within the last two years directly to your Secretary of State. He refused even private discussions at working levels. The Russians feel that the present US Administration is closed to the subject. These men who govern your country are brittle pragmatists. And their pride is dangerous.

"Consequently, the Russians feel that if a US Presidential candidate took a positive stance on unilateral disarmament, and if he were supported by an organization such as ours, he might be able to win in the coming election. This would leave the Russians latitude to gradually reduce their armament in a spirit of cooperation without absolute constraints such as a SALT II or III Agreement might impose. Remember, they still must match the Chinese, a reality that the SALT talks have not encompassed."

"How do I know that the Russians will keep their word?" Welsh asked, mentally making the quantum leap from desire to decision.

"There is no assurance, Clifford. There does not have to be. Should you gain the Presidency and initiate disarmament, you *must* do so on a token basis. If the Russians respond, you will know that you can safely, but cautiously, proceed. If they do not keep their word, you would be under no pressure or obligation to continue the disarmament. But think for a minute. Can you visualize the impact that it would have on world opinion if you, as a future President, were able to accomplish a nuclear-weapon-free world. Think of the great good that could be done in a society that was free from fear!"

Welsh nodded in the starlight.

Chapter 10

Loss met the Kents on the following morning. The three of them stood on the jetty, waiting for the sloop *Mintar* to come alongside. The sun was still low in the east, hammering the sea into silver. Loss inhaled deeply, smelling damp earth scents mixed with the tang of salt. Down to the west, where they would sail to, the mountains of Carriacou jutted up in hills of rock and green—somehow calm and yet dynamic. He exhaled, quite content.

"It looks like a fair day," Kent said. "I look forward to getting slightly drunk and disorderly. What say, Margaret?" He leaned over and ruffled his wife's hair.

"Keep your sticky hands to yourself," she replied, frost on her voice but winking at Loss. "I will be very cross with you, Edwin, if you're not coherent when Mr. Loss introduces us to his lady."

Loss raised his eyebrows in surprise. "You've met Holly?"

Margaret Kent nodded, smiling. "Two days ago. She came up on the lumpy little boat that they deliver eggs and produce on, just for the afternoon. She asked for you, and Edwin did his usual intelligence-gathering routine and dragged the story out of her. To my knowledge, you were off poking around some reef."

Kent smiled at Brian, slowly dropping one eyelid. "Believe that she bought two bottles of champagne to take back with her. From experience, I think it might be something of a peace offering."

His wife made disgusted sounds in her throat and punched her husband lightly in the chest. "Edwin, you're so *crude* at times. Really!"

Loss laughed lightly. "I should have guessed that she'd do something like this. By the way, where is she staying?"

"A place called the Mermaid Tavern," she replied. "But take care, Brian. I take it that she spends quite a bit of time with a young English marine biologist who works down at the marine laboratory. I hear that he's something of a cross between Robert Redford and Flipper. He flys as well. His own plane, private income, and that sort of thing.

Loss felt discomfort at the thought: pleased that Holly was here and irked that she might not care whether he knew. Someone once told him, "All women are bitches, all men are bastards." Perhaps all, he thought, at least to some degree.

The charter sloop came alongside the jetty just before nine and they boarded, Kent swinging aboard easily despite his artificial leg. Giles Tobin, the skipper, led them to the cockpit where he had hot coffee waiting. They all drank from enameled mugs while Giles laid on a block of ice and some provisions for the day's sail, singing under his breath about the sea, the men on and under it, and women left behind.

"Looks the part, doesn't he," Kent said softly to Brian. Tobin did look like a seafarer in some slightly miscast way, Loss thought. In his late twenties, Tobin had an owlish face and lean body with ropy muscles. The aviator sunglasses spanned his face and covered his cheekbones, emphasizing his blank-wise look. Heavily tanned, he wore only cut-off jeans faded nearly white. His hair was long and sun-bleached, but tied neatly in a queue, like some seventeenth century foretopman who sailed before the mast.

Tobin saw them looking his way and called aft, "We'll be underway in another ten minutes. Have some more coffee if you like, and there's beer in the icebox." Loss smiled and nodded his head, recognizing that Tobin, like every other charter skipper or charter pilot that he had ever known, would probably like the work a great deal more if only he didn't have to cart around the people who paid the bills. The bus-driver syndrome he thought, laughing to himself.

Loss watched the shore, anxious to be underway. Some of the small Mini-Mokes were making the rounds of the guest cottages, bringing orders of breakfast to the lazy ones. The grounds staff had begun the day, trimming the flower beds and shrubs, working progressively slower as the sun rose. By noon, the men would be one step removed from the shade of the sea grape trees and a cool bottle of beer. Two figures jogged along the beach near the southern end of the island. He knew that it would be Klist and Welsh. Dutchman Klist or German Klist or Polish Klist, "a man with an international face," Kent had said. The Welshes were with the Klist couple now almost continuously, eating meals in their cottage and only coming to the pavillion for an evening drink. The men kept to themselves, talking intently, and when Loss had approached Welsh yesterday afternoon, Welsh had dismissed him curtly as he would a servant.

Welsh is an odd one, Brian thought. The public image of the lean-tough-honest politician was one thing. But the real man was different. Neither the emulsion of a photograph or the phosphor of a TV tube conveyed his vacillation, his need to be reassured, or his hunger for justification. The man was driven by some inflexible image of himself. For his dead father or perhaps for his wife. For the people of New York or maybe DeSilva. But what Welsh did was not for its own reward. There had to be a prompter in the wings and applause down front.

Welsh was a strange kettle of fish. He was dangerous, because he believed only in things he wanted to believe in, lacking the flexibility to count his options.

And he was moldable. The Klist thing was probably some business deal but it had all the hallmarks of an elaborate setup. Too controlled, too perfect, and now growing too intense. Loss made a mental note to check with the hotel office to find out when the Klists had made their reservations. If it had been prior to Welsh making his own reservations, there was probably nothing to worry about.

Giles Tobin came aft, smiling, his eyes lost in the darkness of his glasses, his hair's queue streaming off the leeward. His frame was awkward and stringy, but the placement of hands and feet was oddly precise, without waste of energy. Perhaps a good man on wet, windy nights, Loss thought.

Tobin spoke, the accent a blurred Midlands English. "We'll be off now, right? Mr. Loss, in on the anchor rope as I come up on it and Mr. Kent, just stand by on the main halyard. You take in the slack and Mr. Loss can get it up. OK?" They nodded, pleased to be a part of the crew.

By 9:30, the *Mintar* was underway; Tobin content in his familiar world and the Kents relaxed and easy, just flowing with the day. And Loss, excited now, feeling the sloop moving easily under his feet in the following sea, was thinking of Holly.

Heiss watched them leave under sail. His 7 x 50 binoculars could pick out the small details of the yacht and the individual faces. He cased the glasses finally and walked down the path along the seafront, watching as the yacht ran off before the wind. Near the southern end of the island, the yacht gybed onto port tack and raised a small staysail, making good time now in the fresh breeze.

Heiss watched the *Mintar* until it was nearly lost from sight, a small speck of white fleeing before the wind. Heiss fantasized, seeing himself as the master of a yacht, creaming through the Mediterranean Sea. Not a sailing boat, he thought, but something strong and powerful; a large diesel yacht that he could control from his fingertips. He would have a German mechanic to maintain those engines. And an Austrian chef. And young Greek men in whites to polish the chrome and keep the yacht spotless.

And he would go from port to port and there would be women for the asking, for the taking. He mentally walked through the master stateroom, his feet cushioned by a thick white pile rug, soft as crepe. Golden tones of teak and spots of gleaming brass.

Heiss slung the case from his shoulders and walked the path to the beach house that Loss occupied, stopping occasionally to examine the flowers and gaze out over the anchorage. He passed two West Indian housekeepers, pushing a linen cart before them, giggling to each other, carefully hiding their mouths to suppress their shared laughter. He drew opposite them and they both became quiet, smiling, polite; playing the automatic role of blacks near whites. He heard them laugh again when he was past them, thinking that they were laughing at him. Black bitches, he thought.

He entered Loss's cottage after knocking first. The room was clean, the bed freshly made, and pillow plumped. Fresh hibiscus had been placed in a vase.

He checked the only recorder, finding no more than 5 inches of tape on the takeup reel. The batteries were now a bit low, the charge indicator showing in the caution zone. He changed them, replacing each cell with a gloved hand so as to leave no print.

This was the first time that Loss had been absent from the island. Heiss methodically inspected the contents of drawers, the pilot's flight case, and a worn B-4 suitcase that still had the faded stencil indicating the owner was Captain Loss, USAF.

The closet yielded a leather briefcase, scarred and discolored, but firmly locked. Heiss carefully noted the position of the case as it rested on the floor and then inspected the entire case with his penlight before moving it, looking for the strand of hair, the bit of paper that would tell its owner of tampering. He then worked with the locks, probing with a small tungsten-bladed tool until they yielded.

He carefully opened the case and found that its contents were mainly the ordinary things a traveler would carry: a passport, several books of traveler's checks and a stack of oil company credit cards bound by a rubber band. But the item of most interest to Heiss was a 9-millimeter Luger, carefully holstered. Heiss eased the weapon from its case. It gleamed in the morning sunlight, dull black with age and oil. He smelled the barrel and then handled the gun, feeling the compact power it gave his extended arm as the ramp sights came together in perfect union.

Interesting, thought Heiss. It was not the type of weapon an agent or bodyguard would carry. Too dangerous to carry with a round in the chamber and subject to misfires. He guessed that Loss would carry the weapon out of habits formed in the service. Interesting, nevertheless. It was helpful to know of the weapon's existence. But he would not report this to Klist. This was a bit of private knowledge that he would save against an uncertain future.

Heiss replaced the weapon in its holster and returned it to the briefcase. After locking it, he replaced the briefcase exactly as it had been, with the handle on the correct side and a tennis sock resting against the edge.

Leaving the cottage after a careful survey of the path and the hill above, Carl Heiss walked slowly toward his own cottage, pausing along the road to poke at flowers as any normal guest would do. All part of the job, he thought sardonically.

The sun was higher in the east now, the pathway hot beneath his sandled feet. Sweat soaked the armpits of his shirt and his scalp prickled with the heat. And his eyes ached with the brightness.

Heiss looked up toward his own cottage and saw the flash of white clothing retreat from the open door of his patio into the dark interior. He paused in the shade of a manchineel tree, breathing heavily from the exertion of the grade, waiting for long minutes to catch some variation in the dark patterns. Cursing himself, he remembered the binoculars he carried. Withdrawing them from the case, he focused the glasses on the interior and picked up the shape of a person moving about; a woman surely, but clothed in a bikini or banded-patterned dress. Not a black.

He strode normally to the cottage pathway, sure that he was highly visible from the darkness of the cottage.

Lousje lay in the chaise lounge, drinking from a chilled glass. Her long legs were crossed in composed grace, the darkness of her tanned skin in strobe contrast to the white of the bikini. The sweat of her body gave a dull sheen to her skin as if she had oiled her body. Dark stains of dampness marked her body's outline on the cotton mat beneath her.

"Sit down and listen, Mr. Bolken," she said without preamble. She gestured toward the caneback chair. He ignored her and walked toward the bar.

She snapped her fingers at him, the report startling in the stone-walled room, unexpected. As if he were a dog to be brought to heel.

"You dumb cunt," he hissed, turning on her. "You're here to provide stage dressing and open your legs on command for Klist. If anyone sees you here, it will be all over the staff quarters in fifteen minutes, discussed in the kitchen in twenty-five and part of the bar conversation by 6:00 PM." He turned away, reaching for the bottle of vodka that rested, lid missing, on the bar shelf. He poured a drink from the bottle and took a long first sip of the smooth fire, pushing it between his teeth, washing his tongue and mouth in the evaporating heat of the alcohol.

He turned toward her. Her face was devoid of expression. She watched him as if he were no more or less of interest than paint on the wall or a swatch of fabric. She spoke quietly, indicating the cane chair with her hand. "Sit down, Heiss. I am here at the suggestion of Welsh. I told him that I needed advice on what type of filter to use for my Pentax." She indicated the camera case resting on the tiles near the patio entrance. "You're wasting time. I have instructions from Klist. And, yes, if it suits you, I am a very good cunt, but I can also arrange to have your balls cut off. Be civil and we'll get along." She licked the top of her lips with a pink tongue and smiled, the gesture intentional.

Heiss sat and watched her, listening. Fascinated. And remembered the touch and smell of her on that Barbados morning.

Lousje Klist spoke quickly and precisely, the lines delivered as if memorized, no inflection in her voice. "You know, of course, that we are interested in Welsh and his political leanings. We feel now that he will fit exactly into a special situation that has been devised." She sipped her drink, looking at him noncommittally over the brim of her glass, then lowered it, licking her upper lip.

"However," she continued, "it is important that all the tapes which have been made of Welsh's conversations with his wife and with us should now be analyzed further before we make any final commitment. Do you have photographs?"

"Yes," he said, lifting his shoulders fractionally.

"How good?"

"Over twenty of Welsh and Klist. Good groupings, full face, profile, running on the beach together. Several more, ten or twelve I think, of him and his wife in bed. They're very high ASA. They should be good, but until I can develop them, I can only guess."

"The photographs are important only for future insurance," she continued. She shifted in the lounge, drawing one leg up like a child accentuating her sexuality, playing with him.

"We must handle Welsh very carefully from now on," she said. "Robert is a very good psychologist, but the importance of reading Welsh's personality must be vetted by others who are more disinterested. Welsh is a fool. But he's a reasonably honest fool, and we cannot simply buy him. His wife wants power and can see herself as . . . " she trailed off the sentence, thinking better of giving Heiss any information that was not essential.

"At any rate," she continued, "you will receive a final briefing sometime this evening; perhaps after Robert has finished with Welsh. You will collect all the tapes and films and be ready to leave tomorrow with them. After they are delivered, I doubt that we will have further need of you."

"Where do I take the material." He was calm now, disinterested in her, thinking only of the money, wondering what the recorder that he had concealed in Klist's own bedroom would reveal. There might be even more money to be made from this little job.

He looked up at her and found her eyes intent upon him. And he knew that she understood him exactly.

"Don't attempt anything beyond the scope of your instructions, Heiss," she said. "You know as well as I what that would ultimately mean. The information is valuable only to the people Robert and I work for. It would be useless to attempt to sell it to others."

She paused, sipping the remains of her drink, swirling the remains of ice against the wall of the glass. The noise was oddly mechanical in the tropical morning. "You will take the material to Mexico."

"How do I get there?" he asked.

She looked out beyond the patio, uninterested in him, unselfconsciously adjusting the top of her bikini, taunting him at some lower level of consciousness. It was a movement as natural as brushing the hair from her eyes, yet designed to provoke.

"Mr. Welsh, pardon me, Senator Welsh will have you flown there in his aircraft. It is being arranged."

Chapter 11

The Junior Senator from New York splashed rum over the ice, added ginger ale, and passed the glass to Robert Klist. They clinked their glasses and drank, both thinking about the last four days.

The sun was in the west; the late afternoon light, brittle and hard, was baking the ground to rock-like consistency. Klist felt the heat burning through the umbrella over their table, through his shirt and skin, heating his blood. He was tired but satisfied. He turned to Welsh, forming a poite smile. "It's been a productive four days, hasn't it?"

Welsh nodded, his eyes refocusing from some distant point. He could smell the tide-washed coral mixed with the scent of night-blooming jasmine. Not unpleasant. "Yes," he answered. "Productive. It seems like—a long time." Welsh rubbed his eyes, blinking. The whites were bloodshot and his facial skin tone was more yellow than tan. His left cheek had a tic. He ground his teeth, thinking that it was idiocy to drink especially when he felt so groggy. The heat and the sun must be affecting me, he thought, and he pushed the glass away.

Each day it had been the same. First, he and Klist would run on the beach to the point of exhaustion and then pause to talk. Together, they would have breakfast at the Klist cottage, Lousje serving from the insulated trays brought by the room staff. The morning and afternoon was a long session; Klist asking a series of unrelated questions ranging from Welsh's personal and religious outlook to political dogma. Even as he thought of it, Welsh could barely remember what had been discussed. But it seemed unimportant. And in the evening they would eat at Welsh's cottage, walk to the pavillion for drinks, and retire early. It seemed almost a ritual.

Klist had seemed unaffected by the grinding routine, always well organized and fresh. And his wife was the same. The perfect companion for Judith, finding interesting things to do and keeping her away from the long discussions. She seemed a nice woman, he thought absently.

Klist watched Welsh carefully, noting the symptoms of disorientation. Lousje was feeding Welsh too much of the drug. It had all seemed like a conjuring act; the palms, the lemon grass, Lousje smoothly doing her manikin's movements with Welsh's wife on the lawn below. And the man opposite him, trying desperately to play out some role, reaching for power. Klist drew his fingertips down the side of the cold glass, drawing lines through the condensed moisture. Only the glass is real, he thought, because it is only the glass I can feel. And I am the only reality. Klist sighed and pushed his tiredness aside.

"Clifford?" Klist was talking to him, and Welsh turned to face the man who was smiling at him from across the table.

"Clifford, I think that we've arrived at a point where we both basically agree. But there are a few last specific points I think we must cover."

Welsh nodded, his mind feeling open and receptive. Klist's accent was shaping the words with the precision of a cutting tool. Mustn't drink so much, he thought. Looks bad.

Klist sat up in his wicker chair and leaned forward on the table, hands clasped. "I have tried to outline our position. I don't think that either of us sees any conflict with our group supporting you through the methods that we have agreed upon. Correct?"

Welsh nodded and pushed his sunglasses back on his forehead.

"Then there are just a few specifics," Klist continued. "We have already discussed and agreed upon the Panama Canal situation. You can initiate that as soon as you return to the US. The Guantánamo Bay situation may take longer to arrange, if it is at all possible."

"So how do you inform me?" Welsh said, trying to focus on the form of Robert Klist. The sun was too bright and his eyes hurt.

"It's relatively simple," Klist explained. "Whenever we feel that there is a situation that we can exploit to your advantage, you will receive a telegram from Orlando, Florida. The message will always be the same. It will simply state 'Best of Luck' with the signature of a George Stratton. When you receive such a cable, you will pick up all the mail accumulated in Box 97 at the Highland Falls Post Office. Is that clear?"

Welsh nodded. "Clear. But what's in the mail?"

"You will find a tape cassette. The tape will contain our analysis of what situations we feel can be controlled, and an outline of what we feel you should present to the public. If it is presented as we suggest, we can almost guarantee that the results will be beneficial to your campaign. There can only be time for two or three situations prior to the election and we will choose them carefully. Of course, each situation is open for your acceptance or rejection. We are forcing nothing on you. This is simply the best method that we can devise to assist you."

"There's a name for this kind of thing," Welsh said, slurring the words. "It's Machiavellian. Heavy stuff." He looked past Klist, out over the aching bright landscape.

Klist made a throwaway gesture with his hand, silently discounting the idea. "It's not that easy, Clifford. I dislike the contrived as well as you do. But it's the essence of politics. And in this situation, the end results will be your election to the Presidency, and, ultimately, peace. This is what you want?"

Welsh nodded, knowing that Klist was right. Klist was always right.

"There is one other thing, Clifford," Klist said easily. "Your personal finances are barely adequate to support this campaign. Eventually, you will have contributions and federal funds, but initially it will be difficult. For this reason, I think it is necessary to discuss the South African gold shares."

Welsh's face turned toward Klist, his mouth opening in question, no words being formed.

Klist continued, raising his hand to forestall the question. "Your father made a very prudent investment in 1948. He lodged over 80,000 dollars with a solicitor in Johannesburg, and those funds were invested in shares of long-term quality mines. The shares have grown enormously in value. The dividends have also been reinvested. Their current worth is probably in excess of three million rand, which would convert to approximately three and a half million US dollars. Annual dividends are approximately 9 percent of that value. You are his sole heir as I understand it?"

Welsh was numb. "My father made no such investment, Klist! Yes, sure he believed in gold. He always fought for hard backing to our currency. But his estate would have shown some record—correspondence, things like that. No, Robert," he said angrily, somehow surfacing from beneath his languor, "this is money that you've planted. I'll accept your help but not the money."

Klist shrugged. "This is beyond my control. The investment was really made. The only plausible reason for the lack of records was that he probably wished this investment to remain outside the US for tax reasons. But the fact remains that these are your shares now. Of course, there is no compulsion on your part to use these funds. But I would think that they might be quite useful in the early stages of your campaign."

Klist withdrew an envelope from his briefcase and handed it to Welsh. "This envelope contains a list of your holdings, receipts for taxes paid in South Africa, and a general form of power of attorney from the solicitor's firm. There is currently a debt of approximately 12,000 rand owed in taxes. This can be easily paid from accumulated dividends, but the legal firm cannot act without your authorization, as your father's arrangements were canceled upon his death and the transfer of the shares into your name."

Welsh exploded. "Go to hell, Klist. You're expecting me to swallow all of this, aren't you? In approximately two minutes, you tell me that I have an estate worth 4 million dollars and then you want me to authorize a firm I've never heard of to pay out 12,000 rand. What sort of a game is this?" Welsh's face had reddened through the tan, and perspiration was staining the underarms of his cotton shirt in dark moons of moisture.

"Calm down, Clifford," the Russian said softly. "The letter in the envelope explains this fully. There are even photocopies of some of your father's original correspondence in there. I think you will find the signatures quite authentic. This information came to light when we were first investigating your background. My group has merely acted in your best interests in obtaining this information and passing it along to you. Believe me, there is nothing illegal about this affair. The investment was made as records will prove, and by law, the shares are yours."

Clifford Welsh dropped heavily back into his chair, his eyes closed. "Why, why in hell didn't my father tell me about this? The whole thing is insane. It wasn't like him to hide things from me." Welsh massaged his throat as if he had been strangled.

"I think that it is good not to question it," Klist said tonelessly. "As I remember, there was some legislation proposed around this time that would prohibit private citizens from carrying more than a nominal amount overseas; a type of currency-control situation such as they have in Great Britain. Of course, it never came about. But I think that this was what prompted your father to make the investment. A sort of self-replenishing fund outside US jurisdiction."

Welsh slowly shook his head, eyes closed. "No," he whispered, "I don't think my father would do something like that." Then he suddenly remembered the two small accounts in Canadian banks that had only come to light three years after his father's death. Perhaps it was possible.

Klist saw the indecision on Welsh's face and smiled. "I think it will work out, Clifford." He reached over and placed his hand on the older man's arm. "The money is yours to use as you wish. I think that it comes at a good time." He leaned back and laughed. "Maybe you will just quit politics and retire to, where is it that wealthy Americans retire to now, Palm Springs?"

Welsh smiled now, partially accepting the idea. "No. Definitely not Palm Springs." He paused, thinking. It was still an impossible thing to accept. Even a million would carry me through the initial stages of a campaign, he thought. And what if the money had come from Klist's group. They have demanded nothing, and there won't be anything to link them to me. It was clean with no strings. He looked up at Klist, who was toying with his glass. "I think that you're right, Robert," Welsh said with a thin smile. "The money does come at a good time, and I can use it in the initial stages. I suppose that I have my father to thank for it."

Klist's expression flickered briefly in amusement. "That's good, Clifford. Let me get both of us a drink."

The two men sat in silence for a long time, watching the progress of a volleyball game on the lawn below Klist's cottage. Welsh nursed the drink, still feeling dull and mentally disjointed. He thought about Judith and realized that since meeting Klist, he had barely spoken with her and that each night had been a long dreamless sleep. He felt as if all sexual drive had left him, and Judith had made no demands as if, she too, were filled with loggy inertia. Welsh thought back to the gold shares and attempted to mentally calculate the value of one day's dividends, but his mind balked at the task. God, I feel terrible, he thought listlessly.

Klist broke the silence. "Loss returns this evening from his sailing expedition?"

"Yes," Welsh answered, remembering that Loss knew nothing of the trip to Mexico for Klist. "I haven't told him as yet but the plane is fueled and serviced. There should be no problems. I think that you'll have to stop in Puerto Rico, however, rather than making a direct flight."

"How is that?" Klist said, scowling.

"The Mexican authorities are a little cool to unannounced arrivals by aircraft. We'll have to check with my pilot, but I believe that you'll need visas as well, besides whatever papers that are normally required for private aircraft."

"I think that stopping in Puerto Rico would be inadvisable," Klist remarked, lighting a Rothman. He exhaled, blowing the smoke in twin streams from his nostrils.

"I believe that the paperwork required should be straightforward. Why would you want to avoid stopping there?" Welsh asked, vaguely uneasy. He watched Klist tapping the nonexistent ash from his cigarette, the lighted end glowing in the wind.

"I think, Clifford, that there should be no record, officially that is, of our connection. Our presence here together is unremarkable. We're simply guests who have met. It's a small place. But your aircraft's entry into Puerto Rico would require a passenger manifest. Your aircraft might be recognized by the markings. I think that the press would be interested. No, Clifford, I would rather fly direct. I will cable my friends in Mexico tonight, and they will make the arrangements. We will be accepted without difficulty. Your pilot will drop me there and return the following day."

Welsh paused, thinking. "Why don't we arrange for commercial connections out of Trinidad, Robert? My Aztec could get you down there in less than an hour. You would be in Mexico City by late afternoon. Please don't misunderstand me. I'm only too happy to put the aircraft at your disposal. It's just that it seems—"

"Shit!" Klist snapped out the word like the report of a high-velocity rifle. Welsh was startled, almost dumbfounded. "Pardon my language," Klist said, the edge of impatience still on his voice. "But I have come here at great expense, much greater than you realize. The moral and financial commitments of my associates are enormous. And you are sitting here, pissing about the use of your aircraft.

"I need that aircraft to get to Mexico immediately. I don't want to go through normal immigration inspections, and I don't want to waste time. I am meeting two of my associates there. We will have a great deal of work to do in a very small space of time if you choose to go ahead with our plans for the Panama Canal." He paused, looking intently at Welsh. "You do plan to go ahead." He said it as a statement.

Welsh nodded.

"All right, Clifford. Then we will do this my way. I have told some of the other guests that I will be meeting a friend who owns a yacht at Union Island tomorrow. We will be taking a cruise in the islands. My wife will supposedly meet us in Grenada at some later date. All this will explain my departure. However, I will actually go to Union Island tomorrow with your pilot, and we will take off from there without a flight plan, directly for Mexico.

"I will be taking Mr. Bolken with me. You probably don't realize this, but Bolken is my personal guard and courier. Your pilot will supposedly take him to Martinique to catch a flight—just a small courtesy on your part. Do you understand thus far?"

Welsh nodded meekly.

"All right," Klist continued. "There are just two more things. I have drafted a simple note that states that you have met with me and independently expressed your desire to pursue the candidacy for the President, based on, among other things, your willingness to advocate unilateral disarmament. I must present some concrete evidence to my associates as confirmation of our discussions. This will enable them to go ahead in all matters that I have committed them to." Klist said this quickly and cleanly. The bottom line.

"And what if I should disagree? Who would see this document?"

"You have, and always will have, the option of ignoring these four days," Klist said. "The document will be shown to my associates in Mexico and then burned in my presence. It is just a formal confirmation from you of the acceptance of our aid. My word alone would not be sufficient for the importance and financial cost involved." He withdrew a single sheet of paper and a pen, laying them both before Welsh. It simply read:

> I, Clifford Tannis Welsh of New York, have met for three days with Robert Klist of the Netherlands. The subject of our discussions has been my decision to declare myself for the candidacy of the President of the United States in the forthcoming election, and to foster a policy of unilateral disarmament, both in my candidacy and, if elected, in my term of office. This decision has been made independently by me without offers of assistance and without coercion.
>
> Clifford T. Welsh

Welsh read it and reread it. He pushed the document aside and looked at Klist, his face now a dark form, the tan deep, the sun behind him.

"Publication of such a document would kill me politically," Welsh said, tapping the edge of the paper with his fingers.

Klist looked disappointed. He ran his finger down the bridge of his nose several times, his eyes now closed. At last he spoke, patiently and with exaggerated precision. "Clifford, public disclosure of the document would negate our hopes as well. I have explained its necessity. It says nothing, other than offering proof of a political course you intend to take. It is simply a key that opens a lock. With the lock opened, the key is thrown away."

Welsh looked steadily at Klist, their eyes meeting. Welsh picked up the document and signed.

Klist took the document, glanced at the signature, and folded it. In fewer than five days, this document would first be photographed and then placed in an underground storage vault at KGB headquarters on Dzerzhinsky Street in Moscow, filed there with the tape recordings and the photographs of Welsh and the Russian together.

Klist relaxed, allowing some warmth into his voice. "And if you wish, I can also return your power of attorney for the South African solicitors. This is up to you, but it should be returned as quickly as possible."

Welsh sighed and opened the envelope and scanned briefly through it. The photocopy of the letter from his father looked authentic, even the scrawl of the signature. He signed the enclosed power of attorney and passed it to Klist. "It would seem that I am committed, Robert," Welsh said. "I simply have to trust you."

Klist nodded and deposited both documents in his briefcase. The sum total of the tapes, photos, and now these documents would ensure future cooperation from Welsh, should that ever be necessary. Inflation is rampant these days, Klist thought. At one time, it only required thirty pieces of silver.

"Yes, and we shall have to trust you as well, Clifford," Klist answered, snapping the clasps shut on his briefcase.

Chapter 12

Sunlight spilled in splashes of gold across the weathered floor, the dark curtains breathing heavily in the wind. The century palms in the courtyard rustled in accompaniment, flicking fronds against the outer walls of their room. There was the sound of bare feet treading down the hallway outside their room and of ice clinking in a pitcher, and then the sound retreated toward the far end of the hall and down the stairs.

"Welcome home," she said, her fingers kneading the small of his back, pulling him into her. "Be still. Just lie like that. I want to be able to feel you for a long time."

He could look down into her eyes, vision blurred at this closeness. Just the tan and darkness of her face, her eyes closed, lashes impossibly long. The white and floral patterns of the pillow beneath her head gave an impressionistic background—abstract Gauguin.

An involuntary surge of desire traversed his frame, but he stilled it, thinking hard about not thinking. Her breasts were points against his chest. He bent his neck to find a hollow against her shoulder, lips against her ear. "This is Carriacou," he said, and she made a marginal nod, breathing more deeply, her exhalations coming in small shudders.

His back was wet with perspiration and felt alternately cool and warm from random gusts of wind and stillness. She moved her hands more strongly, holding his waist, pulling him against her. Tightly, not easing the pressure.

He started to move against her, unconscious of his own thrusts.

"Slowly," she said. Neither statement nor command. Just Holly warm and full, tasting of salt crystals. "Slowly," and her breath was growing more shallow. She started to move under him, no clear direction. More pressure than movement.

He thought of himself suspended in the sea, motionless; the hollow sound of breathing from tanks, the bubbles making bright patterns in the sunlight above. Green world. The vestiges of a deep Pacific swell reaching him at this depth and lifting him in rhythm. Kelp fanning in hazy yellows against the invisible waves. Out beyond the ring of sunlight, darkness.

The rafters creaked in the heat, an outboard humming in the bay. Small sounds without continuity reached his ears. Sounds she made, deep breathing, shallower breathing, sounds of moisture between their skin. Coarse sounds. He realized it was his own lungs drawing for air.

Her body convulsed in small shudders, her breath catching. Seas breaking at the crest but the longer Pacific swells keeping their measure of time, lifting and receding.

She convulsed again, her mouth pressed against his shoulder kissing the skin, saying little monosyllables, her closed eyes spilling tears, fingers tighter now against his back, probing.

"Now," she said. "Please now." And she closed her thighs, forcing her legs up between his, arching her back, cupping his buttocks and drawing him into her.

He came to her, holding her head in his hands, kissing her salty cheeks, saying things stored in the far corners of his mind.

The sun moved west along the sixth parallel, the barometer fell 3 millibars, and the tide checked to the east. During this time they slept and then awoke and made love to each other and slept again.

He awoke at 5:18 PM, arose from the mahogany four-poster, and went to the window overlooking the courtyard. Two blacks sat beneath the almond tree. They were playing checkers and drinking beer from dark green bottles, slamming the wooden men down hard, because that is the way a man shows his confidence in winning. He could hear the rattle of their board, their talk in low tones, and their laughter. The *Mintar* still lay anchored off shore, rolling languorously in the beam swell from Hillsborough Bay. Puffy afternoon cumulus were trooping along in the northern quadrant of the afternoon sky.

"Do you have to go?"

He turned to her. She lay stretched out, arching her feet, hands behind her head.

"Yes, soon," he replied. "Will you come with me?"

"You look funny standing there, speaking to me so seriously, your thing flapping around in the breeze." She brushed her hair from her eyes, laughing. "Men should go into battle naked. They'd be so terrified of having it cut off they'd never fight. But give them a pair of pants . . ."

"Will you go with me?" he asked again, annoyed, pleased, a little embarrassed.

"Yes. Don't you remember that I came to Carriacou to see a friend?"

They met the Kents in the bar below and ordered rum punch after signaling Giles to bring the dingy ashore. Margaret looked at their faces and smiled, knowing, and then to relieve their embarrassment, poured out her purchased treasures of hawksbill turtle bracelets and bric-a-brac. Kent filled in the gaps by telling them of the trip to the hospital up in the hills with the cannon on the front lawn overlooking the bay. Throughout the story, his eyes were laughing.

Giles came and they all had a second punch and then left for the yacht, taking turns rowing the inflatable dingy. By six, they were under way, beating back up the lee coast in light northerly winds.

The sun was setting as it does in the tropics, early and rapidly, leaving no twilight. The vaulted dome above them was streaked with cirrus, which splayed out from the north.

"Windy weather coming, Giles?" Kent asked, sweeping his hand across the sky.

Giles threw his cigarette to leeward and watched the sky thoughtfully, chewing on the corner of his lip. "I don't know," he answered. "We see so much high cloud down here in the winter. Usually means heavy weather further north. If I were in the English Channel, I'd be runnin' for a port." He looked again at the sky in the dying light. "Mare's tails, they're called. Usually what you see a coupla hundred miles in front of a cold front. North of that they'll be thunderstorms and low scud and plenty of rain." He ducked down the companionway, giving the helm to Kent. Five minutes later, he reappeared with a thermos of cocoa and some mugs. "Barometer's down over 6 millibars. Sure to be a front up north and likely to blow like hell tomorrow. Good day for workin' below."

Holly leaned against Loss, edging back against the cockpit coaming. He felt the warmth of her body through the thin material of her windbreaker. Shoving her fingertip into his ribs, she whispered, "If it rains tomorrow, we'll have to stay in bed all day."

He protested, groaning, but thinking of the two bottles of champagne still untouched in her duffel bag. "We could do crossword puzzles," he said, smiling, and she shoved her elbow into his stomach. He looked up to find Kent laughing behind the hand his wife had cupped over his mouth. Margaret was looking noncommitally astern. Good people to share good days with, Loss thought.

The twilight faded and merged into the blackness of the sea. Giles turned on the running lights and binnacle, casting his face in soft red shadows. The stars wheeled west in the dome above them, and they drank their cocoa in silence, listening to the wind and the chuckle of water under the bow, each of them content with the small moment of suspended time.

The *Mintar* tacked up through the reefs to the east of Carriacou, Giles taking bearings over the top of the compass on shore lights from Petit Martinique and Salt Whistle Cay. The yacht was making good time now, eating its way up to windward, chewing bites out of the northerly swell and spitting them out to leeward. They sailed into the anchorage with sheets started, the wind now going light and further into the north.

By 8:40, Giles had laid the sloop alongside the jetty and they wished him good night. He watched them disappear into the darkness beyond the jetty light and powered back to his mooring, taking time to lay out a second storm anchor and place additional gaskets on the sails. Work done on deck, he sat in the companionway, enjoying a final cigarette, and watched the stars in the northern quadrant of the sky become obscured, one by one, with the advancing storm.

The wind had backed into the north and he could feel a surge working its way into the protected anchorage. With the sensitivity of most men who sail alone, he noted the difference in the sound of the seas breaking on the windward reef. They now broke with muffled hollowness like the seas off Corsica before a winter storm.

The wind was coming now in puffs, with short lulls in between. Much drier now, he thought, noting that no dew had formed. And colder. He slipped below and lit the oil lamp which swung from its gimbaled brackets above the salon table. The barometer had paused in its downward race just before sunset, but it was falling again rapidly. The old receiver could barely pick up Miami's marine forecast for the Caribbean, and at the most, he could only hear a garbled voice between crashes of static.

Sighing, he lay out his oil skins on the starboard berth and undressed, setting his alarm for midnight. He would check the anchors then and try to get the Trinidad forecast.

"Bloody fucked-up business, this," he muttered to himself. He snuffed out the flame and eased his body into the narrow bunk.

Loss had seen the message tacked to his cottage door when they returned from Carriacou. On the following morning, he stood in Welsh's cottage, beads of water dripping from his foul weather gear.

Welsh didn't turn to greet him but instead stood by the plate glass windows, watching the channel to the south. The sea was flecked with white and the sky was overcast with black scud racing in from the northeast. Most of the yachts that had been anchored in the lee of the island had left for more protected anchorages, except for the *Mintar*, which was rolling heavily at her mooring.

Welsh sighed and turned to Loss. "Did you get the Barbados forecast?"

Loss pursed his lips and exhaled heavily. He wondered whether Welsh realized that forecasting on the western fringes of the Atlantic was largely dependent on aircraft and ship reports and that in this part of the world, such reports were relatively scarce. "Barbados says there's an extensive low pressure area to the north, coupled with a strong cold front. *Tiros* weather satellite shows extensive cloud cover from Trinidad to the Straits of Florida. Their barometer is down to nine nine two millibars, which is about the bottom of the barrel. They have no reading on winds aloft, and several of the commercial flights have been canceled. In short, the weather's marginal."

Welsh got up and paced the glass-enclosed veranda, looking out to the east. It was the type of day that travel agents don't talk about. He wished fitfully that he was away from this goddamn son-of-a-bitching place. Back up in his home on the Hudson, in the study working on something that he could grasp and control. "Brian, I have to put it this way. Klist is important to me. He has to get to Mexico today. I'm under a good deal of pressure to help him out. Can you make the trip?"

Loss watched the channel for some minutes. The surface wind looked at least 30 knots, and it would be a lot stronger aloft. There was bound to be some icing over the 15,000-foot level, and it would be rough as a cob. "Yes, I can make it," he said. "If not, I'll go into Puerto Rico and wait it out. They've got good instrument approaches into San Juan. But I'm telling you right now, the trip is going to be a real bastard."

Welsh poured himself another cup of coffee and sat down heavily in the chaise longue, spilling some of the liquid on his shirt. He didn't seem to notice. He drank the contents and set the cup down on the tile floor. "Brian, Puerto Rico's out. So is the Dominican Republic. Klist wants—I want you to make the flight direct. You've got plenty of fuel, and I know that we've made much longer trips together, even in bad weather. This trip is politically sensitive. I'm committed, and this trip to Mexico is crucial to the . . ." He paused, groping for words.

"Crucial to what for Christ's sake?" Loss injected, angrily. He was immediately sorry for the verbal punch. Welsh looked ten years older. Dark rings sagged in pouches beneath his eyes, and his tan was a sickly yellow. The perfectly cut hair was unkempt and dull. The man looked as if he were on drugs.

Welsh wheeled on him, his mouth gasping for words, his face flushing. "Loss, you stupid bastard. This is one of the most important things in my life. I pay your salary. I don't have to explain everything I do to you. This is tough enough for me without your kicking comments around."

"Look, *Mister* Welsh, the distance involved is roughly 1300 miles. Even with the long range tanks, it's going to be tight. And if I go direct, I've got no means of radio navigation. I could hit the coast of Mexico 100 miles either side of Cozumel. I'll go, but I'm going to first head for Santo Domingo and get a radio fix there and check the fuel remaining before I start tooling off over 700 miles of open sea. It's either that or I don't go."

Welsh pulled his hand through his hair and slumped back. "You're probably right, Brian. I talked to Klist, and he said that would probably be your reaction. He'll go along with that as long as you keep off the airways and maintain radio silence. If you have to refuel, he's got a place about 80 miles north of Haiti where you can land to get fuel. It's the southernmost of the Bahamas, a place called Great Inagua. The airstrip is unattended, but there's fuel available and he says that if necessary, you can make an instrument approach on the radio beacon. It's not much, but the island's dead flat. You're not going to run into any hillsides."

Loss stared at his employer. "You mean to say that you want me to make this flight without filing a flight plan? And how about Mexico? If I fly into there without clearance, they're going to confiscate the aircraft and put the whole lot of us in one of their fucking jails."

"Why don't you just shut up and listen," Welsh shouted. "Klist says that he has powerful friends down there. He's cabled them this morning and they're making arrangements. He'll use the long-range single-sideband radio to contact them once you're airborne and get confirmation on the clearance before you enter Mexican airspace. The Great Inagua alternative is also being taken care of. He apparently has strings that he can pull in Nassau. So just do like I say, Loss, or start looking for another job."

The anger was starting to rise in Loss's mind. Subconsciously, he tried to restrain it, thinking of the job, but somehow he knew that it was over. He walked over to Welsh and hunched down so that his face was inches away from Welsh's. "What's going on, Welsh?" he said in a hoarse whisper. "Are you running drugs or what? I can lose my license, not to mention spending a good ten years of my life in a Mexican clink."

Welsh started to say something and then closed his eyes, the strain on his face showing. He leaned back again and said, tonelessly, "Just do it, Brian. There's nothing immoral about the flight into Mexico. But this way Klist can't be linked directly to me. That's why the secrecy. I'm willing to give you a one-time bonus of five thousand for the trip." He paused, thinking and then said, "and this person Bolken will be going along. He's some sort of bodyguard or courier for Klist. God, I don't know what he is, but Klist wants it that way. Just get them there and come back the following day. I'll be ready to leave as soon as you return. This whole thing has been too much for me, and I want to get back to New York as soon as possible."

Loss stood up and looked down on the wasted man lying in the chair before him. He ground his teeth together, still angry and then came to a decision. "OK, Welsh. I'll take them. If anything goes wrong, you're the asshole that's going to bail me out. And once we get back to New York, you can start looking for a new pilot to haul you around." He hadn't intended to go this far, but the words lay like rotting fruit in the damp atmosphere of the room, leaving an unpleasant scent. Something you couldn't ignore.

Welsh stood up and looked at him with the contempt of an adult for a rude urchin. "Just fly the airplane, Loss. Klist will take care of the rest of it. And your resignation is gratefully accepted." He turned away from Loss toward the window and looked blindly out to sea, past the raindrops and smears of salt upon the glass.

Chapter 13

The trip from Salt Whistle Cay over to Union Island had been bad. The 4-mile stretch of channel, normally docile, was now a gigantic washing machine—waves slopping up at acute angles and seas breaking at random and without pattern. The helmsman yelled at Loss that it was because the tide was running against the direction of the wind and that there was no real problem. Klist had sat below in the cabin, smoking and reading an ancient *Newsweek* while Bolken hung over the rail, spewing out the remains of his breakfast. Some trip this is going to be, Loss thought.

Rather than going to the main dock in Clifton Harbor, Loss directed the helmsman to steer for the small jetty in the north end of the harbor that was next to the single strip runway. He didn't want to pass the Police Station, which would house the Customs and Immigration Officer as well.

By the time they landed, the rain was hosing down, visibility less than a quarter of a mile. Loss told the boatman not to wait. Mr. Klist was meeting friends here in Union, and he would be taking Mr. Bolken up to Martinique to catch an Air France flight. The black man smiled, cocooned in yellow foul weather gear, and swung away from the dock with a bark of the diesels that was almost smothered in the roar of rain.

The strip was deserted except for a flock of grounded seagulls that preened and pecked at the remains of a broken bag of garbage lying on the grass beside the runway. Loss could barely see the end of the half-mile strip, which terminated at the water's edge. Beyond that was the reef-protected harbor and he could hardly make out the indefinite forms of local trading schooners lurching uneasily at anchor and heeling heavily in the harder gusts.

He herded them into the aircraft, stuffing most of the luggage in the aft compartment, along with their saturated foul weather gear.

Bolken took the back seat, now silent and highly nervous. Despite the sopping condition of his clothes, Loss could smell the stink of fear on Bolken's person. This cabin is going to smell like an overripe mango, he thought, watching Bolken store the camera case. "Strap that thing down with the spare seat belt," Loss said snappishly.

"It's going to be rough?" Bolken said, his eyes worried.

Loss didn't answer, only giving Bolken a wolfish grin and nodding.

Loss eased the seat forward and ran through the checklist. Klist sat in the right front seat, quietly uninterested and yet familiar with the cockpit environment and procedures. He had insisted on taking this position, saying that he had the frequencies and procedures for entering Mexican airspace and would need access to the single-sideband radio. Loss agreed, glad that this part of it would be off his back. He gave Klist a briefing on the radio's operation. Klist indicated that he had operated equipment similar to this and that it would be no problem. Loss shrugged and started the engines.

Minutes later, the Aztec lifted off the runway and accelerated, the gear sucking up into the fuselage. The aircraft flashed out over the harbor, the stubby masts of a schooner disappearing beneath the nose as Loss banked toward the north. He reduced power and rpms for best rate of climb and eased the nose of the aircraft up. Slowly, he milked up the flaps and completed post-takeoff checklist. Below, Loss caught one last glimpse of an offlying reef, smothered in waves from the heavy, rolling sea, and then the aircraft was swallowed by the ragged scud.

On instruments now, Loss carefully trimmed out the aircraft and turned up the panel lights. Heavy rain was rattling against the canopy and the air was turbulent.

Klist leaned over and spoke into Loss's ear. "Pitot heat on?" More angry with himself than Klist, he flicked on the heating element for the airspeed probe, an item he had missed in the checklist. With the probe iced over, he would lose all indications of airspeed, and there was bound to be ice once they had climbed through the freezing level.

Loss looked over at Klist who sat in relaxed composure, watching the instruments. He knew before he asked the question. "Do you fly, Mr. Klist?"

Klist didn't answer, but there was the barest trace of a smile on his lips.

They climbed for half an hour through alternate layers of cloud and rain showers. The turbulence was wild at times, slamming the aircraft in its tracks with hammer blows. Loss donned oxygen at 12,000 feet and instructed them to do the same. At 18,000 they broke out into a blue valley tucked between towering cumulonimbus. He flew the aircraft up through the valley, topping most of the cloud structure at 22,000 feet, their ice-crystaled anvils trailing away in the upper levels of the jet stream.

Loss set the autopilot on a heading of northwest and retrimmed the aircraft for level flight, easing back power and mixture settings for maximum range. The indicated airspeed settled on 145 knots, and fuel flow was running a little higher than he had expected. This would be cutting it very fine. He switched to outboard wing tanks and started timing the fuel flow, determined to squeeze every last drop of fuel from the cells.

"It would seem to me as if you're rather far north of course, Captain Loss," Klist said, holding the oxygen mask back from his lips. He gave an innocent smile and tapped the directional gyro with his fingertips.

"Look, Klist. *Mister* Klist. This trip sucks, and I'm not a fucking airline captain. I'm keeping north of course in case we have to go in somewhere to refuel. Until I can get some reliable radio reception off the Dominican Republic or Haiti, I don't have a clue as to our drift or ground speed. Without that, I'm not turning this pile of junk west toward Mexico. We're pushing the range as it is."

Klist sat slumped in his seat with half a smile before answering. He took a deep breath from the mask and then said, "Yes, I understand, ah, *Mister* Loss. I think that might be wise. As you probably have guessed, I fly as well. Several thousand hours of multi-engine time. But hold your proper heading. I want to stay well south of Puerto Rico's approach control radar. A fix off the Dominican Republic will be quite sufficient." Klist clamped the mask back over his face, sucking on the oxygen, as serene as if he were on a flight between Boston and Washington. The period of time off oxygen seemed to have no effect on him, even at this altitude, Loss observed. The perfect Aryan type, he thought; Klist sat there composed, hair still damp but neatly combed, his nose straight and perfectly formed. And his ice-blue eyes were never still.

Loss swung in his seat to look at Bolken to make sure the man was using his oxygen mask properly. Bolken returned the look, without apparent emotion, his mask concealing his lips, the muscles of his cheeks taut. Congenial couple, this pair, Loss thought sourly.

Loss adjusted number one VOR to Ponce, Puerto Rico. The needle deflected erratically and then recentered, the warning flag exposed to show the reception unreliable. He tried Santo Domingo, and this time raised some indication. He plotted and found, surprisingly enough, that the bearing matched the flight plan with some degree of accuracy. Klist looked sideways at him, his eyes gently reproachful, smiling under his mask. Loss shrugged and noted the time of the bearing, planning to check it again in ten minutes for a rough running fix.

"Do you mind?" Klist asked, pointing to the HF single-sideband radio. Easing his mask into a more comfortable position, Loss shrugged.

"I think that it would be wise if I alerted my people in Mexico," Klist said. "They'll be listening for us and can set up our entry into Mexican airspace."

"It's all right by me, Klist. You seem to know a lot more about this flight than I do. If you have such great contacts, how about getting a weather briefing for Cozumel and a check on their radio beacon. I've found that Mexican navaids are about as reliable as their tap water. But bear in mind that we're not committed as yet. I still want that fix."

Klist nodded, listening to Loss as if he were an anxious child; nodding but not caring. Consulting a notebook, Klist carefully dialed in 6.2893 megahertz and tuned the set carefully. He called briefly in German and waited. A reply came back in English almost immediately.

"Go ahead Zulu Four, over."

"Shifting, over." Klist replied and reached down, readjusting the synthesizer for a frequency 10 kilohertz down and switching to lower sideband.

There was a pause of three or four seconds and a different voice came back, slightly stronger, warped slightly by a slight frequency drift. "Situation and position, Zulu Four. Fox Alpha listening."

Klist shifted frequency again, changing to upper sideband and spoke rapidly in German. The speaker rasped again, this time in yet another voice, replying in German. Klist shifted frequency and sideband again and on all subsequent transmissions, finally terminating the communication with three clicks of the mike key.

As if such procedure were entirely normal, he shut down the set and replaced the mike. He scanned his notes and relaxed back into his seat, now with his mask replaced, breathing deeply on 100 percent oxygen.

Loss sat for some moments, feeling the first prickles of the fear that is bred of uncertainty. A feeling he had last in a C-47 gunship flying north over the DMZ years ago. Klist was no businessman. It was doubtful that he was anything approaching legitimate. Certainly Welsh was implicated in something well over his gullible head. The job was blown at any rate, and it would be better to get this mess on the ground and sort it out from there. He glanced sideways at Klist and found him relaxed with eyes closed. Loss edged into the gentlest of turns, the instruments hardly reflecting the bank, only the sun shifting slowly across the canopy. The Dominican Republic was somewhere on the right wing, moving slowly under the nose.

"Why are you changing course, Loss?" Klist said as he lifted the mask from his mouth. "You will destroy the running fix on Santo Domingo. Get back on your heading, ah, three-four-three degrees, I believe. I have a full weather briefing. We will be getting more of a tailwind as we get further west. Our terminal forecast is three thousand scattered over Cozumel, wind 30 degrees at 18 knots. The fix will give us some idea of our fuel remaining, and *we* can make the decision then. I would like to point out that we are flying into improving weather with a favorable tailwind and a good terminal forecast. What are you frightened of?" Klist then turned to Bolken and spoke to him in muted tones, clearly to keep Loss from understanding. Loss slowly turned back to his heading and noted his watch. Three minutes to run before he could get the other leg of his fix. With that information, he could plot a heading for Santo Domingo. The weather did seem to be slightly improved to the west but the indefinable suggestion of danger still rankled at his subconscious. The suggestion of Klist's, hinting at fear, was real, but it is only those men who have no fear who fly into mountains on dark nights.

At the end of three minutes, Loss centered the VOR needle and read off the bearing and carefully plotted it. Klist leaned over his seat, watching carefully. The legs of the two bearings fell 110 miles south-southwest of Islo Alto Velo, a small island on the southwestern tip of the Dominican Republic. Loss spent several minutes with the hand calculator, working out fuel consumption and fuel remaining. He finally turned to Klist, showing him the results.

"It's marginal. I estimate that this gives us no more than twenty-five minutes of reserve fuel over Cozumel at our present ground speed. Before you say it, I'm not buying your forecast. I know how poor forecasts can be, even in the US. We're going to get fuel in the Dominican Republic. I want to call Welsh and ask him a few questions as well. This whole thing is illegal, and although I'm not concerned about your affair with Welsh, I'm not going to jeopardize either my license or your lives. If Welsh doesn't like it, he can go to hell. I've already told him that I'm dropping this job when we get back to the US."

Klist sat looking at his notes. He then took the folded Enroute Low Altitude Chart and scanned it casually, then replaced it neatly in the clipboard. "Perhaps, Brian, this can be settled without either of us getting upset. Santo Domingo is now behind us. Head for Haiti but let's delay in calling their approach control radio. I think I can convince you of a better alternative."

"It better be damn good," Loss said and selected the frequency of the VOR station in Port-au-Prince, Haiti. Klist had turned and was speaking to Bolken in guarded tones. The consultation was one-sided; Klist in clipped sentences dictating, Bolken grunting acceptance.

Port-au-Prince VOR was starting to show some indications of life on the indicator head and Brian corrected slightly to the north. He waited for Klist to make his pitch, sure that he would push for the Great Inagua alternative.

Klist pulled the mask back from his lips and spoke. "Look here, Loss. You are correct in probably assuming that I'm not a Dutch businessman. But I do represent a group of people who are interested in assisting Senator Welsh in his forthcoming campaign. How we do this is immaterial, but I assure you that it will be in the best interests of both Senator Welsh and your country. But by virtue of the fact that we are European, this assistance must be kept secret. Do you understand what I am saying?"

Loss nodded, believing nothing but listening.

"For this reason," Klist continued, "this flight must be kept quiet. I can assure you that we are not smuggling anything or engaging in any deceptive practice. The Mexican authorities are fully aware of our flight. I cabled my friends in Mexico last night, and as you can see," Klist said, indicating the long range radio, "we are in radio contact with them."

"I anticipated the possibility of a refueling stop, and I have selected Great Inagua Island. This is just 70 miles north of Port-au-Prince. It has a 5000-foot paved runway and a radio beacon you can home on. There is plenty of fuel there and the problems with authorities will be minimal."

"Where is this place?" Loss said.

Klist picked up the Enroute Chart for the Caribbean and pointed to a speck north of Haiti. The island had only one settlement, Mathewtown, and the airport was 4 miles further north along the coast.

Loss expelled his breath. His throat was dry from the oxygen, and he had the start of a headache. He turned to Klist and said, "OK, I'll go along with it. But I want a couple of things understood. First of all, if there are any problems with the local authorities, you're responsible. Secondly, I want you to get on that damned radio and call your friends. By the time we get within 100 miles of Mexico, I want an official clearance from the Mexican Air Traffic Control people to enter their airspace. Understand?"

Klist lifted his hands and dropped them again into his lap in a gesture of decision. "Agreed. I'm going to use your radio again." Without further discussion, Klist switched on the single sideband and called on the last used frequency, again in German.

The reply was almost immediate. The frequency change procedure went into effect again, and Loss realized that with this routine, the chance of anyone monitoring the transmissions would be greatly minimized by the continual alterations of frequency; an effective, makeshift form of scrambling.

This time, Klist's tone was more urgent. There was a delay of several minutes in answer to one of Klist's questions. He finlly signed off and finished writing in his black leather notebook. "My friends say that it is all arranged. You need only contact Cozumel Tower on one-one-eight-point-one when we are 100 miles out, and they will clear you for the approach. You may remain there overnight and return tomorrow. As far as Great Inagua is concerned, I will deal with the local authorities." He patted the wallet in the breast pocket of his jacket and smiled.

"You must have some organization," Loss said, gritting his teeth. "What are you, Klist? German?"

The Russian shrugged. "Does it make any difference, Mr. Loss? It's all in a good cause." He placed the oxygen mask back over his face and breathed deeply.

Loss switched back to the main tanks and prepared for the descent. The weather beneath them had altered little in appearance. There was still an unbroken cloud deck beneath them with high towers of black storm cells probing up through the lesser battlements. He wondered how low the ceiling would be over the sea. Since Great Inagua had no control tower, he would have no way of knowing at what altitude the Aztec would break out of the overcast. If it was anything like this morning, it would be less than 300 feet, but still time enough to get everything squared away for an approach.

He removed the mask and turned to Klist. "I'm going to call Port-au-Prince Approach Control for an altimeter setting and local weather. It should give us some idea of the Mathewtown weather."

Klist sucked the oxygen mask, shaking his head. He removed it and said, "I can well understand where you got your last name, Brian. I keep telling you that we have to minimize our contact with normal air traffic control. If you called them, they would want your registration number, position, and destination." He tapped the VOR indicator with his pencil. "We're almost into Haitian airspace now. It's best that we avoid their radar. Start your descent out to the west and then turn north toward Mathewtown. You can home in on their radio. In this way, we'll stay well out of radar contact with Port-au-Prince, and you'll be letting down over the open sea without any mountains to worry about. However, it wouldn't be a bad idea to monitor the Haitian Approach Control frequency. You might pick up their weather if they're in contact with other aircraft."

Loss nodded. You're just too cute for words, he thought and eased into a turn to the west.

They descended, power back to the stops, the aircraft sinking at over 2000 feet per minute; Port-au-Prince Approach Control frequency silent. Loss tried to estimate the probable altimeter error. If the ceilings in this area were down to about 300 feet over the sea, he would have enough time to level off after breaking out of the overcast. Goddamned fool, he thought.

The Aztec plunged into the murk of a rainshower, the turbulence shaking the aircraft. Loss eased in nose-down trim, trying to keep the airspeed near the top of the airspeed indicator's green arc, retaining control against a stall and yet keeping a safe margin against excessive speed. He adjusted the panel lights to full bright and sank his seat to its lowest position, sweeping the instruments and ignoring the black shroud of sky beyond the windshield.

He could hear retching from the back seat. The stench of vomit would be unbearable when they removed their oxygen masks.

The radio spattered suddenly with an unreadable voice.

The reply was fragmented by heavy static: "—— showers, ——derstorm to the west. Current alt—niner —— five. Wind north at forty gusting fif—"

Loss could feel the shirt soaking on his back, his armpits saturated. A small rivulet of sweat trickled down the edge of his rib cage. The weather could be solid crap right down to the deck, he thought. Wind very strong in the north, and the altimeter setting could be anyone's guess.

He estimated that they were well to the west of Port-au-Prince now, descending rapidly. No time to tune in the ILS for Port-au-Prince now, but the presence of another aircraft to the west, setting up for an instrument approach was a terrifying thought. The odds were enormous against a mid-air collision, but the nightmare persisted.

Passing through eight thousand now. He richened the mixture and eased in slightly more power, checking the rate of descent to 1500 feet per minute.

"Set in the frequency for Great Inagua," he shouted into Klist's ear, the rain hammering against the windshield in a continuous staccato of gunfire. Loss didn't bother to look at Klist, using his eyes to scan the instrument panel. But a hand reached for the ADF radio, set in a frequency, and selected a switch on the audio mixer panel. The faint beat of a frequency punctuated the precipitation hash and coughing static of his speaker; the code identification was unreadable.

Through five thousand now and the rain, if possible, was worse, tricklets of water now forcing through the weather seals of the windows.

The Aztec was suddenly slammed upwards in a bowel-wrenching blow, the G-forces sagging their cheeks, their arms leaden with the sudden weight. The altimeter which had been unwinding in their descent, shuddered and started to climb like some clockworks gone berserk. The instruments once stable, shuddered and blurred with vibration.

Loss pulled back the power to idle-cutoff and still they rose in the core of the storm cell, the rain now mixed with rattles of hail, the aircraft porpoising and rolling erratically. No control movement seemed to dampen the wild tumbling of the Aztec.

Someone or something was shouting in the back seat, a fist beating against his seat.

Fly attitude, he thought. Forget everything else but the attitude indicator. The mask was suffocating, not supplying enough oxygen, and Loss flung it from his face. The control yoke tore from his grip, slamming his knuckles. He grabbed it again, this time with both hands, trying to cushion the shocks, concentrating all his energy and mind on the translation of a simple white bar in a glass-covered cage into some semblance of order for his universe.

The hail intensified, becoming a torrent of sound. Loss thought briefly of damage to the wings, of hail impacting against the thin-skinned aluminum, pounding it into aerodynamic mush. The altimeter blurred through 16,000 feet.

At least we are going up, he thought, and then they went down. The Aztec didn't falter in its climb. It was squashed like a bug with a flyswatter, and then it fell in a waterfall of wind, tumbling over cataracts, smashing against invisible cliffs of air.

The stall warning horn was shrieking in Loss's ears, and the alternator failure light illuminated. His mind registered this, but it seemed trivial. The negative G-forces had scattered map cases, pencils, sunglasses, and trash throughout the cockpit. Klist had lost his Prussian-like composure and was screaming things at Loss in some language, not German, not English.

The vertical velocity indicator was bottomed out at 6000-feet-per-minute down, the needle hard against its peg. Trying twice to reach the throttle quadrant and both times nearly losing control of the aircraft, Loss yelled at Klist, the sound puny in the bedlam of noise. "Give me full power. I can't take my hands off the controls."

Klist stared at him wildly, both hands gripping the central windshield support, trying to dampen the shocks against his body.

Loss screamed at him again. "Klist! The fucking throttles!"

Klist started to react, reaching down to the mixture controls, pulling them back, shutting off the flow of fuel to the engines. The right engine quit immediately, windmilling. The left engine was beginning to stammer.

"Oh, Christ," Loss screamed, smashing his right elbow against Klist's face, forcing him to release his grip on the engine mixture controls. He caught a strobe image of Klist in a lightning flash, blood streaming from his nose and mouth. Klist was howling, his hands pressed against the cabin ceiling, trying to stabilize himself against the buffeting.

The Aztec was yawing heavily to the right, nose high. The right wing dropped, and the Aztec started to spin. In desperation, Loss let go of the yoke with his right hand and slammed the throttle, prop, and mixture controls to full forward position in one sweep of his hand. The Aztec heaved up on her right wingtip, one engine howling to redline and the other backfiring explosively. He rammed the yoke full forward and stood on the left rudder, praying.

The airspeed was beginning to build up rapidly, the altimeter a blur. A lot of hail was impacting against the aircraft now, the sound incredible. Like a truckload of pots falling down an elevator shaft. The turn and bank indicator centered and he eased off the rudder control and pulled back on the power. The spin was broken, but airspeed was building up to maximum allowable—the *never exceed* velocity. Loss started to pull back on the controls, easing the aircraft out of its terminal dive. Still a lot of lightning but the hail was gone, replaced by rain sluicing over the windshield with the pressure of a firehose.

He could feel the G-forces pressing down on him, his face and body tissue sagging under the excessive load. Turbulence less now, he thought, straining to keep his sagging eyelids open, looking for a brief flash of open ocean that he would see a microsecond before impact. Something cracked behind him, and then with an explosive roar, the left rear passenger side window blew out, sucking papers and dust through the opening. Loss was conscious of the sound, but it meant nothing. His eyes flicked down to the altimeter now and watched it unwind through a thousand feet. We're far beyond structural limits, he thought abstractly, but the airspeed was bleeding off. It's worth a try, he thought and hit the flap switch.

The flaps partially extended, slowing the airspeed further and creating lift at a speed 40 knots beyond safe extension speed. The flap motor jammed against the pressure and the circuit breaker blew. But it saved Loss 200 feet of altitude that he would have otherwise lost.

The aircraft slowly eased up into nearly level flight, airspeed rapidly decaying. He felt the buffeting of an accelerated stall. Although he added more power, the aircraft was still sinking.

They broke through the overcast and then were immersed in low stratus again. He glanced down at the altimeter, knowing that it would be in error. It showed something over 400 feet, still unwinding. He had full power in now, and still they were sinking. The Aztec flew out from beneath the overcast again and Loss looked down, horrified to see the wavetops cresting less than 50 feet beneath him. The controls were heavy and he retrimmed, checking to ensure that he was pulling full power. The right engine was running 400 rpm low and he couldn't get anything more out of it. The left was a sweet, steady roar.

Most of the circuit breakers were blown, and he shoved them in with the heel of his hand. Two popped immediately but the alternator warning light extinguished and the radio was coming to life.

He tried to get the flaps up, but the breaker kept blowing. The aircraft was just holding its own now, shuddering on the edge of a stall, but still flying. He chanced a look down at the black sea, each crest frothy and breaking off into spray driven by the storm's wind. The troughs were rippled silk, slick and green between the breaking seas.

He could hear retching from the back seat over the roar of the wind. Klist was upright now, looking over the cowling at the sea below. The blood was a dark stain against his face, the perfect complexion flawed. He stabbed his finger at the side window, indicating the wing. Loos looked and saw the top surface and leading edges coated in rough, irregular ice. That's why she won't fly, he thought. Beside the sheer weight of the ice, the irregular surface was destroying the lift. He checked the deicing equipment and found the circuit breaker blown. He reset it and this time it held.

"Get this thing to land, Loss." Klist's voice was cracked, hoarse from screaming.

Loss scanned the instrument panel and searched the horizon again, a small gray bowl of breaking sea and rain. "I can keep this flying, Klist, but you've got to do some of the work. Get me Port-au-Prince VOR and retune the ADF for Great Inagua. Trim in some left rudder, but, dammit, do it slowly. This thing is hanging right on the edge."

There was a tearing sound from the right wing, and the Aztec yawed suddenly left, Loss automatically compensating with rudder.

Klist shouted something, gesturing toward the wing on his side. A large patch of clear ice had broken away in the warmer air, leaving the wing stripped of paint. The leading edge was a mass of hammered metal unrecognizable from the indentations caused by hail.

"The radios, Klist," Loss shouted. "Just get the radios."

Despite Klist's repeated attempts, the VOR remained dead, the circuit breaker unwilling to reset. The ADF needle showed life, hunting in the general direction of the left wing tip. The code identification was faint but now readable. "That's Mathewtown," Klist said, more composed. "Turn now." The imperial imperative.

"We wait until some of the ice breaks off the left wing, you stupid bastard," Loss said, not looking away from the sea's horizon. "If we turn now, we could dig in a wing tip. Look, the airspeed is up 5 knots. Just relax and do what I tell you to. The engine exhaust-gas analyzer is on your side of the panel. Give me the temperatures for each cylinder of the right engine. It's running ragged as hell."

Klist slowly selected each position, giving the temperature. All but two of the cylinders were overheating, but not badly. Oil pressure low, oil temperature high but in the green. The Aztec flew, just barely, hugging the waves, searching for the cushion of ground effect that would reduce the drag on its tattered airframe. He tried to turn toward the direction of Great Inagua and found he could, using just the smallest increment of bank. The turn took over four minutes.

Ice was beginning to shed off the wings now, and Loss was able to gain over 100 feet of altitude. Life was looking better, he thought. If only the damn right engine would hold together.

They flew on toward the island, slowly gaining altitude. The wave pattern beneath them was changing, becoming more confused but less dangerous looking. Loss realized that his body was aching from the strain of searching ahead for land.

Two bosunbirds flashed by beneath the left wing tip, and the sea took on a yellow cast. Bits of weed from the storm indicated nearby land.

The ice was gone now from the aircraft, the load lighter, but the battered wings were barely providing lift. Loss had maintained power and slowly climbed to 200 feet, just brushing the base of the scud above them.

Out of a rain shower, the shore suddenly appeared: a ragged beach bursting with spray; a single street with frame buildings lining it. They swept by the single radio tower and altered course to the northwest. Brown flats beneath them now. One lone donkey bowed in the rain, rump toward the wind. To the south now, along the coast, the dish antennas of Cable and Wireless appeared and then the runway swept beneath them.

"Tuck in now. Belts on tight." Loss adjusted the power and cycled the flap motor circuit breaker. Useless. He swept out to sea in a wide, flat turn, the aircraft shuddering.

The runway straightened in front of them, 2 miles away. They had only 50 feet of altitude.

"There's a tremendous crosswind and I can't get this thing any slower. When I drop the gear, it's going to produce one hell of a lot of drag. So it's a one-time shot. Klist, when I say 'gear' you drop it and keep your finger on the circuit breaker. If it doesn't extend, we belly it on. Get out as soon as we stop moving."

The Aztec bored down final approach, bucking gusts of 50 knots. Crabbing into the wind to offset drift, the aircraft approached the runway, which was pooled with water and slick black in the failing light. Full power now and the engines shrieked with pain, badly overboosted. The shore was under the wing and Loss called "gear."

The wheels swung outward on their undercarriage, locking seconds before they met the pavement. He chopped the throttles and slammed the nose gear to the asphalt, braking and steering, forcing the aircraft to hold to the centerline. But with diminishing airspeed, the rudder and steering became less effective, and the Aztec entered a series of skidding turns to the left, into the slamming crosswind.

No runway remained now, and Loss savagely applied full left brake. The aircraft drifted into a groundloop, shreading tires; the magnesium rims ignited in a curving trail of flame. Screams now and then silence.

Chapter 14

Loss opened his eyes and closed them again quickly, the intensity of the white-hot sun too great to bear. He ached in some indefinite sort of way, pain overlapping consciousness. Nerve endings dull, no report from the outer periphery. Someone-thing pressing down on his head. Sinking down into the green depths again, bubbles from his mouth drifting upward. He felt the surge of Pacific rollers fanning the sea grass. Like her golden hair. Like fields of wheat in the wind. The wind hot, though. Very dry. The sun, illuminating the waters overhead, just gave brightness to the green depths. He pushed the throttles forward to go higher into the sunlight, but they didn't respond. Very sluggish. Green again. Darker.

His eyes opened again, the sun very small and then a dark shadow. A smell like vodka. An insect stung him as he walked through the field of wheat and he lay down to smell the earth and sleep. And sleep.

A long time of darkness and light and pain. The gunship smelled of carbonic acid. Harris was sitting beside him coughing up blood. The gooney bird was barely flying, and his muscles ached with the effort of holding the controls. Right main gear not down. Someone on the interphone calling him.

"Loss?" The voice female. "Mister Loss?"

He wanted to tell them to shut up. Too much effort. They're dead back there anyway. The whole airplane dead, dying. Burning. Ice on the wings. Have Klist get the gear down.

"Gear down now," he said with great effort, all in slow motion. The sound of his own voice hollow in the interphone, very distant.

His arm hurt again. A burning pain and he heard a door close. The instruments blurred into blackness.

"He come around again," the nurse said, dropping the hypodermic into an autoclave.

The matron nodded and made a notation in the ward book.

"Just three cc's and tetracycline now every twelve hours. Dr. Detrick will prescribe oral medication for the pain. Did he speak, Nurse Wylie?" the matron said, looking up from the desk, tapping the pen against her logbook.

"Yes, mum. Something about gear." The nurse stood there awkwardly, wanting to be dismissed. The white uniform framed and accentuated the blackness of her skin. It was past 2:00 AM. There would be tea for her in the nurses' pantry.

The matron tapped the pen impatiently again, a small tattoo of sound in the silent corridor. The night was sultry, dampness on everything. Insects beat against the screened window, flinging themselves at the single dim light within. The matron sighed, wishing she were in Nassau again, cool and efficient within the air conditioned sanctum of Princess Margaret Hospital. Not here in the Out Islands, with these ignorant people.

She lifted her 190 pounds of bulk in the wicker chair, feeling betrayed by the same black skin that linked her to the girl standing before her, fidgeting like some nervous child.

"Stand properly," the matron said sharply.

"Yes, mum."

"I will tell you for the last time, Nurse Wylie. You are to address me as Matron. You are not my domestic." She sighed, a blend of impatience and resignation, mentally promising herself to apply for transfer back to Nassau—the eighth attempt.

She looked up at the young girl and spoke, her voice mechanical, precise, "Before you go off duty, see to it that the night porter wakes up Dr. Detrick promptly at seven and that he is informed of the white patient's condition. See to it also that Mr. Campbell is informed. He is staying in the government guest house. Dismissed."

The young girl nodded quickly and stepped backwards into the darkness of the corridor, away from the dim pool of light that highlighted the tapping pen of the matron.

Then she turned and walked quickly down the scrubbed wooden floor of the hospital, anxious for the night to be through.

"Fat black bitch," she thought and grimaced.

"I take it that you shouldn't be smoking, Loss." The speaker lifted nonexistent creases with thumb and forefinger and sat heavily in the chair by the window.

"Therefore I shan't offer you one. Rotten things, anyway. Do you mind if I do? No, of course not. Probably smells good. Back with the living, I mean."

The short man tapped a filtered Dunhill against his wrist and placed it between his pursed lips. His hawk-like nose, florid complexion, and the cigarette between his lips gave the illusion of a bird eating a worm. He lit it and inhaled, holding the smoke in his lungs with obvious relish.

Brian Loss lay back against the pillows, not caring who or what this man was. Pain still pulsed through his body, even though the drugs muted it. Twenty-two stitches, the nurse had said, from the bridge of his nose to his right ear. His head was pounding and he felt nauseous. His forearm was burning and oozing beneath the dressings.

"Can't we do this later?"

"I'm sorry, Mr. Loss. I should go away and I will do so as quickly as possible. But I must talk with you before the police do. In your best interest, of course." The florid-faced man tapped the cigarette onto the windowsill, spilling ash across his shirt.

Loss tried to place the stout Englishman and failed. The man had the face of a drinker, burst capillaries beneath the skin, the eyes pouchy, eyelids flickering nervously. Well-trimmed hair, though, and long in a way that the English had always favored.

Brian shaded his eyes against the early morning glare. His right arm hurt like hell.

"Pull the blind, please. The brightness hurts my eyes," he said.

"Yes, of course." And with surprising grace, the visitor leaned over the arm of the chair and drew the blind. The armpits of his white shirt were already dark with perspiration.

"Yes, Mr. Loss," he said, easing back into the chair, "we haven't met. My name is Campbell. Ian Campbell. Of her Majesty's Government. Rather unofficial, of course. The Bahamas is no longer a colony, and I am here on their sufferance."

Loss sighed, tired beyond anything he could recall. He closed his eyes and said, "What branch of the government, Mr. Campbell. Civil aviation, police, what?"

"No, not that at all, Mr. Loss. I expect that I should bring you up to date, all right?" Loss nodded, listening, eyes partially open. His chest was hurting now. The drug's effects probably subsiding.

Campbell resumed. "You crashed off the end of the runway here six days ago. Here, of course, being Mathewtown."

Loss started opening his eyes wide. He attempted to sit up and nearly passed out with the pain.

Campbell made a restraining gesture, his palm flat and down, fingers dark with nicotine. "No, no, Mr. Loss. Please relax. No one has died. You're the primary casualty and you'll live. But the authorities are quite cross with you." He held up his left hand and ticked off his fingers, "One, possession of a firearm, two, stealing an aircraft, three, prohibited narcotics, although I think they'll drop that charge, which, in truth, should be lodged against your friend, Bolken."

Loss groaned, "What in Christ's sake are you talking about? Yes, I carry a firearm in my briefcase. I always have. But I don't carry drugs, and I was directed to make this flight by my employer. I was carrying Bolken and Klist to . . ." He paused, almost having said "Mexico" and thought better of it.

"Who is Klist?" Campbell said carefully, withdrawing a pen from his shirt pocket, rummaging in the pants for a notebook which he withdrew. "Spell the name."

"Klist," Loss replied, impatiently. "K-L-I-S-T. What does he call himself now, and where's Bolken?"

Campbell was silent for a minute, carefully lighting another cigarette from the glowing tip of the first one. He inhaled and coughed, the deep, liquid cough of a man courting emphysema.

"No, Mr. Loss," Campbell said carefully. "There were no passengers other than Bolken. They found you both still in the aircraft, your face smashed into the panel. You took a severe concussion plus a nasty gash across your forehead. One broken rib as well. Bolken was in the right seat, face badly cut. The aircraft had caught fire but apparently an explosion in one of the fuel cells blew the fire out. The rain did the rest. No one got to the airport for probably ten minutes after the crash. It's unattended as you know."

The window blind rattled in the wind, and Loss could hear the low-frequency throb of what was probably a large diesel generator. Footsteps came and went in the hallway, muffled voices in the next room.

"What is your position in this, Mr. Campbell?" he asked, laying his head back into the cleft of the pillow, eyes closed.

Campbell pulled the chair closer to the bed, the feet of the chair grating over the rough floor. He replied in a lowered voice, so close that Brian could smell the staleness of his breath, "Loss. We may not have a lot of time. The local surgeon should be here at any minute. Basically, I am with a division of Her Majesty's Service concerned with the movement of aliens of undesirable political habits within the United Kingdom and even within the Commonwealth. I followed the man you call Bolken from England to Barbados and lost him there. Three, no four days ago it was, the Bahamian authorities contacted Interpol with Bolken's prints. Incidentally, he claims to be Dutch. My department surveys these messages as a routine since political activities sometimes parallel criminal activities. One of the brighter chaps in our section caught it and contacted me. I had traced Bolken only as far as Guadeloupe." He paused, picking at his collar, loosening the tie.

"We have vetted your background and I believe that you are what you say you are. Your employer," he paused to consult his notes, "Senator Welsh, claims that you were instructed to drop Mr. Bolken in Martinique so that he might catch a flight. No mention of this person Klist. The senator states that your absence was not alarming due to the poor weather. Thought you were grounded in Fort de France, enjoying the dollies, etc."

"That's insane," Loss replied, propping himself up, not caring at the pain. "Welsh directed that flight and Bolken and Klist were the reason for it. I was to fly them to Mexico. We got beaten up badly in a storm cell west of Haiti. You must have seen the hail damage on the wings."

"Gently, gently," Campbell said. "Don't shout. I believe you. Let me continue. The local authorities have, of course, removed the aircraft from the runway. There are just two constables, you see. I doubt that a print remains intact. Officially, they view it as simple theft. The plan seems to transfer you to Nassau and charge you with possession of a firearm and stealing an aircraft. Possibly, there will be further charges from the Civil Aviation Department. Bolken is slightly cut up about the face and has a great egg of a lump on his forehead but is staying at the hotel. There was a small quantity of cocaine in his valise, which normally the Bahamian authorities would be most alarmed about. But two days ago, a German lawyer, resident in the Bahamas, arrived from Nassau by chartered flight, and it would appear that the charges have been overlooked for a considerable sum of sterling. Bolken is simply being deported to Haiti by the next flight, which I believe is in two days. Bolken, of course, has made no official statement, but it would seem that he and his lawyer are not entirely friendly. In other words, someone else seems to have arranged for the lawyer, not Bolken himself."

"It looks like I've been screwed, doesn't it?" Loss said numbly.

"It could have been much worse, Mr. Loss," Campbell said. "I examined your aircraft very carefully. I doubt that it is your habit to fly around with the fuel drain cocks open. It would seem now that there was a third party who got out of the aircraft intact and then opened the fuel drains to ensure that the fire consumed the aircraft. Very naughty, wasn't it?"

Loss opened his eyes and stared at the man who sat beside him.

"Yes, Mr. Loss. And I don't think it was Bolken. His goose egg and cuts are real enough. And there is dried vomit in the back seat from what I can determine. Rather thought at first it was chipped beef. Is that where Bolken was actually seated, in the back seat, I mean?"

Loss nodded.

"Yes, then. I'm beginning to see," Campbell said, almost to himself. "It would appear that you've been made the sacrificial goose. Let me check with my people in London about this person Klist plus a few other things. I will need to talk to you again, oh, perhaps this afternoon or tomorrow. In the meanwhile, I would advise you not to make any statement. Say you want a barrister to represent you. Don't muddy up the water. And I'll try to get Bolken detained in some manner as well."

He heaved himself up out of the seat. "Take care," he said and was gone, the latch clicking shut behind him. Loss sighed and drifted back into sleep.

She came much later in the afternoon, across the lawn where children rolled the rims of discarded bicycle wheels over the burned grass. She walked down the cool corridors of the small hospital past empty rooms. Then she stood in the doorway, hesitant to wake him. As he slept, the muscles in his cheek twitched; his face was sallow and unshaven. He had lost a lot of weight. His forehead was bandaged, and his hair was tangled and wild. He stirred and rolled over, burying his face in the crook of his arm, grunting as he moved.

Twenty-two stitches, she thought. The scar would be brutal. The hospital matron said that he had taken six pints of blood in the first day of admission, and she could believe it, having seen the dried brown mess that had been the instrument panel of the Aztec.

"It smells like you're wearing *Caress*," he said, his head still buried in the hollow of his elbow, eyes partly open.

She was slightly startled, his voice unexpected and coarse in texture, as if he had been yelling too much. Sitting down on the edge of the bed, she bent over and kissed him on the nape of the neck. "You're a mess, Loss. But you look like you'll make it. That's the official news, anyway."

He turned over, saying nothing but wincing, bunching the muscles in his cheeks. He grinned at her, his lips dried and cracked, two top teeth badly chipped. "I'm one hell of a mess. Think I ought to give up driving airplanes and associating with politicians." He reached for her hand. "Thanks for coming. How did you get here?"

"Long story." She dug into a straw shopping bag and withdrew a variety of things. "I brought you a doggie bag. Some cheese, a couple of candy bars. Just stuff that I picked up at the local market. These too." She placed two miniatures of cognac on the night stand. "At your discretion. But definitely not for now."

He peeled back the paper on a candy bar and bit into it, wincing occasionally with pain but obviously relishing it. "I had some sort of mush laced with fish bones for lunch. And mashed bananas for breakfast with tea. You don't know how good this tastes."

She watched him eating, feeling like a mother who has had her son come home from a schoolyard fight. Battered but with the spirit left in him. She sat down on the bed, taking his head between her hands and kissed him. "You'll do," she said. He kissed her back, tasting of chocolate.

"You understand what's happened?" he said, wiping his lips on a corner of the sheet.

She was silent, watching his eyes.

"Klist is gone," he said. "Bolken was the only other person in the plane when they got to the crash. The police say that I've stolen the plane. Grand theft. I'm to go up to Nassau to face charges in a couple of days."

She nodded. "There's more," she said. "I can only tell you what I know and what I've been able to piece together. A call came in from the Bahamas the afternoon that you left. From the police in Nassau. Welsh took the call. He then disappeared for about an hour and as far as I can tell, he and Mrs. Klist had a long talk. Then he called back here through the operator in Nassau. I don't know what the call was specifically about, but apparently he got confirmation that the only occupants of the aircraft were you and Bolken. Then he declared that you weren't authorized to take the aircraft. Something about dropping Bolken off at Martinique. He filed charges against you over the phone."

Loss struggled upright. "Christ," he swore. "Certainly there were some people down at the resort that knew Klist left with us."

"No, Brian," she replied, lighting a cigarette. "Most people knew that all of you went to the Union Island airstrip but no mention was made of the flight. You took off in the rain and I doubt that more than one or two local people were around when you boarded the aircraft. Customs and Immigration on Union Island claim you didn't clear with them and that no flight plan was filed. And on top of that, Mrs. Klist said that her husband went over to Union Island to meet some friend of his on a yacht. She said that she was joining them in Grenada in a few days. Then she flew out the next morning by chartered aircraft. Completely unconcerned."

"What about Welsh and his wife?" he said, unconsciously scratching at the growth of beard.

"They're gone too. Back to Barbados and then by commercial flight to the States. He's filed an affidavit with the local police in Union Island, and they've forwarded it to Nassau. He made a big show of putting you down before he left. Talked about you being a heavy drinker and how he had already fired you, effective after they returned to the States from this trip."

He sat there on the bed, feeling tired and broken and trapped. He would lose his license for openers. And forget about being hired for anything other than a pea-patch flying school. But the rest he could fight. Get an attorney and somehow get Bolken detained to serve as a witness. Some witness, he thought.

"Listen," he said gently, "don't worry. You've done everything and more. But there's one thing. You've got to get on the phone to Nassau and dig up a lawyer; I guess they call them barristers here. Start to get my defense together. There are plenty of traveler's checks in the briefcase. The local police must have it in their possession, and then—"

She cut him off, violently shaking her head. "No, Brian," she said, looking down at the bare, scrubbed floors. "No, I've already tried. I've called fourteen different law offices in Nassau and Freeport. No one will take the case. They know all about it. They just listen to me for five minutes and then tell me that their case load is just too great and politely turn me down. It's fixed. Someone has applied really heavy pressure."

He lay back against the pillow, eyes closed. "I can't believe that Welsh could do this to me," he said, almost a whisper.

She sat down next to him. "There's more," she said, her voice low. "Welsh talked to me before he left. Said he was sorry but that it was beyond his control. He's beside himself. The man looks 80 years old. But he told me that if you plead guilty, you'll only get three years. And you'll receive 3000 dollars per month for every month you're in jail, paid into any account you designate. And also that if you fought it, he couldn't personally guarantee your safety. Either way, he said, you'll be found guilty."

"The filthy bastard," he whispered, looking beyond her, as if his stare would penetrate the wooden boarded walls. "The filthy, miserable bastard." He paused and looked at his hands, rubbing them nervously together. "Klist and Welsh have this whole thing wired. And I'm the one chosen to take the fall." He hunched forward, grasping his knees. "The only option left to me is to get the hell out."

She got up and went to the door, opening it and looking down the hallway. Satisfied, she closed it softly, lifting the latch and dropping it quietly in place. She sat down on the bed again and took his hand. "You remember Stroud?"

"The biologist guy you met in Carriacou?"

She nodded. "He was the only one I could turn to. To fly up here commercially would have meant going all the way to Miami and then back down on the feeder airline. He offered to bring me here directly. He's got a little single-engine airplane."

He opened his eyes, listening more carefully. "And?"

"Brian, there's nothing between Stroud and me. It's just that he, well, he loves me in some sort of funny way. Not physical. He understands the situation—that's there's no other option. He's willing to let you take the aircraft. Because of me, because I asked him to."

Loss breathed slowly out, eyes closed, listening to the sound of children playing in the distant field.

Chapter 15

Colonel Anatoli Antonovich Petrov, KGB, Section V, wiped the cold rain from his eyes and watched the Aztec burn. Except for the black smoke from the burning aircraft, the airstrip was devoid of life or movement.

He picked up the two suitcases, one of his own and the other containing Bolken's tapes and photographic film and jogged easily into the tall lemon grass that edged the field. Twice he looked back over his shoulder at the aircraft, now burning with a dense black smoke in the area of the undercarriage.

The rain was harder now, saturating his thin cord suit and plastering his hair flat against his skull. The edges of his jacket flapped violently in the wind and he paused to button it, turning the collar up to offer some protection against the chill that saturated him.

From his estimate, the small settlement of Mathewtown could not be more than 4 miles from the airstrip. The aircraft, as it approached from the sea would have been seen, and he doubted that more than a few more minutes would elapse before someone arrived at the field.

He saw the remains of a 55-gallon oil drum resting in the grass, scrofulous with rust and nearly overgrown. He lay down on the leeward side of the drum, protected slightly from the waves of rain that swept in from the north. The aircraft was burning heavily now. Orange fingers of flame were probing the roots of the wing and the cockpit. He decided to wait, to ensure that the entire aircraft was consumed.

The decision had been easy and automatic as he recalled the final minutes in the Aztec.

Loss had done a superb job landing the aircraft. Petrov doubted that he, himself, could have kept the aircraft from flipping over in the slamming crosswind, which he now estimated at close to 40 knots. The groundloop was unavoidable, and as the aircraft had begun to skid, Petrov had thrown his hands up in front of his face and braced himself against the padded cowling over the instrument panel. Both tires had blown almost simultaneously—muffled reports punctuating the sounds of the shrieking metal, and then the aircraft was still. Petrov had raised his head from the protected position to find the aircraft upright and intact, the nose of the Aztec resting against an embankment four or five yards off the asphalt strip. Loss lay slumped over the controls, his head gashed and bleeding from impact with the corner post of the windshield.

Petrov reached down and shut off the master switch and the magnetos, immediately fearful of the possibility of fire. He turned to find Heiss lying huddled in the back seat, his face and the seat it rested against, pooled in vomit. The stench was unbelievable and Petrov's stomach convulsed, causing him to retch.

Frantically, Petrov opened the passenger door. The impact of driving rain and the cold wind clarified his mind. First, he must destroy the Aztec and Loss. Heiss too. He had accomplished the tape surveillance, and the evidence rested in Heiss's aluminum camera case.

Petrov got out onto the wing and looked down the runway toward the approach end. No vehicle or person in sight. Crawling back into the right front seat, he leaned over and grabbed Loss by the hair and raised him to a sitting position. Loss was groaning now, on the edge of consciousness. Petrov, using Loss's hair as a grip, slammed the pilot into the instrument panel with all the strength at his disposal. Three times he did this, the instruments fragmenting under the impact, blood spattering the panel.

Petrov left Loss slumped over the controls, sure that he was dying. He turned to find Heiss sitting upright, staring with terror at Loss.

"We're getting out of this thing, Heiss. Quickly. Pass me your camera case."

Heiss's eyes were dilated with shock, his face ashen. His thin lips hung slack, exposing the even teeth of his lower jaw.

Petrov swept his knuckles across Heiss's face, the impact flinging partially dried vomit from Heiss's chin.

"Move, you idiot," Petrov screamed into the face that gazed at him, uncomprehending. "The case. Give me the case."

Heiss's hands groped on the floor of the aircraft, raising the aluminum container hesitantly, questioning the eyes of the man before him, almost pleading.

"Yes, yes. Good," Petrov said, taking the case gently from Heiss's grasp.

"Yes, good." Petrov pushed open the aircraft door and backed out onto the wing. Heiss was starting to regain coherence, unstrapping his lap belt and following Petrov onto the wing. Petrov allowed Heiss to move the seat forward and start to step over the door's ledge onto the wing. As his head emerged through the door, Petrov slammed the door in his face. Heiss cried out in pain, almost an animal wail. His hands pushed open the door, almost unbalancing Petrov on the rain-slick wing. Carl Heiss pressed his hands to his face, fully conscious but in shock.

Petrov made another lunge at the man tottering before him, thrusting his stiffened right fingers into the man's solar plexis. Heiss collapsed like a sack of wheat, falling back into the aircraft, sprawled across the right front passenger seat, head lolling back against Loss's slumped form.

It had been less than a minute since the final impact of crash. Petrov stood on the wing, his mind now clean and methodical. He bent down and shoved Heiss's feet into the cockpit, fastened his lap belt with some difficulty, and brought him erect in the seat. Grasping his hair as he had done with Loss, he brought Heiss's head forward in a smashing arc into the control column.

Closing the cabin door now, he jumped lightly to the ground, careful to land in the scarred tracks of the undercarriage. He quickly retrieved his own suitcase from the luggage compartment and carried both items of luggage into the adjacent grass.

Fifty feet back from the aircraft he rested, his breath coming in great gulps, the rain tasting like champagne on his tongue.

There was just a flicker of orange from the right main gear. The tire had blown and the magnesium wheel had caught fire from the friction of the final skid across the runway. Brake fluid dripped down from ruptured lines and was feeding the flame, causing a spluttering sound. The fire was growing in intensity.

I have to make sure, he thought, running back to the aircraft, trying to stay within the torn earth tracks. He bent briefly under the wing, shielding his face from the fire and opened the left main fuel drain. The clear blue fluid drained in a gush over his hands and, panic stricken, Petrov sprinted for the grass. But there was no explosion and even now, as he lay in the tall lemon grass, he was surprised that the aircraft had not gone up in a sheet of flames.

But even as he watched, there was a white-hot pinpoint of light that blossomed into a black-orange rose, sheet metal singing high into the air as a fuel tank exploded. A cloud of black smoke rose, obscuring the aircraft.

Petrov relaxed now, the thing finished. He watched anxiously as the ball of smoke was whipped away in the wind, expecting to see only flame. Instead, the aircraft, minus most of the right wing, had settled in the mud, the landing gear collapsed. Flame still fluttered sporadically around the engine cowlings of the left wing, but it too died in the torrential rain. The remains of the exploded wing were thirty or more feet from the aircraft, engulfed in fire but too far to cause the aircraft to reignite.

A movement far down the runway caught Petrov's eye. He flattened himself into the grass, thinking of the obvious tracks he must have left in the mud around the aircraft. The movement was blanked from sight by the grass, but he could hear the sound of a blaring car horn. Cautiously, he parted the grass, enough to see two black men in foul-weather jackets splashing through the mud and over the debris toward the smoking aircraft. Their movements were shielded from his view as they gained the far side of the aircraft. Petrov could hear muffled shouts, carried by the wind. The two men reemerged from behind the aircraft, dragging two bodies through the mud.

That will obliterate my footmarks, he thought with satisfaction. He could see the vehicle now, parked much too close to the smoldering aircraft. These men were obviously civilians. The car was a mid-fifties Chevrolet, rusted and paint-flaked. A front fender was missing, and the word "taxi" was crudely painted in white across the door. A second vehicle was coming up the runway now, and then a third. Both Land Rovers, dull gray with the black stencils of government service across their hoods.

Petrov flattened himself into the sodden earth, wearied now, his adrenalin level falling. He mentally retraced his steps since the aircraft had crashed and was content that he could have handled the situation in no better manner. It was just bad luck that the explosion had snuffed out the fire. Now Heiss and possibly Loss might live. But if he could reach a telephone or radio, that situation could be rectified.

Petrov's body shook uncontrollably now from the cold torrent of wind and water that swept Great Inagua. But he had known cold before and day after day of walking through mud when he and his mother had resettled their farm near the East German border. And he had known the brilliant, polished cold of Manchurian winters, instructing the Chinese to fly MIG 21s. Cold so intense that metal broke like kindling. And where it was a crime, punishable by death, to stop the engine of a vehicle, for it was certain that the engine would never start again until the spring. Compared to that, this was no more than an inconvenience and he disciplined his body, separating his mind. To think.

A vehicle started up now, the sound carried clearly by the wind. It was raining less now, but it was colder. Another vehicle started, and headlights swept the grass as they turned on the runway and sped off in the direction of the town. One Land Rover remained, the windows fogged with condensation; obviously the man or men left to guard the remains of the demolished Aztec.

Petrov watched the lone sentry vehicle for over half an hour. The motor would start and run for short periods; probably an attempt to keep the cab of the vehicle warm. This served to further fog the windows. Not once did anyone emerge into the gusting rain that swept the bleak landscape in waves.

Satisfied, Petrov slowly retreated through the grass, crawling backwards, dragging the two pieces of luggage in front of him. He encountered a line of scrubby trees that hid him from any possible observation, and rose to a running crouch. Knowing the wind was from the north, he headed south toward the coast.

Twice he met rough asphalt roads, only one lane in width, the roadside strewn with broken glass and empty beer bottles. Crossing these, he kept to the scrub and stunted trees. He topped a rise and although there was no habitation as yet in sight, the ridge of a hill further to the south was transfixed by the monolithic dish antennas of the Cable and Wireless installation that he had seen through the rain-spattered windows of the Aztec on final approach.

This would be the site of the remote transmitter, probably largely unattended. He wished desperately for a cigarette or something warm to drink. The late tropical afternoon, already washed in the gray of the storm, was growing dark. He moved on, resolute, his mind disconnected from his body.

The next rise gave him a clearer view of the transmitter site, and more important, he could see the sea. The southwest coast would probably be the most protected coast and consequently, there would be some type of anchorage for small craft. Cuba lay only 80 kilometers to the west. And Cuba meant the Russian installation at Cienfuegos.

Petrov turned east along the coast, paralleling the beach but staying to the scrub that bordered the wide berm, keeping to the depressions in the grass-covered hillocks. He stopped twice, once to check the contents of Heiss's bag and to extract a sweater from his own bag, which he used as a muffler around his neck. The other stop was unplanned as a small rusted coaster swept down the coast only 200 meters offshore. He watched it as it passed, flattening himself against the sand and weed thrown up by the storm. The coaster carried no flag, and he estimated it to be no longer than 15 meters, a single thudding diesel washing the wake with roiled white in the following sea. Beyond the small pilot house, the decks were clean of superstructure. It was what it appeared to be, a fishing coaster, and he sighed heavily with relief, doubtful that his presence on the shore would be noticed.

The antenna installation was a disappointment. Although uninhabited, a triple strand of barbed wire protected the top of a 4-meter cyclone fence around the perimeter.

He kept to the easterly direction, avoiding the few fishing shacks that dotted the foreshore. Lights glowed within one of them, the dull yellow of kerosene.

The rain had quit now, and the wind was diminishing, the low ceiling having lifted to a more uniform overcast. And the light was failing. Checking his watch, he found it was almost 6:00 PM. He found a dense place in the scrub and settled himself on the two handbags, waiting for darkness, planning ahead to Cuba and beyond. There must be, would be a boat moored along this coast he could steal.

By 6:30, the light was completely gone. His eyes had adjusted to the darkness, and he carefully picked his way west again to intersect the road he was sure would lead toward the small settlement of Mathewtown. The lights of the town were not visible, but they were reflected in the low cloud ceiling. He picked up the road again and turned east along it, walking slowly and carefully on the shoulder, stopping frequently to listen for any approaching vehicle. He noted that the overcast was starting to break up, an occasional glint of a star visible in the ragged patches.

Now civilization was becoming more apparent. He passed two construction sheds, both heavily padlocked, and then the rusted shell of a Volkswagen and a cinderblock house that was set back in from the road by a small lane. A dog barked once and he froze. He heard the slam of a door and an indistinct voice.

The door-sound again, then quiet. He waited patiently for five minutes and then resumed his progress to the west.

The road now ran parallel to the coast, separated from the broad beach by the stunted scrub pines. The smell of the sea gave him fresh energy, its impact tangy and pungent. The breakers were gentle here, less frantic in their beat upon the shore than those to the north. The asphalt track wandered inland again and rose toward the low crest of a hill. To the seaward side of the road on the crest was a two-story building, dimly visible against the light from Mathewtown. The building was dark, and he climbed the hill toward it, finding a pathway lined with conch shells.

He circled the building and found it was built on a low bluff overlooking the sea. A roofed veranda circled the building, providing cover for him for the first time in three hours. He walked along the porch after first removing his shoes and leaving the bags stored near the base of the steps. From here, he could clearly see the main street of Mathewtown, probably less than a kilometer distant. There seemed to be little more than two streets fronting the shore with sparsely placed streetlights blinking through foliage.

More important, he found a sign fixed to the wall near the main door. The sign, faded and dim, read "Great Inagua Aquatic Club, Members Only." So there would be some sort of anchorage or boat basin near here, he thought. In confirmation of this, he found two aluminum masts for small sailboats stacked against the side of the building, sails still bent on and laced with gaskets.

At the back of the building, steps led down to another pathway, this time leading down the bluff toward the sea. Retrieving the bags and his shoes, he followed the path down through arbors of frangipani and bougainvillea. The path branched once and he followed the right-hand deviation only to find it a dead end with a small group of sheds for storage. All were stoutly locked.

He retraced his steps and continued downward, finally breaking out of the arbor onto a rough concrete ramp. Before him was a small basin with mooring space for a small fleet of yachts and commercial craft. Beyond that was the dim outline of a seawall with the opening marked by a single red light.

The basin wasn't much larger than a 100 meters square, a literal hole in the wall. There were no lights on the landing, but Petrov could see the outlines of small sailing boats rafted together on a short trot line. Beyond, there were indistinct shapes of one or two powerboats. On the western edge of the basin, darker against the cliff wall looming over it, was the indistinct spear of a mast and rigging, a vessel larger than the rest.

He walked carefully along the concrete ramp that led to the west side of the basin. The ramp was slick with moss. Things scuttled beneath his feet; the air was fetid with dead marine growth.

A sloop materialized out of the blackness, surprisingly small for the size of her mast and complex rigging. She was painted in some dark color, possibly green. Beyond that the details were too indistinct for Petrov to determine.

He set the bags down on the edge of the ramp and stood in the darkness, his next movement as yet undecided.

Beyond the breakwater, the remains of the storm's swell made a muffled rumble along the rip-rap, almost the sound of a distant train moving slowly over a trestle. The sky was clearer now, batches of stars burning in the blackness above the ragged cumulus.

The small sloop before him moved easily against the restraint of her mooring lines, her mast tracing arcs against the sky. Closer now, he could pick out details of the superstructure and rigging. The lifelines, three strands, circled the deck and were held secure by robust stanchions. And on the stern, were two life rings attached to marker buoys. Even in the darkness, the name of the ship stood out in black-painted letters—*Ulla, Goteborg.*

Without warning, the deck of the yacht was suddenly flooded with light from the two spreaders high in the rigging. Petrov, startled, stood poised to run.

"Yes?" a male voice called from the companionway hatch, more in question than in challenge.

"I'm sorry," Petrov said, his voice strained. "I thought that—well, I—I was looking for the yacht of a friend of mine. Due to arrive today."

"No one in today or even yesterday," the voice replied, young and with a Scandinavian lilt. The spreader lights went out, and a man came up into the cockpit, pausing to turn on a small electric lamp.

He was young and tall, fully bearded. He wore just a large bath towel. The small table lamp illuminated his heavily tanned body and sunburned face.

Petrov, confident now, walked to the edge of the ramp and looked down into the cockpit. The Scandinavian opened a package of cigarettes and took one, offering the opened pack to Petrov.

"Good Swedish cigarettes," he said, smiling. "They taste like cabbage."

Petrov, unsure whether the offer included boarding, took one and then searched his pockets in the universal gesture of looking for a match.

"Oh, come on board," the Swede said. "I have a light."

"I think that I have interrupted you," Petrov said apologetically, swinging easily down to the deck, using the rigging as support.

"Anders is my name," the Swede said, extending a huge hand. "No, you weren't taking me away from anything. I was just sitting there in the dark listening to the radio with the headphones. Trying to get some kind of report on this fuckin' weather." He pointed haphazardly toward the clearing sky. "I think maybe we got what we see tomorrow. Good weather again."

Petrov bent down to accept a light for his cigarette, inhaling the bitter, strange smoke from the cigarette, feeling almost giddy as the smoke filled his lungs. He coughed and looked at the brand name, unable to see it in the dim light.

"I said they were like cabbage," the Swede said, laughing a little. "I only got wine. Would you like some?" he said, moving into the companionway.

"Yes, Anders, I would like that very much," Petrov replied. "My name is Robert Kline. The yacht belongs to a friend of mine. We were meeting here for some diving in the Bahamas. I guess that the storm's held him up."

Anders appeared in the companionway again, handing up a fruit jar of dark wine to Petrov and then coming back up the companionway ladder, a similar jar of wine in his hand.

"Yes, yes. I know. We been here for three days, waiting for this fuckin' storm to get over with. Skoal!"

They lifted the wine in toast and drank for some minutes in silence, each smoking and sipping at the rough wine.

"This seems like a fine yacht," Petrov said finally, noting the obviously well-cared-for condition of the sloop.

"Yes, yes. Thank you. Ulla and me have been sailing her for three years now. We been all over the Med and across the Atlantic. I think maybe now we take her to the Panama Canal and into the Pacific. Before things get much worse there. These guerrillas blow up one US ship. Maybe Swedes next. Pretty soon maybe they blow up the whole fuckin' ditch."

Petrov shrugged. "I doubt it," he said. "The new government will probably make peace with the Americans. Soon, I think."

Anders thought about it and then lifted his jar of wine toward the shore's direction. "All these places are good," he said, "but maybe they don't like white people so much. I think maybe Ulla and me will like it better in the Pacific."

"Ulla is your wife?" Petrov asked, motioning toward the companionway.

"Yes. Well, almost like my wife," the Swede replied, laughing. "Maybe some day we do that. She help me out rebuilding this boat, and she owns half. We sail together. I even cook sometimes. Terrible cooking!" and he laughed again.

Petrov traced his fingers across a sheet winch. "You have good equipment. Barrient winches, I'm told, are the best."

Anders nodded. "Good gear," he agreed. "Sometimes too much of it."

"What do you have in the way of radios?"

The Swede snorted, shaking his head. "Radios. That's the last fuckin' thing we need. Ulla and me, we got no time for radios. They just take up space, and they're no damn good half the time."

Petrov suddenly realized that the Swede was drunk. "You have no radios, then," he asked evenly, swirling the wine in his glass.

"Just the opposite," Anders said, hocking over the rail. "My fuckin' government won't let a small boat go to sea without all them goddamn radios. The little men in their business suits come down and tell you that you can't go here or there without all these radios. We got VHF and low frequency single sideband. They take up space, add weight. I hate the fuckin' things." He deftly dropped down the hatch and reemerged with a 4-liter jerry can of wine. Refilling Petrov's jar and then his own, he sloshed the burgandy onto the clean teak of the cockpit floor.

"You excuse me. I just got a little drunk tonight. Sitting here in this harbor for four days is no good. My father," he paused, drinking nearly half his freshly refilled jar in one long swallow, "my father, we work salvage tugs together, and he always used to say that when in port, ships rot and men go to the devil. He's goddamn right. Me, I never drink at sea. Just here." He speared his thumb toward the shore again.

"You'll leave tomorrow, then?" Petrov asked.

The Swede nodded, picking at the skin of his sunburned nose. His face, splotched by the peeling skin, was nevertheless handsome, both hair and beard bleached white by the sun. His eyes were dull with drink, but his teeth white and even. And he smiled a lot.

"Well, maybe I'll see you again," Petrov said, rising slightly as if to leave. "My friend and I want to do some diving." And then, almost as an afterthought he said, "But I worry about sharks. My friend always has a crew member stand watch with a rifle."

The Swede laughed, shaking his head and lighting another cigarette from the glowing tip of Petrov's. "No, that's stupid." He looked up quickly, his forehead pinched in concern. "Not you, I mean. Just that Ulla and I thought so too, before we came sailing. We thought sharks were like all those films. Attacking people. But we never seen one that bother us. They just nose around. We got this old Husqvarna shotgun, and we used to bathe in the sea, even in the middle of the Atlantic when the wind was calm, with one of us standing guard. But it doesn't matter. And I think if a shark ever decides to get you, you never know about it."

The Swede made a motion with his hand, indicating the slashing attack of a fin. He spilled the wine jar, the small amount left staining his bath towel.

Petrov relaxed, sitting back against the cushions. "Husqvarna," he said. "Fine weapon. My grandfather owned several of them over the years. Would you mind if I looked at yours?"

The Swede looked up smiling and nodded.

Chapter 16

Campbell sat opposite Loss in a disintegrating wicker chair, endlessly flicking his butane lighter. The wind had fallen, and the air was stale and oppressive, even under the shade of the almond tree where they sat. Beyond them, across the baked grounds of the lawn, the small hospital building was aching white in the sunlight.

A black constable, young and filled with self-importance, paced back and forth at a discreet distance from the two men. He watched Loss closely. The white man was bandaged heavily about the forehead, and his arm showed a cuff of white dressings beneath the bathrobe. He had walked with the older man to the chairs beneath the almond tree with a pronounced limp. No, it was doubtful that he would attempt escape.

Elias Wilson switched his baton to the left hand and turned in a wheeling march to the right, back toward the two men. He strained to catch some of their conversation, but it was useless; the afternoon's quiet was overlaid with the cries of the children playing on the cricket pitch across the street.

His superior, Chief Constable Edwards, had been in a foul mood this morning, and Constable Wilson had taken the brunt of it for no good reason. Nassau had called early in the morning and informed them that details for the transfer of the prisoner were complete. Two plainclothes men would be down on tomorrow morning's flight to retrieve Loss. Chief Edwards had wanted to go personally, and now his moment of glory was forfeit. Coupled with this irritation was the annoyance of the Swedish yacht's illegal departure seven days ago. Edwards had really laid into Wilson for that.

With only two men on the force, it was normally Constable Wilson's duty to act as Immigration and Customs Officer. The Swedish yacht had simply left in the night without proper authority, and Elias had taken the brunt of the blame.

Wilson was not overly concerned about the dressing-down. He had stood rigidly at attention before his chief, taking notes where appropriate and had finally departed with a bone-snapping salute. The old man was near retirement, and therefore not important to his career. The reports were filed and queries made to neighboring islands to locate the yacht. He had covered himself well.

His shirt was beginning to prickle against his skin in the blasted heat. We've been self-governing for over ten years now, and we still wear the standard British woolen shirts, he thought. And this *red-leg* honky, Campbell. Some connection with the British Foreign Office. What right does he have to interfere with our affairs. He looked like a parody of the nineteenth century colonial servant.

Wilson completed another leg of his circuit and, transferring the baton to his right hand, he wheeled his dusty brogans through a left turn. He smiled inwardly. In five months, he would be made Chief Constable and then there would be some changes. He watched the two white men carefully.

"It's a complete zero," Campbell said, his eyes averted. "The officials in Nassau are quite adamant that Bolken is being deported on the first flight to Haiti and that you are to be transported to Nassau on tomorrow morning's flight. Very simply, Bolken's lawyer has paid a fine and the matter's closed."

"What did you say Bolken's real name is?" Loss said, flicking his cigarette butt into the dust at his feet.

"Heiss. Carl Heiss. Born in Grossenhain, Germany, 1931. Immigrated with his guardian to England in 1938. Short stint in the British Army in the late forties but discharged for what is termed here as 'maladjustment.' That's a polite name for sexual deviation according to his records." Campbell consulted his notes, flicking through the pages with his thumb as a teller would count bank notes. "Heiss is a photographer by trade; mostly union journals. Four trips back to Germany during the late fifties."

"Why the phony name?"

Campbell wiped the sweat from his florid face and tucked the handkerchief back under his shirt collar. "Some things I can't tell you, Brian. Except that Heiss has done some very nasty jobs for the Russians. More than that I can't say."

Loss came erect in his chair. He bent forward toward Campbell, seeking his eyes. "Are you telling me that Klist also works for the Russians?"

Campbell scratched at his eyebrow, avoiding Loss's stare. "Can't say, Brian. We have no prints, no photos, nothing. He could be anyone. All we know is that the passport was a fake. There's no Klist of this description in Dutch passport files. We know that he entered Barbados, flew by charter flight to Union Island, and stayed at Salt Whistle Cay. Then poof. His wife claimed that he has gone sailing, and now she has conveniently returned to Europe via Venezuela. No forwarding address."

Loss leaned back in his chair and watched the constable pass them. I feel as if I'm in the slammer already, he thought. He turned back to Campbell and said, "I know damn well that Klist must still be on this island. There haven't been any commercial flights in or out in the last seven days. No boat traffic from what Holly has been able to find out. So where is he? Why don't the police try to find him?"

Campbell lifted his hands fractionally. "Because he isn't here. Your lady is not entirely correct, Brian. There was a Swedish yacht moored in the basin the day you arrived. It left sometime that night without proper customs or immigration clearance. I doubt that it will be heard of again."

"Where would he go? He's bound to make port somewhere."

Campbell chuckled. "Yes. At least that's the theory. The Bahamian authorities have requested the other neighboring islands to be on the alert. But I would imagine that our resourceful Mr. Klist headed due west to Cuba, assuming of course that he is linked in some way with the Russians. It's a pleasant little sail of about ten hours, directly downwind. Piece of cake, really."

"What about Heiss?" Brian asked. "Can't he be detained? He's the only one who could verify my story."

Campbell frowned and shook his head. "Heiss is being deported with a minor fine for possession of narcotics. This decision comes straight from Nassau. I've made all the noises that I can to the British High Commissioner and have been told, very politely, mind you, that this is not our jurisdiction any more. In fact, I am to return to London on the first transportation available. Very touchy, politically speaking."

Loss stared at the ground. A column of ants were fighting over his cigarette butt. He looked back up at Campbell. "So what defense do I have? What help can you give me?"

Campbell looked embarrassed. He dropped his notebook into the old-fashioned briefcase and started to rise to his feet and said, "None, Mr. Loss. Absolutely none, I'm afraid. As they would say in an American film, 'You've been had.' Someone in a very high place has been paid handsomely. Your employer, Senator Welsh, claims that you have stolen the aircraft. Heiss denies any knowledge of wrongdoing and is essentially being set free. You *did* possess a firearm in your briefcase, which, in the Bahamas, is punishable by at least one year's confinement." Campbell paused and looked across the lawn to the cricket pitch where the children were playing. "No. I'm afraid that I can do nothing more for you." He extended his hand toward Loss. "I must be on my way."

Loss shook hands with him, finding the grasp firm and surprisingly cool. Campbell turned to go and then, almost as an afterthought, said, "Oh, incidentally, Mr. Loss. Your personal possessions, which will, of course, be forwarded to Nassau, are locked in a rather flimsy filing cabinet in the Chief Constable's office next to the Cable and Wireless building. I have heard it said that the key to the office is generally over the door sill. But then again, these are just rumors. The security is rather lax down here in these islands, as you might well expect it to be. Last murder in 1923, I believe. Very law abiding, really. Well, take care," and he picked up his briefcase.

Loss rose to shake his hand again. Campbell smiled. "You know, Mr. Loss, you really have a lovely young lady. Very resourceful. Asked me to get the weather forecast for tonight and tomorrow, which, I am pleased to report, will be excellent. Something about winds easterly at 15 knots at the 12,000-foot level. Perfectly clear all the way to Miami except for a few isolated afternoon thundershowers. But as you know, weathermen are eternal optimists. Well, cheers." He turned and without looking back, trudged across the burned grass toward the Government Guest House.

Peter Bates Stroud transferred the last of the 5-gallon jerry can's contents into the outboard tank of his aircraft and fastened the tank lid with a firm twist. He checked his watch and, noting that it was 5:18, calculated that he had approximately forty-five minutes remaining before dark. He carefully drained the residue of gasoline from the metal can and placed it on the tarmac, opened neck toward the wind to purge it of fumes.

Next, he checked the oil and although the dipstick showed 8 quarts, he carefully transferred another quart of Shell aviation oil into the filler neck and secured it. With the cowling of the engine compartment still open, he traced each high tension lead and inspected each critical fitting, and only then, satisfied with his preflight inspection, did he close and lock the snap fittings that secured the sheet aluminum cowl.

Stroud continued to work methodically through the late afternoon twilight, examining each part of the aircraft, pausing occasionally to survey the length of the asphalt road that led from Mathewtown to the airport.

The aircraft was a single-engined Piper Comanche; a smaller and older relative to the Aztec that now lay burned and gutted in the grass half a mile down the runway. It was the type of aircraft that a man would buy for himself if he wished to travel a great deal with a large quantity of baggage. Normally, the aircraft could seat four with a moderate amount of luggage, but Stroud had done extensive modifications to the interior so that now the aircraft could carry only two people in comfort. The rest of the space was given over to fuel tanks and storage for his equipment.

Stroud had bought the aircraft in Canada four years previously, and although the blue and white paint was badly faded, the aircraft was mechanical perfection. Contrary to the regulations of the Department of Transport, Stroud did all his own maintenance, allowing certified aircraft mechanics only to inspect and sign off the work in his logbooks. He strongly believed that reliability was a direct function of meticulous and constant care, particularly the reliability of an aircraft that regularly flew over vast stretches of wilderness and most particularly, if he was the man who was flying the aircraft.

Stroud, now 34 years old, had been born to middle-class English parents, nurtured on the pabulum of the welfare system, force-fed with leftist liberalism in the London School of Economics, and, finally, had passed it all out of his system, counting the mutilated bodies of his army comrades in the rain-misted streets of Belfast.

After being mustered out of his national service stint in the British Army, he switched majors, becoming a biologist. From there on in, Stroud spent as much time removed from human habitation as his work and an annual grant would allow.

Having firmly rejected one society, he began to formulate his own by observing the patterns of intelligent mammals, living and playing within complex but logical systems of co-existence. Animals, supposedly lacking the powers of free will, appeared freer than humans, for they seldom subjected themselves to the constraints of a highly structured society, choosing instead a life of freedom and self-determination within loosely defined limits of peaceful cooperation, food gathering, and territorial rights.

In comparison, Stroud observed that man had elected to give up self-determination and, in turn, his own free will, for shallow benefits and the marginal security of a society that progressively extracted more and returned less. It was that simple. He saw no cure for man's dilemma and with this conclusion, strove only for his own salvation. Using his savings and occasional grants, Stroud wandered the wilderness areas of the American continents, studying the infrastructure of select animal societies, totally at peace with himself and as far removed from man as generally possible.

The plane had been a gift to himself. He reasoned that by flying directly to his study site, he would save a great deal of money, frustration, and time. More important, he would retain the twin virtues of flexibility and independence.

With money from a grant for the study of hair seals above the Arctic Circle, Stroud set about first learning to fly and then purchasing an aircraft. Because he would operate in the wilderness areas, he bypassed the chrome-plated pilot factories and instead chose a shaggy Scotsman who flew the Canadian bush, spotting elk migrations. With equal doses of Calvinism and aeronautical instruction, Stroud learned the practical realities of staying alive in a hostile environment.

The choice of an aircraft was more difficult. Since Stroud had 15,000 Canadian dollars to play with, the Scot recommended a high-winged Cessna 182; something that you could put skis or floats on; a plane for all seasons. The Scotsman described it as a "bonny bit of tin."

Stroud, operating in the far Canadian north only during summers and the southern latitudes of Argentina for the balance of the year, chose range, cargo-carrying capacity, and speed instead. With dire warnings and great reluctance, the Scot helped him find and convert such an aircraft. And the Comanche had been a success. In this, his fourth year of ownership, he had never had a failure while accumulating close to 600 hours on the aircraft.

Stroud had been working his way north from Argentina, leaving the South American fall behind, flying into the North American springtime. He wanted to be at his seal observation camp north of Hudson Bay by the time the snows melted. While he waited for the spring thaw in the Canadian Northwest Passage, he worked at the Marine Biology station in Carriacou, studying dolphins and the passing pods of humpback whales.

Stroud had met Hollister Stowe at a depth of 7 fathoms along the reef that protects the windward shore of Carriacou. He happened upon her quite by chance, being primarily intent on following a group of three bottle-nosed dolphins (*tursiops truncatus*), which were playing along the 10-fathom line. She emerged out of the blue depths, swimming opposite to his direction, wearing nothing more than diving tanks and a mask. She waved casually at him as one might do, seeing an acquaintance across a busy street. And then she was gone.

He found her again, two days later, lying on the shingled beach off of Gunn Point, reading Darwin's *Origin of the Species*. In thirty minutes of conversation, Stroud was completely charmed by the only other person he had ever met whom he considered to have a completely free will.

He did not consider himself to be even remotely handsome, and he was right. Stroud's gawky frame of over six feet was topped by a painfully thin face and a brown mop of already thinning hair. His hands, unfulfilled except when working with specimens or flying, were overly large and ill at ease. But in her presence, he felt eloquent and graceful.

He spent two unadulterated days of joy with her, talking of things he had kept within himself for five years. Not once had he touched her hand or smelled her hair, but he was as surely in love as any man can ever be.

That she had left Carriacou with Loss worried him not in the least, for he was content simply to treasure the thought of knowing a free soul. And perhaps this kind of love was better for its distance. Stroud would willingly have given a great deal for her admiration, and the loss of an aircraft now seemed little enough.

The sun was at last swallowed by the horizon, and Stroud adjusted his thick prescription glasses as he watched its ingestion into the western sea. He felt pleased with himself, having foreseen those possibilities that might arise. The aircraft was now parked on the cracked concrete hardstand, awaiting flight. All the tanks had been filled to maximum capacity, and the ten metal jerry cans of fuel were carefully strapped down in the back seat and luggage compartment, allowing a total range of over two thousand miles.

It is considered a very unhealthy practice for one to carry metal containers of 100-octane fuel within the cabin of any aircraft. Fumes from the fuel provide an explosive mixture that can cause catastrophic results with only one small arc of current across a switch contact. Compounding this is the problem of expansion and contraction as the cans are subjected to the pressures of changing altitude. Even such strongly constructed structures as thermos flasks may burst at high altitude if not properly vented.

But Stroud had found it necessary to carry extra fuel on his pilgrimages into the far recesses of the continent in pursuit of his studies. Good fuel was generally unobtainable, and consequently he had devised a system to carry his own reserves. Each individual can was fitted with its own plastic vent tube, which was connected to a brass manifold and vented to the outside air. A separate system allowed the unorthodox accomplishment of in-flight refueling. With the aircraft on autopilot, Stroud would lean into the back seat of the aircraft and individually connect each can of gas to a squeeze-bulb siphon pump, similar to those that are used to connect gasoline tanks to outboard motors. The process was time-consuming but relatively safe; there was only manual energy involved in the transfer of fuel to the main inboard tanks. That such a procedure violated every published standard of safety was all the more reason to use it, for it demonstrated that each man can define his own system and come to live with it. Stroud had developed his own set of rules for safe transfer, and he had committed these to a small index card that was secured to the sunvisor over the pilot's seat.

For Loss's benefit, he had also left detailed written instructions as to the final disposition of the aircraft, whatever its destination, for in order for Stroud to collect the insurance if the aircraft were damaged, there must be evidence of forced entry. This pricked his conscience, but he dismissed it as a necessary measure, even if Lloyds of London were the ultimate aggrieved party.

He looked at the aircraft once more as he got into the rented Ford. It seemed larger, more vital than he had ever remembered, and he wished that it was he who would make this flight with that woman. But it was his gift to her and that was sufficient.

He drove carefully back into Mathewtown, finding the road completely deserted except for scuttling land crabs, which he cautiously avoided. He passed the hospital and the droning shell of the power station and parked in front of Cable and Wireless Ltd. He entered and queried the night switchboard operator for any overseas calls. She replied in a sleepy negative, returning to her magazine without even looking at his face. Stroud thanked her, somewhat embarrassed, and returned into the cool night. He stood in the blackness for some minutes, watching the street that was vacant except for one passing Land Rover going in the direction of the eastern end of town. A small shop further down the street, perhaps two hundred yards distant, throbbed with the reggae beat of a hard-pressed juke box, and there would be men drinking rum and arguing the merits of cricket players. But beyond that, the town had ground to an end of the day.

Stroud adjusted his glasses and nervously glanced through the window of Cable and Wireless. The operator sat slouched behind the counter, absorbed in the magazine. Her hand occasionally strayed beneath the counter to pluck some sweet from a hidden package and convey it to her mouth. But that was all.

He moved softly to the door of the Constable's office and felt along the sill for a key. His fingertips touched a cool metal shape and he retrieved it and inserted it in the lock. He entered the office quickly and closed the door behind him. From his poplin jacket pocket, he withdrew a pair of soiled leather gloves he habitually used for flying. The leather was soft and close fitting, and the scent of the glove gave him momentary assurance, like a friend met in a strange place.

Within three minutes, he had located the filing cabinet and forced it with nothing more than a screwdriver. The briefcase that Holly had described was on the bottom shelf, and he opened it and examined the contents with a penlight. Aside from the books of traveler's checks, passport, and aircraft manuals, the light reflected from the oiled metal of an automatic pistol. He pondered the advisability of leaving the weapon, for this man, Loss, might be the vindictive sort. But in the end, he left the weapon in the briefcase, feeling that it was Loss's decision.

He stood by the curtained window for another two minutes, attempting to scan the street in both directions. It was as silent and deserted as before, and he finally left the office, carefully locking it and replacing the key. He placed the briefcase in the trunk of the Ford along with the gloves and walked off with a light step, almost a bounce, in the direction of the hospital. He was enjoying himself immensely.

Loss was making a nuisance of himself. He briefly checked his watch and noted that it was 5:18. Holly had left roughly ten minutes ago. He rolled on his side and thumbed the buzzer. Far down the corridor, he heard it rasping, like an insistent insect. He waited for another twenty seconds and thumbed the buzzer again, repeatedly. He could hear steps in the hallway, echoing along the bare halls. He smiled and relaxed back into the deep pillows.

The door opened abruptly.

"Yes?"

He looked up at the day nurse and scowled.

"I'd like some water."

"There some on your night table." The nurse was plainly impatient with him; her dark face was devoid of expression, the thick nostrils flaring slightly.

"Yes, I know. But it's warm."

"Matron tell me she replaced your water four times today. That's enough." Nurse Wylie looked at the white man with distaste and shut the door on his objection. Composing herself, she walked briskly down the corridor, the sound of his voice muffled but demanding, following after her.

She paused to stop at the desk and made an entry in her log. She hesitated and counted his calls in the log. Water, codeine, requests that his shirt be washed for the trip to Nassau. And on and on. Fourteen calls since the noon hour. That the man was white didn't bother her. She regarded herself above all that, unlike her brother. But this man was a torment, and she wished him ill. There were only three other patients on the ward and this one asked for, no, demanded more than any patient she had yet experienced in her two years of service.

Loss smiled and settled back in his bed. The girl did have patience, though. If he had been her, he would have long ago ignored the repeated requests. Even though she was inexperienced, she had tended him with care and skill for the first days of consciousness. And she had displayed that almost alarming, total smile that rent the professional mask into honest pleasure as he complimented her for care he honestly felt was superior to any that he had ever seen in any hospital. He regretted doing this thing to her.

After 5:30 now. He withdrew the Comanche flight manual from beneath the covers and read on. The aircraft held no problem for him, but he wanted no fumbling in a darkened cockpit in what might be a tense situation. With the aircraft overgross at 2950 pounds and the center of gravity well aft, he would want 74 knots for lift-off. Visualizing the air speed indicator, he branded the number in his mind, eyes closed with concentration. Maximum range would be the name of the exercise, and he carefully calculated climb speeds and power settings. Best range would be 40 percent power at 15,000 feet. No oxygen, but that was acceptable.

No one here would know of Stroud's jerry-rigged fuel supply, nor would they definitely know that the aircraft came equipped from the factory with optional long range tanks. Stroud would lie to cover this fact. Also, it was logical to assume that any attempt to escape would be at high speed and consequently at high fuel consumption. But Stroud had reasoned differently and had formulated the outline of a workable plan, which Holly had relayed. Stroud would be left tied up at the airport, the infuriated owner of a stolen aircraft. His estimates of range would be initially accepted and later checked, only to confirm that the probable range under average fuel management would be little more than 800 miles. But with careful leaning of the mixture and low power settings plus the fuel provided by both the long-range factory tanks and the mickey-mouse fuel reserve, Loss calculated a range in excess of 2100 miles.

It was useless to turn south into the Caribbean. Most of these countries would have firm diplomatic links with the Bahamas. Mexico was out of the question. Initially, flight into the United States seemed worth consideration—to confront Welsh on his home ground. But in the end, Loss remembered the Kents from Nova Scotia and knew that the dirt airstrip on the Kent farm would be a method of entering the North American continent with minimal chance of detection. From there, he would have time and facilities to deal with Welsh. And be well beyond any accusations voiced in the Caribbean.

There was also the question of what Heiss might know, but the question was how to extract that information.

Loss gritted his teeth and slammed his fist into the pillow. The frustration of being made the scapegoat for something obviously illegal grated continually at the corners of his mind. The fact that Welsh could turn and accuse him of theft, willingly condemning Loss to complete loss of professional reputation and three years of life in a foreign prison seemed unbelievable. What Loss had accepted as fate initially had now become the realization that he was simply a minor character in some play, readily expendable. And for once in his life, Loss was beginning to know the literal meaning of the word hate.

There was a knock at his door, and it opened without his response. Nurse Wylie entered, carrying a food tray. She placed it on the night table without comment and started to leave.

"Take it away."

"I'm sorry, Mister Loss," she enunciated carefully. "This is the food that all patients get. This is what we eat. Perhaps they feed you better in Nassau." She immediately felt regret at lowering herself to conversation with this honky. Her brother was right, in his own way.

Loss softened his tone, leaning back against the pillows and closing his eyes. She could hardly hear his slightly slurred speech.

"Miss Wylie, Nurse Wylie. I'm sorry. I can't eat. Just remove the tray, please, and give me two or three sleeping tablets. No visitors. Nothing. My head really hurts."

She regarded the white man and then understood his irritability. The stitches would be pulling now, and probably the worry of tomorrow bothered him.

"Yes," she said, hesitantly. "Yes, I'll be right back." She removed the tray and left the room, pausing to adjust the blanket that had almost slid off the bed.

She left the room and walked down the corridor, relieved that her professional attitude had not been corrupted by the irritant of Loss's behavior. And now she understood. And with medication for his pain and sleeping tablets, he would be no more trouble for the evening. Tomorrow, he would be gone.

She returned in under five minutes, two separate paper cups containing pills and a fresh glass of cold water balanced on her tray.

He took them without comment and sank back into the pillows.

"Thanks. I still think you're the best nurse I ever saw."

She smiled at him now, relieved.

"I'll be in to see you at eleven. To check your temperature." She watched him with professional pride, the thing now back into a controlled patient-nurse relationship.

"Can't we just skip that this evening? I haven't had a temperature in three days and I want to get a solid night's sleep."

He said it quietly, reasonably. She knew the matron would require it, but she would forget it for this night.

"It will be all right, Mister Loss. Just this once. Sleep well." She smiled as she left the room and closed the door softly.

Loss listened to her steps retreating down the corridor, hollow echoes and then quiet. It was a small risk that his absence would be discovered. But the girl would catch hell in the morning, which he felt genuinely sorry about.

He spit the four capsules into his hand, and washed out his mouth with the water. He discarded the two sleeping tablets in the wastebasket but retained the partially dissolved pain capsules for future use, pocketing them in the robe.

His Rolex showed sixteen minutes after six. He moved to the window and watched the dark hospital grounds and the street beyond. No sign of Stroud's Ford. The power generation station emitted its hollow thrumming, which he could just faintly hear against the prevalent sounds of the trade winds. The Cable and Wireless offices were lighted as they would be until midnight. All the other shops were dark as far as he could see along the sea front with the exception of the rum shop much further along Bay Street toward the eastern edge of town.

He turned reluctantly from the window. Now nineteen past. Rolling a blanket into a tube, he stuffed it beneath the covers. Crude. Maybe enough to pass for a man in the dim light from the corridor. He wanted to shave, to have a shower. But it was an impossibility. He regretted that he had not asked for his billfold and sunglasses. Perhaps even his blood-stained clothing. But there was only the hospital robe. It had to be enough.

The sound of an insect rasping against the screen. He turned and watched a hand draw a fingertip down across the window screen.

"Stroud?"

"Yes." A face appeared, lean, serious, almost comical. His glasses, thick as glass biscuits, reflected doubled pinpoints of light. The face smiled. "Let's get going."

Loss turned the bed lamp off and walked to the window. He watched as Stroud cut a flap in the screening, neatly and without haste, as if he were dissecting a specimen.

His rib hurt as Loss dropped to the ground and the two men grasped hands. Loss felt vaguely embarrassed, as if this were a meeting of two child-conspirators, about to recite a secret oath and then swab the farmer's cows with white paint.

"I'm Stroud." He stood there in the blackness, only the reflection of his glasses and the white teeth visible.

"Yes. You lead. My eyes aren't adapted to night vision yet."

They kept to the dark shadow of the building, trampling the carefully tended flowers; the crushed leaves released a pungent smell. Loss thought of his first date and the scent of lilac. Forever ago.

"The car's over there," Stroud said.

"Did you get the briefcase?"

"Yes. Your weapon too."

Loss paused, seeking the right words. "Stroud, I don't have time to thank you properly for this. Perhaps some day."

Stroud smiled, his teeth bright in the darkness. "It's quite all right. I'm sure you'd do the same. The aircraft is all refueled and preflighted. Use up the main tanks first and then refill them from the reserve cans while you run on the auxiliary tanks. The procedure is on an index card on the left seat sunvisor. I think that you can stretch it to twenty-two hundred some odd miles. There's some tables of actual petrol consumption at various power settings in the dash compartment. You probably will find them helpful."

"Yes, Peter. I understand," Loss said. "Look I don't want to tell you where exactly, but I'm going to try to make Canada. I'll leave the aircraft there in one piece if possible. I'll cover all the expenses and time on the aircraft and leave the money in cash with some friends who will take care of the aircraft. But until then, you just have to convince everyone that it was stolen and, if possible, that the range was short of 800 miles on the fuel available. We'll remove the backseat tanks in Canada and store them so that there won't be any embarrassing questions. Agreed?"

Stroud nodded. "It's fine, Brian. Do whatever you have to do with the aircraft. It's insured. Just don't implicate me on your end, and it will work out. Incidentally, I've overfilled the oil by one quart, but she burns a bit. That should still give you at least minimum oil required by the end of your flight. Just keep the power settings low if you can."

"Thanks. Good to know. Let's move."

The two men watched the street for a few more minutes. The sparsely placed street lamps swung in the wind. Beyond that, there was no movement. They crossed the hospital lawn and then the street, moving carefully and without haste. Loss moved into the back seat allowing Stroud to drive.

"Airport?"

"No," Loss replied. "We've got one other stop to—"

"Get down," Stroud hissed. The door of Cable and Wireless opened, and the night operator moved into the doorway, looking down the street to the east, chewing slowly on some object. Stroud got out of the car immediately, not turning to look at Loss, who hunched down behind the seat.

"Oh, you've received it?" Stroud asked, politely standing just on the edge of the shaded lamp's rim of brightness.

"Get what?" The girl turned to him, scowling, still chewing methodically.

"My cable. I've been waiting for it all day. A cable from Barbados. For me. Peter Stroud." He stood somewhat humbly before her, now moving into the light. He smiled, hesitantly.

"No cable," she said, turning and shutting the door.

Stroud returned to the car and started it, allowing the engine to warm up, not moving yet as if undecided. Finally he pulled away from the dirt parking area onto the asphalt lane and drove slowly away. "Where now," he said.

Loss laughed from the recesses of the back seat. "Very cool." He rose from the back seat floor and said, "OK, Peter. Here comes the harder part. Take the second left down here and go up two blocks. You know the place they call Mary's Beach Cottages? They're not exactly on the beach, but I guess in a town of four or five hundred, you can get away with that." He pointed to the turn. "Here."

They swung left from the bay front and onto a dirt road. The street lights disappeared behind them and only a few scattered houses lined the street—the more prosperous section of town.

"From here on out, Peter, you have to play the captured aircraft owner. I'll have to tie you up with nylon fishing line and gag you. I'll be leaving you in the front seat. Next, I get Heiss out of his cottage and his lawyer as well, if they're rooming together."

Stroud nodded, his face just faintly illuminated in the glow of the dashboard lights.

"The important thing is that you must listen to everything Heiss tells me and report this to the police. When we get to the airfield, I'll question him. It may be a little rough. Both of you will be tied up but well separated. Watch out for him, Peter. Don't trust him an inch. Campbell says that Heiss is violent."

"And then?" Stroud asked, shifting gears smoothly.

"After we find out what we can, Holly and I will take off, leaving you both behind. Your bonds will be loose enough for you to work out of them after a decent period of time. Don't make it seem too quick. Heiss will be really well secured, so don't worry. We'll climb out to the south and then eventually turn north after we're out of sight and hearing. You leave Heiss where he is and trot smartly into town. Give the stolen-aircraft story routine and tell them we departed to the south. Tell them what Heiss has said. From there, just wait until you hear the aircraft has been recovered. Submit an insurance claim as well, I guess. All of this clear?"

"Sounds like good fun," Stroud replied. "Here you are."

Stroud slowed the car and pulled off to the side, extinguishing the lights as he did. A complex of cottages and a central guest house were set back into a grove of white cedar and sea grape trees. The grounds were neatly fenced by low shrubs. The guest house had several lights burning, and movement from within could be seen just as blurred shapes. The sound of a Jim Reeves recording was faint on the humid night wind.

They sat in the darkness for several minutes watching the complex of buildings and the grounds. No real movement except in the main guest house.

"Cottage 4 is the unit Heiss and his lawyer have rented," Loss said, indicating a building set deep into a grove of sea grape trees, far to the left. A light shone dimly behind the drapes.

Stroud rubbed his chin, almost bored. "What's on the program now?"

"That depends. Have you bought the gear that Holly briefed you on?"

"It's in the boot—trunk—whatever you call it. Two hundred-foot coil of eighty-pound test monofilament line. Some adhesive tape. Box of plastic garbage bags and sweets. Chocolate, if you don't mind?"

Loss eased out of the Ford and crouched in its shadow, listening. Satisfied, he opened the trunk and extracted the equipment. He opened his briefcase and groped for his Luger. He released the clip and counted the rounds, snicking his thumbnail down the loading slot. Eight. Loss reinserted the clip and chambered a round. He felt himself slipping past that point of return, where rules made sense.

Loss extracted the monofilament fishing line from the small heap and returned to the driver's side. Stroud obediently turned and crossed his wrists, which Loss bound. Next, the ankles. Finally a tape across the mouth. Loss gently placed Stroud in the right front seat, the Englishman faintly complaining through the gag. Loss squeezed his shoulder and said in a whisper, "Sorry about this. But if I'm caught, just tell them that you were forced. I'm going in to get Heiss now. Stay low on the seat," and he was gone, the Luger cool in his dry hand.

Loss stayed low, running in a crouch along the line of sea grapes that bordered the property. Heiss's cottage was the furthest one, and he gained the wall of the unit without exposure.

His head was pounding now, and he felt weak and lightheaded. The thin bathrobe was a sieve to the night wind, and he rested briefly against the wall of the cottage.

The curtains to the cottage were drawn, but he could hear the sound of a toilet flushing and moments later, a door closing.

Loss felt his way along the edge of the wall to the back of the cottage. One window of a bedroom was opened, the drapes parted, but Loss could not see the full extent of the living room beyond. There were no voices, only the faint strains of the country and western ballad from the main house.

I can't delay this damn thing forever, he thought and retraced his steps along the wall of the cottage to the front door. There was a doorway light recessed in a globe over the sill, and he unscrewed the unlit bulb and cast it aside on the lawn. Tapping lightly with his fingertips on the door, he murmured "Cable, Mistah Bolken" and leaned against the door, Luger leveled at chest height.

The door opened and Loss pushed in, ramming the barrel into Heiss's stomach. Heiss stumbled backwards, tripping and falling heavily to the floor. Loss had the door closed before he had recovered.

"Roll over on your stomach, Heiss, and put your hands behind your back. Where's your so-called lawyer?"

Heiss complied, looking over his shoulder at the man standing over him. Loss stood above him wearing a light blue bathrobe, shod only in tennis shoes. His head was bandaged about the forehead, eyes haggard. The Luger was a black hole, boresighted on his head. He didn't doubt that it was loaded.

"What do you want, Loss? I can't help you. They're deporting me."

"Where's your lawyer, Heiss?"

Heiss started to sit up and Loss stepped back, crouched and raised the weapon to a two-handed combat stance, sighting over the barrel.

Heiss sighed and lay down, rolling over, hands crossed behind his back. "You're a fucking lunatic," Heiss said. "You're only going to get three years and that's at 3000 dollars a month. Any trouble from you and Klist will simply snuff your lights."

"Your lawyer, Heiss. Where is he?" The words came in a hiss.

"He moved to Cottage 1."

"Do you expect him to come over here?"

Heiss shook his head. "No, he's got some sort of a radio schedule to meet."

Loss had fashioned a loop with slip knot from the fishing line. He rammed the Luger's barrel into the cleft in Heiss's buttocks and stood hunched over him, feet straddling the prone form.

"Heiss. Listen carefully. I'm going to tie your hands. Don't move or I'll blow your balls off." A Ranger in Nam had told Loss about this approach. A man can roll with a gun in his back, but the thought of losing his testicles put a prisoner into paralysis. He quickly slipped the loop over Heiss's wrists and pulled it tight, taking subsequent turns to secure the bond.

"Keep still, Heiss. I'm going to do your ankles now. If you twitch, you'll only be fit to sing in church choirs." Heiss felt the long probe of the Luger, hard and alien. He wanted to urinate badly.

"Look, you asshole," Heiss whispered. "If you snuff me, you'll be up for murder. I can't give you any information. Klist is gone. He made it to Cuba; that's why this lawyer is down here. Klist arranged it."

"Why were you with Klist?"

"Just simple stuff. I was recording conversations. Taking pictures. That's the extent of what I know. I don't have any idea of what your boss and Klist were up to. Christ, Loss, can't you see? You're getting in way over your head."

"Listen carefully, Heiss. I'm not going to jail for ten minutes, let alone three years. I want sufficient evidence to clear me. I'm also beginning to think that Welsh is into something that might be very unhealthy, and I want to know more about that. If I have to squeeze your balls in a nutcracker to find out, I will. You and I are going for a little drive, so let me explain the ground rules very carefully."

Heiss lay perfectly still now, his eyes wild.

"This is a garbage bag," Loss said, unfolding the green plastic square. "I am going to place this over your head and shoulders and secure it around your neck with your belt. I will then undo your ankles. We will walk very calmly to a car I have outside. If you run, I don't want to shoot you. I will just clobber you over the head, and since I am not experienced in these matters, I may break something. You have sufficient air in that bag to last for over a minute if, and I emphasize this strongly, if you keep calm. If you run, you either get a broken head, or you suffocate. Understood?"

Heiss closed his eyes and nodded.

Edging back the curtain, Loss looked across the lawn at the complex. No way of knowing which was Cottage 1. But he could see no movement.

Stripping the belt from Heiss's pants, he got an idea. Keeping the weapon trained on Heiss, he backed into the bedroom and swept the closet of clothes hanging there. He brought them into the living room and selected a pair of gray flannel trousers and a pullover sweater of light wool. Exchanging these for the robe, he checked the complex again and then knelt beside Heiss and helped him up. Heiss stood up, tottering slightly. Loss slipped the plastic bag over his head and torso and secured it at the neck with Heiss's belt, taking two turns and tying it loosely. Next, he cut the fishing line bond at the ankles. The bag was expanding and contracting with Heiss's breath now, the appearance almost comical.

"Easy, Heiss. Just conserve your energy and you'll make it." Loss guided him through the doorway and across the yard, keeping to open ground to avoid wasting time.

Opening the back door of the Ford, Loss pushed him in across the seat and paused long enough to retie his ankles before ripping open the bag. Heiss lay gasping, his face bathed in sweat.

Loss closed the door and entered the driver's side. Starting the Ford was an agony, the engine catching and then dying. He tried again, careful not to flood the carburetor. It caught finally, at first firing on just a few cylinders before smoothing out to a steady rhythm.

Loss cursed his own stupidity. He would have to go more carefully. He left the headlights extinguished and backed the car in reverse over one hundred yards before switching on the headlights and turning around.

Stroud lay silent in the seat beside him, Heiss still panting loudly in the back.

The town was relatively deserted as Loss drove through. Near the rum shop two men stood on the dirt pathway that bordered the street, apparently arguing, arms gesturing. No lights in the hospital in his room's wing of the building. His headlights swept across the benches of the park on the western edge of town as he turned onto the coast road. Two people, both black, sat there, apparently just enjoying an evening together. The man was smoking a pipe.

They were beyond the outskirts now, only an occasional house now along the road. He drove past the turnoff to the yacht basin; the club building was dark. For another half a mile, the coastal road ran straight between stunted scrubs, wisps of sand drifting across the asphalt, driven by the wind. To his left, he could catch occasional glimpses of the sea, flecked with light from a slipper moon. At the turnoff to the airport road, he stopped the car and extinguished the headlights. Almost immediately, a cigarette lighter flicked in the blackness ahead and then was extinguished. He relaxed and waited.

She moved along the driver's side, keeping away from the car.

"It's all together," he said. "Use the back seat. Watch out for Heiss. He's tied up. Just push him onto the floor."

She entered the car and leaned over to kiss him. She smelled of lemon grass and sweat.

"Thanks for coming," he said. "Anyone on the road?"

She leaned back into the seat and breathed out heavily. "No, I've been here for about a half hour. I had to come across the fields because it was still daylight. Land crabs and dogs. That's about the sum total."

He accelerated down the narrow highway toward the airport. The highway was obviously less used than the coastal road; cracks in the pavement were filled with sand and weed. He braked sharply and turned left onto the gravel strip near the British Petroleum sign. Slowing, he passed the deserted clapboard terminal and pulled to a stop behind the single-engine Comanche, which shone briefly in his headlights.

He switched off the lights and got out, Holly joining him. He handed her the Luger and opened the rear passenger door, dragging Heiss out feet first and then grasping him under the shoulder blades and dropping him onto the hardstand. Heiss grunted with the impact and then lay over on his side, breathing heavily. Next, Loss opened the right front passenger door and extracted Stroud. He undid the tape and leg bonds, leaving his hands tied. Leaning close to Stroud's ear Loss whispered, "We do our stuff now. Don't overdo it either way. And thanks." Stroud nodded, his smile momentary and almost ironic.

He tied the hands of each man to opposite sides of the front bumper of the Ford, each man sitting on the hardstand, back resting against the bumper. Loss increased the number of turns on Heiss's bonds, checking their security with a penlight he had taken from Stroud's pocket.

Loss lit a cigarette, cupping his hands carefully to shield the match. Exhaling, he sat down on the hardstand in front of the two men. Stroud looked at him intently, his face a mirror of anger. Heiss had leaned his head back against the fender, eyes closed, simply waiting.

"Gentlemen," Loss said, "it is time we began. First of all, I have to apologize to you, Stroud. I know that you were gracious enough to bring Holly up here and we repay you by stealing your aircraft. But that can't be helped. You'll get it back in time."

"Mister Loss," Stroud said between clenched teeth, "I can only advise you to release me. From all appearances, you're in a great deal of trouble already. You don't know how to fly my aircraft, and I warn you that there's relatively little range on the petrol remaining."

"Sorry. I can't stick around. I'll make it to Haiti at least. I can get fuel there tonight before anyone knows I've gotten away. Where are the keys?"

"He keeps them under the floor mat in the baggage compartment," she said. "I think it's unlocked."

"Bad luck, Loss," Stroud said. "The baggage compartment is locked, and the key is back at the hotel. You should have thought of that when you came around tonight waving that Luger."

Loss stood up and walked around to the rear of the Ford. He returned, carrying his briefcase, the plastic garbage sacks, and a tire iron. Handing her the briefcase and tire iron, he said, "If the baggage compartment is locked, force it open with this. Get the keys out and open up the cabin door. Leave the keys in the ignition, but don't touch anything else. And scrounge around in the cabin and see whether you can find any sort of flight manual, operating instructions, maps, that sort of thing. Leave them on top of the dash. We'll be out of here in twenty minutes and sooner if anyone comes. After you get things organized, stay up on the wing of the plane and keep an eye on the approach road. You should be able to see headlights when they're still three or four miles away."

Loss crouched down again in front of them. Laying the Luger within easy reach, he carefully unfolded another plastic garbage bag. This time Heiss watched him carefully, eyes reflecting pinpoints of moonlight, mouth slightly agape.

"All right, Heiss. It's your turn. Loss pulled the bag over Heiss's head and shoulders in one quick motion. Grasping the edge of the bag, he twisted it to form a seal. At first Heiss sat motionless, breathing slowly, the bag wrinkling in and out with slow regularity. Loss counted the seconds mentally.

Thirty-eight, thirty-nine.

The bag was flexing more quickly now.

Fifty-four, fifty-five, fifty-six . . .

Heiss was beginning to struggle now, his chest heaving.

Eighty-one, eighty-two . . .

The body was frantic now, chest and lower torso racked with spasms. Loss caught the acrid odor of urine. Heiss was losing control, his head bucking as if to throw off the bag.

Loss slowly removed the plastic shroud and sat back, listening to Heiss's gasping, lungs racking in fresh air.

"For God's sake," Stroud spat out. "God in heaven—"

Loss cut him off. "Shut up, Stroud. This bastard's name isn't Bolken—it's Heiss. He's a Russian agent or close to it. And he's going to give me information before I leave, and you're going to listen to it and report it word for word to the police. And to the press if you can find anyone who will report it. So look and listen and learn, but keep your mouth shut." Loss turned to Heiss and patted him on the head.

"Very good, Herr Heiss. You lasted nearly a minute and a half. You see, it's not that you're running out of oxygen under there. It's just that all the carbon dioxide you exhale triggers some breathing mechanism and you start to pant, producing more carbon dioxide. That's what suffocation is all about. The

Chinese used it in North Korea. The record is supposed to be over three minutes. Sometimes there is moderate brain damage. You'll probably make a very nice carrot."

Heiss screamed and Loss smashed him across the face with his hand, silencing him abruptly. Blood now streamed from Heiss's nostrils in the dim moonlight.

Loss sighed and sat back on the hardstand. The moon was just a sliver of light, already setting in the west. The sky was cloudless, except for a few thin wisps of cirrus. The wind was as Campbell had reported, moderate and in the east. This thing was gruesome, and he wondered whether he could go through with it. Sighing, he talked to Heiss, almost gently, like a slightly irritated parent would to a son who had dinged the fender of the family car. "Heiss. I don't have all night. I am going to ask you some questions; some of the same questions I asked you back at your cottage. You will answer them. If I think you're lying, I will put the bag over your head again and take a short walk. I will be gone twenty seconds longer than your last exercise in the bag. I don't want to kill you. That will be, very simply, your own free choice. Now, for our English audience here, I want you to repeat who you are, what you did for Klist, and most important, whether I stole the Aztec."

Heiss glared at Loss with hate, his eyes black voids beneath the brows. He said nothing. Loss sighed and opened the bag, preparatory to placing it over his head.

"No, Loss. Don't. Look, I can give you everything I've got if you get me out of here. A Luxembourg account. Just drop me in Trinidad or Venezuela. I've—"

Brian sighed and dropped the bag over Heiss's head, mentally starting to count. Heiss was screaming inside the bag. Loss twisted the bag closed and stood up, brushing off his pants. He could not keep the bag on much more than the first time, but it would seem like an eternity to Heiss.

It was worse this time. No initial attempt to keep still. Heiss was in trouble within thirty seconds.

"Sixty-two, sixty-three . . ."

Heiss was bucking now, trying to stand, actually pushing the car backward, then he collapsed. His body was racked with convulsions.

Removing the bag with a jerk, Loss stood over the body, watching the chest heave, lungs sucking in air. Heiss vomited, gagging, coughing.

Loss walked away quickly and was sick behind the trunk of the Ford. Please Christ, let this thing talk. I've got to get it out of him, he thought, the bile taste thick in his mouth.

He walked back to the front of the car, wiping the spittle from his lips, moving slowly with great calm.

He squatted down directly in front of Heiss. No preliminaries now. "What's your real name?"

"Heiss. Carl Heiss. Jesus. I can't talk. Volgel, the lawyer, will kill me. If he thinks I've talked, he or Klist will kill me."

Loss picked up the bag again, his heart pounding. He opened it, a motion that Heiss reflected in abject terror.

"Yes, Loss, yes. What else," Heiss said in a thin wail.

"Tell Mr. Stroud here why we made the flight."

Heiss was almost incoherent now, the words gushing out between great gulps of air, as if oxygen were forever rationed. "Klist directed the flight. He was aboard. Loss only did what his employer said. He didn't steal the aircraft. Klist got away. To Cuba. By a boat. I don't know how."

"Who's Klist? I mean his real name. His nationality?"

"Petrov. He's Eastern Bloc. He's setting your senator up for something. I wasn't told what. Just that I was supposed to record their conversations. Pictures."

Loss patted his cheek. "Keep going, Heiss. You're going fine. Where are these tapes and films? Did you ever listen to them?"

Heiss shook his head violently, saying nothing.

"You're lying, Heiss. I don't think you can take another session in the bag. If you made the recordings, you probably listened to some of them. Quickly, Heiss." Loss lifted the bag and slowly started to lower it over Heiss's head. Heiss was screaming again, his voice cracked and thin.

"No, Loss. Please, Loss."

Brian snatched the bag off and thrust his face into Heiss's, spitting out each word. "The tapes, you fuckin' bastard. What was on the tapes? I'm going to leave in two minutes and your answer means that you either suck your guts out on dead air or you live." Loss slapped Heiss across the face, his fingers scalding with pain from the force of the blow. "Come *on,* Heiss. I know something about it from Welsh. What . . . was . . . on . . . the . . . tapes?" He was shaking the man now by the hair, slamming Heiss's head against the fender, the frustration of the last five days boiling over, concentrated on one man. This thing.

"I—don't—know," Heiss sobbed, "only—"

"Only what?"

"Only one tape. The rest Petrov—he kept them. He said he had some mark on the tape to show if they had been replayed. I didn't know!" Heiss retched again, this time a dry heaving.

"Go on. Go on. What was on the one tape?"

"I bugged Petrov and that bitch. Just to see if I could find anything to use later. It was all in Russian. I can read it, but I don't speak the language. Just a few words. He said something about Welsh being President and about, something like *hood.* A place, I think. And the word *hussar.* Or *Huzar.* A highway robber."

"What else?"

"Jesus-God, Loss. That was all. I don't know more than that. That's everything. But take me with you. Volgel will—"

"You'll live, Heiss," Loss said, getting to his feet. "Just get in touch with Campbell. I think you've met. He can probably protect you."

Loss paused, standing there in the dim moonlight and looked at the two men. "Stroud. I've got to go now. Your wrists aren't bound too tightly. You should be able to work out of them and if not, they'll find you out here tomorrow morning. There's a flight in from Nassau at 8:15. It's up to you, but I would suggest that you leave Heiss tied up and let the police take care of it. If there is any press coming in on the plane, try to get to them before you talk with the cops."

Stroud nodded. "Perhaps we'll meet again, Loss," he said. "I guess I can understand—everything. Why don't you wait for them yourself? I'll back your story."

Loss shook his head. "No, Peter. I've already committed three or four more crimes they can hold me for. I'll wait until the dust settles. Adios, mother." He said it kindly.

Heiss and Stroud sat there, each bound to the car, watching Loss disappear into the cabin of the aircraft. In three minutes, he had fired up the engine and taxied out to the western end of the runway, lights extinguished but with the blue flame of exhaust pulsing in the blackness.

They heard the growl of the engine, rising in crescendo. The noise grew; the aircraft flashed by them in the moonlight. It cleared the end of the field and climbed, glinting briefly in the moonlight as it turned to the south.

God speed, you Yankee bastard, Stroud thought, smiling thinly. Heiss struggled futilely against his bonds beside him, muttering senseless words against the blackness of night.

Chapter 17

Petrov was seething. He lit another Cuban cigarette and then after inhaling once, submerged it in the remains of his coffee, now grown cold. He rose from his desk and stood over the shoulder of a sandy-haired young rating who sat at a console, headset clamped across his ears. The young man looked up questioningly. Petrov only glowered at him. The operator replied with the merest shake of his head and resumed his concentration.

Petrov walked along the rubber-matted aisle behind the consoles, checking each one in turn. Air conditioning masked the sounds of guarded conversations, the steps of other officers checking the work of their subordinates and the staccato beat of teleprinters.

Petrov regarded the situation display, which was projected on frosted glass that covered the front wall of the command post. The display covered the Caribbean Sea from the Straits of Yucatan on the west to 800 kilometers east into the Atlantic; the coast of Venezuela and Colombia on the south to the Gulf Coast and Florida in the north. Coastlines were projected in red with lines of latitude and longitude etched in lighter traces of white. Tracks of ships were plotted in green and identified by type of ship, nationality, speed, probable destination, and special remarks—all in abbreviated code. Aircraft tracks, which at this minute were Petrov's immediate concern, were in brilliant orange, each aircraft identified in a manner similar to the ships. He watched one track in particular, an elliptical path some 100 kilometers long and only a few kilometers in width, like some super-elongated racetrack. The major axis of this track was placed roughly north-south in the Windward Passage, the body of water that separates Cuba from the Bahamas.

The timer over the display gave a digital wink and registered 22:10 Greenwich Mean Time, or 6:10 PM local time. Too long a wait, he thought, the acid of his stomach burning holes in his composure. He forced a belch, trying to ease the pain. But the raw feeling of doubt remained.

Petrov walked to the desk-console of the senior duty officer. The man, a Lieutenant Commander of the Russian Fleet, Atlantic Division, rose immediately. Petrov motioned him to sit down, noting that the man was grossly overweight and that his uniform was in need of pressing. Thick glasses, a fat wife, and probably entitled to share a dacha on the Black Sea in his retirement. The name tag on his plastic security badge identified him as Lieutenant Commander Vladimirovich Zhivotorskiv.

Petrov bent over the desk, splaying his fingers out over the surface. "Any further transmissions, Commander?"

The naval officer nodded. "Yes, Colonel. But just routine transmissions for our reconnaissance aircraft. Nothing as yet from Comrade—" he paused and looked down at his desk log, "from Comrade Volgel since he reported his position at the airstrip."

Petrov hoped that Volgel was accurate in his assessment of Loss's intentions. It would solve a lot of problems.

Petrov had landed in Cuba seven days before, completely exhausted. After much gun-waving and rough treatment, the Cuban militiamen had delivered him to a Russian interpreter. From there on in, it had been simple to establish his identity. Through the Russian Embassy in Mexico, Petrov had immediately arranged for a sometime-KGB agent in Nassau to fly down to Great Inagua, equipped with a portable transmitter and a weapon. His cover was to be legal counsel for Heiss. The stringer, Ernst Volgel, had done well. Heiss was to be set loose after paying a fine, and Loss was under close surveillance. Both Heiss and Loss would be eliminated; Heiss once he left the Bahamas, and Loss whenever the opportunity presented itself.

It now looked like that opportunity was presenting itself. Volgel had called in the early afternoon on his regular schedule and said emphatically that the small aircraft, a single-engine Comanche, was being prepared for flight by its owner. Petrov had no doubt now that Loss would attempt to escape the loose security of the hospital ward and make a run for it. With the authority granted him by a rapid teleprinter interchange with Moscow, Petrov had ordered a reconnaissance aircraft to maintain station in the Windward Passage. Using this aircraft as an airborne tracking station, Petrov would launch a flight of night interceptors to destroy Loss, once he was over the open sea. Things were resolving themselves nicely, he thought.

"Tell me, Commander," Petrov said, easing down onto the edge of the desk, "what is the capability of your reconnaissance aircraft?"

Commander Zhivotorskiv, well aware that Petrov was KGB, answered promptly, even though their ranks were equal. "It is a Tupulov TU-18. Equipped with radar and infrared scanning. They're presently at 10,000 meters altitude. I'm sure you're familiar with the performance figures." He fished a cardboard box of Red Star cigarettes from his tunic, offering one first to Petrov before taking one for himself. Petrov accepted the brown-paper-wrapped cigarette and bent forward while Zhivotorskiv flicked his western-type Zippo. Petrov noted, in the brief illumination of the lighter that Zhivotorskiv's bald head had a sheen of perspiration.

Petrov turned away and watched the display board for some minutes, smoking the cigarette and tapping the ashes on the polished floor in obvious disregard of the ashtray centimeters from his hand. He hated cigarettes, but when he was nervous, he resorted to them for something to occupy his hands. The thing tasted like dried excrement. In disgust, he dropped it to the floor and ground it under his heel. "And how long have you been stationed here, Commander?" Petrov asked, not really interested but wanting something to ease the waiting.

Surprised that the KGB man should express interest, Zhivotorskiv replied, "Our communications unit was transferred here six years ago. Before that, we were based in East Germany. I would just as soon go back."

"And how so?"

Zhivotorskiv shrugged. "The weather. The food. We don't mix with the Cubans. No opportunities for, well, fun."

Petrov nodded. "And what are your duties specifically?"

The Lieutenant Commander lit another of the foul cigarettes. "Mine personally? Well, I'm shift commander for this section. The Group, of course, monitors all movements of military shipping and air traffic in the Caribbean. We also handle all the communications for the submarine installation up at Cienfuegos on the west coast." He leaned back, relaxing, and continued, "The submarine boys up there get first class treatment. Fresh food flown in from the homeland. New movies. Down here, we eat Cuban dog shit."

Petrov scratched at the rash on his neck. "And the reconnaissance aircraft and fighters. Are they ours or Cuban?"

Zhivotorskiv shook his head. "The recons are ours. Direct support of the subs, of course, and intelligence gathering on the movement of US subs, shots from Cape Kennedy. The usual thing. But the fighters are Cuban. Our noble allies." He snorted in derision.

"They're not competent pilots?" Petrov asked, stifling a yawn.

"Oh, they're good enough, but no discipline. They think these aircraft that we have given them are toys. Incidentally, speaking of the fighters, we've directed Cuban Air Command to position a flight of four MIG-19s on runway alert at the Baracoa fighter strip in Oriente Province. They can be airborne within two minutes of your orders and over Great Inagua in twelve."

Petrov stood up and stretched. "Good. Call me when anything develops. I'll be in the duty officer's day room." He turned and walked away without further comment.

Zhivotorskiv watched him go. Perhaps I've been indiscreet talking about the Cubans, he thought. Petrov was a cold fish. No telling about that kind.

He reached into his desk filing cabinet and reread a copy of the deciphered message that had arrived within two hours after Petrov had first arrived with the Cuban major from Havana. It read:

```
GOSPLAN TO CMDR 288STRATCOM CUBA COMMA
SECURITY LEVEL NINE STOP PERSON NAMED YOUR
INQUIRY IDENTIFIED AS COLONEL ANATOLI
ANTONOVICH PETROV STOP PETROV TO RECEIVE
YOUR FULLEST AND UNQUALIFIED COOPERATION AS
PER HIS VERBAL ORDERS STOP POSITIVE
IDENTIFICATION OF FINGERPRINTS AND PHOTO
BY FOLLOWING DIGITAL SCAN TRANSMISSION STOP
TELEPRINT KGB/5 IN TACTICAL CODE NOVEMBER
COMMA QUOTE SALMACIS UNQUOTE STOP AUTHENTICATION
REPLY IS QUOTE PORT ARTHUR UNQUOTE STOP
SIGNATURE FIRST SECRETARY STOP END MESSAGE
```

Zhivotorskiv read and reread the message form. This man, Petrov, was not to be fooled with. He returned the message form to the file and waited.

Petrov entered the day room. The occupant sat at a desk, engrossed in the playback of a miniature cassette recording, making notations occasionally and then rewinding the tape to verify his conclusions. The voices on the recording were those of Welsh and Klist-Petrov.

"Do you think I'm ready for the theater, Vassel?" Petrov asked, wearily stretching out on the rumpled blanket that covered the iron-framed bunk.

Vassel Rametka, Chief of the Directorate of Special Situations, Order of Lenin, father of children who skated in Gorky Park, shook his head and held his hand up demanding silence. He rewound the tape for a second and replayed the segment.

Petrov could barely hear the conversation, recognizing only the vaguely thick words of Senator Welsh arguing and himself, replying in smooth, even cadence. Very persuasive.

Rametka snapped off the recorder. "Very good, Anatoli," the older man said, unbuttoning his vest and leaning back in the leather chair. "Very good."

"There has been no further transmission from Volgel. The situation remains static," Petrov said, his face lined with fatigue. He bunched up the pillow and fell back into it, his blond hair almost bleached white by the tropic sun. Tanned. But looking very tired.

Rametka removed his steel-rimmed glasses and rubbed the bridge of his nose. The physiological traces of what, in Western circles, was referred to as "jet lag" disturbed him. Disorientation, inability to sleep, a lack of natural timekeeping sense. The flight from the Urals via Moscow to Havana via the Aeroflot Supersonic had stretched over seven hours, but in real time was half a world away. But there was no doubt—Petrov's work with Welsh had been first-class psychology. The rest was a different matter.

Rametka dropped his pen on the desk, the point nicking the worn linoleum. He loosened his tie and as an afterthought, removed it roughly. Petrov still lay back, relaxed. He knows, Rametka thought. He's young and he smells my fear of failure.

Vassel Rametka made a notation on the pad with his gold-plated pen. "Anatoli," he said, "I don't doubt that our psychological analysis of this Senator Welsh was very exact. He reacts in the tapes as was expected. Pavlovian to an exactitude. I think that there can be no question that he will use our help in political situations to further his own career. Should he ever have any doubts about his involvement, we have the photos, tapes, and his signed statement to keep him well within our control."

Petrov nodded, his eyes still closed. "But?" he said, waiting.

"But," Rametka continued, "the plane flight didn't go as we planned it. We have this present situation to contend with and—"

Petrov suddenly sat upright, anger reducing his eyes to stark blue pinpoints. He thrust his finger at Rametka. "But!" he spat out. "*But* for this and *but* for that. Yes, Dr. Vassel Rametka, Order of Lenin, *we* planned the flight. I emphasize the *we*. By utilizing Welsh's plane, Heiss and I were to fly out of the Caribbean into Mexico. The aircraft conveniently is lost at sea on its return trip, eliminating any trace of connection between Welsh and myself. Welsh simply loses his pilot and an aircraft. Another tragedy in the Bermuda Triangle. Welsh returns to the US to resume his role in politics, completely under our control.

"There are three folders in your files concerning the capabilities of the aircraft, the radio equipment in the aircraft, the competence of the pilot. Perfect! Perfect, Comrade Rametka, except for the imponderables of bad weather and the quixotic actions of a pilot who that very morning chose to quit working for Welsh."

Rametka leaned back in his chair. "Go on," he said, sucking the gap between his molars.

Petrov fell wearily back into the bed, disgust evident in his tone. "So this pilot Loss chooses to disregard his employer's instructions and heads for the southern coast of the Dominican Republic in order to judge his flight path and retain the option of refueling. Subsequently, he decides that we have to land to refuel. I strongly suspect that his suspicions were part of this decision."

"So you land in Great Inagua?"

Petrov looked at the scientist. Rametka was making notes with that cheap western pen. More fuel for the report. "Yes, we land in Great Inagua. When Loss made his decision to land, I recontacted our people in Mexico. I had already planned on Great Inagua as a possible alternate because it is close to Cuba, has a minimum of officials, and has good fuel supplies. Loss agreed to this. The rest of the flight was like black dog shit. Uncontrollably violent. Nothing like I have ever seen. The rest of it you know."

Rametka sat silently at the desk, the ball point scratching on the pad. He took the glasses from his face and set them down on the scarred linoleum desk top and thought for several minutes. Finally, he looked up and said, "And what do you intend to do with the Swedish couple and their boat?"

"It will be taken to sea and the seacocks opened. The Swedes should be disposed of. Leave this to the Cubans."

"Is that what you learn in Section V, Anatoli?"

Petrov nodded wearily. "I don't like it either, Vassel. But they are otherwise a liability, even here in Cuba."

"And this man, Volgel?" Rametka said.

"Volgel is a very competent operative. We use him a great deal in Florida. Actually, he is East German."

Rametka raised his eyebrows.

Petrov snorted. "Be realistic, Vassel. Some of us were not born with framed photos of Stalin clutched in our little hands. So it is with Volgel."

"I implied no criticism," Rametka shrugged. "It is just unusual."

"As our American friends say, 'Bullshit.' We are all together in the same cause. Volgel is simply a very competent technician who does occasional work for us. He was the recommendation of the head of the Mexican Department. As soon as I arrived in Cuba, I contacted Mexico and they made the arrangements to send him down there to clean up—I believe the word used was 'sanitize'—the situation involving Loss and Heiss."

Rametka nodded. "How do you see the outcome of tonight?"

Petrov shrugged and fell back heavily on the bed, eyes closed. "You want some sort of equation, don't you, Vassel? Plug in seventeen variables, feed it to the computer and be assured that, within some high percentage of probability, our special situation is under control." He paused, thinking, and then continued, "No, there is no assurance, but to some degree, the situation is within our control. If Volgel does well, then we can go ahead. Until then, you can dream of the order that you wish to have pinned to your imitation western suit upon retirement, and I will sleep."

Forty-three minutes later, the infrared scanners of the TU-18 recognized the thermal signature of the small aircraft on Great Inagua as it started its engine.

Ernest Volgel chewed tentatively at a bit of cuticle on his left index finger. He was slightly nervous and pollen from the weed he lay in was making his eyes water. But his night vision was unimpaired. He watched Loss's movements in front of the sedan. The woman was already in the aircraft. It would not be too long now.

His shirt was damp from contact with the ground and his thin body was sore from lying on the rough terrain. He disliked this assignment. Better in Miami. Clean sheets, clean women. Seldom the necessity for *wet* sanitizing. Most often, just discreet inquiries through credit clearinghouses, public records, or a pickup of film at the *drop* on West Flagler. Just one *wet* job on that Puerto Rican politician. His car had burned well, Volgel thought.

Volgel had been a law student at Leipzig University when the Department had first approached him. He felt neutral about political dogma, but he recognized the corruption in western governments, ultimately realizing that law was written by lawyers for lawyers. Governments were permeated by lawyers who masked themselves as statesmen. Senates and Parliaments, Premierships, and Presidencies were held by lawyers who proclaimed that they were men of the people. He was approached by the KGB to exploit the law for the people and he accepted.

He continued to work in West Germany, moving from one firm to the next, extracting information from dusty files that only a lawyer could distill into intelligence. Items that even he sometimes felt were trivial.

In July, 1964, Volgel boarded a plane for a two-week vacation in Yugoslavia. From there, he flew to the Black Sea resort of Novorossiysk, and from there to Moscow. And in a modishly furnished office of the Komitet Gosudarstvennoi Bezopasnosti on Dzerzhinsky Street, he was awarded citizenship in the USSR and permanent employment in the KGB.

For years he worked in Germany, returning to the Black Sea each summer and then onward to Russia for brief ten-day training assignments. Microphotography, ciphers, and communication procedures at first. Then later, the *wet* stuff. Cyanide gas pistols, weapons training, explosives. Very standard. Fun. Never any politics. And the women from within the KGB were supplied when desired. Clean women and clean sheets. And he thought again of Miami.

The exhaust on the single-engine Comanche barked and belched blue flame, then settled into an even roar. Volgel looked up, somewhat surprised. It hadn't taken much time. So in the end, I was correct, he thought, pleased with his own perception. Loss was going to make the attempt.

He withdrew the small Sony portable and keyed the transmitter that had meticulously been fitted into the small confines of the case. He spoke softly, his breath just catching a bit in anticipation. "Songbird. Seagull here. Engine start. Stand by."

The reply came back almost instantaneously, clear but hollow, like listening down a drain pipe. "Songbird standing by." Volgel smiled and slung the radio over his shoulder by the small leather strap.

The Comanche had taxied to the western end of the runway, its sound swept away by the eastern trades. Volgel stood up, brushing dirt from his pants and shirt. He looked at his watch, pressing a small button. The dial glowed in digital display: 8:21.

Reaching beneath his sports jacket, Volgel extracted a 9-millimeter Walther P-38 and screwed in the gray-aluminum silencer, carefully fitting it to the barrel to prevent cross-threading.

The Comanche was now rolling and Volgel, after chambering a round, ran over the low embankment and down to the edge of the strip. He sat down heavily in the gravel, bracing the elbows of his arms on his knees, the weapon gripped easily in both hands. The moonlight glinted briefly on the aircraft's canopy. It was airborne. He waited. It passed over his head, wheels already being sucked up into the wings; it looked like a cross against the sky. The Walther coughed in his grip twice. And each time, he was sure of a hit in the cockpit area.

He stood and turned to watch the dim silhouette of the aircraft diminish into the blackness of the night. Its profile suddenly altered, banking to the south, the noise of the engine now lost. Puerto Rico? Perhaps.

He unslung the transmitter, turning up the receiver volume.

Songbird, Seagull here. Blackbird off 8:24 to the south."

"Seagull, Songbird back. Confirm the south."

Volgel gritted his teeth. "Affirmative. The south."

A pause, with only the restless brush of static across the black sea.

"Seagull, Songbird back. Any strikes?"

Volgel pressed the transmit switch, smiling. "Two strikes," he said softly.

Another delay. Volgel began to walk toward the parked sedan, half a runway distant. He felt comfortable, loose, the weapon light in his hand, the radio to his ear. Almost lightheaded.

The receiver stuttered, "—itize area. Confirm."

Volgel spoke into the mike, "Songbird, this is Seagull. Say your last transmission again."

"Seagull, Songbird back. I say again. Sanitize area. Confirm."

Volgel broke into an easy jog. Pressing the transmit switch he said, "I confirm sanitize area."

Stroud saw him coming. The fishing line bit into his wrists as he struggled. He wished suddenly for the cold north of Canada, the wild geese honking. The foxes running free across the grass. The man beside him was now frantic, and the disease of fear is communicable.

The man stopped before him, slim and short in stature. Stroud sensed rather than saw the man as poised. Dress well. Something over his shoulder. Something in his hand.

"Where did Loss go?"

Stroud hesitated.

"Where did Loss go?" Volgel repeated, his voice now more insistent, the timbre of his voice dropping to a hoarse whisper.

"I don't know. The south, I think," Stroud replied.

The light blossomed in front of his eyes, pink-white. There seemed to be no sound. Stroud looked up at Volgel, the shock of pain to his chest unbelievable at first. Stroud first thought he had been kicked. His head suddenly cleared. He looked down, and watched with detached interest as his shirt darkened with wetness. There was no pain now. Not even feeling.

"Where did he go?"

Stroud slowly shook his head.

"Thank you," the voice said graciously and the pink-white light blossomed again, going rapidly to red and black. Stroud died with a dim instant vision of a fox running free.

Heiss was making incoherent sounds, jerking against his bonds, the sedan swaying with the force of his effort.

Volgel kneeled down in front of Heiss, his movements those of a priest resting before prayer and supplication. He fished a cigarette from his pocket and lit it, then gently placed it between Heiss's lips.

Volgel spoke first, his words soft and reasonable. "You know that I have to kill you, Carl?"

Heiss nodded dumbly, the cigarette falling from his lips.

"You know as well," Volgel continued, "that I can't negotiate this. It is a matter of you telling me quickly what you told Loss." He picked up the cigarette from Heiss's lap and flung it away into the darkness.

Heiss nodded again, his eyes now closed, arching his head back against the fender, all struggling ceased. The smell of the man beside them was a stench, the fluids now released, his perforated body giving up its life.

"There is no reason to withhold the information," Volgel said. "If you do, you will simply die more slowly. We both know how this is done."

"I told him nothing because I know nothing. Let me make my own way, Volgel," Heiss said, knowing that it was useless.

"I have to ask you again, Carl," Volgel said, a thin edge of impatience on his voice. "Where did Loss go. How much range. What did you tell him? Please spare both of us the lies."

"Loss went south. Haiti, I think, for fuel. He had only short range. Stroud said that he had not refueled. I don't know of these things. Please, Volgel—"

Volgel shot him in the kneecap, using the weapon surgically. There would be a minimum of blood, the pain unbelievable. He had hoped for better cooperation from a man of the same cloth.

Heiss sat there, his mouth open in a silent scream, blood running from the tongue he had partially severed with his own teeth.

Volgel leaned toward him, making the words simple and unmistakable, enunciating each syllable, speaking now in German.

"Carl. Let me finish it cleanly. Once more, Where? And what information did you give away?"

Heiss flung his head from side to side, his teeth sawing into his tongue. "South," he said. "Nothing. I said nothing."

The Walther coughed again, its breath singeing Heiss's face as it disappeared into unrecognizability. His heels beat a tattoo, and he was still.

Volgel got up, feeling the freshness gone, the power spent. He found the gas tank and broached it with a jab of his penknife, the ground saturating with fuel. He waited in the pale moon, allowing the pool to expand, watching the stars wheel. More work now, eliminating the traces of his footsteps, returning to his hotel. The inquiries in the morning. Of course they would think that it had been Loss's actions.

The tank was dry now. Volgel walked upwind, turned, and aimed at the bumper between the two silent forms. He fired once without effect. The second shot struck a spark and the mass of steel, rubber, fuel, and flesh went up in a huge white-hot tongue of flame. Volgel scuttled back up the runway, vaguely dissatisfied with Heiss's sense of loyalty. I would have told, had it been me, he thought, scuffing at the tracks and then climbing the embankment.

"Songbird, this is Seagull, over."

A rush of static. "Go ahead."

Volgel, tired now, his bridgework irritating his gums, body sweating, keyed the transmitter. "South is confirmed. Heiss and Stroud sanitized, over."

"Seagull. This is Songbird. Out."

Volgel walked to his car over the uneven ground. The sedan was now a mass of yellow flame. He turned and entered his Morris Minor, switched on the key, and started the engine. He drove carefully to town, skirting the main street through the back alleys. In his cottage, he stripped and showered, the water blasting against his palid frame. He brushed his bridge and set it in a cup of water. The sheets were cool and clean, and he quickly fell asleep.

Chapter 18

Lieutenant Iosif Sidorov adjusted the gain on the infrared scanner, reducing the blob-like heat source 11,000 meters below to a hard pinpoint of light. He keyed the intercom, making a notation in his log at the same time. "Commander. ECM here."

"ECM. Go ahead, Iosif," the voice tired and with a tinge of boredom.

"Sir, I have a target movement on the airstrip. It's the aircraft we've been monitoring. It's just started its engine at—," he referred to his log, "zero zero two one, GMT."

The aircraft commander of the TU-18 relaxed, the vigil drawing to a close. He hated the Cubans, the Caribbean, and long-range patrol duty in particular. He turned aside to the copilot and nudged him awake, indicating that he take the controls. Then he made a notation on his knee pad. Good, he thought. He keyed the intercom. "Anything else? How about radar contact?"

The electronic-countermeasures officer had anticipated the question. "Negative, sir. The target is still obscured by ground clutter. He won't be visible on the AWA-23 until he's well above 2000 meters. But the infrared scan on him is solid." Lieutenant Sidorov drew heavily on his oxygen mask. Interesting now.

"All right, Iosif," the pilot replied. "Our instructions are to maintain contact on the target aircraft. Call Songbird and give them the information. Use the tactical code frequency that Seagull has been using. Scrambled in Mode 17. I'll start to let down a bit. It might enable you to pick him up on radar as well."

Lieutenant Sidorov keyed the mike in acknowledgement and changed to tactical frequency 249.7. He selected Scramble Mode 17 and called, "Songbird. Eagle here. Copy?"

"We copy. Go ahead."

"Blackbird engine start now."

The reply from Cuba came back immediately. "Affirmative. We have received that information already from Seagull. Give us a track after takeoff, over."

"Affirmative. Understand track heading," Sidorov replied. "Eagle standing by." Very pleased now, the Soviet lieutenant logged the calls and expanded the scale of the scanner to encompass the entire island of Great Inagua. The power plant now showed on the edge of the scope, a truncated orange return. A few other point sources of heat were defined, none of them moving. Homes. Perhaps a stationary vehicle with its engine running. Nothing more.

The frequency crackled. Sidorov anticipated the transmission, but it was between Cuba and the remote unit on the island below.

"Songbird, Seagull here. Blackbird off 8:24 to the south."

Sidorov watched the scope and confirmed that the point source of heat began to move. Good enough, he thought. Once the aircraft is airborne and over the sea, I'll be the only one capable of tracking it. He followed the transmission between Seagull below and the command post in Cuba.

The aircraft was out over the sea now, vectoring south toward Haiti. Sidorov waited until the transmissions between base and Seagull were finished. He caught the interchange between the land stations: the instructions to sanitize. Seagull signed off.

Lieutenant Iosif Sidorov settled into the job. The work was familiar. Another six months of this and back to the Mediterranean Fleet Air Arm. A promotion soon. Which calculated out at 87 rubles more per month.

The aircraft below was climbing out now, the point source of heat strong, as it would be under maximum engine operation. He laid out the cursor over the track and punched data into the computer. The readout gave a track and ground speed of 179 degrees magnetic at 210 kilometers per hour.

"Songbird, Eagle."

The reply transmission from Cuba came back, the voice now a different operator. A slight German accent. "Eagle, go ahead."

Iosif keyed the mike, his voice flat within the confines of the oxygen mask. "Songbird. Eagle here. Target now 12 kilometers south, tracking 179 magnetic." He started to release the mike and realized that a large heat return had blossomed on the infrared scope. The position was right. "And I have a stationary target on the runway. Stand by."

He quickly reduced the gain and contracted the scan to sweep the runway. The point source of heat was the vehicle that had been positioned near the hardstand. There was no doubt about it. It was afire. He keyed the mike again. "Songbird. Eagle here. Target on runway stationary burning vehicle, over."

The German accent again. "Affirmative, Eagle. Maintain information on Blackbird track and speed. We will have four interceptors in the air for your vectors. Their flight leader call sign is Cane Cutter."

"Understand flight leader is Cane Cutter. What type?" Lieutenant Sidorov could imagine the alert klaxon screaming in some dusty fighter base in southern Cuba.

A short pause from Songbird, then, "MIG-19Gs. Do you have radar contact with the target?"

"Negative. I have a solid infrared scan. I should have radar contact when he climbs out. Presently just ground clutter." Iosif rechecked the radar PPI scope.

Nothing. "Stand by, Songbird." He reset the cursor on the infrared scope and noted the still southerly course. The computer readout flickered, minor changes in raw data. He keyed the mike with the foot switch, using his deft, stubby hands to manipulate the controls of the scope.

"Songbird. Eagle here."

A rush of static then, "Eagle. Songbird here. Go ahead."

"I have the target still tracking southerly, course one-eight-eight magnetic, speed 183 kilometers per hour. Eighteen kilometers south. Negative radar return as yet."

Petrov handed the headset back to the young controller and turned to Rametka, smiling. "He's airborne, Vassel."

Rametka nodded without comment. He watched Petrov as the man stalked back and forth along the aisle, highly charged. As if he were waiting for a duck to fly over the blind. His face was now taut, the fatigue faded from the eyes.

Petrov lit another cigarette, disregarding the one smoldering in an ashtray on the edge of the console. His hair, bleached by the sun, was silver-white in the light of the operator's repeater scope. He had a brief conversation with the naval commander, Zhivotorskiv, laughed, and returned to Rametka's side beside the console.

"The fighters scrambled two minutes ago, Vassel. A flight of three MIG-19Gs. The fourth fighter aborted with an overheat. They maintain their aircraft with machetes for tools and idiots for mechanics. The Chinese were better. Much better."

They stood silently now, listening to the controller work the flight of three night fighters, vectoring them south and east to intercept the lone Comanche. The controller's instructions were crisp, economical. Probable contact in eight minutes.

Rametka absorbed the tenseness of the hunt from Petrov. It seemed an electronic game, the bright return of the fighters repositioned on the controller's scope with every sweep of the antennas; the TU-18 slower in its southerly track. No plot on the Comanche, but it was there, over the horizon, below the curvature of the earth. He turned to Petrov and said in a low voice, "Volgel thought he had two hits on the aircraft, is that correct?"

Petrov nodded, more intent on the screen than on the man beside him. "Yes. Just small caliber. Perhaps in the fuel tanks. They would be hard to miss."

Rametka picked at the edge of his nostril. The skin seemed oily, even in the air conditioned environment. "So Heiss is finished. And now Loss and his woman friend. Then the Swedes."

Petrov turned to face Rametka, his forehead furrowed, the radial wrinkles in the corners of his eyes fracturing the hard planes of his face. "Yes, Vassel. They are all finished, in one way or another. Heiss is finished. Like a burned piece of trash. That is what he was. I have no regret. The Swedes—something else." Petrov sat back against the desk behind him and fumbled in his shirt pocket for another cigarette. He found one, slightly crumbled, and lit it. The smoke was wraith-like in the reflected luminescence of the radar scope.

"No," he continued. "I don't like the loss of the Swedes. They are real people. Children. Sailing the world on a kopeck. I do not like to think of them going. You know, when I forced them to take me here to Cuba, the man, Anders, attacked me with a wooden fid. An instrument to splice rope with. I had to shoot him in the leg with the shotgun." Petrov looked down at the glowing tip of the cigarette as if it would give him some answer to his unspoken question. "He lay there, his leg blown away, looking at me. Working over in his mind how he could kill me. I can admire a man like that."

The controller turned to the two men behind him, standing in the half-light of the command post.

"I have a contact. It's the target. Do you want a positive identification, Colonel?"

Petrov nodded wearily. No words. The rating turned to his scope, rapidly fingering a keyboard to the computer terminal. He spoke in terse sentences to the flight of aircraft, giving directional vectors and range. A precise machine of the State. Like competent machines of other States.

It will be a game of machines in the end, thought Petrov, suddenly tired. But satisfied, knowing who would win.

Vassel Rametka edged back, settling on the edge of the desk next to Petrov. He could smell the stink of his own sweat. Or was it Petrov's? "So with Loss's aircraft shot down, will we go ahead?" he asked, watching the blips beginning to merge.

Petrov looked straight ahead, sight unfocused. "Yes, we will go ahead. We would have gone ahead even had Loss reached Nassau alive. He basically knows nothing. He will be blamed for the death of Heiss and Stroud."

"The timing," Rametka said. "Do you feel that it is affected?"

Petrov looked aside at Rametka, feeling marginally sympathetic for the man. From a role of inspector, tutor, and mentor, the man had lost his power. Like all old men, his actions were influenced by the thought of failure. "The timing is good. The device will leave Vladivostok on a Z-Class Fleet Submarine. Three hundred twenty kilometers west of British Columbia, we will transfer it to a small trawler with Canadian markings; really one of our craft that normally fishes in the Gulf of Alaska. From there, it will be carried to a yacht that will be cruising along the northern coast of British Columbia."

Vassel Rametka nodded. He touched his nose again. It was bleeding slightly, the light smear of blood on his fingertip almost black in the harsh cold light of the cathode-ray tube. "The device, there will be handling problems at sea?"

Petrov shook his head curtly. "No, I don't think so. It's packed in a wooden shipping container. It will have a false top container of oceanographic research equipment for any casual inspection. The device is cushioned inside with cellular molded foam. It could be dropped on concrete from 3 meters without damage. It weighs a little in excess of 80 kilos. Three men can easily handle it. Our people on the yacht will tie in on the foredeck of the *Hussar*. I plan to be there when the transfer is made."

"The crew of the yacht?" Rametka questioned.

"There are only two people. Older people. They will present no problem. This type of yacht is largely self-supporting. They cruise these waters during the summer months, from two hundred kilometers north of the Canadian border down into Puget Sound off Washington. The border control by the authorities on such vessels is very limited. Our people will take the device south to the area of Puget Sound. Then they simply wait."

"Will our people know what is within the container?" Rametka said, visualizing the detonation of three megatons within an inland sea, Seattle to the east, Vancouver to the north.

"Of course they will know," Petrov laughed. "As we have *briefed* them, it contains automatic monitoring equipment to measure the magnetic and electrical signature of a Trident submarine. The first of its kind. They will cruise that general area, waiting for the USS *Ohio* to leave on patrol. The waters are shallow and confined in the Hood Canal. They are to approach within 300 meters and switch on the 'recording' equipment."

The controller seated in front of them turned and pointing to the scope with his light pencil said, "Sir. The MIGs have radar contact. The flight leader will be making an identification pass first."

Petrov nodded. "Yes. I want a positive identification first. What type of armament are the MIGs equipped with?"

The controller spoke rapidly into his headset microphone, received a reply and said, "Cannon, sir. Twenty-millimeter rapid-firing cannon. And the flight leader says they're nearly within Haitian airspace."

Petrov turned to Rametka, eyebrows raised. "Not good." To the controller, "Have them finish the identification pass. Then force the small aircraft to turn north before they shoot it down. I don't want the Haitians to catch this on their radar."

The controller turned back to the screen, speaking rapidly in Spanish.

Petrov pointed up at the situation display of the Caribbean. The track of the TU-18 was further south, in the Windward Passage between Cuba and Haiti, still well over 10 kilometers high. The fighters, lower in altitude, were no more than 50 kilometers to the north of Haiti. "I felt sure that Loss would try to fly north," he said, almost to himself. "There is only 100 kilometers between Great Inagua and the north end of Haiti. I can't believe that he would try to escape to the south. Stupid."

Zhivotorskiv, the duty officer, scuttled toward the two men who bent over the shoulder of the radar controller. The fat on his body shifted in waves beneath his taut uniform. His face was florid.

"Colonel Petrov. The Cuban Fighter Command says we can't go further into Haitian air space. They say—"

"Shut up," Petrov snapped. "They've got him now." The points of light on the radar scope were merged.

Chapter 19

Loss stabbed the right brake and wheeled the aircraft around on the end of the runway. The instruments, lighted by dull red illumination, indicated normally. There was no sign of any vehicle as yet. Take your time, he thought, and he carefully read through the checklist.

> Pitch in fine, power run up to 1700 rpm, engine instruments in normal ranges.
> Left magneto drop 125 rpm
> Right magneto drop 110 rpm
> Carburetor heat application. Normal rpm drop, good suction pressure
> Prop cycle from fine through coarse pitch back to fine. Sounds healthy
> Gyros set, altimeter to sea level elevation
> Boost pump on

Just 10 degrees of flap. He looked out the window and could see the flaps cycling down through a small arc in the beam of his pocket penlight.

Leave the navigational and strobe light off. Sometimes, it doesn't pay to advertise.

He looked down the runway. The strip was black on black, the asphalt blotting up the last bit of moonlight. He turned down the instrument panel lights to their lowest level. This time, there was some distinction; the grass edging the runway was a lighter shade of gray. He picked a star that was aligned with the runway, using that for a heading reference. Bellatrix? No, maybe Procyon. Anyway, something in the Canis Minor constellation. "Are you ready?" he said, glancing over at her.

She squeezed his arm lightly. "Let's go," she said.

Loss smoothly applied power, very light on the rudder pedal, trying to keep the track of the aircraft straight. The Comanche accelerated, rpms up at 2350. The controls were growing stiffer with the pressure of the slipstream, and his eyes flicked down and glimpsed 50 knots registered on the airspeed indicator. Then 65. Seconds now. She lifted off with a touch on the controls and was climbing.

He hit the gear switch, starting the retraction. Wait for the flaps just a bit longer. The Lycoming was singing a deep tenor. Bless Stroud and his maintenance, he thought briefly.

The first shot did little damage. It entered the aft section of the cockpit, creasing the fabric on the back of the left front seat. It plowed its way through the fabric liner and insulation of the cabin roof and mushroomed through the top of the fuselage. The sound was lost in the engine's bellow and the noise of the gear retracting into the wells.

Volgel's second shot was spaced one foot further aft and to the right. The 9-millimeter copper-jacketed slug tore through the belly of the Comanche, penetrated the rear seat support that housed the ten containers of fuel, and impacted in the middle container, bursting its walls.

Loss heard the shot this time, only as a muffled crump, followed by the overwhelming stench of raw fuel vapor. At first he thought a fuel line had burst, and he could only think of fire. One spark, or the red hot exhaust manifold. He started to shut down the electrical master switch and stopped in time. One spark from a relay opening as the power was shut down would blow the whole thing.

"Open your door," he shouted across at her. Jesus, not again, he thought.

She was trying now, pushing against the unlocked door with her small frame, pressing against the force of the slipstream that pinned the door inward. She had it open, only a crack.

"Jam it open with something, jam it open," he yelled in her ear. She shook her head, and he knew that she could not do it alone.

He fumbled with one hand on the floor of the cockpit, trying to find something to wedge the door open. Tennis shoe, he thought, and pulled off his right one. Both of them heaved against the door panel, and it opened sufficiently for her to insert the shoe in the howling gap.

The cockpit was vacuumed out of papers and loose dust. A roll of paper towels that Stroud had used to clean the windshield was sucked out through the thin crevice, towels shredding in the wind. Loss leaned back on his side and hunched against the small plexiglas storm window, sucking at the clean, cold air. His lungs felt seared by the fumes and his mind was numb. One of the fuel cans in the back seat had ruptured from—what? They weren't interconnected, so all the banks wouldn't drain through the ruptured one. Most of the fuel would leak through the flooring and find its way back into the hollow shell of the fuselage, where it would rapidly evaporate. Cursing his own stupidity, he belatedly opened the ventilation cowls, bringing more fresh air into the cockpit.

Already, he could tell that the fumes were dissipating. The smell would be there for a long time, but if nothing blew in the next ten minutes, it would be all right. He looked over at her and saw that her face was pressed against the open crack, hair snapping out in the slipstream.

The instruments looked solid; everything in the green. The oil temperature was a little high. He realized that he had not yet reduced the power setting for best climb speed and the engine was overheating. Pulling the throttle back to 23 inches of manifold pressure, he slowly reduced the prop setting to 2350 rpm and waited for the airspeed to stabilize and then retrimmed the controls. His eyes were watering profusely now, and he had a spasm of coughing. He looked over at her, and she was crying and shaking her head as if to clear it of the fumes. He leaned over and tapped her shoulder, giving her the thumbs-up sign. She nodded, head bowed, and closed her eyes.

Loss turned over in his mind what could have gone wrong. The pressure couldn't have done it. Nothing fitted together. Perhaps it would be better to keep the southerly heading in case there were something major wrong with the aircraft. Haiti was the closest lighted airfield, forty, maybe fifty miles to the south. At least there, he would be temporarily safe from the Bahamian authorities. Would they have any sort of extradition treaty? Maybe taking Stroud's airplane qualified as skyjacking. He decided that he would keep to the south, building up altitude and allowing the gas fumes to vent. When it was safe, he would examine the debris in back.

They climbed for another eight minutes, topping a thin cloud deck at 11,000 feet. He retrimmed and leaned the mixture for maximum range. The fuel smell was almost gone now. Before them, they could see the dark form of Haiti in the dying moonlight, and the individual lights of villages and then the blink of the marine beacon on Mole St. Nicholas, the northwestern tip of Haiti.

"How are you feeling now?" he asked. She smiled in the dim glow of the panel lights.

"Better. What happened?" She blew her nose on some paper toweling that was left in the dash compartment.

"That's what I want to find out. Take the penlight and look in the back. You'll have to unstrap your safety belt and crawl back there. I'm going to see whether I can get a bearing on Port-au-Prince. We may go in there if it's anything serious." She started to crawl over the seat, and he said as an afterthought, "Check each fuel can to make sure that the remaining ones are full. I can calculate our range from that."

Loss looked out to the west. The moon was getting lower now. If they had just lost one tank, he could make it. If not, there was always the possibility of putting down somewhere in Florida, refueling and getting airborne again before anyone knew the difference.

"I think you'd better take a look, Brian," she said, playing the penlight over the aft compartment.

He engaged the autopilot, unfastened his seat belt, and turned to face aft. The ten containers were arranged in two rows in the area where the rear seat would normally be. The front middle container was burst along its welded seams. There is only one way that a metal container can be deformed like that.

"And look here," she said and stuck her finger into a hole in the roof upholstery. "Spear?"

"Forty-five caliber spear, maybe," he said, finding the entry hole in the floor and the scar in the upholstery of the seat back.

"Who would have done it?" she said: "Not Heiss. You had him trussed up like a chicken."

"Police, maybe," he replied uneasily, knowing that, somehow, this was Klist's doing. He didn't want to think of Stroud.

"Well, anyway, the other nine containers are full and none of the transfer lines is broken. How does it affect our range?"

He helped her into the front seat, and they withdrew the shoe from the door and locked it.

"Cinderella?" she said handing it to him and he smiled. "Now, how about the range? Do we swim?"

He turned toward her and kissed her lightly on the nose. "No problem. We can still make it direct. If not, then we'll drop in somewhere along the east coast of the US around dawn. I better swing this crate around to the north and get out of here. We're almost over Haiti. By the way, do you have any of those chocolate bars in your—" He froze as he caught a glint of moonlight off beyond their right wingtip. His night vision was bad, both from the gas fumes and from the recently used penlight. He looked again. More definite. A plane with no wing lights.

"Holly. Look out there." He stabbed his finger in the direction.

"What do you see?" she said, looking down toward the sea's surface 2 miles below.

"No, higher. Just level with us."

She looked back, aft of the trailing edge of the wing. Stars. And then she saw it. An airplane. Just the dim outline in the waning moonlight—a reflection of light sliding along its canopy. And it was closing with them, flying a slightly converging heading. "It's an airplane. A jet, I think. He doesn't have any light switched on."

Loss felt fear reaching into his chest. His mind raced. It wouldn't be Bahamian. Haiti, maybe. They had old Mirage IIIs. The paranoia over Cuba. He reached down on the panel and switched on the navigational wingtip lights and the anticollision beacon.

"He's coming in closer," she said, craning her neck to watch the aircraft edge in. "And he's dropping his landing gear!"

Loss handed her the flashlight. "Holly, it's a Haitian night fighter. They probably saw us on radar and sent up this guy to look us over. He's just slowing down to look us over. Take the flashlight and blink morse code for USA . . . dididah . . . dididit . . . didah. Got it?"

She nodded her head and started to flash the message. No reaction from the night fighter, which Loss could see plainly now, just a silhouette 100 yards or less off their right rear quarter. He thought of calling Port-au-Prince approach control and trying to explain. He tried to reason what would look like a non-hostile thing to do. Maybe turn on the interior lights and the landing lights. Start a slow descent for Port-au-Prince. Would this guy be trigger happy? Too close for a firing pass, but then the thought struck him that the rest of his flight would be sitting back half a mile, covering their leader, ready to make a firing pass if ordered. He looked over the cowling. The north coast of Haiti was just under the nose, a thin chain of lights rimming the shore where the coastal road would be. A larger city down to the east.

The jet switched on its landing lights, the dazzle blinding. "He's looking us over. Wave at him!" and Loss realized how ludicrous it would look to the fighter pilot.

The landing lights switched off and the fighter grew in size as it slid in alongside them, no more than 10 yards off their wingtip. Now Loss could see the sharklike profile and the conventional swept wing. The fighter's gear and flaps were down, trying to slow to the speed of the Comanche. But the shape didn't match the delta of a Mirage III.

The fighter was beginning to turn toward them, forcing Loss to turn with him to avoid a collision. The turn was very slow but deliberate. Forcing Loss toward the east, paralleling the coast of Haiti.

Loss looked more closely, the jet's features more apparent in the low luminescence of the splinter moon and starlight. An older subsonic or transsonic fighter. Speed fences on the wing. A bell was ringing in the back of his mind. The insignia of the fuselage was a dark inverted triangle with a white star.

The two aircraft kept turning, slowly, the fighter edging in closer, keeping the turn tight. Compass now rolling through northeast, away from the coast.

No missiles under the wings, he thought. Cannon or rockets housed in the wings or belly. It came to him: MIG. MIG what? Seventeen. Maybe a fifteen. The insignia was *Cuban*. And there would be at least one other bastard sitting back there, radar locked on and firing switches armed. That's why this guy next to him was turning. They wanted him to get away from the Haitian coast, over open water. Loss turned in his seat, looking out the right window, scanning the sky. He couldn't see the other one, but he would be back there. The leader would break away and then there would be the swift firing pass. And it would be like chucking rocks into a garbage can from 3 feet. They couldn't miss. All compliments of Petrov, he thought.

The heading was north now, the jet still on their wing, racked over in the shallow turn that was forcing the Comanche to a northwesterly or westerly heading. Toward Cuba. He could hear the rolling thunder of the jet's engine at high power settings, barely above a stall, mushing along to match the Comanche's speed. The pilot in the cockpit was encased in a helmet with oxygen mask dangling from his face. He was visible in the greenish-white light of the radar scope set in the panel before him. Loss wasn't sure, but he imagined the man was smiling.

He didn't want to wait until the turn was finished. The leader would break off quickly and that would be the end of it. He certainly couldn't outclimb or outdive them, but if there was a way of getting right down on the deck, along the coast of Haiti, he could hide in the radar clutter of the shoreline.

Jesus, he thought. One week or so ago, he had been a normal human being. Life without pain, life without worry, someone to love. Good clothes to wear, and no one to bother him with the aggravations of surviving. Now it seemed that he had fallen to the lower order of those that kill and are killed. Like some mouse, running before the cat, not knowing why he was hunted but sure that the smallest mistake would lead to pain and violent death.

The fighter's rate of turn was decreasing, the wings starting to level. So it's now he thought. He leaned over to her.

"We're getting down to sea level fast. Just read me the altimeter setting at every thousand feet and hold on tight."

Loss pulled on the carburetor heat and then gradually reduced power. The Comanche started to slow immediately; Loss holding the nose up to stay level with the MIG as the airspeed bled off. The MIG was starting to overrun him now, shifting from his wing position to slightly ahead, still banking. Loss could see the flame from his tail cone—a hard feathery blue. Airspeed still decaying rapidly, the airspeed indicator down to eighty and the controls getting mushy. He reached down and switched off the navigational lights and collision beacon. The controls were buffeting now, the Comanche right on the edge of a stall. Loss applied full back pressure on the yoke and stomped full left rudder. The aircraft shuddered for a split second and then the left wingtip dropped, initiating the spin. The pitchdown was violent but then flattening and increasing in rotational speed.

"Ten thousand," she called, her voice tight.

Loss kept the rudder in and the yoke back, watching the stars whirl across the windshield. They were falling like a greased brick now, spinning. Rate of descent well over 3000 feet per minute. But most important, the aircraft was falling in a tight spiral almost straight down. There was a bright flare of light above them, tracers arching away into the night, curving like a scythe as the fighters tried to turn after him.

"Eight thousand," her voice higher pitched now.

The rotational forces were throwing him against the outside of the cockpit, and he wished they would put shoulder belts in these damned aircraft. Stupid, he thought. Stroud should know, should have known better. The nose was starting to tuck down now and this worried him. How much altitude to allow for recovery? She was saying something about thousand, and he saw just the flash of something sweeping across the windshield and a torrent of orange flame from phosphorous tracers licking the sky above him. He felt their passage as the MIG's shockwave buffeted the Comanche.

Three or four turns now, the lights of stars merging with the lights of Haiti. Disorientation.

"*Five thousand!*" Belated, he turned on the boost pump, to keep the fuel pressure up. The engine was barely ticking over now, no power and the black sea below them coming up to meet them. Pretty soon now. Very soon. He rehearsed in his mind the actions he would have to take.

"*Three thousand.* Brian, *three thousand!*" he already had his right foot on the rudder pedal, cramming it into the firewall. The rotation to the left was slowing, but not enough and he pushed harder as if that would do any good. Come on, you bitch, stop! Stop. The Comanche went through one more lazy rotation and stopped turning. He relieved the rudder pressure and dumped the yoke forward, waiting for the controls to firm up. Airspeed picking up now and he slowly applied back pressure. The lights along the shore were bright and individual now. There were cars moving along the coast road and scattered pools of brightness where clusters of houses would be. Beyond that was the shape of dark mountains blotting the southern horizon. The nose was nearly level, and he slowly added power just to check his slow descent. Everything was very quiet now, just the sound of the engine at low revs and the gentle rush of wind past the airframe as they glided for the shoreline.

"Eight hundred," she said, almost softly. He slowly added power as they descended, leveling off above the wavetops. He kept the power setting low, stabilizing the airspeed in the low eighties. The coast was off their right wingtip as he flew east into the trades. Their groundspeed would barely be sixty. Let them find me here, he thought. Sometimes the mouse runs where the cat can't.

He concentrated intently, flying barely above the breaking coastal surf, the minutes ticking by. Nothing else.

She lit him a cigarette, placing it between his lips. He inhaled and she removed the cigarette for him as he exhaled.

"They say you can die from lung cancer," he said.

Chapter 20

Five miles above the Windward Passage, the TU-18 executed a slow bank toward the west. Lieutenant Iosif Sidorov turned up his gain. The three bright infrared returns of the MIGs merged into one as they assumed close formation, streaking westward for the strip in Oriente Province. Of the small aircraft, nothing. It had disappeared in the blackness, the return from its exhaust dying as the flight of MIGs first made contact with it.

He keyed the intercom. "Commander. ECM here. Heading for Camaguey two-eight-eight magnetic. Estimated arrival at thirteen after the hour." As he spoke, he made notations in his log. The oxygen mask was beginning to irritate the bridge of his nose. He knew that they would begin letting down now. Good to suck real air again. Not bottled shit.

The aircraft commander, Major Aksyonov, rolled out on the heading and turned the controls over to his copilot, poking his thumb downwards to indicate a slow descent. The turbojet engines died to a low whine. God, he thought, these things are buckets. Gives one's ass hemorrhoids. He waited, knowing Lieutenant Sidorov would brief him. He had heard the undisciplined chatter on the fighter frequency, but all in Spanish.

"Commander, ECM here."

"Shoot."

"The fighters got the prop aircraft. They're reporting that he spun out after cannon hits. One of the flight followed him down to 1000 meters. The aircraft was single engine. He says it was out of control. It crashed in the sea just 3 kilometers off the coast."

The aircraft commander smiled. It would look good in the debriefing. In the mission report. "Can you confirm their kill?" he asked.

"Affirmative. The infrared return faded just as they closed in. It never reappeared. Just normal heat along the coast. Nothing moving fast, trucks. The power generation plant at Cap Hatier. But definitely no aircraft." His voice was tinged with smugness.

"All right, Iosif. Call Songbird and give them the information. Be sure that your mission log is complete. They'll want seven copies." He settled back in the seat, listening to the ECM officer make his report. Good phraseology. He might make a good officer yet. The commander eyed the altimeter, willing the TU-18 lower, to an altitude where he could remove the oxygen mask and drink tea from the thermos. He started to compose his own mission report mentally, the phrases falling to his mind with ease. But it would be nice, he thought, to know why so much effort had been expended in bringing down the small aircraft. "Enemy of the people" was a standard phrase. He smiled, without humor.

The controller was chattering rapidly in Spanish, writing. He turned to Colonel Petrov. "The aircraft is a confirmed kill, sir. Impacted in the sea just north of Haiti. Here are the coordinates. The flight leader of Cane Cutter says that he positively identified the aircraft as a Comanche. Two passengers in it."

Petrov sighed. He regretted the death of Loss as one pilot regrets the death of another pilot. "And do we have confirmation from the recon aircraft?"

The young enlisted man smiled broadly, showing his fillings. The rest of his teeth were slightly crooked. "Yes, sir. Confirmed. We will have their mission report by morning."

"Have them telephone me when they land. I don't have until morning. We will be in the fleet communications room." Without waiting for an acknowledgment from the young controller, he turned to Rametka, taking him by the arm. "Let's get the messages off, Vassel. And then a few drinks. And sleep."

The two men left the command post, Petrov leading. Rametka noted how the gait and bearing of the young colonel had changed from minutes ago. Petrov was now erect, decisive. A curt nod, perhaps with a smile to the senior duty officer, the quick, offhand scrawl of his hand in the signout register, a friendly word to the security guard in the corridor. They walked along the gray painted corridor leading through the complex to the communications room, through the fluorescent lighted hallways, past security personnel who snapped to attention as they passed.

They entered the communications room, pausing for credentials check by the fleet marine stationed at the double doors, through the massive room partitioned with low walls of acoustic material that separated each operator, and into the duty officer's alcove office. The officer, a plump woman, rose to meet them.

Petrov curtly handed her his security pass for inspection, then a folded teleprinter message. "We will need your office, Lieutenant."

She clicked her heels, a ludicrous gesture, Rametka thought.

"Of course, Colonel. My office is at your disposal. Shall I order tea?"

"Coffee, Lieutenant. Cuban coffee, very strong and black. With cream. And some buns."

She clicked her heels again, the motion transferring minor shockwaves through her body, causing the plump fat of her arms and bosom to jiggle. Rametka almost smiled.

Petrov settled into the officer's still warm chair, Rametka taking the small lounge. In spite of the air conditioning, the room smelled strongly of floral perfume.

They watched the main communications room beyond the office's plate window for some minutes in silence. Petty officers patrolled the perimeter of the room, stopping to examine the logs of each individual radio operator, coding technician, and teleprinter personnel. Perhaps over twenty workers. Unattended facsimile machines recorded weather satellite transmissions, photos and other graphic data, spewing the material into waiting hoppers for collection and dissemination.

The lieutenant returned, carrying a tray. She placed it upon her desk, collected some sheaths of message forms, and, clicking her heels again, withdrew into the main communications room.

They drank their coffee, still not speaking, their eyes meeting only as they tasted the doughy buns. Petrov discarded his into the wastebasket. "We spent 148 billion rubles last year on our military budget. Yet, it doesn't seem that we can afford two kopecks for a decent roll. It's stupid, Vassel." Rametka only nodded, waiting for Petrov to open the conversation for the decisions yet to be made.

Petrov lighted a cigarette and leaned back, placing his feet on the desk. He tried for two consecutive smoke rings and failed. Without preamble he said, "Do you really believe the Cuban fighters got Loss?"

Rametka shrugged. "It seemed obvious, Anatoli. Why do you ask?"

Petrov readjusted his feet, still staring at the ceiling, watching the smoke rise gently upward, then to be sucked into the grillwork of the air conditioning exhaust. "Because I have some doubts. I have flown interceptors as you know. A small plane is a difficult target."

Rametka removed his steel-framed glasses and wiped them on a handkerchief. He placed them in a case and slipped them into the breast pocket of his suit. Momentarily, his hands touched the small enameled badge attached to his lapel, the Order of Lenin, as if to draw reassurance. He sighed. "Does it matter?"

"Perhaps not. But I want to personally question the pilots. And the ECM operator on the TU-18."

"I would think that three aircraft armed with cannon would have no difficulty," Rametka said.

"Yes, possibly. But the point is that in order to match the speed of Loss's aircraft, the fighters would be on the very edge of their lowest operating speed. Loss could easily slow his aircraft well below that figure. Perhaps dive. That is what I would have done. I have been thinking about him, trying to place myself in his situation. He knew the fighters were there after the identification pass." Petrov withdrew his feet from the desk, leaving a heelmark on the green linoleum. Sitting upright, he leaned toward Rametka. "Vassel. Loss was no ordinary private pilot. He has been trained to fly an airplane, not merely drive it as if it were some truck. His file shows extensive military aerobatic training."

"Why wouldn't the fighters be able to keep contact with their radar?"

Petrov gritted his teeth. "Because their radar is designed to search on a horizontal plane. An aircraft, close to them, as Loss was, would be lost from contact if that plane were to gain or lose altitude rapidly. If Loss put his aircraft into a dive, he would be losing altitude at one to two thousand meters per minute, almost straight down."

"And the infrared scan on the reconnaissance aircraft? Their operator confirmed the kill," Rametka said. "No, Anatoli. I think that you are just playing with remote possibilities. Let us make our decision based on facts and be done with it."

"That too is inconclusive, Vassel. Loss would reduce his engine power to an idle. There would still be a return, but much fainter. The operator would have to catch it quickly."

"You liked Loss, didn't you?"

Petrov rubbed the stubble on his chin for a moment and replied, "Yes. I guess I did. Perhaps admired him would be a better word. But his actions were predictable. His attempt to escape by air, his abduction of Heiss. All predictable. The one thing that bothers me was his attempt to fly south. I had guessed that he would try to make the mainland of the US, possibly to some little field there. At any rate, Vassel," he said, his voice tired, "he will not present any problem. He essentially knows nothing. He cannot approach any authorities because of the deaths of Heiss and Stroud, which will naturally be attributed to him. Perhaps he is down in the sea off Haiti. We will want to check carefully with our sources in the Caribbean over the next few days for any signs of the aircraft."

Rametka nodded. "Yes. That should be done. You will question the personnel who took part in the mission?"

Petrov nodded. "Yes. But I think that I will send in the report to Moscow indicating that I accept with reservation their judgment concerning the confirmed kill. Just in case Loss does surface. That way we are covered."

"What about the rest? The device. And Welsh?"

"Yes, we go ahead as planned," Petrov said emphatically. "I'm going to activate the special situation as of tonight. AW-4 will handle the mechanics of routing the device via the Pacific. The Z-Class submarine should be in position in the Gulf of Alaska by August ninth. This will allow a lattitude of four days for the transfer to the fishing vessel. The fishing vessel will then proceed to the north end of Vancouver Island and down into the Queen Charlotte Straits to meet the yacht off North Broughton Island on the sixteenth or seventeenth. From there, the yacht will have four days to position herself in the Hood Canal."

"How positive can we be of the sailing date on the American Trident submarine? And what if they decide to sail at night?"

Petrov momentarily ignored him, tapping on the glass to obtain the attention of the lieutenant. She approached the office. Petrov held up his cold cup of coffee and gestured for two more. She nodded. "The sailing date?" Petrov replied. "Yes. I think we can reasonably be sure of that. August twenty-second. We have people within the US Navy and with the civilian subcontractors. It's just a matter of putting together leave dates of shipboard personnel, supply deliveries of perishable foods for the submarine. The usual thing. As far as the submarine leaving at night is concerned, the best intelligence would seem to argue against that possibility. The USS *Ohio* is quite large, over 150 meters long. About the displacement and general size of a destroyer. It will require tugs, while on the surface. Probably up through the Hood Canal and Puget Sound. This is not the kind of operation normally carried out in darkness." Petrov picked a small particle of roll from between his teeth and continued, "At any rate, the yacht will be positioned at night in the smaller harbor of Squamish at the north end of the Hood Canal. There is an opening bridge through which the submarine would have to pass, which is only one mile away. That would be close enough. Hopefully, the operation will take place in daylight and at a much closer distance."

Vassel Rametka nodded. "Yes," he said. "That would seem reasonable. Our computer estimates indicate that as long as the device is detonated within 500 meters of the vessel, it will appear that the submarine itself detonated. And even if the American Navy claims sabotage, who would believe them? Not the Canadians, I think. Certainly not Western Europe! But we have anticipated their reaction. As long as doubt exists, they will not retaliate and if they do, we would be ready for them." He tapped his pen against his teeth. "Not a pleasant prospect if they do, Anatoli."

Petrov nodded slowly. "Yes," he agreed. "It would not be a pleasant prospect. That is the major element of risk involved. But the American press has been expressing an increasing concern over just such an accident. And the Canadians have been very vocal about having a nuclear sub base only 80 kilometers from their border. If Welsh performs according to cue, the reaction of the American people will be that of outrage. They would disarm overnight." He paused, watching the lieutenant approach with yet another tray of coffee and soggy rolls. "And I think we both agree that such a prize is worth the gamble."

For over thirty minutes, the Comanche kept to the north coast of Hispaniola, first along the shores of Haiti and then across the border and along the coast of the Dominican Republic. Except for the lights of a few villages and vehicles winding their way along the torturous coastal highway, they saw nothing except the flash of white seas breaking on the ragged reefs beneath them.

Loss flew the aircraft between 200 and 500 feet above the sea, keeping always to the coastline, navigation lights extinguished. For the first twenty minutes of the flight along the coast, Loss waited for cannon shells to tear through the thin frame of the aircraft. Fatalistically, almost expected it.

But with increasing time and distance, Loss felt that the interceptors had given up, probably thinking that they had forced him down into the sea. The radius of action of a jet interceptor is not great, particularly at low altitude and low airspeeds, where the turbojet engine is relatively inefficient. And their radar sets would be ineffective, scratching for his presence amongst the clutter of ground return along the coast.

Thirty or more miles to the east, they could see the loom of light from a larger city, probably Puerto Plata, and he decided that they would have to turn north now, away from the coast and north toward the Bahamas.

He turned to her. "Holly, get the maps out of the case. It will be a large one, JNC-47, for this area and the next one north of that, JN-45, I think. Take the penlight and see whether you can find Hispaniola."

She dug into the case, found the chart, and extracted it. The chart was huge when opened and she folded it and refolded it, leaving only the southern Bahamas and Hispaniola displayed.

"What now?"

He looked over briefly at the chart and turned back to concentrate on the controls. "Yes. That's it. Those blocks of lines represent one degree of latitude and longitude. Each block is about 60 miles along an edge. How many blocks are we from the eastern edge of Cuba?"

She arched her thumb and forefinger across one block and walked her fingers across the chart. "I make it to be about three blocks—180 miles and maybe closer to 200 if that is Puerto Plata up ahead." She paused. "Brian. The chart shows a large airfield at Puerto Plata."

He nodded. "Yes. We're not going that far east. We first came south. The fighters bounced us just north of Haiti and we turned east. But I think we've lost them by flying along the coast at low altitude. Now we turn north. I have to stay low for the first 30 miles or so, just in case there is a ground radar station at Puerto Plata." He stole a quick glance at the chart and stabbed a finger at it. "You see the islands north of here?"

She bent down to the chart, penlight shielded. "There are several of them; Grand Turk, North and South Caicos. After that, there are a long string of islands up toward the northwest."

"Grand Turk. That's the one I want. There will be a number shown in a red box next to the letters GT. Give me those numbers. That's the frequency of the radio beacon station."

"Two thirty-two."

He set the frequency into the automatic directional finder and listened for several seconds to the code identification. He heard the letters GT in code barely audible above the static. The needle on the radio compass hunted in a northerly direction, unsteady now, but he knew that as they flew north and gained altitude, it would firm up on a solid bearing.

Easing into a bank, he rolled the aircraft through a shallow turn to the north. There was only the black sea before them now, the coast receding behind them. As they rolled out on the northerly heading, he could pick out Ursa Major and in line with the two stars which formed the lip of the dipper, Polaris low on the horizon—true north. The clock on the panel showed 9:51, airborne now for more than a hour. He noted the time on the back of his wrist with a ballpoint pen. There would be time later to begin to compute fuel consumption and range available, but it would be cutting it fine even with favorable winds. Leaning across the width of the panel, he scanned each instrument carefully looking for any abnormality, the smallest flicker. But they were all solidly in the green. The fuel gauges on the main tank showed slightly more than three-quarter filled and they would lie on the conservative side, he hoped.

Time now for the beginning of fuel conservation. He rummaged in the dashboard locker and found the power-setting tables, written in Stroud's precise hand. One column was outlined in red felt-tip pen, the column heading "55 percent power." He followed the vertical headings of altitude to sea level and across to throttle setting and prop speed. Slowly, he adjusted the throttle back until the manifold pressure registered just over 21 inches and then inched the prop speed back to 2100 rpm. The airspeed slowly stabilized at just short of 150.

The moon was setting in the west now, a dim orange sickle scything into the horizon's haze. They both watched, regretting the fading light. Perhaps a millenium ago, man felt the same, he thought. With the light of the moon gone, there was only blackness and the pinpricks of stars in the heavens above. But the stars were cold and distant. The moon was more personal, a pale sun.

She leaned over and put her hand to the nape of his neck, rubbing and prodding the muscles. "How's that?" she said, watching his profile in the dim illumination of the instruments.

"Not bad. Really tired. My head hurts like hell."

"Can you put it on autopilot? If you tell me what to watch for, I can wake you up if this thing begins to act up."

He stretched his muscles under her probing fingertips. "Nope. Not yet. As long as we're close to the water, I have to hand-fly the aircraft. I wouldn't trust the autopilot. Once we get another ten minutes north of here, I'll start to climb out. But for the present, I want to stay well under any radar that they may have in Puerto Plata."

"Are we going to have enough fuel?" she said, looking down at the gauges.

"I think so. You're looking at the main fuel tank quantity. When I switch over to the auxiliary tanks in a few hours, we have another 500 miles range in them and then another 750 miles in the fuel tanks in the back seat."

"Yes, but haven't we burned up a lot of fuel in the last hour?" She pushed the hair out of her eyes, a gesture that had always stirred Loss.

"Not that much, I think. Maybe twelve gallons. I've kept her as slow as possible. But at any rate, we'll easily make New Jersey, New York state. Somewhere in there. And with good winds, Nova Scotia. It should be dawn tomorrow before we start to go dry."

She sat and thought for several minutes, twirling a strand of hair around a fingertip. She turned to him pointing back to the west. "Those were Cuban aircraft back there?"

He nodded.

"And they were trying to shoot us down?"

He nodded again, edging in nose-up trim to start the shallowest of climbs. The sea was black beneath them, no visual perception of height. The altimeter read six hundred forty feet, the rate of climb indicator nudging upward at fifty feet per minute.

She leaned over next to him, her chin on his shoulder. "Why, Brian?" she asked. "And how did they know that we were there?"

The events of the past spun off in disorder in his mind as he groped for the answer. Klist was Petrov. Bolken was Heiss. Who was Volgel? What was the link between Petrov and Welsh. He shook his head wearily and said, "I just don't know. The fighter that made an identification pass on us must have known the registration number of this aircraft. Even the Cubans don't just shoot down anyone. So they knew." He paused, chewing at the light growth of hair on his lip. How many days without a shave now? "I don't think that it was probably Volgel that shot at us from the ground. Petrov must have gotten to Cuba and Volgel was probably in radio contact with him. They certainly couldn't have used a telephone. But why they would want to shoot us down, I just don't know. Something to do with the deal between Petrov and Welsh. Does that make sense?"

She didn't answer, still lost in thought.

Far out to the east, Loss could see the lights of a ship, plowing southeastward toward Puerto Rico. A cruise liner, perhaps, for its decks were a blaze of light. Going south for days of fun in the sun, nights of romance. Exotic ports, friendly natives. He grimaced, part in envy, part in disgust.

She resumed rubbing his neck, remaining silent. The stimulation to his muscles produced a warm tingling. His forehead still ached, but less so now. If the fuel held out, if the engine held together—. Lots of ifs. Not to think too much about it and just fly the airplane. Even if he couldn't make Canada, he would have a fair trial in the US. Holly would testify. Momentarily, he thought that it might be better to just set the aircraft down in the States and let justice grind away. The only trick was that he was accusing a Senator of the United States of—what?

"Brian?" she said. "If we were shot at by this man Volgel, do you think he would have done anything to Stroud? Or that Heiss person? I mean, if he was willing to shoot at us, wouldn't he try to eliminate any witnesses?"

Loss eased in more power for the climb and watched the airspeed settle to 143. The stars were brighter now as they climbed above the salt air. Ursa Major, the Big Bear, wheeled westward, the Pole Star by itself on the dim horizon.

He shook his head. "I don't know," he said wearily.

Chapter 21

The sky was black but changing, slowly mutating to progressively paler shades of cream. The stars dimmed, one by one in the east, the dissolution spreading west until only Venus and Saturn were left to flicker in the vacant dome.

The dawn was only a dirty red smudge on the horizon, suppressed by a complex frontal system which smeared the eastern horizon with high cirrus, clustered thunderstorms, and rain.

Beneath them, the sea was pocked with oily green-white seas, rolling across the fetch of the Atlantic to break upon the New England coast. A massive supertanker labored southeastward, seas breaking over her superstructure, engulfing her decks with white foam. He watched the ship until she was gone from sight, the only living thing that shared the bleak void of sea and sky.

Loss eased the mixture control back fractionally, watching the cylinder-head temperature waver near the top of the red arc. The Comanche hung on its prop, mushing. But the fuel flow meter fluctuated marginally and stabilized at 7 gallons per hour. He fumbled with the computer, punching in figures, time, and distance. The display gave back an answer of two hours and fourteen minutes to dry tanks, discounting the long slow descent from altitude when fuel consumed would be even less.

He rechecked the computations twice, his mind fuddled with the accumulative effects of high altitude, lack of sleep, and physical fatigue.

He looked down on the sea once more, watching the pattern of the swells from the southeast. Aloft, the wind seemed more southerly, giving the Comanche a boost of 30 miles or more for each hour flown. Or so he guessed. Three hours before, he had passed 90 miles west of Bermuda, using the VOR from Kindley Field to establish his track. The results were generally believable, the tailwind boosting him along, extending his range.

But the information was imprecise, and now, 420 miles to the north, the weather system would have changed and with it, the winds.

Holly stirred in the right seat, curled into a ball, feet drawn up beneath her. Even in sleep, her face was composed and gentle. Loss felt a surge of compassion for her, something far more than love. For three hours last night, while he slept, she had monitored the instruments, alone with her thoughts in a single-engine aircraft 15,000 feet over the black Atlantic. She had awaked him only once to point out the lights of an aircraft passing high overhead to the north, bound toward the mainland. She never once questioned his actions, simply believing his articles of faith; a litany of fuel and time and instruments. Sometime after five, she woke him again and they transferred the last of the fuel from the back seat tanks. By 5:30, an hour before dawn, he ran the auxiliary tanks dry, the engine shuddering and coughing as he switched to the main tanks once more. But now she slept.

Loss selected a frequency of 113.3 on the VOR and watched the indicator for any sign of movements. The needle lay dead in its cage, but the headphones gave out the faint beat of morse code. He listened intently, trying to pick out the individual letters. The station was on the south coast of Nova Scotia, the town of Yarmouth. The Kent farm was 90 miles beyond that, on the eastern coast two miles south of the town of Lunenburg. Kent had described the airstrip as "Grass, cows, and about 2000 feet long. Near the edge of a peninsula." A fragile thing to pin your hopes on, he thought.

He switched on the low frequency ADF radio and dialed through the broadcast bands. The reception was a tumult of voices and crashing static. He found one clear station, probably in Boston. The announcer was giving hockey scores. Then an ad for Fiat electric cars. More hockey scores. Loss fumed, waiting for some means of identifying the station. Finally, a woman's voice:

> Maine, New Hampshire and Vermont will continue to enjoy unseasonably warm weather today with highs around 15 Celsius, winds from the southeast. Some cloudiness this afternoon in northern sections of Vermont and New Hampshire with a 20 percent chance of rain by this evening. Here in Bar Harbor, skies are partly cloudy, temperature 12 degrees Celsius. Barometer ten thirteen millibars and falling. And here's Jack with some good news about saving money on your coal heating bill—

Loss flipped the selector switch of the antenna to ADF and watched the radio compass needle point to the west. That would put him abeam of the station in northern Maine. The bearing wasn't that solid, but it was an indication that the tailwind had been as good as expected, perhaps better. He roughed out the bearing on the enroute low altitude chart and noted the time. Spanning the distance from the bearing to the southern coast of Nova Scotia with his fingers, he estimated 110 nautical miles. No indication yet, he thought, looking at the VOR indicator, which was tuned to Falmouth.

She stirred in the right seat, pushing hair from her face. Sitting up, she squinted out at the eastern horizon and yawned. Leaning over, she kissed him lightly. "Looks cold down there," she said, yawning again. "Where are we?"

"Ninety, maybe a hundred miles from the south coast of Nova Scotia. I think we'll squeak by."

She looked over the cowling of the Comanche. The sea 3 miles below them and to the north looked like a sheet of hammered lead in the spring sunlight. "Do you think anyone has seen us? On radar or whatever they do?" she asked, crossing her arms on the padded instrument cowl and resting her chin on her forearm. Watching the northern horizon.

"Bermuda did, possibly. I doubt it. I don't know about the southern coast of Nova Scotia. Falmouth might have approach control radar."

"What will they do if they see us on radar?"

He scratched at the growth of beard. His mouth felt foul. And the cut over his forehead was starting to throb. "I don't know. Possibly think we were an aircraft out of Halifax. We can fly to the east of them so we'll be on the edge of their radar range. There is a local radio station shown on the sectional map of Nova Scotia about 8 miles from the Kent Farm—CKBW. If we can get a positive identification, we can home in on that."

She nodded and was quiet, watching the north horizon. He withdrew two candy bars from the dash compartment, and they chewed on the chocolate in silence.

The oil temperature was creeping upwards now, fractionally higher than it had been an hour ago. Loss remembered that Stroud had warned him of excessive oil consumption. He opened the engine cooling cowl, disliking the additional drag that it would develop, robbing them of a few miles per hour. Perhaps he could start the descent once the VOR at Falmouth came alive. He looked closely at the sectional, searching for the radio station. He found it, 10 miles to the west of Lunenburg. Dialing in the frequency, he listened. The voice was clear, a Canadian accent, discussing the fisheries program in the Gulf of St. Lawrence. Switching to the ADF function, he watched the needle swing to the northwest, a full 40 degrees to the left of his present heading. He disengaged the autopilot and turned the aircraft left until the needle was centered.

She raised her eyebrows. "What's wrong?"

"Nothing much, I hope," he lied. "We must be further out to sea than I thought. But the ADF needle is locked onto CKBW."

"Will we have enough fuel?"

"I don't know now. We probably have—" he hesitated and looked down at the chart. He checked the time, subtracting the fuel used since the earlier bearing from Bar Harbor. "We probably have about one hour forty minutes worth of fuel left. That translates into about 240 miles, discounting the effects of a wind. And if the engine runs dry, we have about another 40 miles of playing glider."

She looked down at the sea beneath them. "How cold is the sea?" she said, her breath condensing on the perspex of the cabin window, her forehead resting against the pane.

"You'll freeze your balls off," he said, looking down on his side.

"I'm serious."

"So am I. The chart shows that the southern limit of pack ice in March is just north of here. We would last about five minutes in the water. But we're going to make it."

"Yes," she said, leaning against him. "I guess we have to. What about the Kents? It's a lot to expect of them."

Loss laughed. "Not really. Supposedly, I've only stolen two airplanes, left the Bahamas without clearance, and entered Canada illegally."

"Seriously, Brian. He's a retired RCAF officer. It would probably be very difficult for them if we're discovered."

"Holly, I think the Kents are part of a vanishing breed." Unconsciously, he looked at the oil-temperature gauge. It was lower now, but still hovering in the red. More ominously, the oil pressure was down fractionally. He avoided looking at the panel, as if ignorance would keep the engine from betraying them. "The Kents will put us up for the few days that it takes to get this thing sorted out. Stroud will," he paused, thinking about Stroud, "Stroud will be able to clear the thing up in Mathewtown. If I have to, I'll go down to New York to confront Welsh. There has to be some explanation."

She sat up, stretching, working her arms against the tiredness. Looking out over the engine cowling, she scanned the horizon.

"Brian, how far can you see from this altitude?"

He hesitated, eyes scanning the instrument panel. "Oh, about fifty, sixty miles. It's fairly clear."

She pointed ahead and his eyes followed her fingertip toward a brown smear on the horizon. They both watched intently, willing it not to dissolve or change into cloud bank. The smear expanded, slowly filling the horizon. Further to the south, a rocky headland emerged and solidified. And before them, the brown became greens and blues and whites; great forests of fir and spruce dotted with yet-frozen lakes.

Just to the north of their flight path, two great bays, separated by headlands, harbored fleets of fishing vessels. Offshore, but within the protection of the bays, were hundreds of isolated islands, mostly barren except for spots of stunted spruce and birch.

As they passed over the coast, he closed the throttle and began a slow descent.

"Sonovabitch! I still can't believe it." DeSilva, expansive, swirled the 12-year-old Glenlivit in the crystal glass, grinning happily. "Three days! You did in three days what four different Presidents have attempted to do in fourteen years. In-fucking-credible!" and he laughed again, like an 8-year-old child on finding a dollar lying in the dirt at his feet.

Clifford Tannis Welsh sat in the chaise longue, a thin smile set implacably on his lips, his eyes distant. He sipped once again from the brandy snifter and set it down upon the grass beside his armrest. He watched, in the last illumination of the June twilight, as lightning bugs flickered through the maples. Sometimes, it seemed, there were a thousand, all blinking in a screaming silent chorus.

DeSilva was talking again, larding crudeness into each sentence as if it were obligatory grammatical construction. Welsh listened to him, half-heartedly. It was only a dim echo of the media. Of a half-thankful, half-jealous government. Of half-assed idealists. For Welsh now knew where the power lay.

"Did you understand what I said?" DeSilva asked. The malt whiskey sloshed in his glass, spilling clear amber drops across his cardigan. He brushed at the wetness with his hand. "I said that you have, by latest count, invitations to seventeen different speaking engagements, six of them televised. We just can't handle it. I have three more staff as of Thursday, and we still aren't coping with the volume of mail."

"What do they say," Welsh said tonelessly, eyes unfocused, looking beyond the muddy Hudson toward the stain on the horizon that was Manhattan.

"Jesus, Clifford," DeSilva replied. "What do you think they say! You're the new Messiah. Three months ago, we had troops fighting in the streets of the Canal Zone. Two merchant ships hit by mortar fire, one of them sunk. All the UN sticking resolutions up our ass. And with one simple speech in the Senate advocating, as you put it, 'unilateral disentanglement from foreign national domains,' you strike some sort of response from the new government." DeSilva paused, drinking the whiskey. "Christ, I couldn't believe it. Twenty-four hours after the speech, the Republic of Fuckin' Panama invites you down for, as CBS put it, 'bottom line discussions.' And in two days you return with a Panamanian proposal for a cessation of hostilities, peaceful withdrawal of US forces and most important, the face-saving gesture of allowing our ships free passage through the Canal in goddamn perpetuity. The Secretary of State farts around for a couple of days. The White House makes a few noises about the specific language. But every single voter in the US knew that you were the guy that put it all together. We're running an in-depth poll this week to find out where you would stand on voter preference for Governor, but I can tell you right now, unless you declare yourself a raving queer, you're a shoe-in."

"Skip the poll," Welsh said softly. "At least for now."

"For God's sake, why?"

"I said at least for now," Welsh replied, taking a sip of the cognac, letting the warmth bloom on his tongue. The aftertaste was bitter. He turned to DeSilva, examining him in the last vestiges of twilight. DeSilva's clothes, the Blass cardigan, Yves St. Laurent shirt, the slacks, Pucci loafers, were all matched, tastefully selected. But they fit him oddly, as if he were some misshapen manikin. The face, most of all, belonged with working clothes and a hard hat. Coarse black hair, a bulb-like nose, black ferret eyes.

"Harry," Welsh said, "I'm not running for Governor. Or for my seat as Senator. It's the White House I'm after."

"Now wait a minute, Cliff—"

"No, DeSilva. You wait a minute. I have an opportunity that comes just once. I'm going to capitalize on it. I'm going to press everything I can out of this Panama deal, and when that cools off, I'm going for something else like it."

"Balls," DeSilva snorted in disgust. He set his glass down after finishing off the whiskey in one swallow. "Cliff. You've blown this thing all out of proportion. It was a one-shot deal. Great, yes. But not nearly enough to pull you up through five presidential contenders. The convention is only two months away. You weren't in the primaries. You have no national organization, you—"

Welsh cut him off abruptly. "Harry. For once in your life, listen to me. You're a good organization man, yes. But we're going to do this thing my way or you're not going to be part of it. And from here on in, I want you to knock off the swearing, particularly in public."

"Shit."

"Shit, nothing!" Welsh snapped. "Just knock it off. And I mean permanently. And listen carefully. On Monday morning I want you to start getting together a 'Citizens for Welsh Committee.' This has to start spontaneously. Use people we have in the third district. Broad spectrum. Not just teamsters or steelworkers."

DeSilva nodded, subdued now. Rapidly sobering up.

"Model the organization on the McGovern tactics of 1972. It has to be grass roots. I have to play the reluctant statesman being dragged feet first into the nomination. But believe me, Harry, they're going to be screaming for me by August."

DeSilva shook his head in bewilderment. "Cliff," he moaned. "Cliff. It isn't going to be that way. This whole thing has been tried before. Someone pulls off a coup in the election year. Like a crime investigation committee, or ah, a trip to China. Stuff like that. You're everybody's sweetheart for three days. But try to capitalize on it. No fuc—, no way. You don't have the national depth of voter recognition, and those that do know you associate you with free-spending northeastern liberalism. The south hates it, the farmers hate it. Some people in your own party hate it." DeSilva picked up the empty glass, looking morosely at the few remaining drops. He drank those, almost wiping them from the glass with his tongue.

The Welsh children were squealing further down on the broad lawn; small shapes running across the grass, swirling in the gathering darkness like dust devils. Their laughter drifted across the open space, echoing. The two men sat in near-darkness now, watching the shapes collide, turn, flee from one another. Welsh lit a cigarette, the flame of his Ronson etching his features in bas-relief. His face was hardened.

He blew out the smoke in one long stream; the exhalation of a man who is tired of arguing. "Harry. You're one of the best friends I could ever have. I wouldn't be a Senator today unless it were for you. You know the rule book. The polls, the voters. You know how the party works. All these things better than I ever will. But in this situation, you've got to go along with me. I know where it's all at. Are you willing to listen?"

DeSilva nodded. "OK, Cliff. Lay it out for me. I'll listen."

"Good," Welsh said. He leaned back in the chaise longue, folding his hands behind his neck, arching his neck back to watch the night sky. "Good," he repeated. He paused, composing the half-formed words in his own mind, then started to speak. "You're right in some ways. I don't have a national record. Some people know me, but not more than most other junior senators. Everything has already been said twenty times over. Energy, states rights, the economy. It's hacked to death. I can't take any unique position on domestic issues. But the thing that concerns voters most, even though they don't recognize it, is security. Or perhaps I should rephrase that as security from fear. Fear of the Russians, the Chinese, the Middle East. Africa, Indo-China, South America.

"All those people out there, beyond our borders, are hollering for our blood. Because, and only because we represent a threat to them. In other words, they fear us. It isn't our capitalistic system. The Swedes, the Japanese, the Swiss. What are they? Rich capitalistic states, bursting at the seams with consumer goods, healthy children, luxurious standards of living. But no one is sniping at them. The essential difference is that they don't pose a threat. Self-defense within their own borders, but no meddling around in foreign affairs. Do you follow thus far?"

DeSilva remained silent, listening.

Welsh glanced at his watch and continued, "So our essential dilemma is that we have involved ourselves as a nation in the domestic affairs of other countries. We had the muscle once. Following World War II. But we kept it up. It became political dogma for both parties. Berlin. Korea, and then Indo-China. Harry, we've broken our backs carrying the rest of the free world, and the only reward for all this has been the unrelenting hate they spew back at us."

"What are you trying to say?" DeSilva sighed.

"What I'm trying to say is that if we don't withdraw from world affairs, and do it soon, we're going to be confronted in a fight we can't win because we have neither the will to fight nor the weapons to fight with. Withdraw now. Unilateral disengagement, unilateral disarmament."

"Cliff. That kind of talk isn't going to go down well with the conservatives. Military. Defense industries. That sort of thinking in the past has broken the back of every candidate who tried it."

"Yes, Harry. But the operative phrase is 'in the past.' We're talking about the reality of *now*. And tomorrow. Panama was a small example. We unilaterally offer to withdraw and suddenly, the threat is gone. Instead of invective, the countries we're dealing with can offer peace. Friendship. Maybe even like Panama, the concept of cooperation for mutual benefit. The thing you have to understand is that we either withdraw from the arena gracefully or get kicked out."

"OK, Cliff. For the sake of argument, let's assume that you're right. You have the Accord of Panama behind you. But what else can you pull off? And how? The State Department is still wiping egg off its face. They're not going to give you any power base to negotiate from with other countries."

"I don't know exactly," Welsh lied. "I suppose that I could point out that Guantánamo Bay is basically an obsolete facility. A phased withdrawal over two or three years might give Castro the latitude to improve relations."

"That's nothing new," DeSilva replied. "That idea has been kicked around since Kennedy. Besides, Castro is going to take his cue from the Russians."

"Yes. You have a point. But the interesting thing is that if Castro responded favorably now—some gesture of equal magnitude—it could be interpreted as a new beginning toward disinvolvement and even disarmament. With the unspoken accord of the Kremlin."

"And if Cuba doesn't respond, you're going to blow what gains you've made with the voters on the Panama issue. Cliff, don't you see? You've generated tremendously favorable comment already. With TV interviews, we can magnify it, bring your name to bear on the national political scene. But if you try to follow through with a gambit in Cuba and they don't respond down there, which I'm damn sure they won't, you'll end up looking like a three-day wonder."

"But if I got some sort of positive response out of Cuba?"

DeSilva scratched his chin, thinking. He turned toward Welsh, his glasses catching the reflection of the starlight. "If they did respond, Cliff, you would be the darling of the American public. You literally could write your own ticket."

"Yes, that's the way I see it," Welsh replied. He rose from the chaise longue and stretched. "Let's get up to the house. Judith will be getting the kids ready for bed. I've got to say good night to them. Then we can talk some more about this. I've got a rather long list of things for you to do."

Both men strolled slowly across the dark lawn, pausing to watch river traffic crawling up the Hudson.

"That's something I've always wanted to do," DeSilva mused, almost to himself.

"What's that?"

"Drive one of those things. A riverboat." DeSilva turned toward the house, turning away from the river. "I guess it was all the Mark Twain that my father read to us as kids. Cliff?"

"Yes."

"This thing with Panama and now Cuba. Are you telling me everything? You seem so confident. Like it was all arranged."

Welsh laughed. "Harry, you've got no soul. Everything has an angle, doesn't it?"

"You know that I didn't mean it that way."

"Well, you're right in a way," Welsh replied. "The new order of things in a world of politics is emerging. Too few people see the reality that the US is no longer the free world's protector. We have to give up this gung-ho attitude and pull in our horns. I believe that it's the only way we can survive as a nation."

"That may be a difficult concept to sell, Clifford."

"Yes, perhaps. But the people buy results. I intend to produce those results."

They passed the old carriage house and paused in the dark shadow of the greenhouse. DeSilva was puffing slightly from the shallow climb.

The upstairs lights in the front bedroom on the main house blinked on. The great stone mansion stood in stark relief against the night skyline, and Welsh admired it, as he had since he was a boy.

"Do you think they'll call it the White House on the Hudson, Harry?"

DeSilva coughed. "Jesus." He paused. "Sorry about that. Just slipped out."

Welsh laughed softly, feeling power in the reins he held. Perhaps he would have to find a place for DeSilva out of public view eventually. But still, he respected the savvy politician. The polls. That was the crux of being elected, and DeSilva was an expert.

They walked together toward the house, their heels crunching on the gravel pathway.

"Did you finally get payment from the insurance company, Cliff?"

"Yes. About a week ago. The investigator went down to see what was left of the Aztec. It was pretty well stripped out, although God knows what the locals down there would do with damaged aircraft parts."

"Anything more on Loss and the girl?"

"No," Welsh replied. "Two months now and nothing. They think he probably went down at sea from fuel starvation. And there was also some report from Haiti on the same night about an explosion in the sky. About the right place at the right time. But it was from fishermen. Hard to tell."

"What do you think ever possessed Loss to do it? I mean the murders."

Welsh turned to him as they came to the first step of the porch. "Drugs. I don't know. But it's finished now. I don't want to talk about Loss again. Understood?"

He turned and strode up the stairs. DeSilva stood below and watched Welsh enter the house and slam the screen door behind him.

Chapter 22

Ian Campbell shaded his eyes from the hard sunlight with one hand, puffing nervously on the Rothman with the other. The skin on his hands and his face was a bright red, for like most men of his complexion and personal habits, he never tanned. Purplish veins, like tributaries of a river, flowed across his cheeks and nose, the testament of heavy drinking. His chest thudded dully, for even without exertion, his heart could barely maintain the flow of blood to the fat-laden arteries.

He looked across the concourse of the terminal and the service entrance, seeing thousands of people, seeing no one in particular. Grunting softly with relief, he settled himself on the battered leather two-suiter and waited.

His scalp prickled with the heat, and he removed the light woven straw hat, scrubbing the crown on his head with a handkerchief. His hair, wispy around his ears, overlong at the collar, was matted with perspiration. The light breeze felt refreshing.

He checked his watch again, irritated with the delay. Over twenty minutes late. Campbell was a punctual man, and he considered it the rudest of faults for a person to be late, even what is termed fashionably late. If a chap said 3:10, then he should *mean* 3:10. Not 3:15. Or twenty. Like stealing time from the person you were meeting. All very well to be late. Then you were assured that the person was there cooling his heels, waiting for you. Good psychological practice. But damn rude.

He watched the tide of people flowing through the terminal entrance with some curiosity. Canadians? God, they looked *American*! Mod clothes, the ever-present American type of attaché case. Not a decent briefcase with sound leather and good stitching. Plastic things trying to look like leather.

A swept-wing aircraft thundered into the sky to the west, laying down dark tracks of smoke, straining toward the sun. The fuselage was emblazoned with stripes of red and gold and green, the logo of some Canadian airline or another. Looked like a flying stick of candy, he thought.

"Mr. Campbell?"

He turned on the luggage, craning his head toward the speaker, the sun in his eyes.

"Yes, I'm Campbell. You're Kent?"

The man who stood before Campbell nodded his head, economically. "You're alone, Mr. Campbell?"

"Of course. You specified that I was to come alone in the letter."

Edwin Kent nodded and smiled, extending his hand. "Yes, we thought that it might be better. I hope that the information that we included was of some use."

"It was," Campbell grunted, grasping the other man's hand in greeting. "But whether we can do anything with it is another thing."

The two men walked to the dusty Chrysler sedan, Kent limping. The deep, brittle blue of the Nova Scotia early summer was cloudless, vacant. Despite the smells of jet exhaust, Campbell caught the underlying scent of great tracts of spruce and a hint of the salt sea, which lay a few miles to the east.

Campbell had never been in Nova Scotia, but as with most Britons of his era, he had always pictured Halifax as the bitter end of a frayed lifeline across the Atlantic in the early years of the war. For every three ships that left the coast of Nova Scotia, two steamed past the Nab Tower into the Solent to land their cargo on the fire-blackened docks of Southhampton. His son—his only son—had sailed on those convoys and had been lost in a collision off the Irish Coast. Campbell tried not to think about this, ever, but he would want to see the town and the harbor and the place called Pennant Bay from which his son had sailed on the great convoys that had gathered in the winter's dusk.

Kent placed the suitcases in the rear seat and eased himself into the driver's seat, awkwardly lifting his right leg with his hands to swing it over the sill and place it on the floor.

"The war?" Campbell said, nodding toward the leg.

"One of them. The cold one. Not all that bad, this leg. Just can't do some things. They want to refit it with the newer mods.Ced Gears and relays and solid state. That sort of thing. Doubt that I could stand all the whirring. Besides, I'm sort of fond of the old one. Keep telling Margaret, my wife, that I've fitted a rum flask into the calf. Actually found her looking for it one night after I had taken the damn thing off to go to bed." Kent laughed and started the engine.

They traveled south on the expressway, Kent graceful in his driving, handling the machine with casual ease. Campbell thought that Kent would do all things like this with economy of motion, the direct mind-machine link that is the blessing of few.

"Air Marshal, weren't you?" Campbell asked, lighting another Rothman, watching the green blur of spruce rush by.

"Yes, was," Kent replied, watching the road ahead. "Now just on pension. Golden handshake. I miss it sometimes. By the way, it's Ian, isn't it?" Campbell nodded. "Then just call me Kent. Everyone else does, except my wife. Calls me Edwin, which I suppose is a proper Christian name." He paused and then briefly glanced across at the Englishman. Campbell was no fool, he thought. Just looked like one. "Ian, I suppose that you'd like to know about Loss. We have only about thirty minutes before we're back to the farm. I think you need background."

Campbell nodded. "Yes. Everything that you can give me before I start with Loss. And I want to make something clear. For the record, I'm here on holiday. No official function. Depending on Loss and what he may or may not be willing to do, my department may come into it. But it's a very touchy thing right now."

"In what way?"

"Don't you see, Kent? Technically, we're involved in intelligence activities within a foreign 'friendly' country. Neither the RCMP nor the CIA has wind of this. For Loss's safety, I want to keep it that way as long as possible."

Kent lit his pipe, sucking on the flame. He nodded. "It sounds reasonable. But frankly, it seems to me to be a dead end. Loss is really shaken. His confidence is gone."

Campbell pursed his lips briefly. "Yes. I can understand why it would be. But carry on. Tell me about him and the woman."

Kent swung off the expressway and onto an asphalt coastal road, still heading south and west. Through little towns, with clapboard-sided salt boxes, elm-lined streets. Towns with names like Fourteen Mile House and Beechville. The New World, Campbell thought. His son must have liked it here.

"Loss." Kent squinted against the late afternoon July sun. "Yes, Loss. He came two months ago in April. In Stroud's plane. He made it in one direct flight from the Bahamas." He turned to Campbell, explaining. "You see, he had extra fuel. Had it in the back seat. Remarkable that he didn't blow himself up. At any rate, he came into a little cow patch airstrip I have on the farm. There was still a bit of snow around. Muddy too. We had to drag the aircraft off the strip with the tractor. It's in the barn now."

"Did your aviation authorities ever detect the aircraft?"

"No, I doubt it," Kent replied. "Loss was off course, well out to sea. Came into Nova Scotia in an area where there is not too much radar coverage. Besides, this is not an area where there is much of a light-plane security problem. Most of the border smuggling takes place down toward Quebec."

"And then."

"Yes. Well, Loss explained that he had been accused of stealing his employer's aircraft and that the Bahamians were going to jail him for it. To use his words, he said that he was being 'set up.' So he used this other aircraft to escape in with the permission of the owner, this chap Stroud. On top of all this, he was jumped by three jet interceptors shortly after takeoff. The woman confirms his story. I put them up in the guest cottage without contacting the authorities until Loss could sort it out."

Campbell chain-lit another cigarette, spilling ashes across his lapels. He stubbed the fag-end of the used cigarette out in the smoking tray. "I can understand why you would help them," he said. "However, it may be somewhat difficult to explain to the Royal Canadian Mounted if that time comes."

Kent nodded. "Yes, I've thought of that. Margaret, my wife, thinks that the whole thing is slightly insane. At any rate, we got word over CBC that Stroud and this person Heiss were murdered. The authorities in the Bahamas obviously concluded that Loss had done it. So consequently, he can't give himself up to the authorities without some evidence of his innocence, which seems to be severely lacking. Of course, there are also counts of drug smuggling and grand theft against him. He's very depressed about the whole thing. Blames himself for Stroud's death."

"Why doesn't he turn himself in to the American authorities? I would think that he would receive a fair trial."

"I can't reason with him on that score, Ian. He seems to be convinced that Welsh was involved in this whole thing. It would be Welsh's word against Loss's. And as you know, Welsh is presently well thought of in the States. The Panamanian and now this Cuban Accord. Personally, I think Loss is right. Welsh was a part of it, although perhaps unwittingly."

"Loss *is* innocent," Campbell said, yawning. He stretched his arms. "At least on my findings and the conclusions that we can determine from somewhat limited cooperation on the part of the Bahamian government." He ticked off on his stubby fingers like a schoolmaster. "One. Heiss-Bolken was a Russian agent. A very unsavory person. Two. There was a third person aboard that flight as Loss claims. A man known as Klist—Petrov—take your choice. We know nothing about him. But his wife has been traced back to East Germany. Obviously not his wife, but very probably in Russian service. Petrov disappeared, but we think he stole a small yacht. The yacht has never been found.

"Three, and probably most important in terms of Loss's innocence, I found a couple of 9-millimeter cartridge cases quite far down the runway. They are of the same caliber as the weapon that Loss owns, but the extractor marks on the cases don't fit the design of the Luger's extractor. We feel that it was probably a Walther. I have two photographs of the ballistic marks on a bullet we recovered from Stroud. The rifling doesn't match the barrel construction of Loss's type of Luger. Again, evidence indicates that it was from a Walther P-38 type weapon."

"You presented this evidence to the Bahamian police?"

"Yes," Campbell sighed. "But I had a feeling that they didn't want to know. Or at least someone within their department, fairly high on the ladder, didn't. I was told, very politely, mind you, to go back to London."

Kent passed through a small town that seemed to be composed solely of white churches, a boatyard, and a general store. There were children skipping rope in a graveyard. They waved. Near the edge of the village, Kent swung left onto a dirt road and bumped across a cattle guard. He pulled the sedan to a stop beneath the shade of a cluster of maples. Cows, munching on long-bladed grass, raised their heads in dull curiosity and stared, still masticating.

Kent switched off the engine and turned to Campbell. "Then, what you have would help to clear Loss? With the US authorities, I mean."

Campbell nodded. "Yes, in the sense of criminal justice, I think it would. But we see something much more involved than just Loss. Something, perhaps to use a grandiose phrase, of global importance. Loss is just the dog who got his tail caught in the crack of the door. We see this connection between Petrov, Heiss. and Welsh as the main crux of our interest. Very much so now, in view of Welsh's political development. What really further complicates the issue is that Welsh is selling unilateral disarmament to the American people, a view which seems to coincide with our present Labor government's outlook. Our department is essentially nonpolitical. We have reservations about the wisdom of such a policy."

Edwin Kent looked down at his weathered hands, which were tanned and strong from working the fields. His stump hurt like hell. He turned to Campbell, eyes hard and flat gray. "So you can't help Loss? Is that what you've flown from London to tell me?"

Campbell smiled. "No, Kent. Not exactly. I said that one of the conditions was that my department's help might be somewhat limited. We can provide research, contact, surveillance, that sort of thing. But all the links between Senator Welsh and the others—Heiss, Volgel and Petrov—are broken. We can only help Loss if he leaves his burrow and starts to run. Then we shall see who the hounds are."

Margaret Kent removed their coffee cups and withdrew from the study, closing the door behind her.

Kent sat behind a scarred desk, right leg up on a footstool. Behind him on the wall were black and white photos, framed uniformly in plain black molding. Some of the photos were faded, turning shades of sepia. Kent with squadron comrades: serious young men in leather jackets, hands stuffed in pockets, some with mustaches. A spotted dog in the foreground, held by a young man dressed in military blouse and forage cap. Others of Kent alone, sitting in the cockpit of a Hawker Hurricane, smiling shyly.

Book shelves lined two walls of the study, well thumbed, with dust jackets torn or bearing fingermarks. The complete set of Churchill. Jane's *Aircraft of the World,* Bertrand Russell, and surprisingly, a wide-ranging set of volumes on the history of the Canadian Railways.

Campbell rose from the leather ottoman and poured three glasses of cognac neat. He placed one before Kent, handed another to Loss, and retained the third for himself. They raised their glasses in a diminutive toast and drank.

"Confusion to our enemies," Campbell said, wiping his lips with a handkerchief.

"Something like that," Loss muttered. He leaned back in the leather chair, balancing his glass on the upholstered arm. Loss had grown a full beard in the three months he had hidden in Nova Scotia. The cut on his forehead was healed, but the white puckered flesh stood out prominently against the deep tan he had acquired working in the fields. Even now, he wore the faded denims of a field worker, the smell of earth engrained within the fabric. He looked up at Campbell. "So you don't think that the ballistics test would help me?"

Campbell hunched his shoulders. "Inconclusive, Brian. It would only indicate that the weapon used on Stroud and Heiss was not a Luger. That is, assuming that the Bahamian police would accept my work. Look at it from the standpoint of a jury. You take an aircraft from Welsh. He states that you had stolen it. Then you escape from a hospital, abduct both Stroud and Heiss, and take them to the airport. Next, you leave them tied to Stroud's rented car and flee the country in Stroud's aircraft. Both men are found shot and burned to death." He paused for effect, lifting his shaggy eyebrows. "What would be your judgment?"

"Ian, there must be some way out of this. For God's sake—"

Campbell snorted. "Of course there is. Turn yourself in at the border. I'll give you all the help that I can muster. But remember that this is a matter that occurred within Bahamian jurisdiction. You would be extradited and tried there. Back to square one."

Edwin Kent sighed. "The other alternative, Brian, is staying here. You're welcome, you know. An entire lifetime if you choose. I'm too old to keep the farm going, and this leg isn't much help. You and Holly can simply keep the guest house and manage the farm while I sit down and write a history of the Canadian Pacific Railroad."

Loss started to object and Kent interrupted. "No, Brian, hear me out. Margaret and I have talked before about this. We never could have children, and it's nice having you both around the house. Ian can fix you up with documents showing that you're Canadian citizens. Maybe we could buy that old Newfi schooner that's down in Chester. Have David Clark's firm fix her up. Do some sailing. Eventually, we would leave you the farm." Kent was smiling now. "It's a good alternative, Brian."

Loss sat a long time staring at the photographs above the study's fireplace.

"It's true," Campbell added. "Kent and I have talked it over. Regardless of your course of action, you're going to need a new identity. I have Canadian passports for you and Holly. General documents, backgrounds, the whole business." He flicked his hand as if it were nothing. "But, of course, you would have to not reveal the source if you're ever picked up. Very embarrassing to my department."

Loss looked down at his scuffed boots, embarrassed. "I can hardly thank you, Kent, for your offer. Holly and I love it here. Maybe the first time in my life I've been at peace. You and Margaret have been—"

Kent pushed two matchsticks together on his blotter, keeping his face averted. "I mean it, Brian. We want you to stay."

"But you understand, don't you. I've got to find out what the hell made Welsh do this thing. And what his involvement is. If I could nail that down, the rest would begin to fall into place." He looked up at Kent. "If I can get this resolved, if I have any alternatives other than just sitting here for the rest of my life knowing that I've been screwed, then I'll take it."

Campbell refilled their glasses and then lumbered over to the window, watching the quiet countryside change to deeper umber, melting into the twilight. The wind smelled of green growing things. Kent has found his son, he thought. Lucky man. He turned toward Loss, shoving his stubby, veined hands deeply into his pockets. "You talked about an alternative. Are you sure you want one?"

"Yes. It's as I've said before. I want it cleared up. I want Welsh, particularly."

"We have very little to go on, you realize. It may be completely futile."

"What do you have, Ian?"

Campbell retrieved a sealed folder from his briefcase. Breaking the seal with the nail of his thumb, he extracted a perforated computer printout and laid it out across the desk. Line upon line of type, in the misshapen font of computer graphics, covered the sheet. "This is all we have," Campbell said.

Kent pulled the sheet around to read it. "What does it represent?"

Campbell settled back heavily into the ottoman and lit a cigarette. He exhaled, creating a blue haze under the desk lamplight. "It represents the attempt to link the two words that Heiss revealed to Loss. Words that Heiss had heard on a tape recording that he made secretly of Petrov and the woman. Something that Heiss thought he could use later. Perhaps sell to the Americans. Unfortunately, the conversation was in Russian. Heiss picked up only two words, English proper nouns. We have tried to utilize MI-5s data banks to establish the connection between the words *hood* and *hussar*. Either one or both, of course, could be code words for an operation of some sort. But we tend to discount this since the code words originated by the Russians would most likely be Russian words. We have gone on the premise that *hood* is the name of a place. *Hussar* we feel is a *thing*, a name you give to an object. Perhaps a ship, an antique shop, a pub. Something of that sort."

Campbell looked down at the printout. "I don't think that either of you can realize the magnitude of this job. Because we didn't know what we were looking for, it was decided that it would be necessary to optically scan telephone directories, the atlas, trade magazines, etc., ad nauseam, just for the compilation of names and things that matched the key indices. From there, we attempted to obtain matches based on chronological events happening to *things* at *places*. In practice, we favor the latter theory. That is, the establishment of a thing called *hussar* in a place called *hood*.

"Do you have any results?" Loss asked.

"Three believable, all told," Campbell replied. "Some of these matches are tenuous at best. That is not to say that others don't exist."

Loss looked at the sheet. "Only these three?"

"Yes," Campbell replied, picking at a small infection on his cheek. He drew some white matter and then looked at his finger with disgust. He wiped his cheek with a stained handkerchief.

"These digits in the column under *hood* are coordinates?" Loss asked, running his fingernail down the brief set of listings.

Campbell nodded. "Yes. Latitude and longitude. The other adjacent column is the *hussar* link."

"What are they, then? They're all coded, aren't they?"

"We thought that would be wise," Campbell replied. "Most of the printout is flim-flam at any rate. But the three correlations—links if you will—are all in North America. The first is Port Hood on Cape Breton Island. No direct *hussar* link, but there is a pub called The Highwayman. You see, we included various definitions of *hussar* in the search. Most people tend to think of a hussar as a cavalryman. But the word is derived from the Serbian word *huzar*, meaning pirate, or highwayman.

The second match is Port Hood on the Columbia River in Oregon. There is no direct link there except that we feel *Hussar* may be the name of a ship or a smaller vessel." Campbell dabbed at the red splotch on his cheek, examining the handkerchief with each dab to see whether the oozing had stopped. He scowled, somewhat irritated, but continued. "The third match is the Hood Canal in the state of Washington. This is a deep-water seaway leading down from the Strait of Juan de Fuca. Again, the link may be a ship of some sort."

Loss perched himself on the edge of the desk, looking down at the computer printout. "What about ships named *Hussar*. Is there any central registration of names?"

"Lloyds of London," Campbell replied. "Lloyds registers. Covers all commercial shipping. Also Bureau Veritas. Also DOT in Canada and the US. Collecting ship's names was a relatively mundane task. In all, there are sixteen *Hussars*. Some high-tonnage merchant vessels; the balance documented yachts. Of the sixteen, I think that there are only two of interest. One is a sailing yacht with registration in the state of Washington. The other candidate is a Liberian-owned freighter which plies between Seattle, Vancouver, and the Philippines. Both of these vessels might have occasion to navigate the Hood Canal."

Kent doodled on a yellow writing pad. "It all comes down to a few choices then, Ian. The Columbia River, Cape Breton Island, and the Hood Canal."

Campbell shook his head. "Possibly, although I think we can pay less attention to the first two. Port Hood on Cape Breton is not a seaport to speak of. The same holds true of Port Hood on the Columbia River. No, we feel that it is the

Hood Canal. Major shipping area and all that. And the Liberian freighter would seem to be our *Hussar*. The yacht in question, even though she uses these waters, is American-owned. Just plays about on the coast. Never been offshore to speak of. Local boat."

"What's the connection between Welsh and Petrov and the ship?" Loss asked.

Campbell shook his head slowly, jowls sagging, looking down at the printout. "Not the foggiest, Brian. We can only speculate that Petrov wants to ship something or someone in or out of the US. It's my own guess that Petrov's link with the *Hussar* and his link with Welsh are two entirely different operations. Separate but perhaps supportive."

Kent leaned back in the chair, lobbing the pen into the target area of the yellow pad. He looked at the Englishman carefully, as if to detect some visible flaw in the man that would, in turn, invalidate the data. "Ian. Surely, there is some other *Hood-Hussar* link. Or at least places named Hood. It seems to be tossing all your eggs into one basket."

"True on both counts, Kent. There are many places named Hood: Mount Hood, Port Hood, Hoodsport. But note that most of them are named for the Right Honorable Lord Hood, Admiral of the Ocean Seas. Seaports all. There are only four places in North America named for Hood. We have discounted the mountain and a small town in California. I don't intend to demean your thinking. Yes, there are other Hoods. And a few Hussars in the form of pubs, gift shops, and hotels. But most are ships. And ships make port. We think there is a link, and circumstances argue for North America. Agreed?"

Kent nodded. "Agreed." He bent over the desk, looking at his notes. If Campbell was truthful in his description of the complexity of the data collection, there was a great deal of effort and money involved on the part of MI-5. Something more than mere desire to aid Loss. He phrased it bluntly. "What is your government's interest, Ian?"

Campbell ambled over to the fireplace, looking into the dark chasm of blackened brick. He turned and leaned his bulk against the low mantle. "My government's interest? I think you would really mean my department's interest.

"My government's interest is in dealing with the trade unions, the falling standard of living, and the bloody pound sterling. And inventing new methods of putting people on the dole. But, my department's interest is in Soviet intentions. In Europe, in North America. Wherever. The fact that Petrov, who we must presume is a Soviet agent, has in some manner struck a bargain with a US Senator concerns us. Particularly now that your good Senator Welsh is standing in line for a go at the Presidency. On what seems to be a ticket of unilateral disarmament. Very destabilizing."

Kent raised his eyebrows. "Why destabilizing?"

Campbell grunted, shaking his head. "Kent, you of all people know the answer. The nuclear balance of power has worked for thirty years plus. Not the best way to maintain peace, but workable. But once that balance is altered significantly, we feel that the Soviets would exploit any major weakness. It has been argued that were the US and Western Europe disarmed, the Soviets would have no reason to attack. Historically, the Kremlin has proved this concept to be inaccurate."

Loss leaned forward in his chair, mildly irritated. "I don't know, Ian. All three of us were associated with the military for years. We see things—events and national policies—in a different perspective than most people. Too often in recent years, I think we've been wrong. The Russians have shown restraint in the Middle East, in Indo-China. It just could be that with the threat of NATO removed and the US military reduced to home-defense forces, the Russians might turn inward to develop their own standards of living."

"Good argument," Campbell agreed. "And I've heard it at a thousand dull cocktail parties. But it doesn't wash. Willing to hear me out?"

Loss settled back into the chair, watching the Englishman pace erratically before the dark maw of the fireplace. A moth flickered beneath the desk lamp, senselessly beating its wings against the shade.

Kent lit his pipe and shook the match out. "Go on, Ian."

"We tend to equate things," Campbell said, "in terms of what we understand. So we equate the motives and actions of the Russian ruling class in terms of Western thinking. But there *is* a major difference between the two forms of government that we all tend to discount. In the West, the form of national policy is derived, more or less, from the will of the people. Obviously, the people don't always know what is best for them, but it tends to produce governments that are responsive to human desires. And for this reason, there generally is no long-term national policy other than ever increasing the standard of living.

"However, in Russia, there is a national policy that has long-term continuity. Since the death of Stalin, there has been the dominant concept of rule by committee based on the precepts of ultimate world communism. Each of these men who now rule has been programmed by his education and experience to accept this idea as the only workable form of government. They are not responsible to the people; only to themselves and to one central ideal. So the faces and names change, but the ideal goes on. There are sometimes policy shifts within the Russian government that we attempt to analyze in terms of Western thinking, but these policy shifts are really still within the basic framework."

Kent nodded. "I basically agree."

"Let's take a closer look at the construction of 'rule by committee,'" Campbell continued. "In the forties, fifties, and early sixties the Russian government had more individuality. Stalin, Beria, Bulganin, Khrushchev. Each of these individuals was ultimately singled out as ruling by the so-called cult of personality. And ultimately, and in terms of the central ideal of world communism, these rulers were judged to be deviationists. And they fell from grace. Since Brezhnev, we have had a collective group of individuals who have survived all the various purges because they have simply adhered to the central ideal."

"You're saying then that the Central Committee members conduct Russian foreign policy in terms of Marxist idealism," Loss interjected.

"No," Campbell replied. "I'm saying that Russian foreign policy is conducted by a group of men who are afraid to disagree with a central ideal of an expansionistic policy that works. And that policy has been to expand slowly and surely, without direct confrontation. Sometimes there's a hitch and consequently we see the Russians taking two steps forward and one step backwards. But there's a steady net gain. In the meanwhile, the West constructs stop-gap measures to counter the Russians without ever drawing a definite line. And if there ever is a line drawn, it changes with each election of a new US President."

Kent reamed out the dead ashes with a penknife. "Where does it stop?"

"It doesn't," Campbell replied. "Not until the world is under one flag, probably a red one. Do you remember the plaque that was photographed by a UPS stringer in 1974? The one in Stalin's wartime chambers. It read 'He who does not rule is ruled.' Put yourself in their place. As an individual, each man in the Central Committee continues the policy of his predecessor. The policy works. You see the vision of a world united under one flag. No more war. No bickering, lads. Meet your quotas, pay your dues, and enjoy the new era of world socialism. You see Russia as the core of a new and better world order. Divide up the wealth, the food, the industrial production, reserving, of course, a percentage for the Fatherland. Sort of a commission for keeping things on an even keel." Campbell laughed. "It's not hard to visualize. England tried it, as did the Romans. And Germany. Very decent concept, really. Very humane. Except that it violates the precepts of political freedom."

"So you're saying that disarmament by the West would be the removal of the last block to Russian world domination," Loss said.

Campbell picked up a silver mug on the mantlepiece and studied the inscription. He smiled and set it back down, carefully, in its place. "No," he said. "Not quite. Because disarmament is a relative word. The US might withdraw gradually from NATO. Reduce its nuclear strike forces. But there would be a residual force left. Interceptors, some missiles. Perhaps home-defense forces. Still a force to be dealt with. But the important thing is that the US would no longer be able to inflict massive punitive damage on the Russians as a counter threat to a Russian first strike."

"Why would the Russians even consider a preemptive war against us if we were stripped of a strike force?" Loss asked. "It would seem that the US would no longer be a threat."

"Three reasons, Brian," Campbell said. "One. Russia wants your industrial and agricultural output, particularly the latter. Ultimately, food will become the most precious commodity on the face of this planet. The equation is simple—less land to grow foodstuffs on and more mouths to feed. The control of those foodstuffs will ensure long term control of occupied countries. Withdrawal of food supplies will be a form of discipline.

"Two. If the US were to retain its own freedom, it might be possible to rearm. The Russians would find it mandatory to eliminate the potential threat. Permanently.

"And three. If the Russian Presidium has a vision of the world under one flag, they don't want another flag getting in the way. Constant comparison of consumer goods, standards of living, free expression, all that sort of thing is very hard on the morale of the working classes.

"No, Brian, don't delude yourself. If the probability for success is high enough, the Russians will go for an all-out first strike. The trophy for winning is an entire world under Soviet rule. And unilateral disarmament by the US, even to a moderate degree, reduces the risk to the Soviets to an acceptable level."

"You're leading the whole thing back to Welsh, aren't you?" Loss asked.

Campbell smiled. "Yes. Full marks. As we see it, the Russians have picked Welsh as the political key to American disarmament. The Soviets have to be supporting him in these political coups with Cuba and Panama. But even that isn't enough. His chances for the Presidency are still very slim indeed. There's still a missing part to the puzzle. Something that will catapult Welsh into the White House by a landslide. We think it must be the *Hood-Hussar* link—an event that Welsh, and Welsh only, will be able to capitalize on. The 'Man of the Hour' syndrome."

"You really believe this?" Loss asked, frowning.

Campbell picked up the bottle of cognac and refilled his glass. He raised his glass and drank it down, then wiped his lips with the stained handkerchief. "Believe it? I know it! Forgive me if I sound condescending. It comes from being a cynic. But we who live in the so-called free world actually live a fantasy. The good life. And it seems to us that it will go on forever. So we tend to ignore the facts as they are presented, unless they conform to our thinking. God God, man! For the first time in the history of man, a single nation has at its disposal the weapons to conquer the world and more important, the philosophical reason to justify that conquest. We don't see it because we choose to ignore the disagreeable." Campbell paused. "Sorry. I'm getting argumentative. Always get this way with a few tots."

Kent cleared his throat, as if to speak. He refilled his pipe and lit it, puffing deeply to draw the fire down into the bowl. "No, Ian," he said. "You're right, of course. We all stick our heads in the sand. It's all too easy. We can't get used to the continuing fight. No enthusiasm, I expect. Hard concept to sell in a democracy. Ideals and things." He puffed on the pipe but the fire was dead.

Unconsciously, Loss traced the scar on his forehead with his fingertip. "Where does that leave us?"

Campbell jammed his hands in his coat pockets. "Absolutely nowhere. We have the names *Hood* and *Hussar*. And their probable location."

"Why not ring in the CIA and the RCMP," Kent said.

"Too soon," Campbell replied. "And perhaps too dangerous. Either organization might be penetrated. Expose our hand to the wrong people and we might end up getting it cut off." He turned and looked out the window, across the fields. "No, not yet. I can field adequate men. Run down all the bloody *Hoods* and *Hussars*. But it's Loss I really need." He turned on his heel and faced Brian squarely. "Think of it. All the connections severed—Heiss, Stroud, Petrov, his woman. And the Russians must assume that you're dead. And what happens if you surface, poking around, asking questions?"

"I'm dead meat."

"Ultimately," Campbell replied without irony. "But the Russians are meticulous. They would first want to find out how much you knew, who your contacts were, and how you tracked down the *Hood-Hussar* connection. And *then, only then*, would they eliminate you. The theory is that we keep you under round-the-clock surveillance. If any attempt to contact you is made, we intercept it, attempt to track it to its source." He turned to Kent. "Nothing nice or legal. No attempt to obey conventions. We would find out any Russian intentions if it were physically possible. Chemically possible, I perhaps should say. We feel it's that important."

"And if I don't choose to play your way," Loss asked softly.

Campbell pondered the question for a long time, walking back and forth before the gallery of photos. "I suppose that I could inform the Mounties. Hope that you get a fair trial. I would testify on your behalf, of course. But I think that you want to resolve this thing more than me. Or do you want to be a refugee for your entire life? Cowering in one place? I would think not." He sat down heavily in a Morris chair. "Remember that my head's on the chopping block for this one. My department chief's head as well. If we have British agents caught in the States on this operation, it will be the least of our offenses against the Crown or your Constitution."

"Then you're saying that I'm it."

Campbell refilled his glass and then walked to the window, looking out into the dusk. "Yes," he answered. "I suppose that you're it."

Chapter 23

David Fox leaned against the rigging of the *Hussar* and watched the gulls sweep the shore of Booker Lagoon in the last hints of twilight. The yacht lay at anchor close to the eastern edge of the shore in 10 fathoms; bluffs of rock towered above them spotted with small stands of cedar. The anchorage was nearly still; the wind was dying with the sun. The sounds of deer crashing through the brush carried clearly in the damp evening air. Fox sighed with some contentment and sipped at the coffee cup filled with rum.

In the seven weeks of charter, the *Hussar* had wandered through the San Juan Islands, up through the Strait of Georgia and into the far northern reaches of Queen Charlotte Strait. To the east of them lay the still-snowcapped mountains of British Columbia and to the west across the Strait, the hazy land mass of Vancouver Island.

The days had been a mixture of fog and sunshine, rain, and the startling blue of late summer in the high latitudes.

Fox snorted, laughing at himself. The trip had been nearly perfect. Most of the equipment was working well, and there had been ample time to keep the ship well maintained. The charter party itself was the easiest aspect of the trip, consisting of only two men, both of whom were nondemanding and agreeable company. Both were of muddy UK citizenship. Amed had said that he was born in Lebanon to an English father and an Egyptian mother. It looked as if the mother had the more predominant genes. The other, called Trig for some forgotten boyhood reason, was the product of a white Jamaican planter family. Painfully English in his speech and manner.

Both had used the charter, which had been a gift from Amed's father, as a learning experience. Most of their days were ashore, photographing Indian ruins and botanical specimens. But the experience extended to life aboard the yacht. They had adapted to the *Hussar*'s demands with alacrity, immersing themselves in shipboard routine with a will. Fox had taught them the sequences of getting underway and making sail. Amed had proved to be an exceptional helmsman, both under sail and power. Trig had learned the layout of the engine room and now insisted that he take care of the daily maintenance chores on the diesels and generator. They enjoyed it, they said, and Fox offered to let them run the ship as they cared.

Now, the *Hussar* lay in a lagoon at the southern reaches of Broughton Island, with only the Gulf of Aslaska before them to the north. Fox regretted that they would shortly turn south.

Myra emerged from the forecastle hatch, pulling on an oiled wool sweater.

"A good day, wasn't it?" she said easily, slipping an arm around his waist.

"I've seen worse," he laughed. "There, you see? Deer. About five of them just beyond that cluster of rocks."

She couldn't see them in the dim light without her glasses, but she nodded happily. "Davy, you know, we could try it again."

"Try what again?" he said, shifting his position against the shrouds.

"The Caribbean. With the money from this charter and the other one in late September, we would have enough to get down to charter off Mexico and even on the Atlantic side." She turned back to him, looking into his face, which was tanned and had sun wrinkles in the corners of his eyes. He was thinner now and more muscled. "David. We've got to give it a try. If we stay up here through another winter, we'll rot."

He nodded and then sipped at the rum. "Yes, I've thought about the same thing. We know the *Hussar* better now. And Jane looks like she might make a first-rate cook. If I can pick up a good deckhand-engineer around Vancouver, it would lighten the load a lot. Yes," he squeezed her shoulder with his arm, "let's think about it some more, and when this charter is finished, we'll begin to make some definite plans." He turned and started aft toward the cockpit. "Come on. Let me light the cockpit lamp so they'll be able to find us."

She followed him aft into the cushioned cockpit, and he lit the oil lamp. The orange-yellow glow reflected from the polished brass fittings, and the warmth and smell of food cooking drifted up from the galley. She snuggled against him in the coolness of the evening, and they both listened as a loon swept across the water, the sound of the bird's cry ringing back from the cliffs.

"You know, Davy, it really has been perfect these last seven weeks. Trig and Amed are about as easy to please as a couple of kids. And he's so polite, Amed, I mean. They make up their bunks in the morning. It couldn't be better. I almost feel guilty taking their money."

"Don't," he laughed, pleased that it was going so well. "Amed's father is loaded. Oil broker of some sort. Works for the Arabs."

"And Trig. Where does he get the money?"

"He doesn't," Fox said, polishing off the mug of rum. "This is all gratis of Amed's father. Trig is just a former school chum. Now they both work in Europe for the French, so says Amed. Underwater acoustics, magnetohydrodynamics, all very esoteric deep sea stuff. Said that they hoped that we could get down into the Hood Canal to see the first Trident sub. I don't see why not. I'd sort of like to myself."

"Incidentally, what time are they coming back? I've got to tell Jane something about the serving time."

He looked at the luminous dial of his watch and scowled in the half-light. "Should be within twenty minutes. Less, maybe. They said that they wanted to look over a Kwakiutl Indian site down past Cullen Point. Just inshore of where that big trawler anchored this afternoon. Amed said that they might drop by the trawler to see whether they could buy some pipe tobacco." He stood up and stretched. "What's on for dinner tonight?"

"Salmon. Some corn. Butter clams for an appetizer. How does that sound?"

"Tremendous, as usual." He paused in the top of the companionway. "Jane's been quite a help to you. Have you settled on any wages for her?"

Myra hunched her shoulders. "Nope. She says that she asked for the job just to get the experience. Wants to eventually buy a boat with her boyfriend and cruise the Pacific. I wouldn't worry about it. She'll probably get a good tip at any rate. But you're right; she's been a tremendous help. I'm spoiled." She handed her husband an empty glass. "If you're going down, how about fixing me a Beefeaters and tonic."

He raised his hand in salute and backed down the companionway. He passed through the salon, past the gimballed table already laid out with good china and silver, past the staterooms and into the galley.

She looked up from the saucepan and smiled. Beads of perspiration had formed on her bare shoulders and in the cleft between her breasts. She hitched up the apron and wiped her hands on a towel. She smiled again, a more genuine grin. "Are they back yet?"

Fox unconsciously pulled in his stomach and stood straighter. She was attractive with her long blond hair now roped up in a knot. French bun was the word, striking a chord in his memory. He laughed good-naturedly, thinking of French buns. "I'm sorry," he said, laughing harder. "It just got to me." He splashed some Mount Gay into his mug and rummaged in the locker for the Beefeaters.

Holly spilled the remainder of mushrooms into the saucepan and stirred, her face set in a noncommital smile. The whole thing was a waste, she thought, watching the slabs of butter melt. Loss was 200 miles to the south, probing the various *Hood-Hussar* combinations that Campbell had outlined. This one, she thought, was a dead end. The Foxes were normal enough, and the two men in the charter party were shy, almost too polite. In a few more days, the yacht would start south again. She was anxious for the trip to end.

"No, Jane," Fox said, still laughing, a slightly drunken vision washing against the edges of his mind, "they're not back yet. Pretty soon." He saw the look on her face and thought he understood. "I'm sorry, Janey. I'm not laughing at you. Just that Myra and I are—well, we're having a great time. I guess the first in years." He watched her face and seeing no comprehension, changed the subject. "Lucky thing Myra met you. You've been a tremendous help. Great food. We have to pay you for the trip."

"No," she shook her head, her blond hair bobbing. "It was all my doing. I found out from your broker that you had a charter and there were only the two of you. I tracked Myra down and asked for the job. No pay, just experience. I'm happy if you are."

"Myra said you had a friend," he said, standing straighter, trying to focus his eyes.

"He's down in Vancouver." She added lemon juice to the sauce, avoiding his look.

There was silence for a minute; the only sounds were the alcohol stove sputtering and small waves working against the hull. He nodded and left.

They came back a quarter of an hour later, rowing across the lagoon, one of them singing a tuneless song, the sound of their occasional laughter following the splash of a missed oar stroke. Fox turned on the spreader lights and stood near the boarding gate, ready to help them aboard.

A clinker-built rowboat emerged out of the darkness with three men, two rowing in tandem and the third in the stern sheets. The *Hussar*'s inflatable dingy trailed astern of the rowboat, bobbing along like a black rubber duck. Fox quickly dropped fenders over the cap rail and leaned over to receive the painter. Amed turned his face upwards, smiling at Fox. "Yes, Captain Fox. Good evening. I am sorry that we are late." His teeth were brilliant in the light, contrasted by his deeply tanned skin and thick black hair. "We have brought a friend. For only a moment."

The rowboat came alongside, squashing the fenders slightly. There was a confusion of oars being removed from oarlocks and stowed, a laugh, and men crawling up the boarding ladder. Amed came aboard first, extending his hand as he always did, shaking Fox's. Just a quick cool touch. His handsome Arabian features were accentuated by high cheekbones, deeply set brown eyes, and powerful build. Fox could imagine him in a burnoose, bowing, hands pressed together.

Trig next: small, corpulent, and balding, with thin wisps of hair combed straight across his sunburned scalp, glasses forever sliding down the bridge of his nose. He looked up at Fox, smiling hesitantly. "Evening. Really sorry we're late. Long row back," he said, unnecessarily pointing across the black water to the west. Then more formally, "And this is Mr. Krissholm. From the trawler."

Krissholm swung up through the boarding gate and offered his hand. He was tall and thin, without suggestion of frailness. There were several days of blond stubble on his face. His eyes were blue ice. "I'm pleased to meet you, Captain Fox," he said formally. They shook hands and Fox gently herded them aft to the cockpit, automatically offering a drink. Myra introduced herself and went below with drink orders, agitated that supper would be delayed.

David Fox offered each of them cigarettes. Only Krissholm accepted. Fox was vaguely uneasy for no reason that he could specify. He lit Krissholm's, then his own.

"You're from the trawler, then?"

Krissholm nodded. "Yes. *The Franklin Gaines III.* Rather a long name for an old fishboat. I'm just with them for a short while. Really with B.C. Fisheries."

Fox rubbed the side of his nose, unconsciously irritated. He tapped the ashes into a cockpit drain. "You mean, like our Fish and Game people?"

Krissholm nodded. "Yes. About the same. I really invited myself over to see your vessel. And to get away from the smell of fish for a while." He laughed.

Fox couldn't detect the smell of fish, but it wasn't important. "So how is the fishing?" Fox said for lack of anything else to say.

"Not too good, I think. But I really work on the measurement of mercury poisoning. A lot of that up here with our pulp mills. Worse than in the States, I suppose. Keeps me busy at any rate." He looked around the cockpit, noting the radar scope, fathometer, and engine controls. "Very well equipped."

Fox nodded. "Thanks." Myra appeared in the companionway with a tray of drinks. She put a dish of crackers and a plate of cheese on the cockpit table and disappeared below. She's pissed, Fox thought.

"Can you stay for supper?" Fox said, half-heartedly.

"No, thank you. I really came over just to meet you and ask you a favor."

Amed brushed his hair back and leaned forward on his elbows. "Mr. Krissholm has asked *us* a favor, and I suggested that he speak to you."

"Yes, Captain Fox," Krissholm interjected. "I hope that it won't be too much to ask, but I have a box of Nansen bottles that our department has been collecting for the University of Washington's Oceanographic Department. Normally, we would ship these down by the next ferry going south from Alert Bay. But that's ten days from now. It would help greatly to get them down to Port Townsend or Anacortes directly. Amed here has offered to have them forwarded by United Parcel. If you can just carry them as deck cargo . . . " Krissholm smiled depreciatingly, tapping the cigarette ash into his cupped palm.

"Where is the box and how much does it weigh?" Fox said, relieved at the lessened chance of one more for dinner. He wanted to make it an early night.

"About 150 pounds. And it's in my boat. Boxed and labeled. If you can carry it on the foredeck, it shouldn't present much of a problem. I brought two bottles of good Canadian Rye as well. Sort of a bribe." He laughed.

Fox sighed and then smiled. "Yes. That's fine. We'll take care of it. Amed, you know where it goes?"

Amed nodded "Yes. It already has the labels for shipping. It is no problem for us."

Expansive now, a drink in his hand, Fox smiled. "I think it should be OK. Let's get it aboard now, and then we can have another drink." He finished his, not noticing the others had hardly touched theirs.

They went forward, Kirssholm and Amed crawling down the boarding ladder into the rowboat. They passed up a pine box, insisting that Trig help Fox. The box measured less than 3 feet square, was well constructed, and padlocked. Four of them moved it along the teak deck by the rope handles and then secured it with a line that Krissholm provided just aft of the forecastle hatch to ringbolts in the deck.

Krissholm stood up and dusted his hands. "I think that should hold it." He grasped Fox's hand and shook it. "We like to cooperate with the Americans as much as possible. Thanks again, Captain Fox. I mean it. You've been a great help to us."

Fox nodded. "It's my pleasure. Really, would you like to stay for dinner?" The alcohol was heavy on his tongue.

Krissholm squeezed Fox's arm and then walked to the rail. "No. This is quite enough. Many thanks." He shook hands again with Trig, Amed, and Fox. Myra came forward after switching on the spreader lights. He shook her hand formally and stood, momentarily, looking aloft at the rigging and mainmast. "It's a fine yacht you have," he said and then clambered down the boarding ladder. They watched him row off into the blackness.

Holly Stowe watched from the starboard galley porthole. Watched the man lift his hand in farewell as he rowed off into the blackness. She returned to the galley and stirred the burning carrots, turning off the gas. Petrov, she thought, stunned.

Loss paused in the rain outside the arcade, scanning the tarnished brass nameplates that lined the stone facade. He found the one he wanted, wrinkled the corner of his mouth, and entered the shabby foyer. The light in the tiled hallway beyond was dim and he paused, allowing his eyes to adjust to the light. In the reflection of a tarnished mirror, he examined his face. His hair, now long, was artfully cut, falling over his forehead to conceal much of the scar. His beard was full but equally well trimmed. He barred his teeth, wishing he had brushed them. They tasted sour and gritty.

Near the elevator, he found the directory and under "W" a single entry: Western Pacific Shipping,   oom 212. The "R" was missing.

The single elevator registered that it was still poised at floor 7. Loss took the staircase at the back of the musty hallway. At the first landing, he paused to look out through the mottled window and rusted grill, down on the wet Seattle street. The traffic was getting heavier in the late August afternoon, parking lights coming on in the misty rain. A woman scurried across the street, umbrella held like a shield against the oncoming traffic. Loss smiled. I know how you feel, he said, lips barely moving.

The offices of Western Pacific Shipping consisted of one door of pebbled glass in an otherwise deserted hallway. Loss could hear the sound of a lone typewriter, pecking out the truth. He opened the door and entered.

She stopped typing and looked up at him expectantly. "Yes?"

"I'm trying to get some freight schedules on the shipment of some crates from Manila. About three tons. General furniture."

She tapped a type eraser against her teeth, looking at him more closely. Her hair fell straight and black, her eyes almond. Quite beautiful, thought Loss.

"We have two schedules. One on the *Lancer* and one on the *Hussar*. Which ship and who is the consignee?" She started to rummage in a drawer, swore under her breath, and retreated to a filing cabinet.

"*Hussar* and consignee is Golden West Imports," he called across the office. Golden West sounded big enough.

She returned with a dog-eared mimeographed sheet. "*Hussar,* ah, September twenty-eighth Seattle, October fourth Vancouver. And we don't have any loading manifest as yet. Generally don't get it until a couple days after they sail from Manila." She looked at him and grinned.

Loss frowned. "I thought she was due in earlier. Something like about September sixth."

"Boilers. New fire brick or something," she said. A shrug. "Anything else?" She smiled again, displaying several teeth smudged with lipstick.

"I guess not. I'll come in to see the cargo manifest when you get it, which would be about—?"

"About September tenth. We notify all the consignees then. Was it Golden West?" And she made a note that Loss knew would find its way to the trash basket once he cleared the office.

"Correct."

"See ya," and she turned to her ancient IBM.

He left the building, back through the rain-wet streets, past the sullen stores fronting the waterfront area. Stopping often in the entrance to shops, he watched for some sort of pattern in the people who flowed past him. Nothing. None. Never.

Catching a bus for the downtown loop, he swung off it two blocks later and felt like a fool, looking back to glimpse a man who was never there. Running, he stepped squarely in a pothole and splashed down into six inches of grimy rainwater. His leg was soaking.

Shit, he thought, watching up and down the street. Three weeks already gone. He hailed a cab in disgust and went back to the Reno Motel on Route 99.

He popped his head into the office. The night manager, who came on at four, was eating a heavily stuffed salami sandwich, a piece of lettuce attached by mayonnaise to the corner of his mouth. He shook his head without taking his eyes from the game show. "No messages, Mr. Lange. Nothing. Hey, watch this." He stabbed a finger at the screen, his mouth agape. "It's for 12,000 bucks." Loss shut the door on him and ducked under the skimpy eves, edging his way down to the room. The hair on the suitcase was undisturbed, as it had been for three weeks. Nor had there been any tampering with the lock on the briefcase. He sighed and sat heavily down on the hard bed in the stale room and looked at his fingernails. Loss, Lange, Loser.

On impulse, he dialed out direct to a Vancouver operator and placed the call. The phone answered immediately.

"Thurston residence."

"I want to talk to Campbell," Loss said.

"I'm sorry. There's no Campbell at this residence." The voice was male and fruity.

"This is Loss. I'm calling Campbell. Put him on, you asshole."

A long delay, then, "We'll try. I'm putting you on hold." No smile this time.

Loss lit a cigarette, impatiently tapping the ashless tip against a tray. The line clicked twice.

"Mr. Lange?" Campbell's thick mutter on the other end.

"Yes. I'm calling to tell you that it's a dead end down here. The ship doesn't arrive until September twenty-eighth. I've been down to that place on the Columbia River. Also the Canal. Nothing. No one cares whether I walk off with the local banks, it's that dead."

"Yes, I understand." A cough and he cleared his throat, long distance. It sounded like an empty ashcan rolling down an alleyway. "You realize that you were only to call in an emergency?"

Loss sighed. "Does it matter that much? I think we're totally wrong about this. They would have picked me up long ago."

"Perhaps," Campbell mumbled. "We have a small problem up here. Your friend was supposed to just get a look at the yacht, find out who was aboard and where they were going."

"And," Loss said quietly, gripping the receiver.

"And instead, she convinced the wife of the owner that she could serve as a cook. Somehow or another, she tracked the yacht to Britannia Beach, a little town north of Vancouver. They apparently hired her on the spot."

"Where are they, Campbell? You shouldn't have let her—"

"I didn't let her do anything, Brian. She took it upon herself. As best as we can determine, the yacht is up in the northern reaches of Queen Charlotte Strait.

I have one man on it. He reported last night that they were anchored at Broughton Island. Keeping track by chartered seaplane. Damned expensive."

Loss pulled the Rand-McNally folder from its place on the bedside table, flipping through the pages to British Columbia. He picked up the location of the small island, guessing at the distance from Vancouver. One-eighty, maybe two hundred miles.

Campbell was saying something. Loss pushed the map folder aside. "Sorry. I was occupied with something else."

"I was saying that everything seems to be normal up there. The yacht is making normal passages, anchoring each night. My man reports that there is the usual activity on board. Nothing special."

"About the charter party. Anything on them?"

Campbell sniffed. "Normal, we think. They're both British passports. We're checking. But nothing as yet. Seems that one comes from a rather wealthy family. So the yacht charter broker says."

Loss leaned back on the pillow, catching the scent of disinfectant. The bedclothes had a plastic underlay, as if they expected him to wet the bed. "I'm going up there," he said finally.

There was a long silence, and then static, as if the connection had been severed. Campbell came on again, hacking directly into the mouthpiece. "You're to stay put. She's all right. I'm sure that something will more likely occur down there. We've got three men watching you in shifts." Some papers rustled in the background. "I'm told that you had fried clams, salad, and two beers last night. There is one thing, however."

"Which is?"

"Your friend from New York is on the telly tonight. Channel 4, I believe. Touted by some as a major policy speech. The show is *Meet the Media.*"

"Where does he stand now in the polls?"

Campbell was silent but he could hear another voice in the background. Campbell came back on. "Thirty-one percent indicate him as their choice. And it's rising."

"Jesus," Loss swore. "And that in just three months from a nothing."

"Exactly," Campbell said. "Three months from nothing. It's been the Canal and Cuba. Something else now, I should expect in the speech tonight."

The line was empty, each waiting for the other to speak.

Loss spoke first. "Ian, I'm coming back up there. Maybe it *is* the yacht. I'm worried about Holly."

"Brian. Leave this to me. We'll cover her, but your function is to cover that end of things."

Loss was irritated now, listening to Campbell's plodding voice. "I'm telling you, Ian. There's nothing down here. I've covered everything. The Western Pacific Shipping thing isn't due in for more than a month. The Hood Canal is just a natural inland waterway. I've been down most of it in a rented boat. There's no commercial traffic on it. Just yachts and summer cottages."

"Look, Loss," Campbell was the impatient one now. "We're covering her all the time. Stay down there. You can do the best—"

Loss dropped the telephone in its cradle. Lying back on the bed, he stared at the ceiling: stucco with small embedded flakes of silver glitter. The ceiling bulged in the far corner, cracks radiating outward from the corner wall.

The whole thing seemed futile. Three weeks of plodding around, just looking, being highly visible. Whatever Welsh and Petrov had conjured up now seemed unimportant, remote. That I'm alive is probably enough, he thought. Get Holly and drive back across Canada to Kent's place and try to forget it. Raise kids and potatoes.

He rolled over on the bed, tapping the cigarette into the ashtray. His watch said 6:10 PM. Fumbling in the bureau letter drawer, he found *TV Guide*. *Meet the Media* was scheduled for 7:30 Pacific Standard Time.

Loss pulled on his raincoat and left the room, walking a block in the smog-mist-rain to the Oyster Shack on Aurora Avenue. The traffic was heavy now, cars bumper to bumper. The few remaining gasoline stations left open during the shortage were taking only red coupons. Tomorrow was blue. And no fuel at all on the weekend except for black priority card holders and public transportation. Loss scowled, walking quickly through the rain, hands thrust deeply into his raincoat. The world was sliding down the tubes, little chunks at a time.

The Oyster Shack wasn't crowded, and he took a booth, facing the parking lot. He ordered steamers, swordfish, salad, and an Olympia beer. The steamers were gritty and the swordfish tough, and he worked mainly on the beer and the salad, watching the other customers and the parking lot. Halfway through the steamers, an Olds drew up in the parking lot, the driver remaining in the dark interior behind slowly flicking windshield wipers. Loss watched cautiously, raising his eyes only when he drank from the glass. Washington plates on the Olds, but the numbers were unidentifiable in the darkness.

Loss wolfed the rest of the meal and left money on the table. As he passed the parked Olds, the window slid down and a balding man clad in a plaid lumber jacket leaned out and said, "Steamers?" The window slid closed silently, and he could hear the man laughing from within the interior.

Furious, Loss kicked at the fender. Campbell and his merry men. The car pulled away quickly and merged into the southbound traffic on Aurora Avenue.

He got back in time, the thin raincoat soaked through, to catch the opening minutes of the program.

Welsh sat there in a dove-gray suit, face unlined and composed: two-dimensional. The moderator, Louis Rickter of UPI, introduced the panel. Harris from United Press, McKennin from the *Manchester Guardian* and DeRouche of Reuters. The screen dissolved into an ad on home insurance, and Loss made instant coffee from the heater in the bathroom, listening to the mumbled sounds of the ad and the noises of neighboring flushing toilets. He came back and sat on the edge of the bed to watch the man who was responsible for what was left of his life.

RICKTER: It gives me great pleasure to present the US Senator from New York who has so recently caused far-reaching innovations in American foreign policy. Senator Welsh, welcome to *Meet the Media*.

WELSH: Thank you, Lou. It's entirely my pleasure.

RICKTER: First of all, Senator, there has been a great deal of speculation in the media concerning whether you are a candidate for your party's nomination in San Francisco. Would you care to comment on this?

WELSH (lowering his eyes, slightly embarrassed but with a smile): As you know, I didn't participate in any of the primaries. There has been some unofficial grass-roots support for my candidacy, which I am most grateful for. To answer your question, I'm not a candidate at this time. I do plan to go to the convention as (a broader smile) an observer.

General laughter on the panel. Jesus, Loss thought, he's too precious for words. The gestures, the phrasing. Like it was a script.

RICKTER: Yes, we understand, Senator. But what our viewers are interested in is whether you would actually accept your party's nomination if it were tendered?

WELSH: I believe that I would have to evaluate that situation only if and when it occurred. I do feel strongly about contributing to the platform committee on foreign affairs. Of course, I will support whomever our party puts forward in nomination.

HARRIS: Along that same line of thought, Senator, it has been reported from inside sources close to the President that your name is being considered as a possible replacement running mate for the Vice Presidential ticket. What are your feelings about this possibility?

WELSH: I don't believe that I could accept the nomination for the Vice Presidency. In all fairness, I don't believe that my viewpoint is well enough aligned with the present Administration to assist the party in that manner.

In addition, there are still pressing obligations I must consider in terms of my constituency and of the nation. However, as I have already indicated, this sort of discussion is speculative and I would have to evaluate such a circumstance if and when it arose.

DeROUCHE (removing his glasses): Mr. Senator, those of us in Europe have witnessed, within the last three months, some hope for a new understanding in international affairs—a resurgence, if you will, of hope that the United States is seeking meaningful accommodation with the world. Your negotiations with the Republic of Panama and more recently, with The Peoples Democratic Republic of Cuba, have awakened belief that progress can be made through mutual understanding. Can you comment on this?

WELSH (turning to view the camera directly, his perfectly cut hair just slightly gray): Yes, I'd like to. It has always been my belief that the concept of "dealing from strength," as the present Administration likes to term its policy, is a debased form of power politics. Put in another manner, it essentially can be equated as to how much we can shove down someone else's throat.

I believe that in this constantly evolving relationship of nations, those that have the power are in the best position to share that power—to make concessions where need be. (Arching his fingertips together) I feel that there can be a new spirit in American foreign policy, a new era of understanding. Other nations seek accommodation with us, not confrontation. Quite simply stated, we must take the first steps.

HARRIS: Yes, but this sort of idea has been put forth before. In all fairness to your most recent accomplishments, how do you account for your startling degree of success?

WELSH: I think that we all too easily forget that foreign powers are still groups of men. All men respond to an open-handed approach particularly where the stronger of two parties is unilaterally willing to make concessions. My speeches on the Floor of the Senate have tried to suggest pre-concessions which would set an atmosphere of trust and good will in our foreign dealings. I believe that such an attitude represents a new wave in American foreign policy, an attitude that is long overdue.

The station broke for an advertisement. Loss stared blankly at the screen, his coffee untouched and now cold. Welsh's new poise, for a person who knew him intimately, was incredible. Gone were the hesitations of speech, the odd ducking movement of his head when he was asked a question. The words came smoothly, the voice evenly modulated. And yet, he hadn't said a goddamn thing. But it sounded logical unless you listened carefully.

The sixty-second commercial terminated, showing an elderly couple shaking hands with their insurance agent, and the tube dissolved back to the studio.

McKENNIN: Senator Welsh. You disclosed in a press conference yesterday morning that you felt that there were, and I will quote, "Major new avenues of peace to be explored." Can you expand on this statement and tell our viewers what you might specifically have in mind?

WELSH (stroking the bridge of his nose, as if in consideration of what he was about to say): What I have to say concerns the Strategic Arms Limitations Talks, specifically the forthcoming SALT III. We are entering the fourth decade of a cold war with the Soviets. In that period of time, both our countries have built up massive and dangerous arsenals of nuclear weapons. But in this entire frame of time, not once has either country seriously considered going to war with the other. Both countries are now wealthy, powerful, and uncontested. And yet both of us are locked into a useless series of meetings, debating the quotas of weapons that we may each add to our armories.

I feel, and I know every sensible American will understand, that we must do something to reduce and ultimately eliminate this threat. I feel that we are strong enough to initiate the first steps.

McKINNEN: Are you saying, Senator Welsh, that we should unilaterally disarm?

WELSH: I think that we should give immediate and serious consideration to the idea. Not only to lessen tensions but also to avoid an accidental holocaust, which we, ourselves, invite. There are no less than four thousand nuclear weapons stored in this country and at least half as many in Europe. Many of these are located near major cities. I sometimes think that we have more to fear from our own folly than from the Soviets.

RICKTER: You're saying then that the Administration should shelve the SALT III talks and proceed unilaterally.

WELSH (laughing): I'm afraid that you're putting words in my mouth. No, that is a determination of the Administration. There may be reasons why the President feels he must pursue SALT III. But remember, these negotiations are basically conducted by the military and the Department of State. It is against their basic philosophy to eliminate one single rifle from our inventory.

I feel that if we, as a people, take the initiative in starting a disarmament, bypassing so-called military considerations, we may find that the Soviets will respond in kind. A major reduction in arms on our part would prove good faith.

He's done it, Loss thought. Welsh was coming out of his closet for unilateral disarmament. There was a bombardment of questions from the interviewers and Loss turned the volume down, catching only words. Welsh was expanding his view, and Loss caught the words "eliminate NATO." The West Germans will love that, he thought. Shades of Munich in reverse. There was no doubt in Loss's mind now that the Russians would soon issue a statement praising Welsh and hinting at major troop reductions in Eastern Europe.

He watched Welsh manipulate the panel for another five minutes. Seasoned, hard veteran newscasters all, they fed Welsh questions that he smoothly fielded, turning the interview into a political statement.

Something in the interview nagged at Loss. Something that Welsh had said or implied. The unilateral disarmament wasn't that new. He had talked in that vein of thought over five months ago. Something else. Accidental detonation of our own nuclear weapons? The thought solidified. If Welsh were warning of this danger and it actually happened, happened before the convention, then Welsh would be stampeded into the nomination by an electorate *demanding* disarmament.

The idea became more and more concrete in Loss's mind. Petrov would be the cause of the accident, an accident involving the *Hood-Hussar* link. And to be effective, it would have to take place prior to the convention, which would eliminate the freighter. That left the yacht. Loss felt a flush of fear along his neck. Ten, twelve days at the most.

He sat down and direct-dialed Campbell's number. It rang ten times without answer and he redialed it without effect.

Something had to give; there had to be some way of flushing Petrov out into the open. He played with the thought again as he had for the last two weeks. Campbell wouldn't like it. Screw Campbell and his merry men.

Loss called the Washington DC Directory Assistance and obtained the number, then carefully punched in the number.

On the third ring, the line clicked. "Soviet Embassy."

"I'm calling for Mr. Petrov."

A pause and then, "I'm sorry. There is no one in the Embassy or Consulate staff by that name. May I refer you to someone else?" The voice was accentless, a woman.

"Tell him that an old flying friend of his called. L-O-S-S. Brian Loss. I think that you can probably find him. Tell him that I'd like to meet in Vancouver soon."

The connection clicked twice and a male voice came on. Flat, no accent or inflection. "Mr. Louis? This is Mr. Zukinov of Embassy Personnel. I'm afraid that you've made a mistake. We have no Petrov on our staff. I can—"

Loss sliced him off midsentence. "Just get hold of Petrov and tell him that I want to meet him at the lobby to Eatons in Vancouver in three days. At noon on Friday. And the name is Loss." He hung up.

By 10:30, he had packed, paid his bill, and turned the Kents' Chrysler north toward the Canadian border.

Chapter 24

He came to the border at 1:05, slowing the Chrysler under the mercury floodlamps, stopping opposite the booth. A short man with longish gray sideburns accentuating a bony face stooped to his open window. He wore the brown twill and badge of Canadian Customs and his breath smelled of mouthwash.

"Wha' do ya have to declare?" The accent merged with mainstream Canadian but still showed a trace of the highlands.

Loss looked at him in the harsh chrome-yellow light, his beard accentuating his tiredness. "Nothing. Just personal effects. A few packs of cigarettes."

"An' you're from wheer?" Very conversational. His glasses were bifocals, magnifying and dissecting the brown irises of his eyes. He wore a clear plastic mac over the twill.

"Nova Scotia." Loss thought of Kent and the sandy hills spilling down to the sea. "From near Chester, on Mahone Bay."

"Do ya have some identity, Mr. —?"

"Passport, if that's enough. And my name is Lange. Brian Lange." Loss turned and fumbled for the briefcase in the back seat.

A larger man was walking toward him now, dressed in an orange rain slicker, his campaign hat dripping from the rim with sparkling pinpoints of rain, each drop luminous in the cast of the mercury light. He stopped on the passenger side and briskly rapped his knuckles on the glass. Loss leaned over, rolling down the window.

"RCMP." Just a flat statement. Christ, Loss thought, Sergeant Renfrew of the Royal Canadian Mounted. He turned on the interior light and saw the officer was in his early twenties, his face unlined, with the shadow of a moustache growing like a sick weed on his upper lip. "Please pull your vehicle over to the inspection booth." He pointed with a gloved hand toward a turnoff, his eyes steady on Loss.

Loss turned back to the Customs inspector. Another officer had joined the transplanted Scot, standing behind him, clipboard in hand. Loss almost giggled with the idiocy of it; caught at the border because of a routine inspection on a dull, wet night when he would just as soon be sitting in a pub, drinking beer with these men.

"Take booth number one, Mr. Lange," the Scotsman said, noting down his license plate number and passing the slip to the man who stood behind him.

Loss dropped the shift selector into Low and the car drifted forward toward the covered bay. An overhead light snapped on, floodlighting the area. His mind was racing now. The passport would stand up, as would the other identity papers and the credit cards. The Luger, holstered under the front seat, would not. Campbell had warned him of taking it, as had Kent, but he wouldn't part with it. Too old a habit. The decision made, he pounded the pedal to the floor, swerving back into the main lane and streaking for the barrier. He took it at eye level, and it shattered the right windshield into a starry glaze of crystalline pebbles. The Chrysler, like a startled horse from a gate, rushed out of the lights into the blackness. Loss heard the shriek of a police siren and caught the blue flash in his rearview mirror. The old Chrysler would never last three miles in a chase. The road swung gently to the left, blanking out the view behind him. Loss slowed, swung into the left lane and then spun the wheel over to the right, leaping the curb and plowing through bordering shrubs and undergrowth. The bellypan scraped on rock, and the sedan tumbled down a shallow embankment, rolling once as if in slow motion. More glass shattered and his briefcase arced from its place on the back seat into the dashboard, grazing his head in its flight. The car came to rest, making the last roll in micro-time, tottering slowly over to fall heavily back on its wheels. He sat there stunned, thinking that all this had happened before in time. The engine was still running, and he switched it off.

The shriek of the siren passed; blue-light flashes touched the tops of the firs, and then the sound died into the night.

The rain was slanting into the car's interior through the fractured windshield. Loss leaned against the steering wheel letting the wetness saturate his hair, feeling the trickles run down his collar. His ribs ached. He sat like this for what seemed hours, listening to the sound of the wind and the rain and of time unwinding. Slowly, his head cleared. There was no smell of gasoline, and he lit a cigarette, taking time to think. The Mountie might estimate that the bare two-minutes lead time would be enough for Loss to make the turnoff to the coast toward Langley. Three possible routes. They wouldn't set up roadblocks, but the Chrysler with its Nova Scotia plates would be on an all-points bulletin. And they knew his name, at least the name Lange. It was unlikely that they would discover the car's track through the shoulder tonight. Screw it, he thought, and unbuckled his seat belt and climbed into the back seat, opening the sleeping bag and spreading it over himself. He drifted off into fitful sleep.

He awoke around 4:00 AM, the first cracks of light penetrating the cloud bank receding to the east. The sky overhead was clear, the air cool and fresh. He unpacked his shaving gear and using water from the radiator, shaved off his beard and mustache. Surprisingly enough, the shaving part was easy, but the razor kept clogging with hairs, and he changed blades three times, each time throwing the cartridge double edge far into the bushes. It would be helpful if they thought him still fully bearded.

By five, he had changed into old corduroy pants and a leather jacket. He consolidated most of his gear into a nylon duffel bag, leaving only a few shirts and the sleeping bag behind. He disassembled the Luger and tucked the parts in the bottom of the bag. There was no point in burning the car. They had the plate numbers, and Kent would still have to face some awkward questions. So add a stolen car and running a border station to the tally of charges, he thought smiling, and suddenly he didn't care much anymore. Whistling, he walked along the gully and then across a field, intersecting the highway a further half-mile north. By six, he caught a ride from a bakery truck headed for south Vancouver.

The two of them sat together in the cab, the driver singing. The smell of fresh bread was overpowering, yeasty and moist. His stomach rumbled.

"Can I buy a bun?" Loss said, grinning, producing a bill.

"Perks," the florid-faced driver said, his smile easy. "All I can eat. Reach behind me, in the carton."

There were cinnamon buns, and a thermos in a partially opened cookie box. And a stack of styrofoam cups.

"It's got sugar and milk. Help yourself and pour me about a half cup. Too much of the stuff and the caffeine gets to my stomach." He looked down the road, watching the morning traffic wheel north. "Yank, are you?"

"Not likely," Loss answered. "From Nova Scotia. Come out here to keep from freezing my balls off. Better work here, eh?"

The driver stuck a large, gnarled hand toward Loss. The back of his wrist was a mat of red hair. "Corrigan. Michael Corrigan. But they call me Muff."

Brian grasped his hand and shook it. "Lange's mine. Brian Lange." He passed the partially filled foam cup of coffee to Corrigan and filled his own. Loss watched an RCMP pass the other way, toward the border, moving slowly with the traffic. The sun was washing over the pavement now; a little steam rose.

"Great morning," Corrigan said happily, scruffing at his long red sideburns, scratching as a dog will do, just for pleasure.

"Not half bad," Loss said, then filled his mouth with the bun, swilling in coffee.

"Yeah. Thought you were a Yank. Near the border and all that. Can't stand the cheeky bastards. Think they own us, they do."

Loss looked over at him. A face of red skin, unwrinkled, with smile creases. Thin red hair, balding around the crown with an excess flowing down his collar and long red sideburns. His eyes were smoky gray, hard. He would probably be good in a fight.

A favorite Canadian subject: the Americans. Loss nodded, swallowing the mushy bun. "I guess you see a lot of them out here. We're only bothered by them in the summer months. Trailers and campers. They buy nothin'. Just gasoline."

"Same here," Corrigan offered. "They come up in convoys and pick off all the best spots for campin'. Burns my ass, it does. And they truck moose and deer out of here in the fall like they was tryin' to feed Los Angeles. Makes you fair sick."

Corrigan paused to light a vile black cheroot. He puffed on it angrily, clouding the cab with smoke. "Yeah," he grumbled, tapping the ash on the floor. "An' they keep tellin' us how to run our country when they can't even run their own. Worse than the froggies in Kay-bec." He strung out the word like it was a curse. "Won't catch me speaking French, nor my kids either. Let DeGaulle or who ever it is support Kay-bec." He turned to look at Loss, eyes bright with anger. "Ya know, we're still payin' off them O-lympics. They get all the gravy and the fuckin' glory and the rest of Canada has to pay. Terrible."

Loss could hardly keep from smiling. Next Corrigan would start raving about the Indians and the pipelines and socialized medicine. In roughly that order. He had heard it all before.

"And the Indians. Want the whole goddamn province back. Collect checks from the government and laugh at us workin' people." Corrigan ranted on, happily, getting it out of his system for the day, grinding away on the cigar he held between his teeth, reducing the visibility in the cab to instrument approach conditions.

Loss sat back happily and injected grunts and "yeahs," watching the suburbs of Vancouver materialize from the green vacant fields. He could see office buildings on the skyline and mountains as a backdrop to the north. The traffic was heavier now, both lanes filling. They passed an RCMP patrol car, pulled over to the side, light switched off. The Mountie was leaning against his door, watching the vehicles pass. Loss slumped down marginally as they passed and waited, sweating, for the shriek of a siren.

"... and the fuckin' Yank pigboats. Probably blow Vancouver into eastern Alberta. Right on our border. If they don't drop one of them A-bomb rockets when they're loadin', it'll probably be target number one for the Russians." He poked the stub of his second cigar at Loss for emphasis. "Right on our own border, mind you. Pure fuckin' gall, I say."

Loss sat up again, listening to Corrigan. "I didn't catch that. What about the Russians?"

Corrigan flipped the smoldering butt out the vent window. He rubbed his forearm across his mouth, glaring out at the bright hardness of the August sun. "Yeah. I said about the Yank pigboats down in Washington. Right on our border. That's the new submarine missile base. Fuckin' A-bombs piled up all over the place. One accident and poof." Corrigan made a fist and then splayed the fingers in an explosive gesture.

"You mean the Navy base at Bremerton?"

"Shit, no! They're building a new one, just for the new atomic submarines.

Carries twenty-four rockets, an' all of them got A-bomb heads. Base 'em all down in Los Angeles or Las Vegas, I say." The fact that Las Vegas was in the desert was obviously lost on Corrigan.

Loss felt a shiver in the small of his back. "I never heard about it."

Corrigan warmed to the subject, a fount of local knowledge. He lit his third cigar, offering another to Loss. "Cuban cigars. Damn good, eh? Yeah, I was sayin' that they're buildin' a sub missile base down near Seattle. Do all the maintenance down there. The crews stay there, everything. Then them bastards come steamin' up the Hood Canal and fuck off into the Pacific for God knows how long. Six, eight months maybe. Right out the Straits of Juan De Fuca. Right on the Canadian border. One of them subs collides with a freighter and poof. Twenty-four A-bombs turn Vancouver into an ash heap. Big thing about it on the CBC about a month ago."

Loss whitened, his pulse quickening. "Where in Washington?"

"Bangor. Little town down on the Hood Canal," Corrigan replied, pulling out into the left lane and overtaking a school bus. The kids waved at them as they edged past. Bright faces, big bread eaters. Corrigan waved back, his face smothered in a grin.

"I've been down there," Loss said. "I never heard anything about it. Nothing." He wondered how he could be so stupid.

"Doesn't surprise me," Corrigan said to the windshield, blaring his horn at a slow driver in the passing lane. "They don't talk much about it down there. Just got used to the idea, I guess. That and all them atomic power plants. Makes me creep, it does. Think that's what's messing up the weather. Used to—the winters was warmer." He started off in a monologue about atomic energy and the weather, chewing on the long cigar.

The truck penetrated the suburbs, passing the old fair grounds. They stopped at a light. Loss dropped off the truck, thanking Corrigan. They gripped hands and Corrigan gave a broad grin. "Looks like you need some tan where you chopped off the beard. Good luck, Lange. We're all working men, eh?" And he drove off, singing.

The small shopping plaza was still closed, but Loss found a BP gas station with a phone. He dialed Campbell's number, letting it ring twelve times before dropping the handset onto the hook. Then he dialed Kent's farm, reversing charges. Margaret answered. Trans-Canada clicks, the operator's voice spelling out Lange.

"It's me," Loss said, watching the attendant pump gas into a small Morris. "The guy who crashes airplanes."

"Yes," she answered. "Edwin and I thought you might call. They've been checking about the license plate. Edwin told them that he sold the car to you for your summer vacation. There's no real problem here."

"I had to leave it in a ditch."

"Oh, don't fuss so. It's too old anyway. We have insurance. I've been pestering Edwin to get an MG sedan. Edwin says they're too flimsy."

Loss fumed with impatience. "Look," he injected. "You don't understand. They'll probably take fingerprints off the car. They'll find out who I am."

"Oh dear." She paused, then "Here's Edwin."

"Hi," Loss said, weakly.

"Brian. Listen carefully. The local constable called up last night. I told him you borrowed the car but that you had already paid most of the purchase price to me. It's all right. I told them that you probably bolted because you had no proof of ownership." His voice had an echo to it, like the conversation was through a ComSat.

"I wrecked it. I left prints all over it." The attendant was finished serving the Morris now, accepting a credit card and gas rationing coupons. Loss wanted to terminate the conversation quickly.

"Brian. I wouldn't worry just yet. Your prints are only with InterPol. The RCMP will just assume that you're Canadian and check their files. I'll clean it up on this end if I can."

"Thanks, Kent. Sorry to put you in this position."

"Nothing at all, Brian. That's the least I can do. How goes it on your end? Anything yet?"

"Yes. A lot I think. I can't get hold of Campbell, but I think it's the yacht, not the freighter. Something really big. I'm going to write you today. Give you everything I know. In the event anything happens. Look, I've got to go. Much thanks for everything."

"God speed, Brian. And take care. We're waiting for you both to come back." Kent hung up and the line was empty.

Loss spent that day and the next in a motel room in South Vancouver, writing longhand what he knew of the affair from its inception with the trip to the Caribbean. He also made a number of calls, first to the yacht brokers in Seattle that had handled *Hussar*. They had received their commission and weren't concerned with the whereabouts of the yacht. "Up north in the Queen Charlottes," repeated the nasal voice of the woman broker. He did learn that they would probably stop and provision at Nanaimo on Vancouver Island on their way south. The charter terminated in Port Angeles on the Olympic Peninsula on September 30th. They were paid through that date. Was there anything else, because she had a long distance call from a very important client and she would have to put him on hold. No, there was nothing else.

Campbell's phone didn't answer until the second evening.

A different voice this time. "What number are you calling?"

"This one. Put Campbell on."

A longish pause and then the voice again, high-pitched so that Loss could only guess at the sex. Female maybe. He grew impatient.

The voice again. "Mr. Campbell is on the line to London. Give us your number, and he'll call you back in five minutes." Loss gave them the motel's number and extension and hung up, slightly relieved.

Thirty minutes elapsed, and Loss called Campbell's number again, receiving only the distinctive buzz of a busy signal. He finished off the tersely worded twenty pages of events and left the room, TV still switched on, the lights burning. The night desk clerk was a young man, thin and very tall. He was hunched over a book.

"Do you have any manila envelopes?"

The boy pushed back his glasses and looked up nearsightedly at Loss. "Pardon?"

"Manila envelopes. I want to mail something. And some stamps."

Comprehension dawned and the boy got up, still holding the book, reading, from what Loss could see, about invertebrate zoology. Shortly, the boy tendered the envelope and stamps, preoccupied with the book. Loss inserted the thin sheath of papers in the envelope and wrote Kent's address on the label without a return address. Guessing, he plastered three dollars' worth of stamps and paused by the door to mumble his thanks. The kid nodded, engrossed, not looking up.

He posted the envelope half a block down and returned to the motel, cutting across an empty lot. Squeezing past two closely parked cars he paused, looking for his room in the monotonous corridor of brown-birch panel that faced the parking lot. A man stood before his door, plaid jacket wine-red in the dim light. He was not knocking, just listening, ear lightly pressed against the plywood. A newspaper hung over his right hand, folds draped over his wrist like a waiter's towel. Definitely not the law. Plaid Jacket was now testing the knob without success. Beginning to look nervous, glancing back and forth along the corridor of rooms. Finally he knocked, the paper raised with his wrist to waist level.

Loss stooped down, groping along the edging of the parking area for a stone. His fingers felt the shape of a rock, whitewashed and smooth. He pried it loose, conscious of the noise as it broke away from the adjacent stones. Loss stepped out of his loafers, footsteps now silent, as he walked across the asphalt. Closer now, he could see Plaid Jacket held a weapon beneath the paper, the muzzle protruding.

The man heard him and, wheeling, fired two quick shots in succession, both missing low and to the left, zinging away into the night. It was the man from Seattle, Campbell's man who had followed him to the Oyster Shack. The muzzle was coming up, the tube shape of a silencer elongating the barrel. Loss heaved the stone at his chest and fell flat to the pavement. Another round spanged off into the parked cars, the muffled sound of the weapon a light crump.

The weapon clattered to the asphalt, the man making a gasping noise. Loss looked up to see the man reeling away in the dim light, his face a mask of blood, features flattened and unrecognizable. The weapon was lying there, a Colt Lightweight. Loss scrambled to his feet, scooping the .38 up in his left hand and stumbled into the blackness after the man. Plaid Jacket was twenty yards ahead of him, running wildly, ricocheting off the edge of the building near the service entrance, then across the redwood deck of the poolside. There was a splash and clatter of an overturned deck chair. Loss pulled up short of the tiled edging and looked into the water. Wavelets still lapped over the edge, soaking his socks. The man lay face down in the pool, arms grasping his head, legs jerking. A bubble erupted from the surface and the body began to sink, spreading a black stain.

"Oh shit," Loss said as a kind of prayer. He threw the .38 into the pool after the sinking man.

A door was opening behind him preceded by the rattle of a safety chain and the snick of a latch bolt. He ran past the opening door, face down, spitting out words toward the startled face. "Police. Close your goddamn door!" He heard the door slam behind him, shutting off a jumble of voices.

Unlocking his own door, he swept through the room, throwing items of clothing and his shaving gear into the nylon duffel bag. He cleared the room, leaving the lights and TV on, and ran through the parking lot. Picking up his loafers from the ground, he looked back once and, seeing no one, headed toward the street through the adjacent vacant lot. Plaid Jacket didn't walk here, he thought, searching the street. One block down he found the Olds. It was unlocked and he climbed into the driver's seat, brushing aside the remains of a bag of cookies. The passenger side was littered with the remains of take-out containers for hamburgers and a milkshake carton. He found the key in two minutes, hidden under the right seat floor mat.

He drove west through the suburbs for fifteen minutes, his heart pounding and mind a blank. He munched on the remains of Plaid Jacket's cookies, watching cars slide past his windshield. Nice middle class neighborhoods, the occasional pub. Movie theater showing a rerun he'd like to see.

The blur of the last half hour was something he could still reject from his mind. There were images now, but he pushed them back. The Olds was smooth, bucket seats comfortable; it even had a sun roof. He opened it and filled his lungs with the night air. He was feeling just a little sick, the shock overtaking his nervous system.

Suddenly, he felt his stomach heave, and he swerved into a parking lot next to an unlighted store. He vomited over the right front seat, unable to roll down the window in time. His hands and legs were shaking now; they were vibrating, dead, wooden things. He gagged again, felt the shock of fluid filling his mouth, and spewed it out on the leather and over the gear selector. Absentmindedly, he thought that his trousers were ruined. The acrid stink of vomit filled the car, and he gagged again, this time convulsing on an empty stomach, heaving up in spasms, only spittle drooling from the corners of his mouth.

The convulsions subsided and he lay back, his neck cushioned by the headrest, looking at the night sky between the low buildings. Hazy but with pinpricks of stars, yellowed by the coal smog. The air tasted like tin and leaves and bitter ale. How far I've come, he thought. I killed a man. With a rock. Like you kill a rodent, with anything handy. His face had been bloody meat, and it would have been better if he had screamed, but he had just made sucking noises. Almost silent. And running, careening off things, like a wounded animal. And I ate his cookies, he thought irrationally. All his cookies.

He lay down in his own vomit and cried and then slept; dew gathered on his windshield, blanking out the darkness and the light.

He awoke at dawn, feeling used and sick, stomach aching. The Olds started first touch, and he used the wipers to clear the windshield. Loss rejected thinking about last night. Only about Campbell and getting to Eatons at noon. He looked up into the rearview mirror, turning it to see his reflection. A normal set of eyes glared back at him, and his chin looked right but pale without its beard and just a small growth of blue stubble. His nose was still lopsided. All normal.

Loss really wanted a beer. Instead, he chose a McDonalds, changing first into blue cotton slacks and a sweat shirt in the back of the Olds. The vomit was still moist, and the car was putrid. He pulled the floor mats from the car, folding them over carefully, and stuffed them into a white barrel marked "Keep it Clean, Vancouver." He left the sun roof and windows open, venting the car.

He ordered a pair of something McMuffins, noting that he was the thirty-billionth-plus person to make the same selection. He couldn't finish them. But the coffee was ambrosia, and he bought another cup, the girl smiling as she took his change. Indian, with subdued features and high cheekbones, hair black as soot and slender fingers. Where was Corrigan now? Pushing the van up Route 99 singing? Coffee and crullers. Spitting and black Cuban cigars. How easy to know who and what you hated.

He finished the coffee and saw a public phone next to the cigarette machine. On nothing but impulse, he inserted a quarter and punched in the number.

It rang only once and the same voice, clean and shaven and awake, answered. "What number are you calling?"

"This is Loss. Put Campbell on." A long pause—two minutes.

A voice, antiseptic, "Loss, this is Klist. Where are you?"

"Disneyland. Where's Campbell?"

"Out to lunch, I'm afraid. You made a mess last night. They're looking for you."

"Yes, I suppose that I did. Where's Campbell?"

Petrov sighed into the telephone. Loss could hear other voices in the background. "That's a long story, Brian. I'll tell you all about it, but not at Eatons. Too public, I think. You'll be picked up."

"Where then?"

A long pause as if Petrov were thinking, but the line had that muffled quality as if Petrov had his hand over the mouthpiece. And then, "A better place, Brian. Something very public without being crowded. There's a breakwater with a two-lane road on it leading out from the mainland to a ferry terminal in Tsawwassen. It's over a mile in length. Meet me there at noon. Just the two of us and no weapons. Do you know where it is?"

"I'll find it."

"Good." The line went dead.

Loss called again but the number rang without response. He tried twice more and hung up.

He took another coffee to go and left the building. Approaching the Olds, he noted that it had a shallow dent in the left rear fender, as if someone had kicked it. The day was suddenly brighter. Like Corrigan, it was nice to know who you hated. The alternatives now? Still zero until he could bring Petrov in. Out of CIA jurisdiction and if Petrov didn't show, any contact with the RCMP would be the end of it. Petrov had known and that's why he wasn't afraid to keep the appointment. Fine with me, Loss thought.

He drove west and then south, toward Tsawwassen, following the signs. The day was cloudless, trees in the full flush of late summer. Kids playing with garden hoses, shrieking at each other as they ran across well-groomed lawns in bathing suits.

Campbell was gone. Or maybe working with Petrov. Plaid Jacket? Campbell's man or Petrov's. Or both. Too many unanswered questions. And Petrov's only desire now would be to find Brian Loss and kill him, he thought. Fourth try.

A clock over the entrance of a branch of the Royal Bank of Canada showed twenty minutes after nine. Two and a half hours to plan. He found a library on South Twelfth Street and parked the Olds in back. A young woman with a limp was the librarian. She sniffed delicately, catching the odor of dried vomit still hanging on his body. She showed him the shelf and walked gamely away, her left ankle dragging. He caught her looking back, face expressionless. Loss smiled weakly in reply.

He found the *Cruising Guide to Puget Sound and British Columbia* and xeroxed the passage down from Queen Charlotte Strait to the Hood Canal. Under periodicals, he found the British Columbia Ferry schedule. Next, he studied both *Small Arms of the World* and Swindon's *The Luger*. He xeroxed two pages from the latter. For a remaining half hour, Loss sat back in a deep leather chair, a magazine on Canadian wildlife folded across his lap, playing out in his mind the actions of the next four hours.

Petrov would certainly try to kill him. Established. They had nothing to bargain with. *How* was the question. Not by a handgun. The ferry schedule showed the access road as a stark mile of two-lane road leading across riprap, shouldered on each side by walkways and a railing. Petrov wouldn't take a chance of being caught like that.

Sniper, possibly, or by chemical. Loss doubted that Petrov would let him leave the meeting alive. That it should look like an accident would probably be less important than ensuring that I die, he thought, trying to place himself in Petrov's mind. When in Rome, screw the Romans, and he left the library, humming.

Across the street was a shopping complex. He found heavy rubber bands in an office supply store as well as a ball of wrapping twine. Next door was a deli and he stopped for a smoked meat sandwich and an ale. The french fries were served with vinegar, Canadian style. He paid in Canadian change and practiced his Nova Scotia accent. The waitress grinned at him, welcoming him to Canada. "I love the Kojak reruns," she said. "Have a nice visit." Loss winced.

He refueled the Olds at a Shell station, using the men's room to change. Locking the door, Loss stripped and, using a towel and soap, sponged off the smell of vomit. Selecting a pair of denims, he pulled them on and then sat down on the toilet to reread the xeroxed pages copied earlier in the library. Then, withdrawing the Luger from its bed in the bottom of the nylon bag, he carefully disassembled it, removing the grip and trigger mechanism. What remained was the barrel and receiver mechanism, roughly eight inches in length and less than an inch square.

He cocked the toggle and then depressed the sear mechanism with his fingertip, listening to the firing pin snap into the empty chamber. Satisfied, he carefully chambered a cartridge and closed the toggle, binding it to the receiver with ten of the heavy rubber bands. When it did fire, the toggle would not rise. A zip gun, he thought, smiling. He bound the barrel loosely to his forearm with twine, repositioning it twice so that it could be easily extracted from beneath his sleeve and yet not be easily detectable.

When he finished shaving, Loss pulled on a long-sleeved sports shirt, patterned in blue and white checks. He grinned at the mirror and the reflected image leered back, looking no more menacing than a tired commuter. It's all I've got, he thought, leaving the tiled room.

The station owner said that he knew a kid who could do the job for Loss. Within fifteen minutes of the call, the kid pumped into the gas station on a ten-speed, slewing on the gravel as he stopped. Loss explained the layout quickly, implying that it involved a girlfriend and a suspicious wife. The kid said that he understood completely.

They left the Shell station fifteen minutes before twelve. The boy talked endlessly about soccer, rattling off names of teams and players Loss didn't know. He listened dimly to the boy, watching the streets and traffic.

Loss lifted a twenty dollar bill from his wallet, tucking it in the boy's shirt pocket. "That's for the car and expenses." He pulled another twenty and laid it on the seat. "And that's for being quiet. I don't want my wife to get wind of this. Just leave the car on the other side if I don't show up at the ferry. If my wife meets you over there, just say that I was delayed by business and I wanted her to have transportation. She's staying with a cousin. Got it?" He winked into the acned face. The money disappeared into a pant's pocket.

"Got it," the kid said, half smiling, a lieutenant of lechery. Bucking for captaincy.

The kid dropped him off at the midpoint on the causeway, one hundred yards further out from the shore than Petrov, who stood lounging against the rail, camera slung from his neck. He wore slacks and a short-sleeved shirt. They approached each other, Petrov finally sticking out his hand in greeting. Loss ignored it.

Petrov smiled. "Sorry you feel that way, Brian. It's just business. Nothing personal."

Loss looked at the relaxed figure before him, expensive slacks and Lacoste shirt. Petrov's hair was almost bleached white from the sun, contrasting with his strong, tanned face; his eyes were like chips of marble, picking up the blue of the surrounding sea.

"Do I have the name right? Petrov was what Heiss called you," Loss said, watching Petrov's face tighten.

"Call me what you wish," he replied.

"So where's Campbell?" Loss said.

Petrov shook his head and turned to lean on the railing, looking down into the water. "Campbell was an old man. Second rate. He was an administrator, you know. Hadn't run a field operation for ages. And he forgot basic things that he learned over thirty years ago."

"And you've killed him."

Petrov didn't answer for a moment and then turned to look at Loss. "Understand this. Both Campbell and I are in a business where one doesn't make mistakes. He regarded this project as pulling a plum out of the pie. Something nice to retire with: perhaps Queen's Honors List. We started watching him from the time he left Great Inagua. Unfortunately, we didn't follow him to Nova Scotia for the meeting with you and the Kents. Really stupid on my part."

"What's the point of all this, Petrov?"

"The point is, Brian, that when Campbell came out here, we knew that he was on to something. He activated a string of operatives who have worked for the English from time to time. One of these men, the one you killed last night, has been a KGB double for over eight years. So we knew exactly where to find Campbell. We tapped his telephone lines and simply waited until you called. Yes, Campbell is dead. The price we all pay for growing old or careless."

Petrov was smooth and cold like a block of ice. Loss felt his anger rising, but he tried to restrain it, holding it in check, gathering it for the moments to come. "And what are you and Welsh up to?" Loss rubbed his forearm, feeling the barrel beneath the cotton.

Petrov shrugged. "Nothing that Welsh himself doesn't want to do. We agree with his political philosophy. Does it occur to you that Welsh represents a new element in American politics—realism? Russia wants to deal with pragmatists, not dillettantes."

"So you're just helping him along. Panama and Cuba. And now this thing about unilateral disarmament."

Petrov hunched his shoulders fractionally. "I doubt that you would understand, Loss. It all leads to a permanent peace."

Loss gritted his teeth. "So I understand, you prick. Campbell had it worked out. And why did you bother to meet me out here?"

Petrov shrugged again. "Curiosity, I suppose. We had to find out where you were. I didn't think you could resist meeting me. I was half hoping that you wouldn't come."

Loss stepped away from the rail, moving back, but Petrov ignored him, speaking in a conversational tone. "Don't worry, Loss. I'm not armed. But you're covered by a very competent man with a telescopically sighted magnum rifle from up there on the bluff. Both ends of the causeway are covered. It's your stupid mistake, I'm afraid."

Loss looked up at the bluff less than half a mile away. Less than a thousand yards and very little wind. Not a difficult shot. "So what do you want to do now, Petrov?" He watched Petrov's shirt for the beat of his heart; a spot five inches below and to the left of the alligator symbol, where he would want the bullet to enter.

"Nothing particular, Brian." Petrov smiled, showing even teeth. "I thought we'd chat for a few more minutes. And then I will have to leave." He glanced at his watch. "Yes, a few more minutes." He turned to Loss, charming and friendly like an old acquaintance. "I take it you spun out in the Comanche when we sent the MIGs after you?" Loss nodded. Petrov pursed his lips and smiled again. "Yes, I thought you probably did. We had a reconnaissance aircraft airborne with infrared. An older-type set and an overconfident operator. He will lose his commission because of this."

"Pity."

"Yes, I suppose. But there is no use in employing incompetents. So you refueled somewhere along the way and made it to Canada? Quite a flight."

Loss said nothing, watching Petrov's hands for any movement.

"I suppose that you don't know the Kent's farm burned to the ground last night. I'm sorry." Petrov said it flatly.

"Bullshit!" Loss said explosively. He felt his muscles contracting, the sudden surge of anger pumping adrenalin into his veins.

"Don't even move!" Petrov warned, his voice still calm. "It only takes a half a second for the bullet to travel from that muzzle to your chest. The man is an expert. Besides, you have only yourself to blame. You involved them in this, not me." He carefully extracted a cigarette case and lighter from his pocket. He offered one to Loss who stood glaring, a sheen of perspiration on his forehead. "Loss, I know how you feel. But you are the one who involved them without their consent. As you involved Stroud and your woman." Petrov lit the cigarette, blowing smoke against the light wind.

Loss could see the ferry quite close to the shore, the distinctive upper deck making it look more like a floating cake than a ship. He estimated that it would dock in two or three minutes. He rocked back on his heels, visibly relaxing. "And what of the *Hussar,* Petrov? Do you really think you can pull that off?" He watched Petrov's eyes, seeking confirmation.

"You're playing games with yourself, Loss," he said, exhaling smoke through his nostrils, his eyes distant. "Heiss didn't know that much and what he knew died with Kent and Campbell." He started to raise his hand to the camera.

Loss flicked his forearm down, sliding the Luger's barrel into his right hand, his left hand pressing against the sear. He kept both hands low, below the level of the iron railing, removed from the direct sight of the sniper. "Get your fucking hands down, Petrov, and freeze," Loss said quietly, lips parted in a smile for the benefit of the man on the bluff. "This is a one-shot Luger. Don't make any movement except slow, natural ones. You'll die if I die."

The ferry had docked now—one long blast. In a minute, there would be a solid stream of traffic inbound toward the shore.

Petrov started to move his hand carefully upward. "Rather good, Loss. I saw the shape under your sleeve, but I thought it was a knife. I must be—"

Loss cut into his words. "Put your hands on the rail. Like you did before. Very casually," he said slowly, easing air from his lungs. "I don't want any new motions." His heart was pumping now—a staccato. He moved in carefully toward the Russian, keeping the barrel clear of Petrov's elbows. "Last and only chance, Petrov. Where and when does this *Hussar* thing happen. I want an answer in three seconds or you lose your spine."

Petrov kept silent, his breathing rapid and audible. Loss jammed the barrel of the Luger brutally into Petrov's kidney and grabbed the Russian's belt to support him from falling, pinning him against the rail with his body weight. Petrov gasped, air sucking into his lungs in the prelude to a scream. There was the snap of a miniature shockwave as the bullet whined past his face, spanging off the concrete behind them. He pulled Petrov closer, forming a shield toward the bluff.

The cars from the ferry, a whole line of them, were getting closer, disgorging from the ship. Loss watched them draw closer, their image distorted by refraction, wobbling in the waves of heat rising from the causeway.

"*Now*, goddamn your ass, Petrov." He rammed the barrel in again, hearing a scream of pain that seemed oddly dim in his ears. Petrov started coughing violently now, saying something between the spasms. The cars were almost to them. Loss jerked the camera strap over Petrov's neck, smashing the camera to the concrete. As the mechanism impacted on the concrete, the lens disintegrated, releasing a gas. Loss grabbed Petrov by the shirt collar, shoved him into the roadway, then dragged him into the lane opposite to the approaching cars. "With me, Petrov! You're coming with me or I'll kill you." The Russian was stumbling now, bent over and retching. Concrete chips shattered from the roadbed ahead of them as another bullet whined off into space beyond.

They cleared the first one, a small Fiat. Loss caught a brief vision of the driver, a white-faced woman, too startled to reach for the horn. Behind her was a solid stream of cars, imposing a barrier between him and the sniper. He bent low, dragging Petrov, running for the ferry terminal half a mile further out from the shore. Petrov was gagging now and then he stumbled, falling to his knees. Loss turned to drag him to his feet just as Petrov's face exploded, showering the pavement around him in a red mist. Loss never heard the bullet. A horn was blaring and he turned toward the traffic to see a Turbo-Corvette that had pulled out across the solid yellow line and was accelerating in an attempt to pass the few vehicles in front of it. Loss dove for the sidewalk, regained his feet and ran hard, head tucked low, toward the terminal. He heard the squeal of brakes and turned momentarily, still moving forward, to see the Corvette's massive taillights illuminated brilliant red as the car slewed sideways in a panic stop. The Corvette suddenly hunched forward with the impact and Loss saw a ragged lump tumble over the turtleback of the sports car. Petrov landed, limbs flopping, against the grilled railing.

There was another whine, and this time Loss felt the passage of the bullet as it plucked at the fabric of his shirt. He bent low and ran back into the right lane, keeping within feet of the passing traffic. The first half of the distance to the terminal took less than two minutes, but his lungs were searing, sucking hot exhaust-laden air. There were no more snaps of high velocity slugs that he could hear, but his senses were remote and dull; he felt now only the ache of his legs beating against the pavement and the triphammer of his heart pounding against the walls of his chest.

Loss looked over his shoulder, slowing to a jog. The shoreward stream of vehicles was stopped, a large crowd gathering around the lump that had been Petrov. And as he watched, a rust-red open-bed pickup truck wheeled through a U-turn and came back out the causeway, heading for him. It had Alberta plates, two faces perched in the high cab. He waved them down, standing in the roadway.

Loss ran to the driver's window and rapped on the glass. The man, complexion ruddy with sunburn, the face of a farmer, was wearing a flowered sports shirt. The woman's face was pale. He pulled the ball cap back on his head. "What's yer problem?"

Panting, Loss pointed toward the ferry and terminal building.

"That guy—" he swallowed for breath. "Got to get an ambulance." He panted, the explanation incomplete.

"Get in the bed of the truck. That's why we was goin' back. Ain't goin' to do much good though. He looks like a butchered steer."

Loss nodded, still panting and pulled himself up over the tailgate. He felt exposed, the bluff in clear view. He slumped down in the bed of the truck, picking up what protection he could from the side panels.

They stopped at the ticket gate briefly and then were waved through, Loss low in the bed of the truck, undetected. The truck squealed to a stop near a low concrete building, and the driver yelled back at Loss something about a telephone and loped off toward the building's door, fat moving in waves beneath his bulging shirt.

The Luger barrel was still in his hand, its still-cool form a black extension of his fingers. He slid it back up beneath the sleeve, using two loops of the twine to secure it, and crawled out of the bed of the truck. The grating for the ramp was only twenty yards further from the building, and he walked calmly onto the *Queen of Victoria,* capacity 48 cars and 2000 tons, 8 dollars round trip Tsawwassen-Vancouver Island and back.

He passed a deckhand in an orange vest, who was chaining the gates. "Guy killed back there in traffic," Loss said. The man nodded, not looking up.

The passenger deck above him was crowded with a mass of people looking down at the causeway. Several were taking pictures, proof of their touch with death. No one was looking down at him.

He passed from the sunlight into the tunnel gloom of the starboard side, amongst the parked vehicles. There were only fifteen or so on this side and he couldn't see the Olds. He stood next to a camper, letting his eyes adjust to the darkness. Petrov had said that both ends of the causeway were covered. Loss had no doubt. They obviously would know the Olds' registration, but did they know he was using it?

When his eyes were better adjusted and he was breathing calmly, he walked through the midship passageway, checking the port side. The Olds was last in line, the second lane outboard. He watched the lines of cars and his own for over a minute, suddenly feeling very tired. The deck plates were vibrating under his feet now as the ferry went astern. Three long blasts on the ship's siren. There was no movement on the car deck. Only the sounds of the engine thrashing beneath his feet and bulkhead doors slamming. He headed for the Olds, walking softly on the balls of his feet.

The car was empty, the passenger side locked. He walked around the rear of the car, looking back across the empty loading deck to watch the shore recede. A crewman in jeans and a denim shirt walked across the loading platform and swung through a bulkhead door, pulling it shut after him. The shore was more distant now, green and white roiled seas foaming under the stern. Gulls were following the ship.

Loss moved down the left side of the car and tried the driver's door. It was open and he dropped into the thick upholstered seat. The keys were not in the ignition, but he found them in the ashtray, buried in burned-out ends of cigarettes. Smart kid, he thought.

He caught the first movement, a flash of yellow in the rearview mirror. A man running toward him. Loss cursed, wishing he had used the time to reassemble the Luger. He was fumbling for the barrel lashed to his forearm when a movement to his left startled him. He raised his hand defensively, diminishing the impact as a tubular object smashed into his forehead. Loss clearly read the speedometer as he fell to the cushions. It told him that he was going nowhere.

Chapter 25

He awoke to the sound of chain roaring through an iron pipe. It diminished slowly, then ceased. There was movement beneath him, as if he were slewing sideways. All his senses were responding now, confused messages back from the perimeter of his consciousness. A feeling of dampness and smells of mustiness. Loss opened his eyes to watch a fly traverse a painted wooden beam within an arm's span above his head. He tried to move his arm and couldn't. No movement possible in his leg either, but his foot could flex.

He shut his eyes again and just rested, absorbing sounds. His mind was reeling as if he had too much to drink too quickly. There was a vague, unpleasant acid taste in his mouth; his tongue felt spongy and dry.

A door opened, rasping on the sill as if poorly fitted. He opened his eyes and craned his neck up from the prone position.

A woman stood there, hands thrust into cardigan pockets, peering at him, expressionless. Loss thought she might be in her late thirties and then decided she was older; her straight black hair, which was clipped severely at shoulder level, had traces of silver. The skin of her face was without crease or furrow. No smiles, no frowns. No emotion. Her high cheekbones and the hint of almond in her eye structure suggested she might be oriental. But not a face to remember.

"Do you wish more air, Loss?" Her voice was that of a child's; high and thin but soft. "You may not talk loudly." She pushed the door fully open and entered, moving to a porthole and opening it. He felt the breath of fog.

"Where am I? What's happened?" He listened to his own voice and found it hoarse. "I want some water."

"In a short time," she said and closed the door behind her.

He had no means of telling time, since his arms were restrained by some sort of strap secured to the bunk he lay on. The light through the small brass porthole was the washed-out white of thick fog. It could be morning or evening. Or in between.

The room he lay in was triangular in shape; the apex was formed by a wedge-shaped bunk he lay on and the deckhead above him had beams of oak with teak planking. The rest of the room at the foot of the bunk had limited standing room under a raised coach roof. The only light was from the two portholes. By its shape and general construction, he guessed that he was confined in the forecastle of a small power cruiser. An iron pipe of about 4-inch diameter ran from the center of the compartment through the deckhead. Spurling pipe? The source of the noise that woke him? It guided the chain up from the locker beneath the cabin sole through the deckhead and over the windlass. So they were anchored in the fog—where?

He heard a muttered conversation aft, beyond the door, and then the starting cough of a small generator that settled to a low hum, more vibration than sound. He lay his head back on the bunk and rested, his left temple a dull throb. He slept again.

Loss awoke minutes or hours later. There had been no apparent passage of time. The porthole still was muzzled in the gray light of thick fog. A man bent over him, shaking him gently by the shoulder. "Do you feel like some food now, Mr. Loss?"

He felt the chest straps being released. The man bent down to undo the bindings on his legs and Loss caught a glimpse of a slightly balding figure as he stooped.

"Who are you?" Loss said, easing himself up onto his elbows.

"Call me James. Come out into the main cabin. We have some food prepared, but I warn you that I want no violence or noise. Otherwise you will be sedated." He turned and left the cabin, a thin figure in blue corduroys and a thick Navy peajacket. Loss followed him, stretching his tendons, reeling slightly from dizziness. James indicated a position at the gimballed mahogany table where a setting of utensils and a napkin had been laid. Loss slumped down onto the settee and leaned on the table, head between his hands. The woman set a plate covered with fried eggs and hash browned potatoes before him. She added to this two slices of toast and then a large enameled mug of black coffee next to his elbow.

"Eat now," she said and walked aft down a passageway toward, what Loss supposed, were the sleeping cabins.

Loss ate slowly at first, ignoring his surroundings and the man who sat opposite him. He ate with total concentration, the food delicious, almost separable into individual flavors of salt and bitter, sweet and sour. As if each individual taste bud responded in a separate totality. He closed his eyes, chewing on the toast. Each kernel of wheat, each molecule of yeast, each salted trace of butter seemed to leap to his senses. The coffee was incredible, unbelievably good. He mopped the plate with the last crust and leaned back. James offered him a cigarette and a package of wooden kitchen matches. Loss's hand shook as he lit the match and inhaled. "She cooks well," he commented, extinguishing the match, exhaling. God, he thought, I've never tasted food before. Not food like that.

"It's a side effect of the medication," James offered, opening a notebook which lay closed beside him on the settee.

Loss carefully studied the man opposite him. Like the woman, he had light Asian features, and he was balding with straight black hair cut very short by contemporary standards. His eyes, encased behind yellow-tinted glasses, were birdlike: bright and black and unwinking. The rest of his face was unremarkable except for the fine, hard line that his lips formed. Loss resisted the compulsion to say "Ah, so!"

"You find this situation funny?" he said, staring at Loss.

"No," he replied, "not funny. Just that I'm washed out."

James nodded. "I suppose so. Again, part of the side effects." He made a notation in the notebook and snapped it shut. He started without preamble. "Brian Loss, born thirty-nine years ago, US citizen. Former service in the US Air Force. Pilot to Clifford Welsh. And, there's much more here."

"Where am I?"

James looked down at his watch. "You've been unconscious for, for, ah, fifty-two hours. The vessel is the *Sunflower*. And presently we are anchored in Squamish Harbor on the Olympic Peninsula of Washington."

"On the Hood Canal."

James nodded. "Yes, on the Hood Canal."

"And you are . . .?"

"James. As I said before, you can call me James. I think that you would have to say that I am with the government. A division of external security."

"What division? CIA?"

James nodded. "Something like that. We cooperate with the CIA on situations such as this." He paused, looking down at his fine-boned hands. "There is a very large segment of Chinese and Japanese Americans on the West Coast. As with blacks and chicanos, caucasians do not readily notice us." He hesitated, stroking his forehead with a delicate fingertip. "Do you dislike orientals, Mr. Loss?"

Brian shrugged. "I've never thought of it much. Like or dislike, I mean. I have unpleasant memories of Viet Nam. People tried to kill me on occasion." Surprisingly, Loss found that he wanted to cry. His hand was shaking again, and he hid it beneath the table.

"Don't be concerned with your reactions, Mr. Loss. Your nervous system has been heavily strained. One night of normal sleep and you'll be fine. More coffee?"

Loss nodded, leaning back against the cushions, his eyes closed. James left the compartment and returned in a few minutes with the cup refilled. "There is sugar and dried cream in the locker behind you." He ruffled through several pages of his notebook until he found what he was looking for. "An interesting experience, Mr. Loss. I suppose that you will be interested to know that Petrov's dead. The police in Vancouver termed it an accidental death. There wasn't enough left to determine the real cause. The Dutch Embassy made arrangements for his burial."

"Petrov's a Russian. Was. Or one of their agents—"

James nodded. "Yes. We are quite aware of that. But he was carrying a Dutch passport in the name of Klist. No forwarding address. He was buried in North Vancouver yesterday afternoon."

"You mentioned medication. What kind of drugs?"

James raised his eyebrows. "Drugs that I'm sure you wouldn't be familiar with. But we had no time for half-truths or opinions. We wanted everything you knew and very quickly. I suppose that you would term them truth drugs, but that would not be quite accurate."

A wave of nausea and disorientation hit Loss. He gagged, trying to keep the bile down.

"Put your head between your knees," James said curtly, removing the cigarette from Loss's hand. "It will pass. I would suggest that you refrain from smoking for a few hours. Loss kept his head tucked down, and with his eyes closed, he felt motion as if he were tumbling in space and then, just as quickly, his mind cleared.

Slowly he sat up and looked at James. "Jesus, you bastards don't fool around. Whatever you gave me is crap. And fuck-all unnecessary. I would have gladly told you everything that I knew."

James studied Loss for a moment before replying. "I doubt that, Mr. Loss. You would have told us what you *thought* you knew or what you wanted us to know. In this manner, we were able to extract, as you would say in industry, raw data. I'm sorry that we ah, violated your civil liberties. You can take that up with the proper authorities if you care to when the time comes. But I might point out that without our group, you would be dead."

"For Christ's sake, James, stop the Charlie Chan act. You're here to tell me something or ask me something. Otherwise you'd have me stuffed away in a cell or a padded room. Isn't that what you guys usually do? Get to the fuckin' point."

James stood up and turned his back to Loss, obviously angered. His hands were slowly clenching and unclenching as he fought down a retort. Finally, he turned to face Loss, his face utterly expressionless, his eyes calm. His voice was even as he spoke. "Mr. Loss. I would like you to refrain from vulgarity. I find it offensive. Your present reaction is that of confusion and fear. I am here to inform. Nothing else. From the information you gave us, I feel that you will be prepared to do one final task in this affair." He sat down on the settee and opened the notebook. "Do I make myself clear?"

Loss nodded, without speaking, looking down at his bare feet. James was right, of course. It was the fear and the tension of the last five days that produced the anger. "All right, James. Go ahead. What happened at the ferry?"

"Much better, Mr. Loss. And please try to absorb as much of this as possible. It may be to your benefit. Concerning the ferry, one of Petrov's men was aboard, apparently covering that end of the causeway. As a precaution, we had assigned one of our people to cover him. When you arrived, Petrov's man was in position behind a camper one row over. It was he that struck you on the forehead. He was about to use this on you when our agent, the woman, who incidentally prepared your breakfast, intervened." James produced a small plastic atomizer with the label of a nasal decongestant. He set it on the table before Loss. "Prussic acid. A very near thing, Mr. Loss."

Brian examined the plastic container, as he would a dead rat, probing it with a spoon. "I'll take your word for it. And then?"

"Then she simply moved Petrov's man into the vehicle with you, injected you both with a sedative, and strapped the pair of you upright in the front seat with the shoulder harness. It would seem to any passerby that you were both sleeping."

"No one on the ferry noticed this, this whole thing?"

James shook his head. "As far as we can tell, no. The trip over to Vancouver Island takes roughly two hours. Most of the car passengers make use of the upper deck or the snack bar, rather than remaining in their vehicles." James touched the edge of his glasses, a curiously delicate gesture. "From there, she brought you both to a rendezvous with this vessel in Nanaimo where the *Hussar* was then located."

"Suppose you go back to the beginning, Mr. James, or is it just James? How did you find out about the Welsh-Petrov thing. Campbell?"

"As I said before, just call me James. The beginning? We didn't know about Welsh or Petrov. Our knowledge of the affair started in Russia. Through sources there, we knew that the Russians had produced three nuclear weapons at the Zhignask installation, and that one of these had been tested underground. There were several curious things about this weapon. First, it was produced in only a quantity of three; an unusually low number for what presumedly will be a production weapon. More important, from our analysis of intelligence and from limited sampling of some of the alloys that were used in the production of the cases, we found that there was a remarkable resemblance with a weapon presently being manufactured in the US for use in the Poseidon C-3 warhead. That made it something surely worth watching.

"We traced the movement of one of the warheads to Vladivostok where it was placed aboard one of the older Z-Class Fleet submarines. From there, we tracked it across the Pacific with one of our own nuclear submarines. The device was transferred to a Russian trawler with Canadian Fish and Game markings off the coast of British Columbia and then onto the *Hussar* at Broughton Island. Petrov either accompanied the weapon all the way from Russia or was on the trawler. We don't know this for sure. We do know that he had the device placed aboard the *Hussar*, which two men working for the Russians had chartered."

"He saw Holly then?"

"No, it doesn't seem that way. He was only on board for a few minutes, seeing to the transfer of the weapon. Your woman friend must have been below-decks because I feel that Petrov would surely have recognized her. The other two men apparently didn't know her identity and thought that she was a normal part of the crew."

"So she was still aboard the *Hussar*?"

James nodded. "Yes, we saw her on the yacht in Nanaimo. Everything seemed to be quite normal. The device is on the foredeck of the yacht, lashed down with rope. It appears to be marked with an address, as if it were a parcel of cargo. We can't tell as yet."

"You mean that you haven't stopped the whole operation yet? Jesus Christ! What are you waiting for?" Loss stood up, infuriated, immediately feeling a wave of dizziness sweep his consciousness.

The woman came immediately into the cabin and pushed Loss back down onto the settee, gently but with an undisguised trace of distaste. She handed him a tablet and indicated that he should wash it down with the remaining coffee. James was mute during this, placidly thumbing through his notes and checking the weather through the opened porthole. When Loss was quiet, slumping back against the settee, James continued. "You see, Mr. Loss, your heart has been heavily strained over the last few days. The drugs unfortunately account for this. One good night's sleep and you will be normal, but you must remain calm."

The woman looked at James for any further instructions. He replied by a fractional shake of his head. She left the room, closing the door softly behind her. James removed his glasses and, laying them aside, massaged the bridge of his nose. "No, Mr. Loss. What you don't seem to realize is that the Russians cannot simply be arrested. To do that would expose a situation that would be recognized as an attempt by Russia to detonate a nuclear device within the confines of the US. The only response for the United States would be to accuse Russia and possibly precipitate a total war." He paused to think and then said, "I believe all that would be counterproductive. The way that this must be handled is to neutralize the weapon and simply eliminate all the people connected with Petrov. The result will be a warning to the Russians, a hardening of US policy, and perhaps, some degree of rearmament by the US to reachieve a parity in military power. The public should not be informed of this. Welsh, of course, must be removed permanently."

Loss heard the deep moan of a foghorn in the distance. It was so muffled and distorted that it seemed like the moan of some animal. He looked down at his hands. There were still occasional tremors, but his feeling of disorientation was subsiding. "How did you find out about me?"

James made a scratching noise in his throat. "Through Petrov. After he placed the weapon aboard the yacht, he returned to the trawler. We thought that he would put to sea, but instead, the trawler took him down to Alert Bay and landed him there. The following morning, he flew to Vancouver. From there on in, we followed his movements, which eventually led to your meeting on the causeway at Tsawwassen. Through you, we've been able to put all the unknowns in place. His plan is quite evident, now."

"And that is?" Loss interjected.

"That the Soviets have subverted an American presidential hopeful by arranging situations within their control. The Cuban reaction to Guantánamo was stage-managed by the Russians, as was the Panamanian Accord. As you had noticed, Mr. Loss, in Welsh's last television interview, he made a statement about the proliferation of nuclear weapons and the dangerous practice of having so many within US borders. It would seem that they planned to transport the device to the Hood Canal in time to detonate it as close as possible to the first Trident submarine leaving on patrol with fully loaded and armed missiles. The detonation would appear to have originated with the submarine, thus fulfilling Welsh's predictions of playing with fire. His election would have nearly been assured. All in all, a very clever scenario."

"But Petrov's dead now."

"Ah, but that doesn't matter. The weapon is in place and I doubt that the men on board the *Hussar* have any idea that there is anything wrong. Typical Russian compartmentation of espionage. Each element works independently of the other."

"How many men?" Loss said.

James stood up and walked over to the navigational table. He returned with a pile of black and white photographs and lay them in front of Loss. "Only these two. Do you recognize either one of them?"

Loss leafed through the stack. All were obviously taken with a telephoto lens, with characteristic foreshortening of the background. One of them was a man with Arabic features, almost handsome. The other, nondescript, a typical anyman. Loss shook his head.

"No, I thought not," James said half to himself. "The caucasian one," he tapped the first photo, "is English. We can find nothing concerning him except that he had a fellowship at Cambridge in biophysics. Also a good linguist. The other one, the Arab, we know much more about. Amed Menkar. A young Libyan naval officer, something of an expert in acoustics and hydromagnetics. Attended the University of Leningrad in the late sixties. Now a Russian citizen. A strange pair to select for what would seem a suicide mission."

"Do you think that's the idea?" Loss rubbed his forehead, feeling slightly sick. "I mean, that it's a suicide thing?"

"Not very likely," James replied. "They probably think it's some sort of surveillance device. Their backgrounds would indicate that such is the case. They have probably been instructed to place the yacht in a position as close to the submarine as possible. There might be a switch that they activate to start the equipment. On the other hand, their role might be passive as far as the device is concerned. It could be activated by an outside source such as a transmitter or even, in some way, the presence of the submarine itself."

"Look, James. All this is very nice. I'm truly impressed. The drugs I don't mind. I admit that you probably got more out of me than I would have freely given. But there is only one essential thing that has to be done. Stop those two guys on the *Hussar*. And get the crew off safely. There are only two men. Surely, you can contrive some situation where they will be both on deck at one time. Knock them off with automatic weapons."

The muscles in James's cheeks tightened, giving his face a hard, angular tone. "Loss, we don't know how that weapon is to be triggered. It could be by some switching device on the storage box, but it could also be by radio impulse. Eliminating those two men doesn't guarantee us that we stop the device from detonating. Besides the people living in this area, Seattle is less than twenty miles to the east of here, directly downwind."

Loss hammered his fist down on the table, upsetting the coffee mug. "For Christ's sake, James, what in hell do you expect to do. Do you have to have an Act of Congress to move your ass?" He started to rise and then sat down suddenly, the sensation of his senses tumbling flooded him in a wave of nausea.

James reached over and felt Loss's pulse. "Not good," he said softly. "Keep your emotions under control, Mr. Loss." He stood up and walked over to the porthole, looking at the fuzzy forms of boats anchored in the bay. It seemed to be thinning out. He turned back to Loss and sat down, exhaling heavily. "I have already made preparations for taking the *Hussar*. I am only waiting on approval from people further up in the government."

"What are you planning?" He tried to watch James's face, but he had trouble keeping it in focus.

"The *Hussar* is anchored on the other side of the bay. The USS *Ohio* is scheduled to put to sea tomorrow morning at 5:00 AM in company with four tugs. We doubt that the *Hussar* will move before dawn. Consequently, we plan to destroy the nuclear device tonight."

"Destroy it how? Don't you run the risk of detonating it?"

"Unlikely," James replied. "The heart of the weapon is basically an atomic bomb, a fission weapon. This is first triggered to create the intense heat necessary for a hydrogen fusion reaction. This atomic 'trigger' is a ball of plutonium encased with a special type of high explosive that must be detonated by electrical impulses in a highly complex sequence. If we fracture that high explosive, the trigger mechanism is destroyed. The result at worst would be an explosion of perhaps twelve kilos of high explosive. The core material would be shattered and there would be some radioactive contamination of the local area. But no nuclear detonation."

"How do you know that it will happen this way?"

"We don't exactly," James replied looking down at his notebook. "But this is the best estimate that our technicians can provide. If we are fortunate, there will not even be any high explosive yield."

"How about the crew?" Loss asked.

"There are no guarantees. Destruction of the nuclear weapon comes first. If there is no high explosive yield, we will attempt to get them off the *Hussar*."

"Oh, my God!" Loss buried his face in his hands.

"Yes, I know. I'm sorry. But with the time remaining, there is no other way. We will take the *Sunflower* very close alongside the *Hussar,* as if we were re-anchoring closer to shore. We must be close enough that the first shell from the recoilless rifle cannot miss. We cannot chance having to fire a second time."

"James, you can't—"

"There is no alternative to this plan, Mr. Loss. We will follow the recoilless rifle with satchel charges if there is no detonation. We must be positive that the device is destroyed."

Loss looked up, tears of anger spilling down his face. "You cold-blooded prick! And who pulls the trigger? There are five people on that yacht. And you're the bastard that gets a medal for defending flag and country!"

James looked smaller and fragile in the pale light. He rubbed the back of his neck reflectively, looking up at the overhead. "For flag and country? That's an odd expression." He paused, thinking. "I suppose so, Mr. Loss. Ultimately, it is for flag and country. More to the point, because we are ordered to do it." He smiled at Loss, his lips compressed. "We will have to be no more than fifteen meters from the device when we launch our attack. I will be one of the men firing the recoilless rifle."

"Jesus Christ," Loss shouted. He staggered to his feet, reeling. "What kind of a bullshit organization is this? Some CIA Kamikaze team?" He suddenly faltered, feeling sick, tears flooding his eyes. He sat down on the cabin sole, trying to neither giggle nor cry.

There were muttered voices in the background, and he felt the needle sliding into his arm before he could protest. His last image of James was a pair of tennis shoes attached to legs rising to a body beyond his contracting vision.

Chapter 26

He slid back into consciousness as cold water saturated his clothing. There was the sound of an engine beneath him, running at very low revs, and the smell of bilge water and diesel fuel filled his nostrils. Trying to move, he found that his wrists and ankles were bound, although loosely. A figure sat aft by the tiller, black against a clear night sky, stars by the thousands framing the helmsman.

Loss tried rolling to one side and nudged a prone figure lying next to him. The body was that of a man, breathing shallowly but regularly. But not conscious.

The engine throttled down to an idle and the helmsman appeared above him, a small penlight held in one hand; a knife in the other. His ankle bonds were cut in one stroke.

"You can sit next to me, Mr. Loss." It was the woman. She helped him to his feet and guided him to a seat beside her on the after thwart. Even in the starlight, her face was blank.

"Do you realize what has happened, Mr. Loss?"

"No, only that you keep shoving needles in me. Where's James?"

She was silent for a moment, throwing the gear lever into forward and advancing the engine's revs. "James directed me to take you to the shore in the launch. He won't be coming."

"Where's the *Hussar*?" The cold night air was clearing his mind now, and he was beginning to connect events.

"James died two hours ago," she said softly. "Both the *Hussar* and the *Sunflower* are gone. But there was no nuclear detonation."

"They all died?" he said, choking.

She nodded. "Everyone."

"Oh, Jesus," he moaned. "Oh, Good Jesus." The girl with the dog, walking on the Montana road. Swimming in the shallows of the Mad River together and tracing castles and rabbits in the afternoon cumulus as they lay on their backs. "Oh, Jesus," he repeated over and over as he wept, tears mixing with the salt air as his body convulsed in spasms.

She sat beside him, only her hand moving on the tiller, guiding the launch through the silent reaches of Possession Sound as they moved northeast toward distant lights.

When he was quiet, she cut his wrist bonds and handed him a bottle. He took it, drinking the brandy down and then coughing and drinking again.

She took the bottle from him. "That is enough. There is coffee in a flask under the seat."

"Where are we going?"

"I will drop you ashore south of Elliot Point just after dawn. From there, I will go further north to Everett. My embassy has made arrangements for your intelligence authorities to meet me there. We have some documentation of Petrov's affairs. Tapes, photographs; many things. And of course, they will question me for a long time."

"Your embassy?"

She turned to look at him carefully. "Yes, I thought James would have told you. His name was Lin Po Sung. He comes from the same province as our Chairman—Hunan."

"You mean mainland China?" he said, incredulous.

"There is only *one* China, Mr. Loss."

Loss watched the shore lights gliding past, unreal and distant. "Why did you do this? What concern was it of yours—of your government?"

"Because we know the Soviets, Mr. Loss. We have shared a common border with them for sixty years. In your country, you have a Munich mentality, a belief in peace at any price. As our country has, your country must finally reconcile itself to meet them with strength. Otherwise, they will slaughter you. Our only concern is that we wish to see a balance between world powers. Your country presently provides that balance and that is what I hope has been retained tonight."

"What of Welsh?" The first thin cracks of dawn were fracturing the eastern horizon.

"Our group obtained no direct evidence to tie him to this. There is only your word that there was any link between them." She pointed toward the form that lay next to the engine housing. "The man who tried to kill you on the Tsawwassen ferry. A pig of a Russian. But I don't think that even he knew who Petrov really was, or of Welsh's connection."

"Will you tell them what you know about Welsh?"

She nodded. "But not for three or four days, longer if I can hold up to their questioning. But enough to give you time."

"Where is he now?"

She shrugged. "Probably in New York. He had a speaking engagement there. But he will be at the opening of the party's national convention in San Francisco the day after next. It is more than likely that he will receive the nomination."

The launch ran slowly north in Possession Sound, stemming the tide. Just at dawn, she nudged the launch in against the beach south of Elliot Point, the keel grating lightly on the shingle and sand.

She pointed to the blue nylon bag. "You can go ashore here. Everything that you need is in the bag. They won't know about you or Welsh for three or four days. That's all the time you have."

He picked up the bag and moved forward to the bow and then turned to face her. "This is what James meant when he said that I had something more to do?"

She had on a cardigan and she must have been cold, he thought. Her hands were stuffed in the pockets and she looked no more sinister than a slightly plump aunt. "Yes. That is what he had in mind, Mr. Loss. I think you understand why."

"I suppose that will be the end of it?"

She shook her head. "No, I don't think so, Mr. Loss. For us, this is just a waiting period. What we have done was in our own interest. There will be a day in the future when your country will have to deal with us as well."

She put the gear selector in reverse and backed away form the beach as Loss leaped down to the sand. He watched her as she put the tiller over and then shifted to forward, moving slowly against the tide. She never looked back or smiled; just sat there, eyes straight ahead, looking north. He watched her until she was out of sight beyond the point.

He changed into dry clothes and checked the contents of the nylon bag. There was his Lange passport, over a thousand dollars in cash, and a sheet of typed paper giving Welsh's known schedule. In addition, there was an Armalite rifle with folding stock and a telescopic sight. The ammunition in the clip had expanding tips, the type that mushrooms as it passes through the target.

He headed east toward the highway, savoring the smell of dawn. Once he was finished, there would be time enough to mourn the dead.

As he picked his way through the trees, he wondered whether the media would call it a conspiracy.

Cozumel

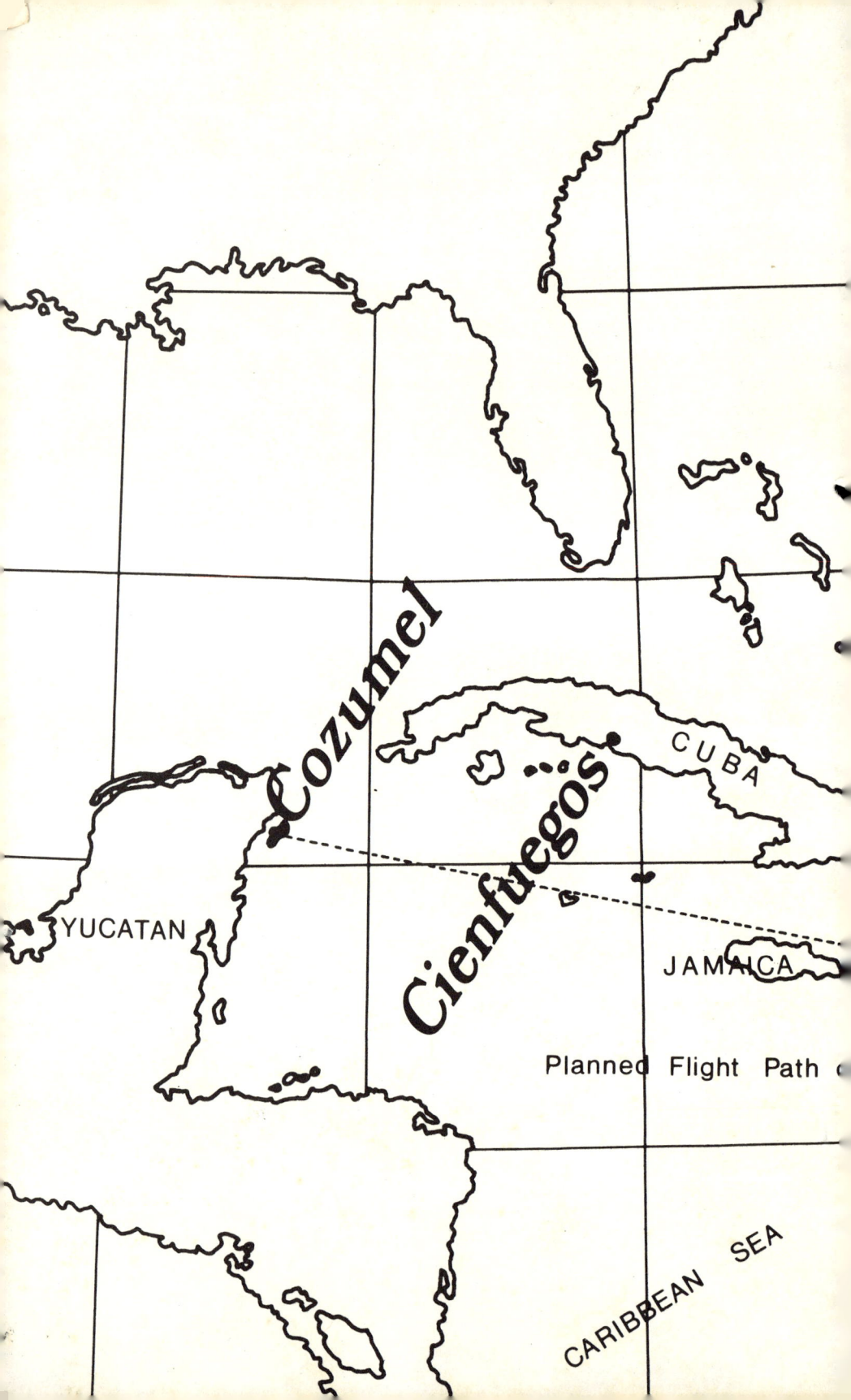

Cienfuegos

YUCATAN

CUBA

JAMAICA

Planned Flight Path

CARIBBEAN SEA